·

THE
VICTORIAN
FAIRY TALE
BOOK

·

THE VICTORIAN FAIRY TALE BOOK

Edited and with an Introduction by

MICHAEL PATRICK HEARN

With illustrations from the original editions

PANTHEON BOOKS · *New York*

All rights reserved under International and Pan-American Copyright
Conventions. Published in the United States by Pantheon Books, a
division of Random House, Inc., New York, and simultaneously in
Canada by Random House of Canada Limited, Toronto.

Library of Congress Cataloging-in-Publication Data

The Victorian fairy tale book.
Summary: A collection of classic Victorian fairy tales
by such authors as John Ruskin, Charles Dickens, and Oscar Wilde.
1. Fairy Tales—Great Britain.   2. English fiction—19th century.
[1. Fairy tales. 2. Short stories]
I. Hearn, Michael Patrick.
PR1309.F26V48   1988   823'.8'08 [Fic] 87-36039
ISBN 0-394-56594-0

Designed by Sara Reynolds
Manufactured in the United States of America
First Edition

PICTURE CREDITS

I am indebted to the following for helping me obtain examples of the
original illustrations for these works:

Cynthia Hearn Dorfman, for "Goblin Market"; Barry Klugerman, for
Peter Pan in Kensington Gardens; The Library of Congress, for *The King
of the Golden River*, "The Fairies," "The Golden Key," *The Little Lame
Prince and His Travelling-Cloak*, "The Necklace of Princess Fiorimonde," "The Selfish Giant," and "The Deliverers of Their Country";
and The New York Public Library, for "The Pied Piper of Hamelin,"
The Rose and the Ring, "Melilot," and "Rocking-Horse Land."

For Laura Jane Musser

M. P. H.

ACKNOWLEDGMENTS

I am grateful to the following people who have helped, in one way or another, towards the completion of *The Victorian Fairy Tale Book*: Cynthia Hearn Dorfman, Michael Emyrs, Rodney K. Engen, Brigitte Heinrich, Daniel Hirsh, Barry Klugerman, C. A. McDonald, Bernard McTigue, Glenn Edward Sadler, Justin G. Schiller, Barbara Seaman, Jane Yolen, and Jack Zipes. And of course Wendy, Mitch, and Helena.

M. P. H.

A lake and a fairy boat
To sail in the moonlight clear,—
And merrily we would float
From the dragons that watch us here!

Thy gown shall be snow-white silk,
And strings of orient pearls,
Like gossamers dipp'd in milk,
Should twine with thy raven curls!

Red rubies should deck thy hands,
And diamonds should be thy dow'r—
But Fairies have broken their wands,
And wishing has lost its pow'r!

THOMAS HOOD
"Song: For Music"

Contents

Contents

Contents

Introduction

ONCE UPON A TIME—but not so long ago—the fairies were not welcome in the British nursery. The battle over Elfland raged for centuries. With the coming of Christianity to the British Isles towards the end of the Roman Era, the Celtic faërie kings and queens went underground as ancient local traditions were absorbed or transformed by the country's new religion. Those who in the old legends were merely amoral were now, in the eyes of the early church fathers, evil.

Yet a wealth of fairy lore still survived in French and English medieval romances and ballads. King Arthur and his chivalric knights consorted with fays, Sir Gawain battled with the Green Knight, Thomas the Rhymer was spirited off by the Queen of Elfland, and fair maidens were deflowered by Young Tam Lin, the Elfin Knight. Even so, by the Elizabethan age, the very existence of fairies was widely disputed. In 1584, Reginald Scot argued in his *Discoverie of Witchcraft* that only "sicke folke, children, women and cowards" still believed such superstitious nonsense. The preaching of the Gospel had, he said, largely driven out most of the old legends. But ancient beliefs were not so quickly uprooted. King James VI of Scotland was so outraged by Scot's treatise that he wrote his own repudiation, *Daemonologie*, declaring the reality of fairies and brownies; and on ascending the throne of Great Britain as King James I, he ordered *The Discoverie of Witchcraft* publicly burned.

The sixteenth and early seventeenth centuries were a renaissance of fairy literature in England. The works of Ben Jonson, Edmund Spenser, Michael Drayton, Robert Herrick, John Lyly, and, of course, William Shakespeare eagerly explored the wonders of fairyland. However, with the exception of Spenser, whose *Faerie Queene* (1590, 1596) was lovingly modeled on the old romances, these poets did not take elfin tradition seriously. Thus the powerful Queen Maeve of Irish legend became Mab, the fairies' midwife, in *Romeo and Juliet*. Perhaps the clearest expression of the Elizabethan decadent attitude to fairyland is Drayton's *Nimphidia* (1627), his parody of courtly romance, in which the diminutive fairy knight Pigwiggen

> quickly Armes him for the Field,
> A little Cockle-shell for his Shield,
> Which he could bravely wield:
>   Yet it could not be pierced:
> His Speare a Bent both stiffe and strong,
> And well-neere of two Inches long;
> The Pyle was of a Horse-flyes tongue,
>   Whose sharpnesse naught reversed.

The old fairy lore, if remembered at all, was now considered fit only for children and peasants and circulated as old wives' tales and in chapbooks, the cheap pamphlets hawked about the provinces by itinerant dealers, offering the histories of Tom Thumb and Jack the Giant-Killer.

The Puritans had no patience with such petty amusements. In their pursuit of a temporal state based upon the Word of God, they denounced all forms of popular literature as pernicious trash. Hugh Rhodes warned parents in *The Book of Nurture* (1554) to keep their boys and girls "from reading feigned fables, vain fantasies, and wanton stories, and songs of love, which bring much mischief to youth." In *A Candle in the Dark* (1656), Thomas Ady told parents to beware of old wives "who sit talking, and chatting of many fake old stories of Witches, and Fairies, and Robin Good-Fellow . . . all which lying fancies people are more naturally to listen after than the Scriptures."

Religious zealots all but exiled the fairies from Britain's shores. With the Revolution of 1688, after which even the celebrating of Christmas was outlawed, "Farewell, rewards and fairies!" resounded throughout the land. Yet even Puritan literature was not wholly free of the fairies' spell: no matter what its pious intent, John Bunyan's *Pilgrim's Progress* (1678, 1684), with all its fearsome giants and marvelous monsters, was no more than an allegorical fairy tale.

Meanwhile, the fairies found refuge in France, at the court of Louis XIV. Bored with the popular novels of the day, the lords and ladies who attended Mme. Marie-Catherine d'Aulnoy's salon coddled one another with fairy tales. So fashionable did these diversions become that *Le Cabinet des fées* (1785–1789), the authoritative collection of these stories, reached forty-one volumes by the fall of the Ancien Régime. Designed to entertain their upper-class audience, they tended to be overwrought extravaganzas, and consequently most have long been forgotten. The best, composed by a minor member of the French Academy named Charles Perrault, still endure. His classic retellings of "Cinderella," "Little Red Riding Hood," "The Sleeping Beauty in the Wood," "Bluebeard," and "Puss in Boots" appeared in 1697 in *Histoires ou contes du temps passé*, which was first published in English in 1729 and became popularly known as "Tales of Mother Goose." Although variants of these stories were known prior to Perrault, so charming were his versions that they immediately entered the world's folklore. While retaining the simplicity and directness of the oral originals, Perrault transformed them according to the high standards he set for a literature designed specifically for children. Dedicating the small volume to a niece of Louis XIV, Perrault removed all the licentiousness that he felt had marred earlier versions and might corrupt the virtue of princesses. In the manner of La Fontaine's fables, he appended little morals in verse to each selection, but happily his well-meant lessons do not intrude on the graceful storytelling.

The term "fairy tale" apparently did not exist in English prior to 1699, when Mme. D'Aulnoy's *contes des fées* (popularly known in England as "Tales of Mother Bunch") were first translated. It has proved a threadbare phrase to describe so vast a form. It rarely concerns fairies, what J. R. R. Tolkien dismissed as "that long line of flower-fairies and fluttering sprites with antennae that I so disliked as a child, and which my children in their turn detested. . . . *Faerie* contains many things besides elves and fays, and besides dwarfs, witches, trolls, giants, or dragons: it holds the seas, the sun, the moon, the sky; and the earth, and all things that are in it: tree and bird, water and stone, wine and bread, and ourselves, mortal men, when we are enchanted." Perhaps a more accurate translation is "tale of enchantment," which thus embraces every story in which occurs, according to Joseph Jacobs, "something 'fairy,' something extraordinary—fairies, giants, dwarfs, speaking animals."

While both Mother Goose and Mother Bunch were readily welcomed to many British firesides, not everyone approved of these foreign fairies. The Age of Reason was quickly advancing upon the nursery. While arguing for the introduction of instruction through amusement, John Locke, in *Some Thoughts Concerning Education* (1693), cautioned against fairy tales, chapbooks, and old wives' tales, which with all their wild bugaboos might damage impressionable infant minds; the only book he thought fit for boys and girls was Aesop's fables.

Considering both the advent of the Enlightenment and the persistence of English Puritanism throughout the eighteenth century, it is no surprise that there was no great revival of the writing of fairy tales in Great Britain concurrent with that in France. If one did appear in some children's book, it had to reflect Lockean philosophy. Sarah Fielding included two in *The Governess* (1749), but with the stiff warning from Mrs. Teachum that "Giants, Magic, Fairies and all Sorts of supernatural Assistances in a Story, are only introduced to amuse and divert: For a Giant is called so only to express a Man of great Power; and the magic Fillet round the Statue was intended only to shew you, that by Patience you will overcome all difficulties. Therefore, by no means let the Notions of Giants or Magic dwell upon your Minds."

"Fairy tales," the *Monthly Review* noted in 1788, "were formerly thought to be the proper and almost the only reading for children; it is with much satisfaction, however, that we find them gradually giving way to the publications of a far more interesting kind, in which instruction and entertainment are judiciously blended, without the intermixture of the marvelous, the absurd, and things totally out of nature." This decline of the old nursery lore in favor of contemporary moral stories was promoted by such pious journals as Sarah Trimmer's *Guardian of Education* (1802–1806), arguing that "there is not a species of Books for Children and Youth . . . which has not been made some way or other an engine of mischief," and that none was more mischievous than the fairy tale.

As the century progressed, the war against the fairy tale found a formidable ally in an American, Samuel Griswold Goodrich. When a boy in Connecticut, Goodrich was given a collection containing "Little Red Riding Hood," "Jack the Giant-Killer," and "some other tales of horror" he found "calculated to familiarize the mind with things shocking and monstrous" and "to make criminals of a large part of the children who read them." To combat such nursery stories, Goodrich began in 1827 to publish, under the pseudonym "Peter Parley," a series of "reasonable and truthful" books for boys and girls. Designed "to enlarge the circle of Knowledge, to invigorate the understanding, to strengthen the moral nerve, to justify and exalt the imagination," these books became internationally successful. Clearly juvenile literature was expected to be as wholesome as a breakfast food.

But there were also powerful defenders of the fairy tale in this age of unbelief. Charles Lamb was outraged to find that moral and educational stories had all but "banished the old classics of the nursery." "Damn them!" he wrote Samuel Taylor Coleridge in 1802 about the instructional tales' authors, "those Blights and Blasts of all that is Human in man and child . . . Think what you would have been now, if instead of being fed Tales and old wives' fables in childhood, you had been crammed with geography and natural history?" Coleridge himself avowed that "from my early reading of fairy tales . . . my mind had been habituated *to the Vast*. . . . I know of no better way of giving the mind a love of the Great and the Whole." And his fellow poets, Blake, Shelley, Keats, and others, paid the tales they had known in their own childhood the great compliment of making free use of fairy lore in their verse.

Oddly, however they may have adored the old stories, the English Romantics left it to their German contemporaries to revive the form. Thus the *Kunstmärchen*, the German art fairy tale, evolved into as rich and grand a tradition as the French *conte des fées* a century earlier. But it was the *Volksmärchen*, the local folktale, as recorded by Jakob Ludwig and Wilhelm Karl Grimm between 1812 and 1814, that most significantly altered world literature. The first edition in English, *German Popular Stories*, appeared in 1823, to be quickly followed by a second volume in 1826, both translated by Edgar Taylor. These books did more than any other to usher a new era of imagination into English juvenile literature. Despite the scholarly apparatus of the volumes, Taylor was mindful to have, as he admitted to the Grimms, "the amusement of some young friends principally in view," and therefore he was "compelled to conciliate local feelings and deviate a little from strict translation." "Here was once again the true unadulterated fairy tale," declared Charlotte M. Yonge, the novelist, "and happy the child who was allowed to revel in it—perhaps the happier if under protest, and only permitted a sweet daily taste." The extraordinary reception of the Grimms' and Hans Christian Andersen's fairy tales (first available in English in 1846) encouraged the publication in England of many other collections of the world's folk and fairy tales. British folklorists, following the Grimms' example, now began the great task of preserving their native oral literature before it passed from the memory of the common people. And the time was now ripe for a revival in the writing of original fairy tales in England.

The coronation of Victoria in 1837 marked the arrival of a golden age for the literary British fairy tale. Even though initially there was still considerable resistance to these innocent amusements, by the queen's fiftieth jubilee fairy tales were no longer regarded as the engines of mischief Mrs. Trimmer had called them, but rather, as Edward Salmon declared in *Juvenile Literature As It Is* (1888), "as engines for the propulsion of all virtues into the little mind in an agreeable and harmless form." Clearly, their authors were mindful of the criticisms of earlier nursery lore. The new fairy tales were cleansed of the savagery and ethical ambiguity that had characterized many traditional stories: here there were no ogres who cut off children's heads, as there were in Perrault's "Hop o' My Thumb," and no rewards for the liar, as in "Puss in Boots." Even when not overtly moralizing, these tales were always moral.

Good always triumphed over Evil in these optimistic fantasies. By the time of Victoria's death in 1901, hundreds of new fairy books had been published, a surprising number of which have become classics, remarkable for their abundant invention, literary distinction, and philosophical depth.

The first Victorian fairy tale of lasting importance was a youthful work by John Ruskin. He fell in love with *German Popular Stories* at ten years old, and his admiration did not dim with the years. He later praised the Grimms' tales for children for "animating for them the material world with inextinguishable life, fortifying them against the glacial cold of selfish science, and preparing them submissively, and with no bitterness of astonishment, to behold, in later years, the mystery—divinely appointed to remain such to all human thought—of the fates that happen alike to the evil and the good." This high purpose Ruskin retained in the fairy tale he himself wrote, *The King of the Golden River*, which was (he admitted) "a good imitation of Grimm and Dickens, mixed with a little Alpine feeling of my own." Composed in 1841 to amuse twelve-year-old Effie Gray, his future wife, it was not published until 1851, and then anonymously. He later scoffed at this early effort in his autobiography, *Praeterita* (1889), judging it "totally valueless. . . . I can no more write a story than compose a picture." Yet, of all his many writings, *The King of the Golden River* may ensure Ruskin's immortality.

Borrowing patterns and motifs from German folklore, particularly "The Golden Goose" and "The Water of Life," Ruskin spun a classic ecological parable, enriched with his fervent observations of Nature. In this simple fairy tale lie the seeds of the mighty social consciousness that blossomed in his mature writing: the Black Brothers' selfish (and thus sinful) materialism is severely punished, and the good youngest brother is rewarded for selflessly restoring the regenerative balance between Man and Nature. Ruskin also refined the paganism of the Grimms' tales by introducing a medieval Christian argument, buffered by English Romanticism, that Nature was God's picture book addressed to Mankind, with "the sole and evident purpose of talking to him and teaching him."

When a boy, Ruskin had been as charmed by the pictures in *German Popular Stories* as by the text. The book was the first illustrated edition of Grimm in any language, and its plates by George Cruikshank revolutionized juvenile book illustration. Here were, as William Makepeace Thackeray argued, "the first real, kindly agreeable, and infinitely amusing and charming illustrations for a child's book in England."

Throughout his life Ruskin remained a loyal defender of Cruikshank's etchings for Grimm (and appropriately *The King of the Golden River* was illustrated by one of Cruikshank's most gifted disciples, Richard Doyle).

Ruskin generously provided the introduction to a reissue of Taylor's translation with the original pictures. Learning that Cruikshank was desperately in need of money in 1866, Ruskin proposed that the two collaborate on a collection of the critic's favorite fairy tales. To test the artist, he sent him the Grimm version of "The Blue Light" and Robert Browning's retelling of the German legend "The Pied Piper of Hamelin," perhaps the greatest fairy tale written for children in English verse. (The poet had composed it to amuse a friend's son and only reluctantly included it in 1842 in *Dramatic Lyrics*.) Cruikshank completed the two etchings, but Ruskin abandoned the project, concluding that "the dear old man has . . . lost his humour. He may still do impressive and moral subjects, but I know by this group of children [in the "Pied Piper" plate] that he can do fairy tales no more." Ruskin was too harsh: Cruikshank's etching is a charming illustration, and it is here published for the first time with Browning's poem.

Despite these few triumphs of early Victorian fairy lore, many people still adhered to the old principle of instruction through amusement by providing what Thackeray called "abominable attempts" to "cram science down [children's] throats as calomel used to be administered under the pretence of a spoonful of currant-jelly." Utilitarians had no use for fairy tales. Among the voices raised at this time in defense of the old nursery stories, none was more eloquent than that of Charles Dickens. Unlike Ebenezer Scrooge, Dickens never forgot his earliest childhood reading. "Little Red Riding-Hood," he confessed, "was my first love. I felt that if I could have married Little Red Riding-Hood, I should have known perfect bliss." On recalling the first time he read *The Arabian Nights*, Dickens found "all things become uncommon and enchanted to me! All lamps are wonderful; all rings are talismans!" References to fairy tales abound everywhere in his novels. *Hard Times* (1854) decries the injustice done to people denied works of fancy in their childhood. "Now, what I want is Facts," declares Thomas Gradgrind, the proprietor of a model school. "Facts alone are wanted in life . . . nothing else will ever be of any service to them." Consequently, none of his children "had ever associated a cow in a field with that famous cow with the crumpled horn . . . or that yet more famous cow who swallowed Tom Thumb . . . and had only been introduced to a cow as a graminivorous ruminating quadruped with several stomachs." The dismal results of such intense instruction are the Smallweeds of *Bleak House* (1853), boys and girls who have "discarded all amusements, discountenanced all storybooks, fairy tales, fictions, and fables," and thus "bear a likeness to old monkeys with something depressing on their minds."

Woe to him who dared to alter the tales beloved by Dickens in his childhood! When Cruikshank rewrote the old favorites "to inculcate, at *the earliest age*, A Horror of Drunkeness, and a recommendation of Total Abstinence from All Intoxicating Liquors" in his *Fairy Library* (1853), Dickens charged "fraud on the fairies." He believed that more than ever, in this utilitarian age, the stories must remain in their true, original state to continue "in their usefulness . . . in their simplicity, and purity, and innocent extravagance, as if they were actual fact."

Dickens' interest in fairy tales was by no means limited to those he had read in his childhood. He was acquainted with Andersen's works through his own children, and the Danish writer was his houseguest on a trip to England. *Household Words*, Dickens' magazine, reviewed new collections and published originals by Henry Morley, an editor and noted literary scholar. Morley believed that "there is in all literature nothing that can be produced which shall represent the essential spirit of a man or of a people so completely as a legend or a fairy tale." He collected the stories he told his own children as *Fables and Fairy Tales* (1860) and *Oberon's Horn* (1861). Their illustrator, Charles Henry Bennett, aptly assured the writer, "Your fairy tales are fuller of notions, conceits, and good honest daring absurdity than anything modern I know." Morley's highly inventive tales deserve to be better known today.

Despite his great support of the fairies' cause, Dickens himself wrote only one children's story of any consequence, "The Magic Fish-Bone," from his serial *Holiday Romance* (1868). This mock fairy tale, purportedly the work of "Miss Alice Rainbird, Aged Seven," retains the naivety of its supposed child author but nevertheless has its clear Victorian lesson. The villain here is poverty. Although the little heroine possesses the magic fish-bone throughout the story, she does not use the one wish it can grant her until after her father has tried every way he can to help his struggling family. "When we have done our very, very best, papa, and that is not enough," Princess Alicia realizes, "then I think the right time must come for asking help of others."

While wry, "The Magic Fish-Bone" is not as broadly comic as William Makepeace Thackeray's fairy tale *The Rose and the Ring* (1855). Then living in Italy, the novelist drew at his daughters' request a number of Twelfth Night characters to entertain them during the holidays; when recovering from a bout of malaria, he amused himself by inventing an elaborate story based on these pictures. He tested the narrative, chapter by chapter, on the bedridden daughter of his friend William Wetmore Story, the American sculptor. Here were the King, the Queen, the Dame, the Dandy, and all the other stock characters of the pantomime, the traditional British Christmas stage show that combined fairy stories with broad comedy and elaborate spectacle. Under the pen-name "Michael Angelo Titmarsh," Thackeray wrote and illustrated (in the manner of Cruikshank) his "Fire-Side Pantomime" about "a little *misfortune*" bestowed by the Fairy Blackstick on innocent Prince Giglio of Paflagonia and Princess Rosalba of Crim Tartary. *The Rose and the Ring* is a delightful Christmas confection by a master humorist, a deft parody not only of British pantomime but also of contemporary melodrama, studded with an abundance of puns and topical jokes as amusing to adults as to children. While mercilessly burlesquing fairy tale conventions, *The Rose and the Ring* is the first masterpiece of prose nonsense in English juvenile literature, anticipating the higher comedy of *Alice in Wonderland* by a number of years.

Dickens' and Thackeray's light-hearted works for children confirmed that the fanciful had become fashionable. A wealth of fairy stories appeared in the middle years of Victoria's reign—some of them, however, of dubious quality. Some Victorian storytellers are too long-winded, others too precious for modern sensibilities. Many, evidently intent on writing nineteenth-century equivalents of *Pilgrim's Progress*, are preoccupied more with moral and pious discourses than with the marvels of fairyland. Perhaps the trouble with many Victorian stories is that, as Andrew Lang noted in *The Lilac Fairy Book* (1910), "the three hundred and sixty-five authors who try to write new fairy tales are very tiresome. . . . These fairies try to be funny, and fail; or they try to preach, and succeed."

The Reverend Charles Lutwidge Dodgson, as "Lewis Carroll," may have called *Alice's Adventures in Wonderland* (1865) and *Through the Looking-Glass* (1871) "fairy tales," but their genius is really of an entirely different sort. Tolkien argued that "since the fairy-story deals with 'marvels,' it cannot tolerate any frame or machinery suggesting that the whole story in which they occur is a figment or an illusion." The dream narrative is no more a true fairy tale than is the beast fable; there is nothing especially enchanted in the latter, for the talking animals are merely symbols of human frailties. Carroll's most ambitious, most earnest work for children, *Sylvie and Bruno* (1889, 1893), does concern fairies, but this late Victorian attempt to combine instruction with amusement only proves Lang's point: it tries to be funny, and fails; it tries to preach, and succeeds.

Still, a good deal of the new literature proved to be more than fairy gold. Charles Kingsley's *The Water-Babies* (1863), a naturalist's parable, is admired now less for its overt social message than for its author's marvelous storytelling and inventive wordplay. Although little read today, Dinah M. Mulock Craik wrote several distinguished fairy books. Her most famous children's story is *The Little Lame Prince and His Travelling-Cloak* (1875), a fairy novella which, despite its pitiful hero and deathbed scenes, is never too maudlin or sentimental.

Arguably, the Pre-Raphaelite Brotherhood made the greatest contribution to Victorian fairy literature. This self-consciously archaic group of artists, poets, and critics redefined English literature as profoundly as it did contemporary painting. It swiftly led into the Arts and Crafts Movement, that late-nineteenth-century protest against the vulgarities of high Victorian design and manufacture. Its proponents wished to discard the Industrial Revolution and return to an earlier, simpler state where romance and social justice could flourish, and Man could be in harmony with Nature. It is remarkable how many other lives crossed those of the Pre-Raphaelites. Ruskin championed them, Carroll photographed them, Mrs. Craik's husband published them. William Allingham secured haunting wood engravings from his friends Dante Gabriel Rossetti, John Everett Millais, and Arthur Hughes for his collection of poetry, *The Music Master* (1855), in which appeared his most celebrated verse, "The Fairies." Rossetti showed his sister's poetry to Allingham and Ruskin before getting it published and providing the book's extraordinary frontispiece and pictorial title page. The lush sensuality of the title selection of Christina Rossetti's *Goblin Market and Other Poems* (1862) introduced not only the Pre-Raphaelite but also the "Fleshly School" of British verse, best exemplified by her brother Dante's and Algernon Charles Swinburne's poetry.

Mary De Morgan was the spirited, funny, outspoken sister of William De Morgan, the prominent Arts and Crafts designer and novelist. She was also a superb storyteller who entertained the children of her friends Edward Burne-Jones and William Morris, as well as the young Rudyard Kipling and his sister, with her own fairy tales. Her first collection, *On a Pincushion* (1877), was graced with her brother's pictures; another, *The Necklace of Princess Fiorimonde* (1880), with elegant wood engravings by Walter Crane; she dedicated her last anthology, *The Windfairies* (1900), to Burne-Jones' grandchildren. Hers are among the most skillfully told fairy tales of the period, full of the marvels of the French *contes* but with a Victorian moral sensibility.

The last phase of these Pre-Raphaelite fairy tales is represented by Ford Madox Ford's *The Brown Owl* (1891). This rambling youthful romance, written to entertain the author's sister when he was only nineteen years old, so enchanted their grandfather, the painter Ford Madox Brown, that the old man found a publisher and contributed two illustrations to the book. It was sold outright for ten pounds, of which the author's mother gave him ten shillings; it sold several thousand copies, more in the author's lifetime than any other book Ford ever wrote.

Unquestionably, the master of the Victorian fairy tale was George MacDonald. His stories, like those of the Pre-Raphaelites, were moral yet more symbolic than didactic or allegorical, as were many of his contemporaries' efforts. His adult fantasies, *Phantastes* (1858) and *Lilith* (1895), marked the beginning and the end of his distinguished literary career. His children's books include several of the most extraordinary works of the imagination in juvenile literature: *Dealings with the Fairies* (1867), *At the Back of the North Wind* (1871), *The Princess and the Goblin* (1872), and *The Princess and Curdie* (1883), all exquisitely illustrated by Arthur Hughes. "For my part," MacDonald explained, "I do not write for children, but for the childlike, whether of five, or fifty, or seventy-five." His stories contain a mystial resonance rare in books for boys and girls, and he never wrote a more beautiful fairy tale than "The Golden Key," from *Dealings with the Fairies*.

Just as MacDonald reached the pinnacle of the Victorian fairy tale, the form entered its decline. "At the present moment," Mrs. E. M. Field reported in *The Child and His Book* (1889), "the fairy tale seems to have given way entirely in popularity to the children's story of real life." But she immediately had to amend this statement by acknowledging in a footnote the popularity of Andrew Lang's *The Blue Fairy Book* (1889). So successful did this collection of classic folk and literary fairy tales prove that it became merely the first volume in a successful series of ten big books of the world's fairy lore. Lang was surprisingly lean on British legends, but another folklorist, Joseph Jacobs, found enough to fill *English Fairy Tales* (1890), *More English Fairy Tales* (1894), *Celtic Fairy Tales* (1892), and *More Celtic Fairy Tales* (1894). Jacobs' research was supplemented by William Butler Yeats' fine early collections, *Fairy and Folk Tales of the Irish Peasantry* (1888), *Irish Fairy Tales* (1892), and *The Celtic Twilight* (1893), as well as his celebrated verses taken from folklore. Probably the most haunting of these is "The Stolen Child," from *The Wanderings of Oisin* (1889).

The Decadents entered the fairy sphere as quickly as they did the rest of British life and art, with the publication of Oscar Wilde's *The Happy Prince and Other Tales* (1888) and *The House of Pomegranates* (1891). The design of these sumptuous volumes, the first embellished by Walter Crane and Jacomb Hood, the second by Charles Ricketts and Charles Shannon, beautifully reflects the artificiality of their texts. What Wilde admired in ancient art, "the Greeks' joy in the visible aspect of things, all the Greeks' sense of delicate and delightful detail, all the Greeks' pleasure in beautiful textures, and exquisite materials, and imaginative designs," is everywhere evident in these elegant stories. Wilde may have taken his theme of Christian self-sacrifice from Andersen, but these tales are really all about marvelous surfaces. They express a world-weariness tinged with misogyny and homoeroticism not common to earlier English fairy literature. They are more introspective, less concerned with society than with the individual. Wilde's violences, whether physical or psychological, are generally self-inflicted: his monsters turn upon themselves rather than upon others. (He was horrified when Yeats told an old tale about blood-thirsty giants that brought Wilde's son Cyril to tears.) The simplest and clearest of Wilde's fairy tales, the one most free of the excesses of his aestheticism, is "The Selfish Giant," from *The Happy Prince*. It is, as Walter Pater assured its author, "perfect in its kind."

An aestheticism much like Wilde's permeates Laurence Housman's exquisite stories. Their verbal filigree is as ornate as the fine line drawings he provided for his collections, *A Farm in Fairyland* (1894), *The House of Joy* (1895), *The Field of Clover* (1898), and *The Blue Moon* (1904). Delight was his chief concern in composing them. "The true end and object of a fairy-tale is the expression of the joy of living," Housman explained. "There begins and ends the morality of the fairy-tale: its value consists in its optimism. So for the true and unpolluted air of fairyland we have to go back to the old and artless tales of a day purer and simpler than our own." "Rocking-Horse Land," the first tale in his first collection, *A Farm in Fairyland*, beautifully embodies this ideal of fairy literature.

Wilde, Housman, or any other Decadent could have posed for the monster in Kenneth Grahame's "The Reluctant Dragon," from *Dream Days* (1898). Grahame's aesthetic creature is no more than a "happy Bohemian," more concerned with poetry than pillaging. He does not want to hurt anyone. But all true red-blooded Englishmen are, Grahame explains, "the most awful beggars for getting up fights. . . . Dogs, bulls, dragons—anything so long as it's a fight." Grahame, just like his civilized dragon, had no use for this muscular Christianity, and he implies here that he had none for the aims of the British Empire as well.

The most robust of these *fin-de-siècle* fairy tale authors was a woman, Edith Nesbit Bland, who signed her work simply "E. Nesbit." Her attitude towards fairyland was refreshingly matter-of-fact. Perhaps her greatest gift as a fantasist, as is evident in the Five Children trilogy (*The Five Children and It*, 1902; *The Phoenix and the Carpet*, 1904; and *The Story of the Amulet*, 1905) as well as her other modern fairy tales, was her ability to effortlessly transfer her young characters from contemporary London to lands of enchantment. The earliest example of this power lies in "The Deliverers of Their Country," first serialized in the *Strand Magazine* (May 1899) and republished in her collection *The Book of Dragons* (1901). This short story possesses all the verve, wit, and self-assured inventiveness one finds in Nesbit's more celebrated books.

If, by this time the Empire was truly fading, so too were its traditions. The glories of the Victorian fairy tale would pass with the creation of Peter

Pan. He made his first appearance in several chapters of James M. Barrie's novel *The Little White Bird* (1902), which were later printed separately as *Peter Pan in Kensington Gardens* (1906), opulently illustrated by Arthur Rackham. The more famous play *Peter Pan* did not open until 1904, to be followed by the novel *Peter and Wendy* in 1911. Perhaps no other character in modern juvenile literature is more misunderstood than poor Peter Pan; even in his first manifestation, in *Peter Pan in Kensington Gardens*, the boy who couldn't grow up is a tragic figure. Beneath the story's gossamer charm lies a tale of abandonment, loss, and death, written by a sad little man so distressed with the present that he longed to go back to his past.

The last gasp of the grand old tradition came with Rudyard Kipling's *Puck of Pook's Hill* (1906) and its sequel, *Rewards and Fairies* (1910). But they lack conviction: their fairy machinery is no more than pastework and tinsel, and the stories are crammed more with British history than with fairy lore. The optimism so vital to their predecessors could not survive the horrors of the First World War. Science fiction, the imagination looking forward, supplanted the fairy tale, the imagination looking backward, with the coming of the Modern Age.

The Victorian Fairy Tale Book does not pretend to embrace all aspects of this vast and varied genre. Instead, it includes only outstanding examples of imaginative fiction and poetry, several by writers who were among the greatest authors of their time. Remarkably, though works of fancy, most never intended as anything more than children's stories, they reflect Victoria's England better than most of the earnest novels and social tracts of that era. After all, Henry Morley observed, "everybody knows that fairy tales and other compositions of that kind represent the spirit of the age and nation out of which they spring." Some amuse, some enchant, some satirize, some criticize—after all, no one creates an alternative world who is content with his own. Whatever their authors' intentions, these selections, reunited with illustrations from their original editions, display the abundant riches to be found in the Victorian fairy tale.

THE
VICTORIAN
FAIRY TALE
BOOK

The King of the Golden River

O R

The Black Brothers

J O H N   R U S K I N

I

How the Agricultural System of the Black Brothers Was
Interfered with by South West Wind, Esquire

In a secluded and mountainous part of Stiria, there was, in old time, a
valley of the most surprising and luxuriant fertility. It was surrounded,
on all sides, by steep and rocky mountains, rising into peaks, which were
always covered with snow, and from which a number of torrents descended
in constant cataracts. One of these fell westward, over the face of a crag so
high, that, when the sun had set to everything else, and all below was
darkness, his beams still shone full upon this waterfall, so that it looked
like a shower of gold. It was, therefore, called by the people of the neigh-
bourhood, the Golden River. It was strange that none of these streams fell
into the valley itself. They all descended on the other side of the mountains,
and wound away through broad plains and by populous cities. But the clouds
were drawn so constantly to the snowy hills, and rested so softly in the
circular hollow, that in time of drouth and heat, when all the country round
was burnt up, there was still rain in the little valley; and its crops were so
heavy, and its hay so high, and its apples so red, and its grapes so blue,
and its wine so rich, and its honey so sweet, that it was a marvel to every
one who beheld it, and was commonly called the Treasure Valley. The whole
of this little valley belonged to three brothers, called Schwartz, Hans, and
Gluck. Schwartz and Hans, the two elder brothers, were very ugly men,
with overhanging eyebrows and small dull eyes, which were always half shut,
so that you couldn't see into *them*, and always fancied they saw very far into

3
.

you. They lived by farming the Treasure Valley, and very good farmers they were. They killed everything that did not pay for its eating. They shot the blackbirds, because they pecked the fruit; and killed the hedgehogs, lest they should suck the cows; they poisoned the crickets for eating the crumbs in the kitchen, and smothered the cicadas, which used to sing all summer in the lime-trees. They worked their servants without any wages, till they would not work any more, and then quarrelled with them, and turned them out of doors without paying them. It would have been very odd, if with such a farm, and such a system of farming, they hadn't got very rich; and very rich they *did* get. They generally contrived to keep their corn by them till it was very dear, and then sell it for twice its value; they had heaps of gold lying about on their floors, yet it was never known that they had given so much as a penny or a crust in charity; they never went to mass; grumbled perpetually at paying tithes; and were, in a word, of so cruel and grinding a temper, as to receive from all those with whom they had any dealings, the nick-name of the "Black Brothers." The youngest brother, Gluck, was as completely opposed, in both appearance and character, to his seniors as could possibly be imagined or desired. He was not above twelve years old, fair, blue-eyed, and kind in temper to every living thing. He did not, of course, agree particularly well with his brothers, or rather, they did not agree with *him*. He was usually appointed to the honourable office of turnspit, when there was anything to roast, which was not often; for, to do the brothers justice, they were hardly less sparing upon themselves than upon other people. At other times he used to clean the shoes, floors, and sometimes the plates, occasionally getting what was left on them, by way of encouragement, and a wholesome quantity of dry blows, by way of education.

Things went on in this manner for a long time. At last came a very wet summer, and everything went wrong in the country round. The hay had hardly been got in, when the haystacks were floated bodily down to the sea by an inundation; the vines were cut to pieces with the hail; the corn was all killed by a black blight; only in the Treasure Valley, as usual, all was safe. As it had rain when there was rain nowhere else, so it had sun when there was sun nowhere else. Every body came to buy corn at the farm, and went away pouring maledictions on the Black Brothers. They asked what they liked, and got it, except from the poor people, who could only beg, and several of whom were starved at their very door, without the slightest regard or notice.

It was drawing towards winter, and very cold weather, when one day the two elder brothers had gone out, with their usual warning to little Gluck, who was left to mind the roast, that he was to let nobody in, and give nothing out. Gluck sat down quite close to the fire, for it was raining very hard, and the kitchen walls were by no means dry or comfortable-looking. He turned and turned, and the roast got nice and brown. "What a pity," thought Gluck, "my brothers never ask anybody to dinner. I'm sure, when they've got such a nice piece of mutton as this, and nobody else has got so much as a piece of dry bread, it would do their hearts good to have somebody to eat it with them."

Just as he spoke, there came a double knock at the house door, yet heavy and dull, as though the knocker had been tied up—more like a puff than a knock. "It must be the wind," said Gluck; "nobody else would venture to knock double knocks at our door." No it wasn't the wind: there it came again very hard, and what was particularly astounding, the knocker seemed to be in a hurry, and not to be in the least afraid of the consequences. Gluck went to the window, opened it, and put his head out to see who it was. It was the most extraordinary-looking little gentleman he had ever seen in his life. He had a very long nose, slightly brass-coloured, and expanding towards its termination into a development not unlike the lower extremity of a key bugle. His cheeks were very round, and very red, and might have warranted a supposition that he had been blowing a refractory fire for the last eight-and-forty hours. His eyes twinkled merrily through long silky eyelashes, his moustaches curled twice round like a cork-screw on each side of his mouth, and his hair, of a curious mixed pepper-and-salt colour, descended far over his shoulders. He was about four feet six in height, and wore a conical pointed cap of nearly the same altitude, decorated with a black feather some three feet long. His doublet was prolonged behind into something resembling a violent exaggeration of what is now termed a "swallow-tail," but was much obscured by the swelling folds of an enormous black, glossy-looking cloak, which must have been very much too long in calm weather, as the wind, whistling round the old house, carried it clear out from the wearer's shoulders to about four times his own length.

Gluck was so perfectly paralyzed by the singular appearance of his visitor, that he remained fixed without uttering a word, until the old gentleman, having performed another and a more energetic concerto on the knocker, turned round to look after his fly-away cloak. In so doing he caught sight of Gluck's little yellow head jammed in the window, with its mouth and eyes very wide open indeed.

"Hollo!" said the little gentleman, "that's not the way to answer the door: I'm wet, let me in."

To do the little gentleman justice, he *was* wet. His feather hung down between his legs like a beaten puppy's tail, dripping like an umbrella; and from the ends of his moustaches the water was running into his waistcoat pockets, and out again like a mill-stream.

"I beg pardon, sir," said Gluck, "I'm very sorry, but I really can't."

"Can't what?" said the old gentleman.

"I can't let you in, sir,—I can't indeed; my brothers would beat me to death, sir, if I thought of such a thing. What do you want, sir?"

"Want?" said the old gentleman petulantly. "I want fire, and shelter; and there's your great fire there blazing, crackling, and dancing on the walls, with nobody to feel it. Let me in, I say; I only want to warm myself."

Gluck had had his head, by this time, so long out of the window, that he began to feel it was really unpleasantly cold, and when he turned, and saw the beautiful fire rustling and roaring, and throwing long bright tongues up the chimney, as if it were licking its chops at the savoury smell of the leg of mutton, his heart melted within him that it should be burning away for nothing. "He does look *very* wet," said little Gluck; "I'll just let him in for a quarter of an hour." Round he went to the door, and opened it; and as the little gentleman walked in, there came a gust of wind through the house, that made the old chimneys totter.

"That's a good boy," said the little gentleman. "Never mind your brothers. I'll talk to them."

"Pray, sir, don't do any such thing," said Gluck. "I can't let you stay till they come; they'd be the death of me."

"Dear me," said the old gentleman, "I'm very sorry to hear that. How long may I stay?"

"Only till the mutton's done, sir," replied Gluck, "and it's very brown."

Then the old gentleman walked into the kitchen, and sat himself down on the hob, with the top of his cap accommodated up the chimney, for it was a great deal too high for the roof.

"You'll soon dry there, sir," said Gluck, and sat down again to turn the mutton. But the old gentleman did *not* dry there, but went on drip, drip, dripping among the cinders, and the fire fizzed, and sputtered, and began to look very black, and uncomfortable; never was such a cloak; every fold in it ran like a gutter.

"I beg pardon, sir," said Gluck at length, after watching the water spreading in long, quick-silver-like streams over the floor for a quarter of an hour; "mayn't I take your cloak?"

"No, thank you," said the old gentleman.

"Your cap, sir?"

"I am all right, thank you," said the old gentleman rather gruffly.

"But—sir,—I'm very sorry," said Gluck, hesitatingly; "but—really, sir,—you're—putting the fire out."

"It'll take longer to do the mutton then," replied his visitor drily.

Gluck was very much puzzled by the behaviour of his guest; it was such a strange mixture of coolness and humility. He turned away at the string meditatively for another five minutes.

"That mutton looks very nice," said the old gentleman at length. "Can't you give me a little bit?"

"Impossible, sir," said Gluck.

"I'm very hungry," continued the old gentleman. "I've had nothing to eat yesterday, nor to-day. They surely couldn't miss a bit from the knuckle!"

He spoke in so very melancholy a tone, that it quite melted Gluck's heart. "They promised me one slice to-day, sir," said he. "I can give you that, but not a bit more."

"That's a good boy," said the old gentleman again.

Then Gluck warmed a plate, and sharpened a knife. "I don't care if I do get beaten for it," thought he. Just as he had cut a large slice out of the mutton, there came a tremendous rap at the door. The old gentleman jumped off the hob, as if it had suddenly become inconveniently warm. Gluck fitted the slice into the mutton again, with desperate efforts at exactitude, and ran to open the door.

"What did you keep us waiting in the rain for?" said Schwartz, as he walked in, throwing his umbrella in Gluck's face. "Ay! what for, indeed, you little vagabond?" said Hans, administering an educational box on the ear, as he followed his brother into the kitchen.

"Bless my soul!" said Schwartz when he opened the door.

"Amen," said the little gentleman, who had taken his cap off, and was standing in the middle of the kitchen, bowing with the utmost possible velocity.

"Who's that?" said Schwartz, catching up a rolling-pin, and turning to Gluck with a fierce frown.

"I don't know, indeed, brother," said Gluck in great terror.

"How did he get in?" roared Schwartz.

"My dear brother," said Gluck, deprecatingly, "he was so *very* wet!"

The rolling-pin was descending on Gluck's head; but, at the instant, the old gentleman interposed his conical cap, on which it crashed with a shock that shook the water out of it all over the room. What was very odd, the rolling-pin no sooner touched the cap, than it flew out of Schwartz's hand, spinning like a straw in a high wind, and fell into the corner at the further end of the room.

"Who are you, sir?" demanded Schwartz, turning upon him.

"What's your business?" snarled Hans.

"I'm a poor old man, sir," the little gentleman began very modestly, "and I saw your fire through the window, and begged shelter for a quarter of an hour."

"Have the goodness to walk out again, then," said Schwartz. "We've quite enough water in our kitchen, without making it a drying-house."

"It is a cold day to turn an old man out in, sir; look at my grey hairs." They hung down to his shoulders, as I told you before.

"Ay!" said Hans, "there are enough of them to keep you warm. Walk!"

"I'm very, very hungry, sir; couldn't you spare me a bit of bread before I go?"

"Bread, indeed!" said Schwartz; "do you suppose we've nothing to do with our bread, but to give it to such red-nosed fellows as you?"

"Why don't you sell your feather?" said Hans, sneeringly. "Out with you."

"A little bit," said the old gentleman.

"Be off!" said Schwartz.

"Pray, gentlemen."

"Off, and be hanged!" cried Hans, seizing him by the collar. But he had no sooner touched the old gentleman's collar, than away he went after the rolling-pin, spinning round and round, till he fell into the corner on the top of it. Then Schwartz was very angry, and ran at the old gentleman to turn him out; but he also had hardly touched him, when away he went after Hans and the rolling-pin, and hit his head against the wall as he tumbled into the corner. And so there they lay, all three.

Then the old gentleman spun himself round with velocity in the opposite direction; continued to spin until his long cloak was all wound neatly about him; clapped his cap on his head, very much on one side (for it could not stand upright without going through the ceiling), gave an additional twist to his cork-screw moustaches, and replied with perfect coolness: "Gentlemen, I wish you a very good morning. At twelve o'clock to-night, I'll call again; after such a refusal of hospitality as I have just experienced, you will not be surprised if that visit is the last I ever pay you."

"If ever I catch you here again," muttered Schwartz, coming half frightened out of the corner—but, before he could finish his sentence, the old gentleman had shut the house-door behind him with a great bang: and there drove past the window, at the same instant, a wreath of ragged cloud, that whirled and rolled away down the valley in all manner of shapes; turning over and over in the air; and melting away at last in a gush of rain.

"A very pretty business, indeed, Mr. Gluck!" said Schwartz. "Dish the mutton, sir. If ever I catch you at such a trick again—bless me, why the mutton's been cut!"

"You promised me one slice, brother, you know," said Gluck.

"Oh! and you were cutting it hot, I suppose, and going to catch all the gravy. It'll be long before I promise you such a thing again. Leave the room, sir; and have the kindness to wait in the coal-cellar till I call you."

Gluck left the room, melancholy enough. The brothers ate as much mutton as they could, locked the rest in the cupboard, and proceeded to get very drunk after dinner.

Such a night as it was! Howling wind, and rushing rain, without intermission. The brothers had just sense enough left to put up all the shutters, and double-bar the door, before they went to bed. They usually slept in the same room. As the clock struck twelve, they were both awakened by a tremendous crash. Their door burst open with a violence that shook the house from top to bottom.

"What's that?" cried Schwartz, starting up in his bed.

"Only I," said the little gentleman.

The two brothers sat up on their bolster, and stared into the darkness. The room was full of water, and by a misty moonbeam, which found its way through a hole in the shutter, they could see in the midst of it an enormous foam globe, spinning round, and bobbing up and down like a cork, on which, as on a most luxurious cushion, reclined the little old gentleman, cap and all. There was plenty of room for it now, for the roof was off.

"Sorry to incommode you," said their visitor, ironically. "I'm afraid your beds are dampish; perhaps you had better go to your brother's room: I've left the ceiling on, there."

They required no second admonition, but rushed into Gluck's room, wet through, and in an agony of terror.

"You'll find my card on the kitchen table," the old gentleman called after them. "Remember, the *last* visit."

"Pray Heaven it may!" said Schwartz, shuddering. And the foam globe disappeared.

Dawn came at last, and the two brothers looked out of Gluck's little window in the morning. The Treasure Valley was one mass of ruin, and desolation. The inundation had swept away trees, crops, and cattle, and left in their stead, a waste of red sand, and grey mud. The two brothers crept shivering and horror-struck into the kitchen. The water had gutted the whole first floor; corn, money, almost every moveable thing had been swept away, and there was left only a small white card on the kitchen table. On it, in large, breezy, long-legged letters, were engraved the words:—SOUTH WEST WIND, ESQUIRE.

I I

Of the Proceedings of the Three Brothers After the Visit
of South West Wind, Esquire; and How Little Gluck Had
an Interview with the King of the Golden River

South West Wind, Esquire, was as good as his word. After the momentous visit above related, he entered the Treasure Valley no more; and, what was worse, he had so much influence with his relations, the West Winds in general, and used it so effectually, that they all adopted a similar line of conduct. So no rain fell in the valley from one year's end to another. Though everything remained green and flourishing in the plains below, the inheritance of the Three Brothers was a desert. What had once been the richest soil in the kingdom became a shifting heap of red sand; and the brothers, unable longer to contend with the adverse skies, abandoned their valueless patrimony in despair, to seek some means of gaining a livelihood among the cities and people of the plains. All their money was gone, and they had nothing left but some curious old-fashioned pieces of gold plate, the last remnants of their ill-gotten wealth.

"Suppose we turn goldsmiths?" said Schwartz to Hans, as they entered the large city. "It is a good knave's trade; we can put a great deal of copper into the gold, without any one's finding it out."

The thought was agreed to be a very good one; they hired a furnace, and turned goldsmiths. But two slight circumstances affected their trade: the first, that people did not approve of the coppered gold; the second, that the two elder brothers, whenever they had sold anything, used to leave little Gluck to mind the furnace, and go and drink out the money in the ale-house next door. So they melted all their gold, without making money enough to buy more, and were at last reduced to one large drinking-mug, which an uncle of his had given to little Gluck, and which he was very fond of, and would not have parted with for the world; though he never drank anything out of it but milk and water. The mug was a very odd mug to look at. The handle was formed of two wreaths of flowing golden hair, so finely spun that it looked more like silk than metal, and these wreaths descended into and mixed with a beard and whiskers, of the same exquisite workmanship, which surrounded and decorated a very fierce little face, of the reddest gold imaginable, right in the front of the mug, with a pair of eyes in it which seemed to command its whole circumference. It was impossible to drink out of the mug without being subjected to an intense gaze out of the side of these eyes; and Schwartz positively averred that once, after emptying it full of Rhenish seventeen times, he had seen them wink! When it came to the mug's turn to be made into spoons, it half broke poor little Gluck's heart; but the brothers only laughed at him, tossed the mug into the melting-pot, and staggered out to the ale-house; leaving him, as usual, to pour the gold into bars, when it was all ready.

When they were gone, Gluck took a farewell look at his old friend in the melting-pot. The flowing hair was all gone; nothing remained but the red nose, and the sparkling eyes, which looked more malicious than ever. "And no wonder," thought Gluck, "after being treated that way." He sauntered disconsolately to the window, and sat himself down to catch the fresh evening air, and escape the hot breath of the furnace. Now this window commanded a direct view of the range of mountains, which as I told you before, overhung the Treasure Valley, and more especially of the peak from which fell the Golden River. It was just at the close of the day, and, when Gluck sat down at the window, he saw the rocks of the mountain-tops, all crimson and purple with the sunset; and there were bright tongues of fiery cloud burning and quivering about them; and the river, brighter than all, fell, in a waving column of pure gold, from precipice to precipice, with the double arch of a broad purple rainbow stretched across it, flushing and fading alternately in the wreaths of spray.

"Ah!" said Gluck aloud, after he had looked at it for a little while, "if that river were really all gold, what a nice thing it would be."

"No it wouldn't, Gluck," said a clear metallic voice, close at his ear.

"Bless me, what's that?" exclaimed Gluck, jumping up. There was nobody there. He looked round the room, and under the table, and a great many times behind him, but there was certainly nobody there, and he sat down again at the window. This time he didn't speak, but he couldn't help thinking again that it would be very convenient if the river were really all gold.

"Not at all, my boy," said the same voice, louder than before.

"Bless me!" said Gluck again, "what *is* that?" He looked again into all the corners, and cupboards, and then began turning round and round, as fast as he could, in the middle of the room, thinking there was somebody behind him, when the same voice struck again on his ear. It was singing now very merrily "Lala-lira-la"; no words, only a soft running effervescent melody, something like that of a kettle on the boil. Gluck looked out of the window. No, it was certainly in the house. Up stairs, and down stairs. No, it was certainly in that very room, coming in quicker time, and clearer notes, every moment. "Lala-lira-la." All at once it struck Gluck that it sounded louder near the furnace. He ran to the opening, and looked in: yes, he saw right, it seemed to be coming, not only out of the furnace, but out of the pot. He uncovered it, and ran back in a great fright, for the pot was certainly singing! He stood in the farthest corner of the room, with his hands up, and his mouth open, for a minute or two, when the singing stopped, and the voice became clear, and pronunciative.

"Hollo!" said the voice.

Gluck made no answer.

"Hollo! Gluck, my boy," said the pot again.

Gluck summoned all his energies, walked straight up to the crucible, drew it out of the furnace, and looked in. The gold was all melted, and its surface as smooth and polished as a river; but instead of reflecting little Gluck's head, as he looked in, he saw meeting his glance, from beneath the gold, the red nose and sharp eyes of his old friend of the mug, a thousand times redder and sharper than ever he had seen them in his life.

"Come Gluck, my boy," said the voice out of the pot again, "I'm all right; pour me out."

But Gluck was too much astonished to do anything of the kind.

"Pour me out, I say," said the voice rather gruffly.

Still Gluck couldn't move.

"*Will* you pour me out?" said the voice passionately. "I'm too hot."

By a violent effort, Gluck recovered the use of his limbs, took hold of the crucible, and sloped it, so as to pour out the gold. But instead of a liquid stream, there came out, first, a pair of pretty little yellow legs, then some coat-tails, then a pair of arms stuck akimbo, and, finally, the well-known head of his friend the mug; all which articles, uniting as they rolled out, stood up energetically on the floor, in the shape of a little golden dwarf, about a foot and a half high.

"That's right!" said the dwarf, stretching out first his legs, and then his arms, and then shaking his head up and down, and as far round as it would go, for five minutes, without stopping; apparently with the view of ascertaining if he were quite correctly put together, while Gluck stood contemplating him in speechless amazement. He was dressed in a slashed doublet of spun gold, so fine in its texture, that the prismatic colours gleamed over it, as if on a surface of mother-of-pearl; and, over this brilliant doublet, his hair and beard fell full half-way to the ground, in waving curls, so exquisitely delicate, that Gluck could hardly tell where they ended; they seemed to melt into air. The features of the face, however, were by no means finished with the same delicacy; they were rather coarse, slightly inclining to coppery in complexion, and indicative, in expression, of a very pertinacious and intractable disposition in their small proprietor. When the dwarf had finished his self-examination, he turned his small sharp eyes full on Gluck, and stared at him deliberately for a minute or two. "No it wouldn't, Gluck, my boy," said the little man.

This was certainly rather an abrupt and unconnected mode of commencing conversation. It might indeed be supposed to refer to the course of Gluck's thoughts, which had first produced the dwarf's observations out of the pot; but whatever it referred to, Gluck had no inclination to dispute the dictum.

"Wouldn't it, sir?" said Gluck, very mildly and submissively indeed.

"No," said the dwarf, conclusively. "No it wouldn't." And with that, the dwarf pulled his cap hard over his brows, and took two turns, of three feet long, up and down the room, lifting his legs up very high, and setting them down very hard. This pause gave time for Gluck to collect his thoughts a little, and, seeing no great reason to view his diminutive visitor with dread, and feeling his curiosity overcome his amazement, he ventured on a question of peculiar delicacy.

"Pray, sir," said Gluck, rather hesitatingly, "were you my mug?"

On which the little man turned sharp round, walked straight up to Gluck, and drew himself up to his full height. "I," said the little man, "am the King of the Golden River." Whereupon he turned about again, and took two more turns, some six feet long, in order to allow time for the consternation which this announcement produced in his auditor to evaporate. After which, he again walked up to Gluck and stood still, as if expecting some comment on his communication.

Gluck determined to say something at all events. "I hope your Majesty is very well," said Gluck.

"Listen!" said the little man, deigning no reply to this polite inquiry. "I am the King of what you mortals call the Golden River. The shape you saw me in was owing to the malice of a stronger king, from whose enchantments you have this instant freed me. What I have seen of you, and your conduct to your wicked brothers, renders me willing to serve you; therefore attend to what I tell you. Whoever shall climb to the top of that mountain from which you see the Golden River issue, and shall cast into the stream, at its source, three drops of holy water, for him, and for him only, the river shall turn to gold. But no one failing in his first can succeed in a second attempt; and if any one shall cast unholy water into the river, it will overwhelm him, and he will become a black stone." So saying, the King of the Golden River turned away, and deliberately walked into the centre of the hottest flame of the furnace. His figure became red, white, transparent, dazzling—a blaze of intense light—rose, trembled, and disappeared. The King of the Golden River had evaporated.

"Oh!" cried poor Gluck, running to look up the chimney after him. "Oh, dear, dear, dear me! My mug! my mug! my mug!"

I I I

How Mr. Hans Set Off on an Expedition to the
Golden River, and How He Prospered Therein

The King of the Golden River had hardly made the extraordinary exit related in the last chapter, before Hans and Schwartz came roaring into the house, very savagely drunk. The discovery of the total loss of their last piece of plate had the effect of sobering them just enough to enable them to stand over Gluck, beating him very steadily for a quarter of an hour; at the expiration of which period they dropped into a couple of chairs, and requested to know what he had got to say for himself. Gluck told them his story, of which of course they did not believe a word. They beat him again, till their arms were tired, and staggered to bed. In the morning, however, the steadiness with which he adhered to his story obtained him some degree of credence; the immediate consequence of which was, that the two brothers, after wrangling a long time on the knotty question, which of them should try his fortune first, drew their swords, and began fighting. The noise of the fray alarmed the neighbours, who, finding they could not pacify the combatants, sent for the constable.

Hans, on hearing this, contrived to escape, and hid himself; but Schwartz was taken before the magistrate, fined for breaking the peace, and, having drunk out his last penny the evening before, was thrown into prison till he should pay.

When Hans heard this, he was much delighted, and determined to set out immediately for the Golden River. How to get the holy water, was the question. He went to the priest, but the priest could not give any holy water to so abandoned a character. So Hans went to vespers in the evening for the first time in his life, and, under pretence of crossing himself, stole a cupful, and returned home in triumph.

Next morning he got up before the sun rose, put the holy water into a strong flask, and two bottles of wine and some meat in a basket, slung them over his back, took his alpine staff in his hand, and set off for the mountains.

On his way out of the town he had to pass the prison, and as he looked in at the windows, whom should he see but Schwartz himself peeping out of the bars, and looking very disconsolate.

"Good morning, brother," said Hans; "have you any message for the King of the Golden River?"

Schwartz gnashed his teeth with rage, and shook the bars with all his strength; but Hans only laughed at him, and, advising him to make himself comfortable till he came back again, shouldered his basket, shook the bottle of holy water in Schwartz's face till it frothed again, and marched off in the highest spirits in the world.

It was, indeed, a morning that might have made any one happy, even with no Golden River to seek for. Level lines of dewy mist lay stretched along the valley, out of which rose the massy mountains—their lower cliffs in pale grey shadow, hardly distinguishable from the floating vapour, but gradually ascending till they caught the sunlight, which ran in sharp touches of ruddy colour along the angular crags, and pierced, in long level rays, through their fringes of spear-like pine. Far above, shot up red splintered masses of castellated rock, jagged and shivered into myriads of fantastic forms, with here and there a streak of sunlit snow, traced down their chasms like a line of forked lightning; and, far beyond, and far above all these, fainter than the morning cloud, but purer and changeless, slept, in the blue sky, the utmost peaks of the eternal snow.

The Golden River, which sprang from one of the lower and snowless elevations, was now nearly in shadow; all but the uppermost jets of spray, which rose like slow smoke above the undulating line of the cataract, and floated away in feeble wreaths upon the morning wind.

On this object, and on this alone, Hans' eyes and thoughts were fixed; forgetting the distance he had to traverse, he set off at an imprudent rate of walking, which greatly exhausted him before he had scaled the first range of the green and low hills. He was, moreover, surprised, on surmounting them, to find that a large glacier, of whose existence, notwithstanding his previous knowledge of the mountains, he had been absolutely ignorant, lay between him and the source of the Golden River. He entered on it with the boldness of a practised mountaineer; yet he thought he had never traversed so strange or so dangerous a glacier in his life. The ice was excessively slippery, and out of all its chasms came wild sounds of gushing water; not monotonous or low, but changeful and loud, rising occasionally into drifting passages of wild melody, then breaking off into short melancholy tones, or sudden shrieks, resembling those of human voices in distress or pain. The ice was broken into thousands of confused shapes, but none, Hans thought, like the ordinary forms of splintered ice. There seemed a curious *expression* about all their outlines—a perpetual resemblance to living features, distorted and scornful. Myriads of deceitful shadows, and lurid lights, played and floated about and through the pale blue pinnacles, dazzling and confusing the sight of the traveller; while his ears grew dull and his head giddy with the constant gush and roar of the concealed waters. These painful circumstances increased upon him as he advanced; the ice crashed and yawned into fresh chasms at his feet, tottering spires nodded around him, and fell thundering across his path; and though he had repeatedly faced these dangers on the most terrific glaciers, and in the wildest weather, it was with a new and oppressive feeling of panic terror that he leaped the last chasm, and flung himself, exhausted and shuddering, on the firm turf of the mountain.

He had been compelled to abandon his basket of food, which became a perilous incumbrance on the glacier, and had now no means of refreshing himself but by breaking off and eating some of the pieces of ice. This, however, relieved his thirst; an hour's repose recruited his hardy frame, and, with the indomitable spirit of avarice, he resumed his laborious journey.

His way now lay straight up a ridge of bare red rocks, without a blade of grass to ease the foot, or a projecting angle to afford an inch of shade from the south sun. It was past noon, and the rays beat intensely upon the steep path, while the whole atmosphere was motionless, and penetrated with heat. Intense thirst was soon added to bodily fatigue with which Hans was now afflicted; glance after glance he cast on the flask of water which hung at his belt. "Three drops are enough," at last thought he; "I may, at least, cool my lips with it."

He opened the flask, and was raising it to his lips, when his eye fell on an object lying on the rock beside him; he thought it moved. It was a small dog, apparently in the last agony of death from thirst. Its tongue was out, its jaws dry, its limbs extended lifelessly, and a swarm of black ants were crawling about its lips and throat. Its eye moved to the bottle which Hans held in his hand. He raised it, drank, spurned the animal with his foot, and passed on. And he did not know how it was, but he thought that a strange shadow had suddenly come across the blue sky.

The path became steeper and more rugged every moment; and the high hill air, instead of refreshing him, seemed to throw his blood into a fever. The noise of the hill cataracts sounded like mockery in his ears: they were all distant, and his thirst increased every moment. Another hour passed, and he again looked down to the flask at his side; it was half empty, but there was much more than three drops in it. He stopped to open it, and again, as he did so, something moved in the path above him. It was a fair child, stretched nearly lifeless on the rock, it breast heaving with thirst, its eyes closed, and its lips parched and burning. Hans eyed it deliberately, drank, and passed on. And a dark grey cloud came over the sun, and long, snake-like shadows crept up along the mountain-sides. Hans struggled on. The sun was sinking, but its descent seemed to bring no coolness; the leaden weight of the dead air pressed upon his brow and heart, but the goal was near. He saw the cataract of the Golden River springing from the hill-side, scarcely five hundred feet above him. He paused for a moment to breathe, and sprang on to complete his task.

At this instant a faint cry fell on his ear. He turned, and saw a grey-haired old man extended on the rocks. His eyes were sunk, his features deadly pale, and gathered into an expression of despair. "Water!" he stretched his arms to Hans, and cried feebly. "Water! I am dying."

"I have none," replied Hans; "thou hast had thy share of life." He strode over the prostate body, and darted on. And a flash of blue lightning rose out of the East, shaped like a sword; it shook thrice over the whole heaven, and left it dark with one heavy, impenetrable shade. The sun was setting; it plunged towards the horizon like a red-hot ball.

The roar of the Golden River rose on Hans' ear. He stood at the brink of the chasm through which it ran. Its waves were filled with the red glory of the sunset: they shook their crests like tongues of fire, and flashes of bloody light gleamed along their foam. Their sound came mightier and mightier on his senses; his brain grew giddy with the prolonged thunder. Shuddering, he drew the flask from his girdle, and hurled it into the centre of the torrent. As he did so, an icy chill shot through his limbs; he staggered, shrieked, and fell. The waters closed over his cry. And the moaning of the river rose wildly into the night, as it gushed over THE BLACK STONE.

I V

How Mr. Schwartz Set Off on an Expedition to the Golden River, and How He Prospered Therein

Poor little Gluck waited very anxiously alone in the house, for Hans' return. Finding he did not come back, he was terribly frightened, and went and told Schwartz in the prison all that had happened. Then Schwartz was very much pleased, and said that Hans must certainly have been turned into a black stone, and he should have all the gold to himself. But Gluck was very sorry, and cried all night. When he got up in the morning, there was no bread in the house, nor any money; so Gluck went, and hired himself to another goldsmith, and he worked so hard, and so neatly, and so long every day, that he soon got enough money together to pay his brother's fine, and he went, and gave it all to Schwartz, and Schwartz got out of prison. Then Schwartz was quite pleased, and said he should have some of the gold of the river. But Gluck only begged he would go and see what had become of Hans.

Now when Schwartz had heard that Hans had stolen the holy water, he thought to himself that such a proceeding might not be considered altogether correct by the King of the Golden River, and determined to manage matters better. So he took some more of Gluck's money, and went to a bad priest, who gave him some holy water very readily for it. Then Schwartz was sure it was all quite right. So Schwartz got up early in the morning before the sun rose, and took some bread and wine in a basket, and put his holy water in a flask, and set off for the mountains. Like his brother, he was much surprised at the sight of the glacier, and had great difficulty in crossing it, even after leaving his basket behind him. The day was cloudless, but not bright: there was a heavy purple haze hanging over the sky, and the hills looked lowering and gloomy. And as Schwartz climbed the steep rock path, the thirst came upon him, as it had upon his brother, until he lifted his flask to his lips to drink. Then he saw the fair child lying near him on the rocks, and it cried to him, and moaned for water.

"Water indeed," said Schwartz; "I haven't half enough for myself," and passed on. And as he went he thought the sunbeams grew more dim, and he saw a low bank of black cloud rising out of the West; and, when he had climbed for another hour, the thirst overcame him again, and he would have drunk. Then he saw the old man lying before him on the path, and heard him cry out for water. "Water, indeed," said Schwartz, "I haven't half enough for myself," and on he went.

Then again the light seemed to fade from before his eyes, and he looked up, and, behold, a mist, of the colour of blood, had come over the sun; and the bank of black cloud had risen very high, and its edges were tossing and tumbling like the waves of the angry sea. And they cast long shadows, which flickered over Schwartz's path.

Then Schwartz climbed for another hour, and again his thirst returned; and as he lifted his flask to his lips, he thought he saw his brother Hans lying exhausted on the path before him, and, as he gazed, the figure stretched its arms to him, and cried for water. "Ha, ha," laughed Schwartz, "are you there? remember the prison bars, my boy. Water, indeed! do you suppose I carried it all the way up here for *you*?" And he strode over the figure; yet, as he passed, he thought he saw a strange expression of mockery about its lips. And, when he had gone a few yards further, he looked back; but the figure was not there.

And a sudden horror came over Schwartz, he knew not why; but the thirst for gold prevailed over his fear, and he rushed on. And the bank of black cloud rose to the zenith, and out of it came bursts of spiry lightning, and waves of darkness seemed to heave and float, between their flashes, over the whole heavens. And the sky where the sun was setting was all level, and like a lake of blood; and a strong wind came out of that sky, tearing its crimson clouds into fragments, and scattering them far into the darkness. And when Schwartz stood by the brink of the Golden River, its waves were black, like thunderclouds, but their foam was like fire; and the roar of the waters below and the thunder above met, as he cast the flask into the stream. And, as he did so, the lightning glared in his eyes, and the earth gave way beneath him, and the waters closed over his cry. And the moaning of the river rose wildly into the night, as it gushed over the TWO BLACK STONES.

V

How Little Gluck Set Off on an Expedition to the Golden River, and How He Prospered Therein; with Other Matters of Interest

When Gluck found that Schwartz did not come back, he was very sorry, and did not know what to do. He had no money, and was obliged to go and hire himself again to the goldsmith, who worked him very hard, and gave him very little money. So, after a month, or two, Gluck grew tired, and made up his mind to go and try his fortune with the Golden River. "The little king looked very kind," thought he. "I don't think he will turn me into a black stone." So he went to the priest, and the priest gave him some holy water as soon as he asked for it. Then Gluck took some bread in his basket, and the bottle of water, and set off very early for the mountains.

If the glacier had occasioned a great deal of fatigue to his brothers, it was twenty times worse for him, who was neither so strong nor so practised on the mountains. He had several very bad falls, lost his basket and bread, and was very much frightened at the strange noises under the ice. He lay a long time to rest on the grass, after he had got over, and began to climb the hill just in the hottest part of the day. When he had climbed for an hour, he got dreadfully thirsty, and was going to drink like his brothers, when he saw an old man coming down the path above him, looking very feeble, and leaning on a staff. "My son," said the old man, "I am faint with thirst, give me some of that water." Then Gluck looked at him, and when he saw that he was pale and weary, he gave him the water: "Only pray don't drink it all," said Gluck. But the old man drank a great deal, and gave him back the bottle two-thirds empty. Then he bade him good-speed, and Gluck went on again merrily. And the path became easier to his feet, and two or three blades of grass appeared upon it, and some grasshoppers began singing on the bank beside it; and Gluck thought he had never heard such merry singing.

Then he went on for another hour, and the thirst increased on him so that he thought he should be forced to drink. But, as he raised the flask, he saw a little child lying panting by the road-side, and it cried out piteously for water. Then Gluck struggled with himself, and determined to bear the thirst a little longer; and he put the bottle to the child's lips, and it drank all but a few drops. Then it smiled on him, and got up, and ran down the hill; and Gluck looked after it, till it became as small as a little star, and then turned, and began climbing again. And then there were all kinds of sweet flowers growing on the rocks, bright green moss, with pale pink starry flowers, and soft belled gentians, more blue than the sky at its deepest, and pure white transparent lilies. And crimson and purple butterflies darted hither and thither, and the sky sent down such pure light, that Gluck had never felt so happy in his life.

Yet, when he had climbed for another hour, his thirst became intolerable again; and, when he looked at his bottle, he saw that there were only five or six drops left in it, and he could not venture to drink. And, as he was hanging the flask to his belt again, he saw a little dog lying on the rocks, gasping for breath—just as Hans had seen it on the day of his ascent. And Gluck stopped and looked at it, and then at the Golden River, not five hundred yards above; and he thought of the dwarf's words, "that no one could succeed, except in their first attempt"; and he tried to pass the dog, but it whined piteously, and Gluck stopped again. "Poor beastie," said Gluck, "it'll be dead when I come down again, if I don't help it." Then he looked closer and closer at it, and its eye turned on him so mournfully, that he could not stand it. "Confound the King and his gold too," said Gluck; and he opened the flask, and poured all the water into the dog's mouth.

The dog sprang up and stood on its hind legs. Its tail disappeared; its ears became long, longer, silky, golden; its nose became very red; its eyes became very twinkling; in three seconds the dog was gone, and before Gluck stood his old acquaintance, the King of the Golden River.

"Thank you," said the monarch, "but don't be frightened, it's all right"; for Gluck showed manifest symptoms of consternation at this unlooked-for reply to his last observation. "Why didn't you come before," continued the dwarf, "instead of sending me those rascally brothers of yours, for me to have the trouble of turning into stones? Very hard stones they make too."

"Oh dear me!" said Gluck, "have you really been so cruel?"

"Cruel!" said the dwarf, "they poured unholy water into my stream: do you suppose I'm going to allow that?"

"Why," said Gluck, "I am sure, sir—your Majesty, I mean—they got the water out of the church font."

"Very probably," replied the dwarf; "but," and his countenance grew stern as he spoke, "the water which has been refused to the cry of the weary and dying is unholy, though it had been blessed by every saint in heaven; and the water which is found in the vessel of mercy is holy, though it had been defiled with corpses."

So saying, the dwarf stooped and plucked a lily that grew at his feet. On its white leaves there hung three drops of clear dew. And the dwarf shook them into the flask which Gluck held in his hand. "Cast these into the river," he said, "and descend on the other side of the mountains into the Treasure Valley. And so good-speed."

As he spoke, the figure of the dwarf became indistinct. The playing colours of his robe formed themselves into a prismatic mist of dewy light: he stood for an instant veiled with them as with the belt of a broad rainbow. The colours grew faint, the mist rose into the air; the monarch had evaporated.

And Gluck climbed to the brink of the Golden River, and its waves were as clear as crystal, and as brilliant as the sun. And, when he cast the three drops of dew into the stream, there opened where they fell a small circular whirlpool, into which the waters descended with a musical noise. Gluck stood watching it for some time, very much disappointed, because not only the river was not turned into gold, but its waters seemed much diminished in quantity. Yet he obeyed his friend the dwarf, and descended the other side of the mountains, towards the Treasure Valley; and, as he went, he thought he heard the noise of water working its way under the ground. And, when he came in sight of the Treasure Valley, behold, a river, like the Golden River, was springing from a new cleft of the rocks above it, and was flowing in innumerable streams along the dry heaps of red sand. And as Gluck gazed, fresh grass sprang beside the new streams, and creeping plants grew and climbed among the moistening soil. Young flowers opened suddenly along the river-sides, as stars leap out when twilight is deepening, and thickets of myrtle, and tendrils of vine, cast lengthening shadows over the valleys as they grew. And thus the Treasure Valley became a garden again, and the inheritance, which had been lost by cruelty, was regained in love. And Gluck went in, and dwelt in the valley, and the poor were never driven from his door; so that his barns became full of corn, and his house of treasure. And, for him, the river had, according to the dwarf's promise, become a River of Gold. And, to this day, the inhabitants of the valley point out the place where the three drops of holy dew were cast into the stream, and trace the course of the Golden River under the ground, until it emerges in the Treasure Valley. And, at the top of the cataract of the Golden River, are still to be seen two BLACK STONES, round which the waters howl mournfully every day at sunset; and these stones are still called by the people of the valley, THE BLACK BROTHERS.

1851

Designed & Etched by George Cruikshank. Sep.r 27.th 1866

The Pied Piper of Hamelin

ROBERT BROWNING

I

Hamelin town's in Brunswick,
   By famous Hanover city;
   The River Weser, deep and wide,
   Washes its wall on the southern side;
   A pleasanter spot you never spied;
But, when begins my ditty,
   Almost five hundred years ago,
To see townsfolk suffer so
   From vermin, was a pity.

I I

   Rats!
They fought the dogs, and killed the cats,
   And bit the babies in the cradles,
   And ate the cheeses out of the vats,
     And licked the soup from the cook's own ladles,
   Split open the kegs of salted sprats,
   Made nests inside men's Sunday hats,
   And even spoiled the women's chats,
     By drowning their speaking
     With shrieking and squeaking
In fifty different sharps and flats.

I I I

At last the people in a body
  To the Town Hall came flocking:
" 'Tis clear," cried they, "our Mayor's a noddy;
  And as for our Corporation—shocking
To think we buy gowns lined with ermine
For dolts that can't or won't determine
What's best to rid us of our vermin!
You hope, because you're old and obese,
To find in the furry civic robe ease?
Rouse up, sirs! Give your brains a racking
To find the remedy we're lacking,
Or, sure as fate, we'll send you packing!"
At this the Mayor and Corporation
Quaked with a mighty consternation.

I V

An hour they sate in council,
  At length the Mayor broke silence:
  "For a guilder I'd my ermine gown sell,
  I wish I were a mile hence!
It's easy to bid one rack one's brain—
I'm sure my poor head aches again
I've scratched it so, and all in vain.
Oh for a trap, a trap, a trap!"
Just as he said this, what should hap
At the chamber door but a gentle tap?
"Bless us," cried the Mayor, "what's that?"
(With the Corporation as he sat,
Looking little though wondrous fat;
Nor brighter was his eye, nor moister
Than a too-long-opened oyster,
Save when at noon his paunch grew mutinous

For a plate of turtle green and glutinous.)
"Only a scraping of shoes on the mat?
Anything like the sound of a rat
Makes my heart go pit-a-pat!

V

"Come in!"—the Mayor cried, looking bigger:
And in did come the strangest figure!
His queer long coat from heel to head
Was half of yellow and half of red;
And he himself was tall and thin,
With sharp blue eyes, each like a pin,
And light loose hair, yet swarthy skin,
No tuft on cheek nor beard on chin,
But lips where smiles went out and in—
There was no guessing his kith and kin!
And nobody could enough admire
The tall man and his quaint attire:
Quoth one: "It's as my great-grandsire,
Starting up at the Trump of Doom's tone,
Had walked this way from his painted tombstone!"

V I

He advanced to the council-table:
And, "Please your honours," said he, "I'm able,
By means of a secret charm, to draw
All creatures living beneath the sun,
That creep, or swim, or fly, or run,
After me so as you never saw!
And I chiefly use my charm
On creatures that do people harm,
The mole, and toad, and newt, and viper;
And people call me the Pied Piper."
(And here they noticed round his neck

A scarf of red and yellow stripe,
To match with his coat of the selfsame cheque;
And at the scarf's end hung a pipe;
And his fingers, they noticed, were ever straying
As if impatient to be playing
Upon this pipe, as low it dangled
Over his vesture so old-fangled.)
"Yet," said he "poor piper as I am,
In Tartary I freed the Cham,
Last June, from his huge swarms of gnats;
I eased in Asia the Nizam
Of a monstrous brood of vampire-bats:
And, as for what your brain bewilders,
If I can rid your town of rats
Will you give me a thousand guilders?"
"One? fifty thousand!"—was the exclamation
Of the astonished Mayor and Corporation.

V I I

Into the street the Piper stept,
  Smiling first a little smile,
As if he knew what magic slept
  In his quiet pipe the while;
Then, like a musical adept,
To blow the pipe his lips he wrinkled,
And green and blue his sharp eyes twinkled
Like a candle flame where salt is sprinkled;
And ere three shrill notes the pipe uttered,
You heard as if an army muttered;
And the muttering grew to a grumbling;
And the grumbling grew to a mighty rumbling;
And out of the houses the rats came tumbling:
Great rat, small rats, lean rats, brawny rats,
Brown rats, black rats, grey rats, tawny rats,
Grave old plodders, gay young friskers,
  Fathers, mothers, uncles, cousins,
Cocking tails and pricking whiskers,

Families by tens and dozens,
Brothers, sisters, husbands, wives—
Followed the Piper for their lives.
From street to street he piped advancing,
And step for step they followed dancing,
Until they came to the River Weser
Wherein all plunged and perished
—Save one who, stout as Julius Cæsar,
Swam across and lived to carry
(As he the manuscript he cherished)
To Rat-land home his commentary,
Which was, "At the first shrill notes of the pipe,
I heard a sound as of scraping tripe,
And putting apples, wondrous ripe,
Into a cider-press's gripe:
And a moving away of pickle-tub boards,
And a leaving ajar of conserve-cupboards,
And the drawing the corks of train-oil flasks,
And a breaking the hoops of butter-casks;
And it seemed as if a voice
(Sweeter far than by harp or by psaltery
Is breathed) called out, Oh rats, rejoice!
The world is grown to one vast drysaltery!
So munch on, crunch on, take your nuncheon,
Breakfast, supper, dinner, luncheon!
And just as a bulky sugar-puncheon,
All ready staved, like a great sun shone
Glorious scarce an inch before me,
Just as methought it said, Come, bore me!
—I found the Weser rolling o'er me."

VIII

You should have heard the Hamelin people
Ringing the bells till they rocked the steeple;
"Go," cried the Mayor, "and get long poles!
Poke out the nests and block up the holes!
Consult with carpenters and builders,

And leave in our town not even a trace
Of the rats!"—when suddenly up the face
Of the Piper perked in the market-place,
With a "First, if you please, my thousand guilders!"

I X

A thousand guilders! The Mayor looked blue;
So did the Corporation too.
For council dinners made rare havock
With Claret, Moselle, Vin-de-Grave, Hock;
And half the money would replenish
Their cellar's biggest butt with Rhenish.
To pay this sum to a wandering fellow
With a gipsy coat of red and yellow!
"Beside," quoth the Mayor, with a knowing wink,
"Our business was done at the river's brink;
We saw with our eyes the vermin sink,
And what's dead can't come to life, I think.
So, friend, we're not the folks to shrink
From the duty of giving you something for drink,
And a matter of money to put in your poke;
But, as for the guilders, what we spoke
Of them, as you very well know, was in joke.
Beside, our losses have made us thrifty;
A thousand guilders! Come, take fifty!"

X

The Piper's face fell, and he cried,
"No trifling! I can't wait, beside!
I've promised to visit by dinner-time
Bagdad, and accept the prime
Of the Head Cook's pottage, all he's rich in,
For having left, in the Caliph's kitchen,
Of a nest of scorpions no survivor—

With him I proved no bargain-driver,
With you, don't think I'll bate a stiver!
And folks who put me in a passion
May find me pipe to another fashion."

X I

"How?" cried the Mayor, "d'ye think I'll brook
Being worse treated than a cook?
Insulted by a lazy ribald
With idle pipe and vesture piebald?
You threaten us, fellow? Do your worst,
Blow your pipe there till you burst!"

X I I

Once more he stept into the street;
   And to his lips again
Laid his long pipe of smooth straight cane;
   And ere he blew three notes (such sweet
Soft notes as yet musician's cunning
   Never gave the enraptured air)
There was a rustling, that seemed like a bustling
Of merry crowds justling at pitching and hustling,
Small feet were pattering, wooden shoes clattering,
Little hands clapping, and little tongues chattering,
And, like fowls in a farm-yard when barley is scattering,
Out came the children running.
All the little boys and girls,
With rosy cheeks and flaxen curls,
And sparkling eyes and teeth like pearls,
Tripping and skipping, ran merrily after
The wonderful music with shouting and laughter.

XIII

The Mayor was dumb, and the Council stood
As if they were changed into blocks of wood,
Unable to move a step, or cry
To the children merrily skipping by—
And could only follow with the eye
That joyous crowd at the Piper's back.
But how the Mayor was on the rack,
And the wretched Council's bosoms beat,
As the Piper turned from the High Street
To where the Weser rolled its waters
Right in the way of their sons and daughters!
However he turned from South to West,
And to Koppelberg Hill his steps addressed,
And after him the children pressed;
Great was the joy in every breast.
"He never can cross that mighty top!
He's forced to let the piping drop,
And we shall see our children stop!"
When, lo, as they reached the mountain's side,
A wondrous portal opened wide,
As if a cavern was suddenly hollowed;
And the Piper advanced and the children followed,
And when all were in to the very last,
The door in the mountain-side shut fast.
Did I say, all? No! One was lame,
And could not dance the whole of the way;
And in after years, if you would blame
His sadness, he was used to say,—
"It's dull in our town since my playmates left!
I can't forget that I'm bereft
Of all the pleasant sights they see,
Which the Piper also promised me;
For he led us, he said, to a joyous land,
Joining the town and just at hand,
Where waters gushed and fruit-trees grew,

And flowers put forth a fairer hue,
And everything was strange and new;
The sparrows were brighter than peacocks here,
And their dogs outran our fallow deer,
And honey-bees had lost their stings,
And horses were born with eagles' wings;
And just as I became assured
My lame foot would be speedily cured,
The music stopped and I stood still,
And found myself outside the Hill,
Left alone against my will,
To go now limping as before,
And never hear of that country more!"

X I V

Alas, alas for Hamelin!
 There came into many a burgher's pate
 A text which says, that Heaven's Gate
 Opes to the Rich at as easy rate
As the needle's eye takes a camel in!
The Mayor sent East, West, North, and South
To offer the Piper by word of mouth,
 Wherever it was men's lot to find him,
Silver and gold to his heart's content,
If he'd only return the way he went,
 And bring the children behind him.
But when they saw 'twas a lost endeavour,
And Piper and dancers were gone for ever,
They made a decree that lawyers never
 Should think their records dated duly
If, after the day of the month and year,
These words did not as well appear,
"And so long after what happened here
 On the Twenty-second of July,
Thirteen hundred and Seventy-six":
And the better in memory to fix
The place of the children's last retreat,

They called it, the Pied Piper's Street—
Where any one playing on pipe or tabor
Was sure for the future to lose his labour.
Nor suffered they Hostelry or Tavern
    To shock with mirth a street so solemn;
But opposite the place of the cavern
    They wrote the story on a column,
And on the Great Church Window painted
The same, to make the world acquainted
How their children were stolen away;
And there it stands to this very day.
And I must not omit to say
That in Transylvania there's a tribe
Of alien people that ascribe
The outlandish ways and dress
On which their neighbours lay such stress,
To their fathers and mothers having risen
Out of some subterraneous prison
Into which they were trepanned
Long time ago in a mighty band
Out of Hamelin town in Brunswick land,
But how or why, they don't understand.

X V

So, Willy, let you and me be wipers
Of scores out with all men—especially pipers:
And, whether they pipe us free from rats or from mice,
If we've promised them aught, let us keep our promise.

1842

The Rose and the Ring

O R

The History of Prince Giglio and Prince Bulbo

WILLIAM MAKEPEACE

THACKERAY

I

Shows How the Royal Family Sate Down to Breakfast

This is Valoroso XXIV, King of Paflagonia, seated with his Queen and only child at their royal breakfast table, and receiving the letter which announces to his Majesty a proposed visit from Prince Bulbo, heir of Padella, reigning King of Crim Tartary. Remark the delight upon the monarch's royal features. He is so absorbed in the perusal of the King of Crim Tartary's letter, that he allows his eggs to get cold, and leaves his august miffins untasted.

"What! that wicked, brave, delightful Prince Bulbo!" cries Princess Angelica; "so handsome, so accomplished, so witty—the conqueror of Rim-bombamento, where he slew ten thousand giants!"

"Who told you of him, my dear?" asks his Majesty.

"A little bird," says Angelica.

"Poor Giglio?" says mamma, pouring out the tea.

"Bother Giglio!" cries Angelica, tossing up her head, which rustled with a thousand curl-papers.

"I wish," growls the King—"I wish Giglio was . . ."

"Was better? Yes, dear, he is better," says the Queen. "Angelica's little maid, Betsinda, told me so when she came to my room this morning with my early tea."

"You are always drinking tea," said the monarch, with a scowl.

"It is better than drinking port or brandy-and-water," replies her Majesty.

"Well, well, my dear, I only said you were fond of drinking tea," said the King of Paflagonia, with an effort as if to command his temper. "Angelica! I hope you have plenty of new dresses; your milliners' bills are long enough. My dear Queen, you must see and have some parties. I prefer dinners, but of course you will be for balls. Your everlasting blue velvet quite tires me: and, my love, I should like you to have a new necklace. Order one. Not more than a hundred or a hundred and fifty thousand pounds."

"And Giglio, dear," says the Queen.

"GIGLIO MAY GO TO THE—"

"Oh, sir," screams her Majesty. "Your own nephew! our late King's only son."

"Giglio may go to the tailor's, and order the bills to be sent in to Glumboso to pay. Confound him! I mean bless his dear heart. He need want for nothing; give him a couple of guineas for pocket-money, my dear; and you may as well order yourself bracelets while you are about the necklace, Mrs. V."

Her Majesty, or *Mrs. V.*, as the monarch facetiously called her (for even royalty will have its sport, and this august family were very much attached), embraced her husband, and, twining her arm round her daughter's waist, they quitted the breakfast-room in order to make all things ready for the princely stranger.

When they were gone, the smile that had lighted up the eyes of the *husband* and *father* fled—the pride of the *King* fled—the MAN was alone. Had I the pen of a G. P. R. James, I would describe Valoroso's torments in the choicest language; in which I would also depict his flashing eye, his distended nostril—his dressing-gown, pocket-handkerchief, and boots. But I need not say I have *not* the pen of that novelist; suffice it to say, Valoroso was alone.

He rushed to the cupboard, seizing from the table one of the many egg-cups with which his princely board was served for the matin meal, drew out a bottle of right Nantz or Cognac, filled and emptied the cup several times, and laid it down with a hoarse "Ha, ha ha! now Valoroso is a man again."

"But oh!" he went on (still sipping, I am sorry to say), "ere I was a king, I needed not this intoxicating draught; once I detested the hot brandy wine, and quaffed no other fount but nature's rill. It dashes not more quickly o'er the rocks, than I did, as, with blunderbuss in hand, I brushed away the early morning dew, and shot the partridge, snipe, or antlered deer! Ah! well may England's dramatist remark, 'Uneasy lies the head that wears a crown!' Why did I steal my nephew's, my young Giglio's—? Steal! said I? no, no, no, not steal, not steal. Let me withdraw that odious expression. I took, and on my manly head I set, the royal crown of Paflagonia; I took, and with my royal arm I wield, the sceptral rod of Paflagonia; I took, and in my outstretched hand I hold, the royal orb of Paflagonia! Could a poor boy, a snivelling, drivelling boy—was in his nurse's arms but yesterday, and cried for sugar-plums and puled for pap—bear up the awful weight of crown, orb, sceptre? gird on the sword my royal fathers wore, and meet in fight the tough Crimean foe?"

And then the monarch went on to argue in his own mind (though we need not say that blank verse is not argument) that what he had got it was his duty to keep, and that, if at one time he had entertained ideas of a certain restitution, which shall be nameless, the prospect by a *certain marriage* of uniting two crowns and two nations which had been engaged in bloody and expensive wars, as the Paflagonians and the Crimeans had been, put the idea of Giglio's restoration to the throne out of the question: nay, were his own brother, King Savio, alive, he would certainly will away the crown from his own son in order to bring about such a desirable union.

Thus easily do we deceive ourselves! Thus do we fancy what we wish is right! The King took courage, read the papers, finished his muffins and eggs, and rang the bell for his Prime Minister. The Queen, after thinking whether she should go up and see Giglio, who had been sick, thought, "Not now. Business first; pleasure afterwards. I will go and see dear Giglio this afternoon; and now I will drive to the jeweller's, to look for the necklace and bracelets." The Princess went up into her own room, and made Betsinda, her maid, bring out all her dresses; and as for Giglio, they forgot him as much as I forget what I had for dinner last Tuesday twelvemonth.

I I

How King Valoroso Got The Crown, and Prince Giglio Went Without

Paflagonia, ten or twenty thousand years ago, appears to have been one of those kingdoms where the laws of succession were not settled; for when King Savio died, leaving his brother Regent of the kingdom, and guardian of Savio's orphan infant, this unfaithful regent took no sort of regard of the late monarch's will; had himself proclaimed sovereign of Paflagonia under the title of King Valoroso XXIV, had a most splendid coronation, and ordered all the nobles of the kingdom to pay him homage. So long as Valoroso gave them plenty of balls at Court, plenty of money and lucrative places, the Paflagonian nobility did not care who was king; and, as for the people, in those early times they were equally indifferent. The Prince Giglio, by reason of his tender age at his royal father's death, did not feel the loss of his crown and empire. As long as he had plenty of toys and sweetmeats, a holiday five times a week, and a horse and gun to go out shooting when he grew a little older, and, above all, the company of his darling cousin, the King's only child, poor Giglio was perfectly contented; nor did he envy his uncle the royal robes and sceptre, the great hot uncomfortable throne of state, and the enormous cumbersome crown in which that monarch appeared from morning till night. King Valoroso's portrait has been left to us; and I think you will agree with me that he must have been sometimes *rather tired* of his velvet, and his diamonds, and his ermine, and his grandeur. I shouldn't like to sit in that stifling robe, with such a thing as that on my head.

No doubt, the Queen must have been lovely in her youth; for though she grew rather stout in after life, yet her features, as shown in her portrait, are certainly *pleasing*. If she was fond of flattery, scandal, cards, and fine clothes, let us deal gently with her infirmities, which, after all, may be no greater than our own. She was kind to her nephew; and if she had any scruples of conscience about her husband's taking the young Prince's crown, consoled herself by thinking that the King, though a usurper, was a most respectable man, and that at his death Prince Giglio would be restored to his throne, and share it with his cousin, whom he loved so fondly.

The Prime Minister was Glumboso, an old statesman, who most cheerfully swore fidelity to King Valoroso, and in whose hands the monarch left all the affairs of his kingdom. All Valoroso wanted was plenty of money, plenty of hunting, plenty of flattery, and as little trouble as possible. As long as he had his sport, this monarch cared little how his people paid for it: he engaged in some wars, and of course the Paflagonian newspapers announced that he gained prodigious victories: he had statues erected to himself in every city of the empire; and of course his pictures placed everywhere, and in all the print-shops: he was Valoroso the Magnanimous, Valoroso the Victorious, Valoroso the Great, and so forth;—for even in these early times courtiers and people knew how to flatter.

This royal pair had one only child, the Princess Angelica, who, you may be sure, was a paragon in the courtiers' eyes, in her parents', and in her own. It was said she had the longest hair, the largest eyes, the slimmest waist, the smallest foot, and the most lovely complexion of any young lady in the Paflagonian dominions. Her accomplishments were announced to be even superior to her beauty; and governesses used to shame their idle pupils by telling them what Princess Angelica could do. She could play the most difficult pieces of music at sight. She could answer any one of *Mangnall's*

Questions. She knew every date in the history of Paflagonia, and every other country. She knew French, English, Italian, German, Spanish, Hebrew, Greek, Latin, Cappadocian, Samothracian, Ægean, and Crim Tartar. In a word, she was a most accomplished young creature; and her governess and lady-in-waiting was the severe Countess Gruffanuff.

Would you not fancy, from this picture, that Gruffanuff must have been a person of the highest birth? She looks so haughty that I should have thought her a Princess at the very least, with a pedigree reaching as far back as the Deluge. But this lady was no better born than many other ladies who give themselves airs; and all sensible people laughed at her absurd pretensions.

The fact is, she had been maid-servant to the Queen when her Majesty was only Princess, and her husband had been head footman; but after his death or *disappearance*, of which you shall hear presently, this Mrs. Gruffanuff, by flattering, toadying, and wheedling her royal mistress, became a favourite with the Queen (who was rather a weak woman), and her Majesty gave her a title, and made her nursery governess to the Princess.

And now I must tell you about the Princess's learning and accomplishments, for which she had such a wonderful character. Clever Angelica certainly was, but as *idle as possible*. Play at sight, indeed! she could play one or two pieces, and pretend that she had never seen them before; she could answer half-a-dozen *Mangnall's Questions*; but then you must take care to ask the *right* ones. As for her languages, she had masters in plenty, but I doubt whether she knew more than a few phrases in each, for all her pretence; and as for her embroidery and her drawing, she showed beautiful specimens, it is true, but *who did them?*

This obliges me to tell the truth, and to do so I must go back ever so far, and tell you about the FAIRY BLACKSTICK.

I I I

Tells Who the Fairy Blackstick Was, and Who Were Ever So Many Grand Personages Besides

Between the kingdoms of Paflagonia and Crim Tartary, there lived a mysterious personage, who was known in those countries as the Fairy Blackstick, from the ebony wand or crutch which she carried; on which she rode to the moon sometimes, or upon other excursions of business or pleasure, and with which she performed her wonders.

When she was young, and had been first taught the art of conjuring by the necromancer, her father, she was always practising her skill, whizzing about from one kingdom to another upon her black stick, and conferring her fairy favours upon this prince or that. She had scores of royal godchildren; turned numberless wicked people into beasts, birds, millstones, clocks, pumps, bootjacks, umbrellas, or other absurd shapes; and in a word was one of the most active and officious of the whole College of fairies.

But after two or three thousand years of this sport, I suppose Blackstick grew tired of it. Or perhaps she thought, "What good am I doing by sending this princess to sleep for a hundred years? by fixing a black pudding on to that booby's nose? by causing diamonds and pearls to drop from one little girl's mouth, and vipers and toads from another's? I begin to think I do as much harm as good by my performances. I might as well shut my incantations up, and allow things to take their natural course.

"There were my two young goddaughters, King Savio's wife, and Duke Padella's wife: I gave them each a present, which was to render them charming in the eyes of their husbands, and secure the affection of those gentlemen as long as they lived. What good did my Rose and my Ring do these two women? None on earth. From having all their whims indulged by their husbands, they became capricious, lazy, ill-humoured, absurdly vain, and leered and languished, and fancied themselves irresistibly beautiful, when they were really quite old and hideous, the ridiculous creatures! They used actually to patronize me when I went to pay them a visit;—*me*, the Fairy Blackstick, who knows all the wisdom of the necromancers, and who could have turned them into baboons, and all their diamonds into strings of onions, by a single wave of my rod!" So she locked up her books in her cupboard, declined further magical performances, and scarcely used her wand at all except as a cane to walk about with.

So when Duke Padella's lady had a little son (the Duke was at that time only one of the principal noblemen in Crim Tartary), Blackstick, although invited to the christening, would not so much as attend; but merely sent her compliments and a silver papboat for the baby, which was really not worth a couple of guineas. About the same time the Queen of Paflagonia presented his Majesty with a son and heir; and guns were fired, the capital illuminated, and no end of feasts ordained to celebrate the young Prince's birth. It was thought the Fairy, who was asked to be his godmother, would at least have presented him with an invisible jacket, a flying horse, a Fortunatus's purse, or some other valuable token of her favour; but instead, Blackstick went up to the cradle of the child Giglio, when everybody was admiring him and complimenting his royal papa and mamma, and said:

"My poor child, the best thing I can send you is a *little misfortune*;" and this was all she would utter, to the disgust of Giglio's parents, who died very soon after, when Giglio's uncle took the throne, as we read in Chapter I.

In like manner, when CAVOLFIORE, King of Crim Tartary, had a christening of his only child, ROSALBA, the Fairy Blackstick, who had been invited, was not more gracious than in Prince Giglio's case. Whilst everybody was expatiating over the beauty of the darling child, and congratulating its parents, the Fairy Blackstick looked very sadly at the baby and its mother, and said:

"My good woman—(for the Fairy was very familiar, and no more minded a Queen than a washerwoman)—my good woman, these people who are following you will be the first to turn against you; and, as for this little lady, the best thing I can wish her is a *little misfortune*." So she touched Rosalba with her black wand, looked severely at the courtiers, motioned the Queen an adieu with her hand, and sailed slowly up into the air out of window.

When she was gone, the Court people, who had been awed and silent in her presence, began to speak.

"What an odious Fairy she is (they said)—a pretty Fairy, indeed! Why, she went to the King of Paflagonia's christening, and pretended to do all sorts of things for that family; and what has happened—the Prince, her godson, has been turned off his throne by his uncle. Would we allow our sweet Princess to be deprived of her rights by any enemy? Never, never, never, never!"

And they all shouted in a chorus, "Never, never, never, never!"

Now, I should like to know, how did these fine courtiers show their fidelity? One of King Cavolfiore's vassals, the Duke Padella just mentioned, rebelled against the King, who went out to chastise his rebellious subject.

"Any one rebel against our beloved and august monarch!" cried the courtiers; "any one resist *him*? Pooh! He is invincible, irresistible. He will bring home Padella a prisoner, and tie him to a donkey's tail, and drive him round the town, saying, 'This is the way the great Cavolfiore treats rebels.' "

The King went forth to vanquish Padella; and the poor Queen, who was a very timid, anxious creature, grew so frightened and ill, that I am sorry to say she died; leaving injunctions with her ladies to take care of the dear little Rosalba.—Of course they said they would. Of course they vowed they would die rather than any harm should happen to the Princess. At first the *Crim Tartar Court Journal* stated that the King was obtaining great victories over the audacious rebel: then it was announced that the troops of the infamous Padella were in flight: then it was said that the royal army would soon come up with the enemy, and then—then the news came that King Cavolfiore was vanquished and slain by his Majesty, King Padella the First!

At this news, half the courtiers ran off to pay their duty to the conquering chief, and the other half ran away, laying hands on all the best articles in the palace; and poor little Rosalba was left there quite alone—quite alone; and she toddled from one room to another, crying, "Countess! Duchess! (only she said 'Tountess, Duttess,' not being able to speak plain) bring me my mutton sop; my Royal Highness hungy! Tountess! Duttess!"

And she went from the private apartments into the throne-room and nobody was there;—and thence into the ball-room and nobody was there;—and thence into the pages' room and nobody was there;—and she toddled down the great staircase into the hall and nobody was there;—and the door was open, and she went into the court, and into the garden, and thence into the wilderness, and thence into the forest where the wild beasts live, and was never heard of any more!

A piece of her torn mantle and one of her shoes were found in the wood in the mouths of two lioness's cubs, whom KING PADELLA and a royal hunting-party shot—for he was King now, and reigned over Crim Tartary.

"So the poor little Princess is done for," said he; "well what's done can't be helped. Gentlemen, let us go to luncheon!" And one of the courtiers took up the shoe and put it in his pocket. And there was an end of Rosalba!

I V

How Blackstick Was Not Asked to the
Princess Angelica's Christening

When the Princess Angelica was born, her parents not only did not ask the Fairy Blackstick to the christening party, but gave orders to their porter absolutely to refuse her if she called. This porter's name was Gruffanuff, and he had been selected for the post by their Royal Highnesses because he was a very tall fierce man, who could say "Not at home" to a tradesman or an unwelcome visitor with a rudeness which frightened most such persons away. He was the husband of that Countess whose picture we have just seen, and as long as they were together they quarrelled from morning till night. Now this fellow tried his rudeness once too often, as you shall hear. For the Fairy Blackstick coming to call upon the Prince and Princess, who were actually sitting at the open drawing-room window, Gruffanuff not only denied them, but made the most *odious vulgar sign* as he was going to slam the door in the Fairy's face! "Git away, hold Blackstick!" said he. "I tell you, Master and Missis ain't at home to you:" and he was, as we have said, *going* to slam the door.

But the Fairy, with her wand, prevented the door being shut; and Gruffanuff came out again in a fury, swearing in the most abominable way, and asking the Fairy "whether she thought he was a-going to stay at that there door hall day?"

"You *are* going to stay at that door all day and all night, and for many a long year," the Fairy said, very majestically; and Gruffanuff, coming out of the door, straddling before it with his great calves, burst out laughing, and cried "Ha, ha, ha! this *is* a good un! Ha—ah—what's this? Let me down—O—o—H'm!" and then he was dumb!

For, as the Fairy waved her wand over him, he felt himself rising off the ground, and fluttering up against the door, and then, as if a screw ran into his stomach, he felt a dreadful pain there, and was pinned to the door; and then his arms flew up over his head; and his legs, after writhing about wildly, twisted under his body; and he felt cold, cold, growing over him, as if he was turning into metal; and he said, "O—o—H'm!" and could say no more, because he was dumb.

He *was* turned into metal! He was, from being *brazen, brass!* He was neither more or less than a knocker! And there he was, nailed to the door in the blazing summer day, till he burned almost red-hot; and there he was, nailed to the door all the bitter winter nights, till his brass nose was dropping with icicles. And the postman came and rapped at him, and the vulgarest boy with a letter came and hit him up against the door. And the King and Queen (Princess and Prince they were then) coming home from a walk that evening, the King said, "Hullo, my dear! you have had a new knocker put on the door. Why, it's rather like our porter in the face! What has become of the boozy vagabond?" And the housemaid came and scrubbed his nose with sand-paper; and once, when the Princess Angelica's little sister was born, he was tied up in an old kid glove; and another night, some *larking* young men tried to wrench him off, and put him to the most excruciating agony with a turnscrew. And then the Queen had a fancy to have the colour of the door altered, and the painters dabbed him over the mouth and eyes, and nearly choked him, as they painted him pea-green. I warrant he had leisure to repent of having been rude to the Fairy Blackstick!

As for his wife, she did not miss him; and as he was always guzzling beer at the public-house, and notoriously quarrelling with his wife, and in debt to the tradesmen, it was supposed he had run away from all these evils, and emigrated to Australia or America. And when the Prince and Princess chose to become King and Queen, they left their old house, and nobody thought of the Porter any more.

V

How Princess Angelica Took a Little Maid

One day, when the Princess Angelica was quite a little girl, she was walking in the garden of the palace, with Mrs. Gruffanuff, the governess, holding a parasol over her head, to keep her sweet complexion from the freckles, and Angelica was carrying a bun, to feed the swans and ducks in the royal pond.

They had not reached the duck-pond, when there came toddling up to them such a funny little girl! She had a great quantity of hair blowing about her chubby little cheeks, and looked as if she had not been washed or combed for ever so long. She wore a ragged bit of a cloak, and had only one shoe on.

"You little wretch, who let you in here?" asked Gruffanuff.

"Dive me dat bun," said the little girl, "me vely hungry."

"Hungry! what is that?" asked Princess Angelica, and gave the child the bun.

"Oh, Princess!" says Gruffanuff, "how good, how kind, how truly angelical you are! See, your Majesties," she said to the King and Queen, who now came up, along with their nephew, Prince Giglio, "how kind the Princess is! She met this little dirty wretch in the garden—I can't tell how she came in here, or why the guards did not shoot her dead at the gate!— and the dear darling of a Princess has given her the whole of her bun!"

"I didn't want it," said Angelica.

"But you are a darling little angel all the same," says the governess.

"Yes, I know I am," said Angelica. "Dirty little girl, don't you think I am very pretty?" Indeed, she had on the finest of little dresses and hats; and, as her hair was carefully curled, she really looked very well.

"Oh, pooty, pooty!" says the little girl, capering about, laughing, and dancing, and munching her bun; and as she ate it she began to sing, "Oh, what fun to have a plum bun! how I wis it never was done!" At which, and her funny accent, Angelica, Giglio, and the King and Queen began to laugh very merrily.

"I can dance as well as sing," says the little girl. "I can dance, and I can sing, and I can do all sorts of ting." And she ran to a flower-bed, and, pulling a few polyanthuses, rhododendrons, and other flowers, made herself a little wreath, and danced before the King and Queen so drolly and prettily, that everybody was delighted.

"Who was your mother—who were your relations, little girl?" said the Queen.

The little girl said, "Little lion was my brudder; great big lioness my mudder; neber heard of any udder." And she capered away on her one shoe, and everybody was exceedingly diverted.

So Angelica said to the Queen, "Mamma, my parrot flew away yesterday out of its cage, and I don't care any more for any of my toys; and I think this funny little dirty child will amuse me. I will take her home, and give her some of my frocks."

"Oh, the generous darling!" says Gruffanuff.

"Which I have worn ever so many times, and am quite tired of," Angelica went on; "And she shall be my little maid. Will you come home with me, little dirty girl?"

The child clapped her hands, and said, "Go home with you—yes! You pooty Princess!—Have a nice dinner, and wear a new dress!"

And they all laughed again, and took home the child to the palace, where, when she was washed and combed, and had one of the Princess's frocks given to her, she looked as handsome as Angelica, almost. Not that Angelica ever thought so; for this little lady never imagined that anybody in the world could be as pretty, as good, or as clever as herself. In order that the little girl should not become too proud or conceited, Mrs. Gruffanuff took her old ragged mantle and one shoe, and put them in a glass box, with a card laid upon them, upon which was written, "These were the old clothes in which little BETSINDA was found when the great goodness and admirable kindness of her Royal Highness the Princess Angelica received this little outcast." And the date was added, and the box locked up.

For a while little Betsinda was a great favourite with the Princess, and she danced, and sang, and made her little rhymes, to amuse her mistress. But then the Princess got a monkey, and afterwards a little dog, and afterwards a doll, and did not care for Betsinda any more, who became very melancholy and quiet, and sang no more funny songs, because nobody cared to hear her. And then, as she grew older, she was made a little lady's-maid to the Princess; and though she had no wages, she worked and mended, and put Angelica's hair in papers, was never cross when scolded, and was always eager to please her mistress, and was always up early and to bed late, and at hand when wanted, and in fact became a perfect little maid. So the two girls grew up, and, when the Princess came out, Betsinda was never tired of waiting on her; and made her dresses better than the best milliner, and was useful in a hundred ways. Whilst the Princess was having her masters, Betsinda would sit and watch them; and in this way she picked up a great deal of learning; for she was always awake, though her mistress was not, and listened to the wise professors when Angelica was yawning or thinking of the next ball. And when the dancing-master came, Betsinda learned along with Angelica; and when the music-master came, she watched him, and practised the Princess's pieces when Angelica was away at balls and parties; and when the drawing-master came, she took note of all he said and did; and the same with French, Italian, and all other languages—she learned them from the teacher who came to Angelica. When the Princess was going out of an evening she would say, "My good Betsinda, you may as well finish what I have begun." "Yes, Miss," Betsinda would say, and sit down very cheerful, not to *finish* what Angelica began, but to *do* it.

For instance, the Princess would begin a head of a warrior, let us say, and when it was begun it was something like this—

But when it was done, the warrior was like this—

(only handsomer still if possible), and the Princess put her name to the drawing; and the Court and King and Queen, and above all poor Giglio, admired the picture of all things, and said, "Was there ever a genius like

Angelica?" So, I am sorry to say, was it with the Princess's embroidery and other accomplishments; and Angelica actually believed that she did these things herself, and received all the flattery of the Court as if every word of it was true. Thus she began to think that there was no young woman in all the world equal to herself, and that no young man was good enough for her. As for Betsinda, as she heard none of these praises, she was not puffed up by them, and being a most grateful, good-natured girl, she was only too anxious to do everything which might give her mistress pleasure. Now you begin to perceive that Angelica had faults of her own, and was by no means such a wonder of wonders as people represented her Royal Highness to be.

V I

How Prince Giglio Behaved Himself

And now let us speak about Prince Giglio, the nephew of the reigning monarch of Paflagonia. It has already been stated, in Chapter 2, that as long as he had a smart coat to wear, a good horse to ride, and money in his pocket, or rather to take out of his pocket, for he was very good-natured, my young Prince did not care for the loss of his crown and sceptre, being a thoughtless youth, not much inclined to politics or any kind of learning. So his tutor had a sinecure. Giglio would not learn classics or mathematics, and the Lord Chancellor of Paflagonia, SQUARETOSO, pulled a very long face because the prince could not be got to study the Paflagonian laws and constitution; but, on the other hand, the King's gamekeepers and huntsmen found the Prince an apt pupil; the dancing-master pronounced that he was a most elegant and assiduous scholar; the First Lord of the Billiard Table gave the most flattering reports of the Prince's skill; so did the Groom of the Tennis Court; and as for the Captain of the Guard and Fencing Master, the *valiant* and *veteran* Count KUTASOFF HEDZOFF, he avowed that since he ran the General of Crim Tartary, the dreadful Grumbuskin, through the body, he never had encountered so expert a swordsman as Prince Giglio.

I hope you do not imagine that there was any impropriety in the Prince and Princess walking together in the palace garden, and because Giglio kissed Angelica's hand in a polite manner. In the first place they are cousins; next, the Queen is walking in the garden too (you cannot see her, for she happens to be behind that tree), and her Majesty always wished that Angelica and Giglio should marry: so did Giglio: so did Angelica sometimes, for she thought her cousin very handsome, brave, and good-natured: but then you know she was so clever and knew so many things, and poor Giglio knew nothing, and had no conversation. When they looked at the stars, what did Giglio know of the heavenly bodies? Once, when on a sweet night in a balcony where they were standing, Angelica said, "There is the Bear." "Where?" says Giglio. "Don't be afraid, Angelica! if a dozen bears come, I will kill them rather than they shall hurt you." "Oh, you silly creature!" says she: "you are very good, but you are not very wise." When they looked at the flowers, Giglio was utterly unacquainted with botany, and had never heard of Linnæus. When the butterflies passed Giglio knew nothing about them, being as ignorant of entomology as I am of algebra. So you see, Angelica, though she liked Giglio pretty well, despised him on account of his ignorance. I think she probably valued *her own learning* rather too much; but to think too well of one's self is the fault of people of all ages and both sexes. Finally when nobody else was there, Angelica liked her cousin well enough.

King Valoroso was very delicate in health, and withal so fond of good dinners (which were prepared for him by his French cook Marmitonio), that it was supposed he could not live long. Now the idea of anything happening to the King struck the artful Prime Minister and the designing old lady-in-waiting with terror. For, thought Glumboso and the Countess, "when Prince Giglio marries his cousin and comes to the throne, what a pretty position we shall be in, whom he dislikes, and who have always been unkind to him. We shall lose our places in a trice; Gruffanuff will have to give up all the jewels, laces, snuff-boxes, rings, and watches which belonged to the Queen, Giglio's mother; and Glumboso will be forced to refund two hundred and seventeen thousand millions, nine hundred and eighty-seven thousand, four hundred and thirty-nine pounds, thirteen shillings, and sixpence halfpenny, money left to Prince Giglio by his poor dear father." So the Lady of Honour and the Prime Minister hated Giglio because they had done him a wrong; and these unprincipled people invented a hundred cruel stories about poor Giglio, in order to influence the King, Queen, and Princess against him; how he was so ignorant that he could not spell the commonest words, and actually wrote Valoroso Valloroso, and spelt Angelica with two l's; how he drank a great deal too much wine at dinner, and was always idling in the stables with the grooms; how he owed ever so much money at the pastry-cook's and the haberdasher's; how he used to go to sleep at church; how he was fond of playing cards with the pages. So did the Queen like playing cards; so did the King go to sleep at church, and eat and drink too much; and, if Giglio owed a trifle for tarts, who owed him two hundred and seventeen thousand millions, nine hundred and eighty-seven thousand, four hundred and thiry-nine pounds, thirteen shillings, and sixpence halfpenny, I should like to know? Detractors and tale-bearers (in my humble opinion) had much better look at *home*. All this backbiting and slandering had effect upon Princess Angelica, who began to look coldly on her cousin, then to laugh at him and scorn him for being so stupid, then to sneer at him for having vulgar associates; and at Court balls, dinners, and so forth, to treat him so unkindly that poor Giglio became quite ill, took to his bed, and sent for the doctor.

His Majesty King Valoroso, as we have seen, had his own reasons for disliking his nephew; and as for those innocent readers who ask why?—I beg (with the permission of their dear parents) to refer them to Shakespeare's pages, where they will read why King John disliked Prince Arthur. With the Queen, his royal but weak-minded aunt, when Giglio was out of sight he was out of mind. While she had her whist and her evening-parties, she cared for little else.

I dare say *two villains*, who shall be nameless, wished Doctor Pildrafto, the Court Physician, had killed Giglio right out, but he only bled and physicked him so severely, that the Prince was kept to his room for several months, and grew as thin as a post.

Whilst he was lying sick in this way, there came to the Court of Paflagonia a famous painter, whose name was Tomaso Lorenzo, and who was Painter in Ordinary to the King of Crim Tartary, Paflagonia's neighbour. Tomaso Lorenzo painted all the Court, who were delighted with his works; for even Countess Gruffanuff looked young and Glumboso good-humoured in his pictures. "He flatters very much," some people said. "Nay!" says Princess Angelica, "I am above flattery, and I think he did not make my picture handsome enough. I can't bear to hear a man of genius unjustly cried down, and I hope my dear papa will make Lorenzo a knight of his Order of the Cucumber."

The Princess Angelica, although the courtiers vowed her Royal Highness could draw so *beautifully* that the idea of her taking lessons was absurd, yet chose to have Lorenzo for a teacher, and it was wonderful, *as long as she painted in his studio*, what beautiful pictures she made! Some of the performances were engraved for the Book of Beauty: others were sold for enormous sums at Charity Bazaars. She wrote the *signatures* under the drawings, no doubt, but I think I know who did the pictures—this artful painter, who had come with other designs on Angelica than merely to teach her to draw.

One day, Lorenzo showed the Princess a portrait of a young man in armour, with fair hair and the loveliest blue eyes, and an expression at once melancholy and interesting.

"Dear Signor Lorenzo, who is this?" asked the Princess. "I never saw any one so handsome," says Countess Gruffanuff (the old humbug).

"That," said the painter, "that, madam, is the portrait of my august young master, his Royal Highness Bulbo, Crown Prince of Crim Tartary, Duke of Acroceraunia, Marquis of Poluphloisboio, and Knight Grand Cross of the Order of the Pumpkin. That is the Order of the Pumpkin glittering on his manly breast, and received by his Royal Highness from his august father, his Majesty King PADELLA I., for his gallantry at the battle of Rimbombamento, when he slew with his own princely hand the King of Ograria and two hundred and eleven giants of the two hundred and eighteen who formed the King's body-guard. The remainder were destroyed by the brave Crim Tartar army after an obstinate combat, in which the Crim Tartars suffered severely."

What a Prince! thought Angelica: so brave—so calm-looking—so young—what a hero!

"He is as accomplished as he is brave," continued the Court Painter. "He knows all languages perfectly: sings deliciously: plays every instrument: composes operas which have been acted a thousand nights running at the Imperial Theatre of Crim Tartary, and danced in a ballet there before the King and Queen; in which he looked so beautiful, that his cousin, the lovely daughter of the King of Circassia, died for love of him."

"Why did he not marry the poor Princess?" asked Angelica, with a sigh.

"Because they were *first cousins*, madam, and the clergy forbid these unions," said the Painter. "And, besides, the young Prince had given his royal heart *elsewhere*."

"And to whom?" asked her Royal Highness.

"I am not at liberty to mention the Princess's name," answered the Painter.

"But you may tell me the first letter of it," gasped out the Princess.

"That your Royal Highness is at liberty to guess," says Lorenzo.

"Does it begin with a Z?" asked Angelica.

The Painter said it wasn't a Z; then she tried a Y; then an X; then a W, and went so backwards through almost the whole alphabet.

When she came to D, and it wasn't D, she grew very much excited; when she came to C, and it wasn't C, she was still more nervous; when she came to Be, *and it wasn't B*, "O dearest Gruffanuff," she said, "lend me your smelling-bottle!" and, hiding her head in the Countess's shoulder, she faintly whispered, "Ah, Signor, can it be A?"

"It was A; and though I may not, by my Royal Master's orders, tell your Royal Highness the Princess's name, whom he fondly, madly, devoutedly, rapturously loves, I may show you her portrait," says the slyboots: and leading the Princess up to a gilt frame, he drew a curtain which was before it.

O goodness! the frame contained A LOOKING GLASS! and Angelica saw her own face!

V I I

How Giglio and Angelica Had a Quarrel

The Court Painter of his Majesty the King of Crim Tartary returned to that monarch's dominions, carrying away a number of sketches which he had made in the Paflagonian capital (you know, of course, my dears, that the name of the capital is Blombodinga); but the most charming of all his pieces was a portrait of the Princess Angelica, which all the Crim Tartar nobles came to see. With this work the King was so delighted, that he decorated the Painter with his Order of the Pumpkin (sixth class), and the artist became Sir Tomaso Lorenzo, K.P., thenceforth.

King Valoroso also sent Sir Tomaso his Order of the Cucumber, besides a handsome order for money, for he painted the King, Queen, and principal nobility while at Blombodinga, and became all the fashion, to the perfect rage of all the artists in Paflagonia, where the King used to point to the portrait of Prince Bulbo, which Sir Tomaso had left behind him, and say, "Which among you can paint a picture like that?"

It hung in the royal parlour over the royal sideboard, and Princess Angelica could always look at it as she sat making the tea. Each day it seemed to grow handsomer and handsomer, and the Princess grew so fond of looking at it, that she would often spill the tea over the cloth, at which her father and mother would wink and wag their heads, and say to each other, "Aha! we see how things are going."

In the meanwhile poor Giglio lay upstairs very sick in his chamber, though he took all the doctor's horrible medicines like a good young lad; as I hope *you* do, my dears, when you are ill and mamma sends for the medical man. And the only person who visited Giglio (besides his friend the Captain of the Guard, who was almost always busy or on parade), was little Betsinda the housemaid, who used to do his bedroom and sitting-room out, bring him his gruel, and warm his bed.

When the little housemaid came to him in the morning and evening, Prince Giglio used to say, "Betsinda, Betsinda, how is the Princess Angelica?"

And Betsinda used to answer, "The Princess is very well, thank you, my lord." And Giglio would heave a sigh, and think, if Angelica were sick, I am sure *I* should not be very well.

Then Giglio would say, "Betsinda, has the Princess Angelica asked for me to-day?" And Betsinda would anwer, "No, my lord, not to-day"; or, "she was very busy practising the piano when I saw her"; or, "she was writing invitations for an evening-party, and did not speak to me": or make some excuse or other, not strictly consonant with truth: for Betsinda was such a good-natured creature, that she strove to do everything to prevent annoyance to Prince Giglio, and even brought him up roast chicken and jellies from the kitchen (when the Doctor allowed them, and Giglio was getting better), saying, "that the Princess had made the jelly or the bread-sauce with her own hands, on purpose for Giglio."

When Giglio heard this he took heart, and began to mend immediately; and gobbled up all the jelly, and picked the last bone of the chicken— drumsticks, merry-thought, sides'-bones, back, pope's-nose, and all—thanking his dear Angelica: and he felt so much better the next day, that he dressed and went downstairs, where, whom should he meet but Angelica going into the drawing-room? All the covers were off the chairs, the chandeliers taken out of the bags, the damask curtains uncovered, the work and things carried away, and the handsomest albums on the tables. Angelica had her hair in papers: in a word, it was evident there was going to be a party.

"Heavens, Giglio!" cries Angelica: "*you* here in such a dress! What a figure you are!"

"Yes, dear Angelica, I am come downstairs, and feel so well to-day, thanks to the *fowl* and *jelly*."

"What do I know about fowls and jellies, that you allude to them in that rude way?" says Angelica.

"Why, didn't—didn't you send them, Angelica dear?" says Giglio.

"I send them indeed! Angelica dear! No, Giglio dear," says she, mocking him, "*I* was engaged in getting the rooms ready for his Royal Highness the Prince of Crim Tartary, who is coming to pay my papa's Court a visit."

"The—Prince—of—Crim—Tartary!" Giglio said, aghast.

"Yes, the Prince of Crim Tartary," says Angelica, mocking him. "I daresay you never heard of such a country. What *did* you ever hear of? You don't know whether Crim Tartary is on the Red Sea or on the Black Sea, I dare say."

"Yes, I do, it's on the Red Sea," says Giglio, at which the Princess burst out laughing at him, and said, "O you ninny! You are so ignorant, you are really not fit for society! You know nothing but about horses and dogs, and are only fit to dine in a mess-room with my royal father's heaviest dragoons. Don't look so surprised at me, sir: go and put your best clothes on to receive the Prince, and let me get the drawing-room ready."

Giglio said, "O Angelica, Angelica, I didn't think this of you. *This* wasn't your language to me when you gave me this ring, and I gave you mine in the garden, and you gave me that k———"

But what k——— was we never shall know, for Angelica, in a rage, cried, "Get out, you saucy, rude creature! How dare you to remind me of your rudeness? As for your little trumpery twopenny ring, there, sir, there!" And she flung it out of the window.

"It was my mother's marriage-ring," cried Giglio.

"*I* don't care whose marriage-ring it was," cries Angelica. "Marry the person who picks it up if she's a woman; you sha'n't marry *me*. And give me back *my* ring. I've no patience with people who boast about the things they give away! *I* know who'll give me much finer things than you ever gave me. A beggarly ring indeed, not worth five shillings!"

Now Angelica little knew that the ring which Giglio had given her was a fairy ring: if a man wore it, it made all the women in love with him; if a woman, all the gentlemen. The Queen, Giglio's mother, quite an ordinary-looking person, was admired immensely whilst she wore this ring, and her husband was frantic when she was ill. But when she called her little Giglio to her, and put the ring on his finger, King Savio did not seem to care for his wife so much any more, but transferred all his love to little Giglio. So did everybody love him as long as he had the ring; but, when, as quite a child, he gave it to Angelica, people began to love and admire *her*; and Giglio, as the saying is, played only second fiddle.

"Yes," says Angelica, going on in her foolish ungrateful way, "I know who'll give me much finer things than your beggarly little pearl nonsense."

"Very good, miss! You may take back your ring, too!" says Giglio, his eyes flashing fire at her, and then, as if his eyes had been suddenly opened, he cried out, "Ha! what does this mean? Is *this* the woman I have been in love with all my life? Have I been such a ninny as to throw away my regard upon *you*? Why—actually—yes—you are a little crooked!"

"O, you wretch!" cries Angelica.

"And, upon my conscience, you—you squint a little."

"Eh!" cries Angelica.

"And your hair is red—and you are marked with the small-pox—and what? you have three false teeth—and one leg shorter than the other!"

"You brute, you brute, you!" Angelica screamed out: and as she seized the ring with one hand, she dealt Giglio one, two, three smacks on the face, and would have pulled the hair off his head had he not started laughing, and crying,

"O dear me, Angelica, don't pull out *my* hair, it hurts! You might remove a great deal of *your own*, as I perceive, without scissors or pulling at all. O, ho, ho! ha, ha, ha! he, he, he!"

And he nearly choked himself with laughing, and she with rage; when, with a low bow, and dressed in his Court habit, Count Gambabella, the first lord-in-waiting, entered and said, "Royal Highnesses! Their Majesties expect you in the Pink Throne-Room, where they await the arrival of the Prince of CRIM TARTARY."

VIII

How Gruffanuff Picked the Fairy Ring Up,
and Prince Bulbo Came to Court

Prince Bulbo's arrival had set all the Court in a flutter: everybody was ordered to put his or her best clothes on: the footmen had their gala liveries; the Lord Chancellor his new wig; the Guards their last new tunics; and Countess Gruffanuff you may be sure was glad of an opportunity of decorating *her* old person with her finest things. She was walking through the court of the Palace on her way to wait upon their Majesties, when she spied something glittering on the pavement, and bade the boy in buttons who was holding up her train, to go and pick up the article shining yonder. He was an ugly little wretch, in some of the late groom-porter's old clothes cut down, and much too tight for him; and yet, when he had taken up the ring (as it turned out to be), and was carrying it to his mistress, she thought he looked like a little Cupid. He gave the ring to her; it was a trumpery little thing enough, but too small for any of her old knuckles, so she put it into her pocket.

"O, mum!" says the boy, looking at her, "how—how beyoutiful you do look, mum, to-day, mum!"

"And you, too, Jacky," she was going to say; but, looking down at him—no, he was no longer good-looking at all—but only the carrotty-haired little Jacky of the morning. However, praise is welcome from the ugliest of men or boys, and Gruffanuff, bidding the boy hold up her train, walked on in high good-humour. The guards saluted her with peculiar respect. Captain Hedzoff, in the ante-room, said, "My dear madam, you look like an angel to-day." And so, bowing and smirking, Gruffanuff went in and took her place behind her Royal Master and Mistress, who were in the throne-room, awaiting the Prince of Crim Tartary. Princess Angelica sat at their feet, and behind the King's chair stood Prince Giglio, looking very savage.

The Prince of Crim Tartary made his appearance, attended by Baron Sleibootz, his chamberlain, and followed by a black page, carrying the most beautiful crown you ever saw! He was dressed in his travelling costume, and his hair was a little in disorder. "I have ridden three hundred miles since breakfast," said he, "so eager was I to behold the Prin—the Court and august family of Paflagonia, and I could not wait one minute before appearing in your Majesties' presences."

Giglio, from behind the throne, burst out into a roar of contemptuous laughter; but all the royal party, in fact, were so flurried, that they did not hear this little outbreak. "Your R. H. is welcome in any dress," says the King. "Glumboso, a chair for his Royal Highness."

"Any dress his Royal Highness wears *is* a Court dress," says Princess Angelica, smiling graciously.

"Ah! but you should see my other clothes," said the Prince. "I should have had them on, but that stupid carrier has not brought them. Who's that laughing?"

It was Giglio laughing. "I was laughing," he said, "because you said just now that you were in such a hurry to see the Princess, that you could not wait to change your dress; and now you say you come in those clothes because you have no others."

"And who are you?" says Prince Bulbo, very fiercely.

"My father was King of this country, and I am his only son, Prince!" replies Giglio, with equal haughtiness.

"Ha!" said the King and Glumboso, looking very flurried; but the former, collecting himself, said, "Dear Prince Bulbo, I forgot to introduce to your Royal Highness my dear nephew, his Royal Highness Prince Giglio! Know each other! Embrace each other! Giglio, give his Royal Highness your hand!" And Giglio, giving his hand, squeezed poor Bulbo's, until the tears ran out of his eyes. Glumboso now brought a chair for the royal visitor, and placed it on the platform on which the King, Queen, and Prince were seated; but the chair was on the edge of the platform, and as Bulbo sat down, it toppled over, and he with it, rolling over and over, and bellowing like a bull. Giglio roared still louder at this disaster, but it was with laughter; so did all the Court when Prince Bulbo got up; for though when he entered the room he appeared not very ridiculous, as he stood up from his fall for a moment, he looked so exceedingly plain and foolish, that nobody could help laughing at him. When he had entered the room, he was observed to carry a rose in his hand, which fell out of it as he tumbled.

"My rose! my rose!" cried Bulbo; and his chamberlain dashed forwards and picked it up, and gave it to the Prince, who put it in his waistcoat.

Then people wondered why they had laughed; there was nothing particularly ridiculous in him. He was rather short, rather stout, rather red-haired, but, in fine, for a prince, not so bad.

So they sat and talked, the royal personages together, the Crim Tartar officers with those of Paflagonia—Giglio very comfortable with Gruffanuff behind the throne. He looked at her with such tender eyes, that her heart was all in a flutter. "Oh, dear Prince," she said, "how could you speak so haughtily in presence of their Majesties? I protest I thought I should have fainted."

"I should have caught you in my arms," said Giglio, looking raptures.

"Why were you so cruel to Prince Bulbo, dear Prince?" says Gruff.

"Because I hate him," says Gil.

"You are jealous of him, and still love poor Angelica," cries Gruffanuff, putting her handkerchief to her eyes.

"I did, but I love her no more!" Giglio cried. "I despise her! Were she heiress to twenty thousand thrones, I would despise her and scorn her. But why speak of thrones? I have lost mine. I am too weak to recover it—I am alone, and have no friend."

"Oh, say not so, dear Prince!" says Gruffanuff.

"Besides," says he, "I am so happy here *behind the throne*, that I would not change my place, no, not for the throne of the world!"

"What are you two people chattering about there?" says the Queen, who was rather good-natured, though not over-burthened with wisdom. "It is time to dress for dinner. Giglio, show Prince Bulbo to his room. Prince, if your clothes have not come, we shall be very happy to see you as you are." But when Prince Bulbo got to his bedroom, his luggage was there and unpacked; and the hairdresser coming in, cut and curled him entirely to his own satisfaction; and when the dinner-bell rang, the royal company had not to wait above five-and-twenty minutes until Bulbo appeared, during which time the King, who could not bear to wait, grew as sulky as possible. As for Giglio, he never left Madam Gruffanuff all this time, but stood with her in the embrasure of a window, paying her compliments. At length the Groom of the Chambers announced his Royal Highness the Prince of Crim Tartary! and the noble company went into the royal dining-room. It was quite a small party; only the King and Queen, the Princess, whom Bulbo took out, the two Princes, Countess Gruffanuff, Glumboso the Prime Minister, and Prince Bulbo's chamberlain. You may be sure they had a very good dinner—let every boy or girl think of what he or she likes best, and fancy it on the table.*

---

* Here a very pretty game may be played by all the children saying what they like best for dinner.

The Princess talked incessantly all dinner time to the Prince of Crimea, who ate an immense deal too much, and never took his eyes off his plate, except when Giglio, who was carving a goose, sent a quantity of stuffing and onion-sauce into one of them. Giglio only burst out a laughing as the Crimean Prince wiped his shirt-front and face with his scented pocket-handkerchief. He did not make Prince Bulbo any apology. When the Prince looked at him, Giglio would not look that way. When Prince Bulbo said, "Prince Giglio, may I have the honour of taking a glass of wine with you?" Giglio *wouldn't* answer. All his talk and his eyes were for Countess Gruffanuff, who you may be sure was pleased with Giglio's attentions—the vain old creature! When he was not complimenting her, he was making fun of Prince Bulbo, so loud that Gruffanuff was always tapping him with her fan, and saying,

"O you satirical Prince! O fie, the Prince will hear!"

"Well, I don't mind," says Giglio, louder still.

The King and Queen luckily did not hear; for her Majesty was a little deaf, and the King thought so much about his own dinner, and, besides, made such a dreadful noise, hob-gobbling in eating it, that he heard nothing else. After dinner, his Majesty and the Queen went to sleep in their arm-chairs.

This was the time when Giglio began his tricks with Prince Bulbo, plying that young gentleman with port, sherry, madeira, champagne, marsala, cherry-brandy, and pale ale, of all of which Master Bulbo drank without stint. But in plying his guest, Giglio was obliged to drink himself, and, I am sorry to say, took more than was good for him, so that the young men were very noisy, rude, and foolish when they joined the ladies after dinner; and dearly did they pay for that imprudence, as now, my darlings, you shall hear!

Bulbo went and sat by the piano, where Angelica was playing and singing, and he sang out of tune, and he upset the coffee when the footman brought it, and he laughed out of place, and talked absurdly, and fell asleep and snored horridly. Booh, the nasty pig! But as he lay there stretched on the pink satin sofa, Angelica still persisted in thinking him the most beautiful of human beings. No doubt the magic rose which Bulbo wore, caused this infatuation on Angelica's part; but is she the first young woman who has thought a silly fellow charming?

Giglio must go and sit by Gruffanuff, whose old face he too every moment began to find more lovely. He paid the most outrageous compliments to her:—There never was such a darling. Older than he was?—Fiddle-de-dee! He would marry her—he would have nothing but her!

To marry the heir to the throne! Here was a chance! The artful hussy actually got a sheet of paper, and wrote upon it, "This is to give notice that I, Giglio, only son of Savio, King of Paflagonia, hereby promise to marry the charming and virtuous Barbara Griselda Countess Gruffanuff, and widow of the late Jenkins Gruffanuff, Esq."

"What is it you are writing? you charming Gruffy!" says Giglio, who was lolling on the sofa, by the writing-table.

"Only an order for you to sign, dear Prince, for giving coals and blankets to the poor, this cold weather. Look! the King and Queen are both asleep, and your Royal Highness's order will do."

So Giglio, who was very good-natured, as Gruffy well knew, signed the order immediately; and, when she had it in her pocket, you may fancy what airs she gave herself. She was ready to flounce out of the room before the Queen herself, as now she was the wife of the *rightful* King of Paflagonia! She would not speak to Glumboso, whom she thought a brute, for depriving her *dear husband* of the crown! And when candles came, and she had helped to undress the Queen and Princess, she went into her own room, and actually practised, on a sheet of paper, "Griselda Paflagonia," "Barbara Regina," "Griselda Barbara, Paf. Reg.," and I don't know what signatures besides, against the day when she should be Queen, forsooth!

I X

How Betsinda Got the Warming-Pan

Little Betsinda came in to put Gruffanuff's hair in papers; and the Countess was so pleased, that, for a wonder, she complimented Betsinda. "Betsinda!" she said, "you dressed my hair very nicely to-day; I promised you a little present. Here are five sh—no, here is a pretty little ring, that I picked— that I have had some time." And she gave Betsinda the ring she had picked up in the court. It fitted Betsinda exactly.

"It's like the ring the Princess used to wear," says the maid.

"No such thing," says Gruffanuff, "I have had it this ever so long. There— tuck me up quite comfortable; and now, as it's a very cold night (the snow was beating in at the window) you may go and warm dear Prince Giglio's bed, like a good girl, and then you may unrip my green silk, and then you can just do me up a little cap for the morning, and then you can mend that hole in my silk stocking, and then you can go to bed, Betsinda. Mind, I shall want my cup of tea at five o'clock in the morning."

"I suppose I had best warm both the young gentlemen's beds, ma'am," says Betsinda.

Gruffanuff, for reply, said, "Hau-au-ho!—Grau-haw-hoo!—Hong-hrho!" In fact, she was snoring sound asleep.

Her room, you know, is next to the King and Queen, and the Princess is next to them. So pretty Betsinda went away for the coals to the kitchen, and filled the royal warming-pan.

Now, she was a very kind, merry, civil, pretty girl; but there must have been something very captivating about her this evening, for all the women in the servants'-hall began to scold and abuse her. The housekeeper said she was a pert, stuck-up thing: the upper-housemaid asked, how dare she wear such ringlets and ribbons, it was quite improper! The cook (for there was a woman-cook as well as a man-cook) said to the kitchen-maid that *she* never could see anything in that creetur: but as for the men, every one of them, Coachman, John, Buttons the page, and Monsieur, the Prince of Crim Tartary's valet, started up, and said—

"My eyes!"
"O mussey!"
"O jemmany!"   "What a pretty girl Betsinda is!"
"O ciel!"

"Hands off; none of your impertinence, you vulgar, low people!" says Betsinda, walking off with her pan of coals. She heard the young gentlemen playing at billiards as she went upstairs: first to Prince Giglio's bed, which she warmed, and then to Prince Bulbo's room.

He came in just as she had done; and as soon as he saw her, "O! O! O! O! O! what a beyou—oo—ootiful creature you are! You angel—you peri— you rosebud, let me be thy bulbul—thy Bulbo, too! Fly to the desert, fly with me! I never saw a young gazelle to glad me with its dark blue eye that had eyes like thine. Thou nymph of beauty, take, take this young heart. A truer never did itself sustain within a soldier's waistcoat. Be mine! Be mine! Be Princess of Crim Tartary! My royal father will approve our union: and, as for that little carrotty-haired Angelica, I do not care a fig for her any more."

"Go away, your Royal Highness, and go to bed, please," said Betsinda, with the warming-pan.

But Bulbo said, "No, never, till thou swearest to be mine, thou lovely, blushing, chambermaid divine! Here, at thy feet, the Royal Bulbo lies, the trembling captive of Betsinda's eyes."

And he went on, making himself so *absurd and ridiculous*, that Betsinda, who was full of fun, gave him a touch with the warming-pan, which, I promise you, made him cry "O-o-o-o!" in a very different manner.

Prince Bulbo made such a noise that Prince Giglio, who heard him from the next room, came in to see what was the matter. As soon as he saw what was taking place, Giglio, in a fury, rushed on Bulbo, kicked him in the rudest manner up to the ceiling, and went on kicking him till his hair was quite out of curl.

Poor Betsinda did not know whether to laugh or to cry; the kicking certinly must hurt the Prince, but then he looked so droll! When Giglio had done knocking him up and down to the ground, and whilst he went into a corner rubbing himself, what do you think Giglio does? He goes down on his own knees to Betsinda, takes her hand, begs her to accept his heart, and offers to marry her that moment. Fancy Betsinda's condition, who had been in love with the Prince ever since she first saw him in the palace garden, when she was quite a little child.

"Oh, divine Betsinda!" says the Prince, "how have I lived fifteen years in thy company without seeing thy perfections? What woman in all Europe, Asia, Africa, and America, nay, in Australia, only it is not yet discovered, can presume to be thy equal? Angelica? Pish! Gruffanuff? Phoo! The Queen? Ha, ha! Thou art my Queen. Thou art the real Angelica, because thou art really angelic."

"Oh, Prince! I am but a poor chambermaid," says Betsinda, looking, however, very much pleased.

"Didst thou not tend me in my sickness, when all forsook me?" continues Giglio. "Did not thy gentle hand smooth my pillow, and bring me jelly and roast chicken?"

"Yes, dear Prince, I did," says Betsinda, "and I sewed your Royal Highness's shirt-buttons on too, if you please, your Royal Highness," cries this artless maiden.

When poor Prince Bulbo, who was now madly in love with Betsinda, heard this declaration, when he saw the unmistakable glances which she flung upon Giglio, Bulbo began to cry bitterly, and tore quantities of hair out of his head, till it all covered the room like so much tow.

Betsinda had left the warming-pan on the floor while the Princes were going on with their conversation, and as they began now to quarrel and be very fierce with one another, she thought proper to run away.

"You great big blubbering booby, tearing your hair in the corner there; of course you will give me satisfaction for insulting Betsinda. *You* dare to kneel down at Princess Giglio's knees and kiss her hand!"

"She's not Princess Giglio!" roars out Bulbo. "She shall be Princess Bulbo, no other shall be Princess Bulbo."

"You are engaged to my cousin!" bellows out Giglio.

"I hate your cousin," says Bulbo.

"You shall give me satisfaction for insulting her!" cries Giglio in a fury. "I'll have your life."

"I'll run you through."

"I'll cut your throat."

"I'll blow your brains out."

"I'll knock your head off."

"I'll send a friend to you in the morning."

"I'll send a bullet into you in the afternoon."

"We'll meet again," says Giglio, shaking his fist in Bulbo's face; and seizing up the warming-pan, he kissed it, because, forsooth, Betsinda had carried it, and rushed downstairs. What should he see on the landing but his Majesty talking to Betsinda, whom he called by all sorts of fond names. His Majesty had heard a row in the building, so he stated, and smelling something burning, had come out to see what the matter was.

"It's the young gentlemen smoking, perhaps, sir," says Betsinda.

"Charming chambermaid," says the King (like all the rest of them), "never mind the young men! Turn thy eyes on a middle-aged autocrat, who has been considered not ill-looking in his time."

"Oh, sir! what will her Majesty say?" cries Betsinda.

"Her Majesty!" laughs the monarch. "Her Majesty be hanged. Am I not Autocrat of Paflagonia? Have I not blocks, ropes, axes, hangmen—ha? Runs not a river by my palace wall? Have I not sacks to sew up wives withal? Say but the word, that thou wilt be mine own—your mistress straightway in a sack is sewn, and thou the sharer of my heart and throne."

When Giglio heard these atrocious sentiments, he forgot the respect usually paid to Royalty, lifted up the warming-pan, and knocked down the King as flat as a pancake; after which, master Giglio took to his heels and ran away, and Betsinda went off screaming, and the Queen, Gruffanuff, and the Princess, all came out of their rooms. Fancy their feelings on beholding their husband, father, sovereign in this posture!

X

How King Valoroso Was in a Dreadful Passion

As soon as the coals began to burn him, the King came to himself and stood up. "Ho! my captain of the guards!" his Majesty exclaimed, stamping his royal feet with rage. O piteous spectacle! the King's nose was bent quite crooked by the blow of Prince Giglio! His Majesty ground his teeth with rage. "Hedzoff," he said, taking a death-warrant out of his dressing-gown pocket, "Hedzoff, good Hedzoff, seize upon the Prince. Thou'lt find him in his chamber two pair up. But now he dared, with sacrilegious hand, to strike the sacred nightcap of a king—Hedzoff, and floor me with a warming-pan! Away, no more demur, the villain dies! see it be done, or else—h'm!—ha!—h'm! mind thine own eyes!" and followed by the ladies, and lifting up the tails of his dressing-gown, the King entered his own apartment.

Captain Hedzoff was very much affected, having a sincere love for Giglio. "Poor, poor Giglio!" he said, the tears rolling over his manly face, and dripping down his moustachios; "my noble young Prince, is it my hand must lead thee to death?"

"Lead him to fiddlestick, Hedzoff," said a female voice. It was Gruffanuff, who had come out in her dressing-gown when she heard the noise. "The King said you were to hang the Prince. Well, hang the Prince."

"I don't understand you," says Hedzoff, who was not a very clever man.

"You Gaby! he didn't say *which* Prince," says Gruffanuff.

"No; he didn't say which, certainly," said Hedzoff.

"Well then, take Bulbo, and hang *him*!"

When Captain Hedzoff heard this, he began to dance about for joy. "Obedience is a soldier's honour," says he. "Prince Bulbo's head will do capitally," and he went to arrest the Prince the very first thing next morning.

He knocked at the door. "Who's there?" says Bulbo. "Captain Hedzoff? step in, pray, my good Captain; I'm delighted to see you; I have been expecting you."

"Have you?" says Hedzoff.

"Sleibootz, my Chamberlain, will act for me," says the Prince.

"I beg your Royal Highness's pardon, but you will have to act for yourself, and it's a pity to wake Baron Sleibootz."

The Prince Bulbo still seemed to take the matter very coolly. "Of course, Captain," says he, "you are come about that affair with Prince Giglio?"

"Precisely," says Hedzoff, "that affair of Prince Giglio."

"Is it to be pistols, or swords, Captain?" asks Bulbo. "I'm a pretty good hand with both, and I'll do for Prince Giglio as sure as my name is my Royal Highness Prince Bulbo."

"There's some mistake, my Lord," says the Captain. "The business is done with *axes* among us."

"Axes? That's sharp work," says Bulbo. "Call my Chamberlain, he'll be my second, and in ten minutes, I flatter myself, you'll see Master Giglio's head off his impertinent shoulders. I'm hungry for his blood. Hoo-oo, aw!" and he looked as savage as an ogre.

"I beg your pardon, sir, but by this warrant I am to take you prisoner, and hand you over to—to the executioner."

"Pooh, pooh, my good man!—Stop, I say—ho!—hulloa!" was all that this luckless Prince was able to say, for Hedzoff's guards seizing him, tied a handkerchief over his mouth and face, and carried him to the place of execution.

The King, who happened to be talking to Glumboso, saw him pass and took a pinch of snuff, and said, "So much for Giglio. Now let's go to breakfast."

The Captain of the Guard handed over his prisoner to the Sheriff, with the fatal order,

AT SIGHT CUT OFF THE BEARER'S HEAD.
VALOROSO XXIV

"It's a mistake," says Bulbo, who did not seem to understand the business in the least.

"Poo—poo—pooh," says the Sheriff. "Fetch Jack Ketch instantly. Jack Ketch!"

And poor Bulbo was led to the scaffold, where an executioner with a block and a tremendous axe was always ready in case he should be wanted.

But we must now revert to Giglio and Betsinda.

X I

What Gruffanuff Did to Giglio and Betsinda

Gruffanuff, who had seen what had happened with the King, and knew that Giglio must come to grief, got up very early the next morning, and went to devise some plans for rescuing her darling husband, as the silly old thing insisted on calling him. She found him, walking up and down the garden, thinking of a rhyme for Betsinda (*tinder* and *winda* were all he could find), and indeed having forgotten all about the past evening, except that Betsinda was the most lovely of beings.

"Well, dear Giglio," says Gruff.

"Well, dear Gruffy," says Giglio, only *he* was quite satirical.

"I have been thinking, darling, what you must do in this scrape. You must fly the country for a while."

"What scrape?—fly the country? Never without her I love, Countess," says Giglio.

"No, she will accompany you, dear Prince," she says, in her most coaxing accents. "First, we must get the jewels belonging to your royal parents, and those of her and his present Majesty. Here is the key, duck; they are all yours, you know, by right, for you are the rightful King of Paflagonia, and your wife will be the rightful Queen."

"Will she?" says Giglio.

"Yes; and having got the jewels, go to Glumboso's apartment, where, under his bed, you will find sacks containing money to the amount of £217,000,000,987,439 13s.6½d., all belonging to you, for he took it out of your royal father's room on the day of his death. With this we will fly."

"*We* will fly?" says Giglio.

"Yes, you and your bride—your affianced love—your Gruffy!" says the Countess, with a languishing leer.

"*You* my bride!" says Giglio. "You, you hideous old woman!"

"Oh, you—you wretch! didn't you give me this paper promising marriage?" cries Gruff.

"Get away, you old goose! I love Betsinda, and Betsinda only!" And in a fit of terror he ran from her as quickly as he could.

"He! he! he!" shrieks out Gruff; "a promise is a promise if there are laws in Paflagonia! And as for that monster, that wretch, that fiend, that ugly little vixen—as for that upstart, that ingrate, that beast Betsinda, Master Giglio will have no little difficulty in discovering her whereabouts. He may look very long before finding *her*, I warrant. He little knows that Miss Betsinda is—"

Is—what? Now, you shall hear. Poor Betsinda got up at five on a winter's morning to bring her cruel mistress her tea; and instead of finding her in a good humour, found Gruffy as cross as two sticks. The Countess boxed Betsinda's ears half-a-dozen times whilst she was dressing; but as poor little Betsinda was used to this kind of treatment, she did not feel any special alarm. "And now," says she, "when her Majesty rings her bell twice, I'll trouble you, miss, to attend."

So when the Queen's bell rang twice, Betsinda came to her Majesty and made a pretty little curtsey. The Queen, the Princess, and Gruffanuff were all three in the room. As soon as they saw her they began.

"You wretch!" says the Queen.

"You little vulgar thing!" says the Princess.

"You beast!" says Gruffanuff.

"Get out of my sight!" says the Queen.

"Go away with you, do!" says the Princess.

"Quit the premises!" says Gruffanuff.

Alas! and woe is me! very lamentable events had occurred to Betsinda that morning, and all in consequence of that fatal warming-pan business of the previous night. The King had offered to marry her; of course her Majesty the Queen was jealous: Bulbo had fallen in love with her; of course Angelica was furious: Giglio was in love with her, and oh, what a fury Gruffy was in!

"Take off that $\left\{\begin{array}{l} \text{cap} \\ \text{petticoat} \\ \text{gown} \end{array}\right\}$ I gave you," they said, all at once, and

began tearing the clothes off poor Betsinda.

"How dare you flirt with $\left\{\begin{array}{l} \text{the King?"} \\ \text{Prince Bulbo?"} \\ \text{Prince Giglio?"} \end{array}\right\}$ cried the Queen, the

Princess, and Countess.

"Give her the rags she wore when she came into the house, and turn her out of it!" cries the Queen.

"Mind she does not go with *my* shoes on, which I lent her so kindly," says the Princess; and indeed the Princess's shoes were a great deal too big for Betsinda.

"Come with me, you filthy hussy!" and taking up the Queen's poker, the cruel Gruffanuff drove Betsinda into her room.

The Countess went to the glass box in which she had kept Betsinda's old cloak and shoe this ever so long, and said, "Take those rags, you little beggar creature, and strip off everything belonging to honest people, and go about your business;" and she actually tore off the poor little delicate thing's back almost all her things, and told her to be off out of the house.

Poor Betsinda huddled the cloak round her back, on which were embroidered the letters PRIN . . . . ROSAL . . . and then came a great rent.

As for the shoe, what was she to do with one poor little tootsey sandal? The string was still to it, so she hung it round her neck.

"Won't you give me a pair of shoes to go out in the snow, mum, if you please, mum?" cried the poor child.

"No, you wicked beast!" says Gruffanuff, driving her along with the poker—driving her down the cold stairs—driving her through the cold hall—flinging her out into the cold street, so that the knocker itself shed tears to see her!

But a kind fairy made the soft snow warm for her little feet, and she wrapped herself up in the ermine of her mantle, and was gone!

. . .

"And now let us think about breakfast," says the greedy Queen.

"What dress shall I put on, mamma? the pink or the pea-green?" says Angelica. "Which do you think the dear Prince will like best?"

"Mrs. V.!" sings out the King from his dressing-room, "let us have sausages for breakfast! Remember we have Prince Bulbo staying with us!"

And they all went to get ready.

Nine o'clock came, and they were all in the breakfast-room, and no Prince Bulbo as yet. The urn was hissing and humming: the muffins were smoking—such a heap of muffins! the eggs were done, there was a pot of raspberry jam, and coffee, and a beautiful chicken and tongue on the side-table. Marmitonio the cook brought in the sausages. Oh, how nice they smelt!

"Where is Bulbo?" said the King. "John, where is his Royal Highness?"

John said he had a took up his Roilighnessesses shaving-water, and his clothes and things, and he wasn't in his room, which he sposed his Royliness was just stepped hout.

"Stepped out before breakfast in the snow! Impossible!" says the King, sticking his fork into a sausage. "My dear, take one Angelica, won't you have a saveloy?" The Princess took one, being very fond of them; and at this moment Glumboso entered with Captain Hedzoff, both looking very much disturbed.

"I am afraid your Majesty—" cries Glumboso.

"No business before breakfast, Glum!" says the King. "Breakfast first, business next. Mrs. V., some more sugar!"

"Sire, I am afraid if we wait till after breakfast it will be too late," says Glumboso. "He—he—he'll be hanged at half-past nine."

"Don't talk about hanging and spoil my breakfast, you unkind vulgar man you," cries the Princess. "John, some mustard. Pray who is to be hanged?"

"Sire, it is the Prince," whispers Glumboso to the King.

"Talk about business after breakfast, I tell you!" says his Majesty, quite sulky.

"We shall have a war, sire, depend on it," says the Minister. "His father, King Padella . . . "

"His father, King *who*?" says the King. "King Padella is not Giglio's father. My brother, King Savio, was Giglio's father."

"It's Prince Bulbo they are hanging, sire, not Prince Giglio," says the Prime Minister.

"You told me to hang the Prince, and I took the ugly one," says Hedzoff. "I didn't, of course, think your Majesty intended to murder your own flesh and blood!"

The King for all reply flung the plate of sausages at Hedzoff's head. The Princess cried out "Hee-karee-karee!" and fell down in a fainting-fit.

"Turn the cock of the urn upon her Royal Highness," said the King, and the boiling water gradually revived her. His Majesty looked at his watch, compared it by the clock in the parlour, and by that of the church in the square opposite; then he wound it up; then he looked at it again. "The great question is," says he, "am I fast or am I slow? If I'm slow, we may as well go on with breakfast. If I'm fast, why, there is just the possibility of saving Prince Bulbo. It's a doosid awkward mistake, and upon my word, Hedzoff, I have the greatest mind to have you hanged too."

"Sire, I did but my duty; a soldier has but his orders. I didn't expect after forty-seven years of faithful service that my sovereign would think of putting me to a felon's death!"

"A hundred thousand plagues upon you! Can't you see that while you are talking my Bulbo is being hanged?" screamed the Princess.

"By Jove! she's always right, that girl, and I'm so absent," says the King, looking at his watch again. "Ha! Hark, there go the drums! What a doosid awkward thing though!"

"O papa, you goose! Write the reprieve, and let me run with it," cries the Princess—and she got a sheet of paper, and pen and ink, and laid them before the King.

"Confound it! where are my spectacles?" the Monarch exclaimed. "Angelica! Go up into my bedroom, look under my pillow, not your mamma's; there you'll see my keys. Bring them down to me, and—Well, well! what impetuous things these girls are!" Angelica was gone, and had run up panting to the bedroom, and found the keys, and was back again before the King had finished a muffin. "Now, love," says he, "you must go all the way back for my desk, in which my spectacles are. If you *would* but have heard me out . . . Be hanged to her! There she is off again. Angelica! ANGELICA!" When his Majesty called in his *loud* voice, she knew she must obey, and came back.

"My dear, when you go out of a room, how often have I told you, *shut the door*. That's a darling. That's all." At last the keys and the desk and the spectacles were got, and the King mended his pen, and signed his name to a reprieve, and Angelica ran with it as swift as the wind. "You'd better stay, my love, and finish the muffins. There's no use going. Be sure it's too late. Hand me over that raspberry jam, please," said the Monarch. "Bong! Bawong! There goes the half-hour. I knew it was."

Angelica ran, and ran, and ran, and ran. She ran up Fore Street, and down High Street, and through the Market-place, and down to the left, and over the bridge, and up the blind alley, and back again, and round by the Castle, and so along by the haberdasher's on the right, opposite the lamp-post, and round the square, and she came—she came to the *Execution place*, where she saw Bulbo laying his head on the block!!! The executioner raised his axe, but at that moment the Princess came panting up and cried "Re-prieve!" "Reprieve!" screamed the Princess. "Reprieve!" shouted all the people. Up the scaffold stairs she sprang, with the agility of a lighter of lamps; and flinging herself in Bulbo's arms, regardless of all ceremony, she cried out, "O my Prince! my lord! my love! my Bulbo! Thine Angelica has been in time to save thy precious existence, sweet rosebud; to prevent thy being nipped in thy young bloom! Had aught befallen thee, Angelica too had died, and welcomed death that joined her to her Bulbo."

"H'm! there's no accounting for tastes," said Bulbo, looking so very much puzzled and uncomfortable, that the Princess, in tones of tenderest strain, asked the cause of his disquiet.

"I tell you what it is, Angelica," said he: "since I came here yesterday, there has been such a row, and disturbance, and quarrelling, and fighting, and chopping of heads off, and the deuce to pay, that I am inclined to go back to Crim Tartary."

"But with me as thy bride, my Bulbo! Though wherever thou art is Crim Tartary to me, my bold, my beautiful, my Bulbo!"

"Well, well, I suppose we must be married," says Bulbo. "Doctor, you came to read the Funeral Service—read the Marriage Service, will you? What must be, must. That will satisfy Angelica, and then, in the name of peace and quiet, do let us go back to breakfast."

Bulbo had carried a rose in his mouth all the time of the dismal ceremony. It was a fairy rose, and he was told by his mother that he ought never to part with it. So he had kept it between his teeth, even when he laid his poor head upon the block, hoping vaguely that some chance would turn up in his favour. As he began to speak to Angelica, he forgot about the rose, and of course it dropped out of his mouth. The romantic Princess instantly stooped and seized it. "Sweet rose!" she exclaimed, "that bloomed upon my Bulbo's lip, never, never will I part from them!" and she placed it in her bosom. And you know Bulbo *couldn't* ask her to give the rose back again. And they went to breakfast; and as they walked, it appeared to Bulbo that Angelica became more exquisitely lovely every moment.

He was frantic until they were married; and now, strange to say, it was Angelica who didn't care about him! He knelt down, he kissed her hand, he prayed and begged; he cried with admiration; while she for her part said she really thought they might wait; it seemed to her he was not handsome any more—no, not at all, quite the reverse; and not clever, no, very stupid; and not well bred, like Giglio; no, on the contrary, dreadfully vul——

What, I cannot say, for King Valoroso roared out *"Pooh,* stuff!" in a terrible voice. "We will have no more of this shilly-shallying! Call the Archbishop, and let the Prince and Princess be married off-hand!"

So, married they were, and I am sure for my part I trust they will be happy.

XII

How Betsinda Fled, and What Became of Her

Betsinda wandered on and on, till she passed through the town gates, and so on the great Crim Tartary road, the very way on which Giglio too was going. "Ah!" thought she, as the diligence passed her, of which the conductor was blowing a delightful tune on his horn, "how I should like to be on that coach!" But the coach and the jingling horses were very soon gone. She little knew who was in it, though very likely she was thinking of him all the time.

Then came an empty cart, returning from market; and the driver being a kind man, and seeing such a very pretty girl trudging along the road with bare feet, most good-naturedly gave her a seat. He said he lived on the confines of the forest, where his old father was a woodman, and, if she liked, he would take her so far on her road. All roads were the same to little Betsinda, so she very thankfully took this one.

And the carter put a cloth round her bare feet, and gave her some bread and cold bacon, and was very kind to her. For all that she was very cold and melancholy. When after travelling on and on, evening came, and all the black pines were bending with snow, and there, at last, was the comfortable light beaming in the woodman's windows; and so they arrived, and went into his cottage. He was an old man, and had a number of children, who were just at supper, with nice hot bread-and-milk, when their elder brother arrived with the cart. And they jumped and clapped their hands; for they were good children; and he had brought them toys from the town. And when they saw the pretty stranger, they ran to her, and brought her to the fire, and rubbed her poor little feet, and brought her bread-and-milk.

"Look, father!" they said to the old woodman, "look at this poor girl, and see what pretty cold feet she has. They are as white as our milk! And look and see what an odd cloak she has, just like the bit of velvet that hangs up in our cupboard, and which you found that day the little cubs were killed by King Padella, in the forest! And look, why, bless us all! she has got round her neck just such another little shoe as that you brought home, and have shown us so often—a little blue velvet shoe!"

"What," said the old woodman, "what is all this about a shoe and a cloak?"

And Betsinda explained that she had been left, when quite a little child, at the town with this cloak and this shoe. And the persons who had taken care of her had—had been angry with her, for no fault, she hoped, of her own. And they had sent her away with her old clothes—and here, in fact, she was. She remembered having been in a forest—and perhaps it was a dream—it was so very odd and strange—having lived in a cave with lions there; and, before that, having lived in a very, very fine house, as fine as the King's, in the town.

When the woodman heard this, he was so astonished, it was quite curious to see how astonished he was. He went to his cupboard, and took out of a stocking a five-shilling piece of King Cavolfiore, and vowed it was exactly like the young woman. And then he produced the shoe and the piece of velvet which he had kept so long, and compared them with the things which Betsinda wore. In Betsinda's little shoe was written, "Hopkins, maker to the Royal Family;" so in the other shoe was written, "Hopkins, maker to the Royal Family." In the inside of Betsinda's piece of cloak was embroidered, "PRIN ROSAL;" in the other piece of cloak was embroidered "CESS BA. No. 246." So that when put together you read, "PRINCESS ROSALBA. No. 246."

On seeing this, the dear old woodman fell down on his knee, saying: "O my princess, O my gracious royal lady, O my rightful Queen of Crim Tartary,—I hail thee—I acknowledge thee—I do thee homage!" And in token of his fealty, he rubbed his venerable nose three times on the ground, and put the Princess's foot on his head.

"Why," said she, "my good woodman, you must be a nobleman of my royal father's Court!" For in her lowly retreat, and under the name of Betsinda, HER MAJESTY ROSALBA, Queen of Crim Tartary, had read of the customs of all foreign courts and nations.

"Marry, indeed am I, my gracious liege—the poor Lord Spinachi, once—the humble woodman these fifteen years syne. Ever since the tyrant Padella (may ruin overtake the treacherous knave!) dismissed me from my post of First Lord."

"First Lord of the Toothpick and Joint Keeper of the Snuff-box? I mind me! Thou heldest these posts under our royal Sire. They are restored to thee, Lord Spinachi! I make thee knight of the second class of our Order of the Pumpkin (the first class being reserved for crowned heads alone). Rise, Marquis of Spinachi!" And with indescribable majesty, the Queen, who had no sword handy, waved the pewter spoon with which she had been taking her bread-and-milk, over the bald head of the old nobleman, whose tears absolutely made a puddle on the ground, and whose dear children went to bed that night Lords and Ladies Bartolomeo, Ubaldo, Catarina, and Ottavia degli Spinachi!

The acquaintance HER MAJESTY showed with the history, and *noble families* of her empire, was wonderful. "The House of Broccoli should remain faithful to us," she said; "they were ever welcome at our Court. Have the Articiocchi, as was their wont, turned to the Rising Sun? The family of Sauerkraut must sure be with us—they were ever welcome in the halls of King Cavolfiore." And so she went on enumerating quite a list of the nobility and gentry of Crim Tartary, so admirably had her Majesty profited by her studies while in exile.

The old Marquis of Spinachi said he could answer for them all; that the whole country groaned under Padella's tyranny, and longed to return to its rightful sovereign; and late as it was, he sent his children, who knew the forest well, to summon this nobleman and that; and when his eldest son, who had been rubbing the horse down and giving him his supper, came into the house for his own, the Marquis told him to put his boots on, and a saddle on the mare, and ride hither and thither to such and such people.

When the young man heard who his companion in the cart had been, he too knelt down and put her royal foot on his head; he too bedewed the ground with his tears; he was frantically in love with her, as everybody now was who saw her: so were the young Lords Bartolomeo and Ubaldo, who punched each other's little heads out of jealousy: and so, when they came from east and west at the summons of the Marquis degli Spinachi, were the Crim Tartar lords who still remained faithful to the House of Cavolfiore. They were such very old gentlemen for the most part, that her Majesty never suspected their absurd passion, and went among them quite unaware of the havoc her beauty was causing, until an old blind lord who had joined her party told her what the truth was; after which, for fear of making the people too much in love with her, she always wore a veil. She went about privately, from one nobleman's castle to another: and they visited among themselves again, and had meetings, and composed proclamations and counter-proclamations, and distributed all the best places of the kingdom amongst one another, and selected who of the opposition party should be executed when the Queen came to her own. And so in about a year they were ready to move.

The party of Fidelity was in truth composed of very feeble old fogies for the most part; they went about the country waving their old swords and flags, and calling "God save the Queen!" and King Padella happening to be absent upon an invasion, they had their own way for little, and to be sure the people were very enthusiastic whenever they saw the Queen; otherwise the vulgar took matters very quietly, for they said, as far as they could recollect, they were pretty well as much taxed in Cavolfiore's time, as now in Padella's.

X I I I

How Queen Rosalba Came to the Castle of the Bold Count Hogginarmo

Her Majesty, having indeed nothing else to give, made all her followers Knights of the Pumpkin, and Marquises, Earls, and Baronets; and they had a little court for her, and made her a little crown of gilt paper, and a robe of cotton velvet; and they quarrelled about the places to be given away in her court, and about rank and precedence and dignities;—you can't think how they quarrelled! The poor Queen was very tired of her honours before she had had them a month, and I dare say sighed sometimes even to be a lady's-maid again. But we must all do our duty in our respective stations, so the Queen resigned herself to perform hers.

We have said how it happened that none of the usurper's troops came out to oppose this Army of Fidelity: it pottered along as nimbly as the gout of the principal commanders allowed: it consisted of twice as many officers as soldiers: and at length passed near the estates of one of the most powerful noblemen of the country, who had not declared for the Queen, but of whom her party had hopes, as he was always quarrelling with King Padella.

When they came close to his park gates, this nobleman sent to say he would wait upon her Majesty: he was a most powerful warrior, and his name was Count Hogginarmo, whose helmet it took two strong negroes to carry. He knelt down before her and said "Madam and leige lady! it becomes the great nobles of the Crimean realm to show every outward sign of respect to the wearer of the Crown, whoever that may be. We testify to our own nobility in acknowledging yours. The bold Hogginarmo bends the knee to the first of the aristocracy of his country."

Rosalba said, "The bold Count of Hogginarmo was uncommonly kind." But she felt afraid of him, even while he was kneeling, and his eyes scowled at her from between his whiskers, which grew up to them.

"The first Count of the Empire, madam," he went on, "salutes the Sovereign. The Prince addresses himself to the not more noble lady! Madam, my hand is free, and I offer it, and my heart and my sword to your service! My three wives lie buried in my ancestral vaults. The third perished but a year since; and this heart pines for a consort! Deign to be mine, and I swear to bring to your bridal table the head of King Padella, the eyes and nose of his son Prince Bulbo, the right hand and ears of the usurping Sovereign of Paflagonia, which country shall thenceforth be an appanage to your—to *our* Crown! Say yes; Hogginarmo is not accustomed to be denied. Indeed I cannot contemplate the possibility of a refusal; for frightful will be the result; dreadful the murders; furious the devastations; horrible the tyranny; tremendous the tortures, misery, taxation, which the people of this realm will endure, if Hogginarmo's wrath be aroused! I see consent in your Majesty's lovely eyes—their glances fill my soul with rapture!"

"O, sir!" Rosalba said, withdrawing her hand in great fright. "Your Lordship is exceedingly kind; but I am sorry to tell you that I have a prior attachment to a young gentleman by the name of—Prince—Giglio—and never—never can marry any one but him."

Who can describe Hogginarmo's wrath at this remark? Rising up from the ground, he ground his teeth so that fire flashed out of his mouth, from which at the same time issued remarks and language, so *loud, violent, and improper*, that this pen shall never repeat them! "R-r-r-r-r—Rejected! Fiends and perdition! The bold Hogginarmo rejected! All the world shall hear of my rage; and you, madam, you above all shall rue it!" And kicking the two negroes before him, he rushed away, his whiskers streaming in the wind.

Her Majesty's Privy Council was in a dreadful panic when they saw Hogginarmo issue from the royal presence in such a towering rage, making footballs of the poor negroes—a panic which the events justified. They marched off from Hogginarmo's park very crestfallen; and in another half-hour they were met by that rapacious chieftain with a few of his followers, who cut, slashed, charged, whacked, banged, and pommelled amongst them, took the Queen prisoner, and drove the Army of Fidelity to I don't know where.

Poor Queen! Hogginarmo, her conqueror, would not condescend to see her. "Get a horse-van!" he said to his grooms, "clap the hussy into it, and send her, with my compliments, to his Majesty King Padella."

Along with his lovely prisoner, Hogginarmo sent a letter full of servile compliments and loathsome flatteries to King Padella, for whose life, and that of his royal family, the *hypocritical humbug* pretended to offer the most fulsome prayers. And Hogginarmo promised speedily to pay his humble homage at his august master's throne, on which he begged leave to be counted the most loyal and constant defender. Such a *wary* old *bird* as King Padella was not to be caught by Master Hogginarmo's *chaff*, and we shall hear presently how the tyrant treated his upstart vassal. No, no; depend on't, two such rogues do not trust one another.

So this poor Queen was laid in the straw like Margery Daw, and driven along in the dark ever so many miles to the Court, where King Padella had now arrived, having vanquished all his enemies, murdered most of them, and brought some of the richest into captivity with him for the purpose of torturing them and finding out where they had hidden their money.

Rosalba heard their shrieks and groans in the dungeon in which she was thrust; a most awful black hole, full of bats, rats, mice, toads, frogs, mosquitos, bugs, fleas, serpents, and every kind of horror. No light was let into it, otherwise the gaolers might have seen her and fallen in love with her, as an owl that lived up in the roof of the tower did, and a cat, you know, who can see in the dark, and having set its green eyes on Rosalba, never could be got to go back to the turnkey's wife to whom it belonged. And the toads in the dungeon came and kissed her feet, and the vipers wound round her neck and arms, and never hurt her, so charming was this poor Princess in the midst of her misfortunes.

At last, after she had been kept in this place *ever so long*, the door of the dungeon opened, and the terrible KING PADELLA came in.

But what he said and did must be reserved for another chapter, as we must now go back to Prince Giglio.

X I V

What Became of Giglio

The idea of marrying such an old creature as Gruffanuff, frightened Prince Giglio so, that he ran up to his room, packed his trunks, fetched in a couple of porters, and was off to the diligence office in a twinkling.

It was well that he was so quick in his operations, did not dawdle over his luggage, and took the early coach, for as soon as the mistake about Prince Bulbo was found out, that cruel Glumboso sent up a couple of policemen to Prince Giglio's room, with orders that he should be carried to Newgate, and his head taken off before twelve o'clock. But the coach was out of the Paflagonian dominions before two o'clock; and I daresay the express that was sent after Prince Giglio did not ride very quick, for many people in Paflagonia had a regard for Giglio, as the son of their old sovereign; a Prince who, with all his weaknesses, was very much better than his brother, the usurping, lazy, careless, passionate, tyrannical, reigning monarch. That Prince busied himself with the balls, fêtes, masquerades, hunting-parties, and so forth, which he thought proper to give on occasion of his daughter's marriage to

Prince Bulbo; and let us trust was not sorry in his own heart that his brother's son had escaped the scaffold.

It was very cold weather, and the snow was on the ground, and Giglio, who gave his name as simple Mr. Giles, was very glad to get a comfortable place on the coupé of the diligence, where he sat with the conductor and another gentleman. At the first stage from Blombodinga, as they stopped to change horses, there came up to the diligence a very ordinary, vulgar-looking woman, with a bag under her arm, who asked for a place. All the inside places were taken, and the young woman was informed that if she wished to travel, she must go upon the roof; and the passenger inside with Giglio (a rude person, I should think), put his head out of the window, and said, "Nice weather for travelling outside! I wish you a pleasant journey, my dear." The poor woman coughed very much, and Giglio pitied her. "I will give up my place to her," says he, "rather than she should travel in the cold air with that horrid cough." On which the vulgar traveller said, "*You'd* keep her warm, I am sure, if it's a *muff* she wants." On which Giglio pulled his nose, boxed his ears, hit him in the eye, and gave this vulgar person a warning never to call him *muff* again.

Then he sprang up gaily on to the roof of the diligence, and made himself very comfortable in the straw. The vulgar traveller got down at the next station, and Giglio took his place again, and talked to the person next to him. She appeared to be a most agreeable, well-informed, and entertaining female. They travelled together till night, and she gave Giglio all sorts of things out of the bag which she carried, and which indeed seemed to contain the most wonderful collection of articles. He was thirsty—out there came a pint bottle of Bass's pale ale, and a silver mug! Hungry—she took out a cold fowl, some slices of ham, bread, salt, and a most delicious piece of cold plum-pudding, and a little glass of brandy afterwards.

As they travelled, this plain-looking, queer woman talked to Giglio on a variety of subjects, in which the poor Prince showed his ignorance as much as she did her capacity. He owned, with many blushes, how ignorant he was; on which the lady said, "My dear Gigl—my good Mr. Giles, you are a young man, and have plenty of time before you. You have nothing to do but to improve yourself. Who knows but that you may find use for your knowledge some day? When—when you may be wanted at home, as some people may be."

"Good heavens, madam!" says he, "do you know me?"

"I know a number of funny things," says the lady. "I have been at some people's christenings, and turned away from other folks' doors. I have seen some people spoilt by good fortune, and others, as I hope, improved by hardship. I advise you to stay at the town where the coach stops for the night. Stay there and study, and remember your old friend to whom you were kind."

"And who is my old friend?" asked Giglio.

"When you want anything," says the lady, "look in this bag, which I leave to you as a present, and be grateful to—"

"To whom, madam?" says he.

"To the Fairy Blackstick," says the lady, flying out of the window. And when Giglio asked the conductor if he knew where the lady was?

"What lady?" says the man; "there has been no lady in this coach, except the old woman, who got out at the last stage." And Giglio thought he had been dreaming. But there was the bag which Blackstick had given him lying on his lap; and when he came to the town he took it in his hand and went into the inn.

They gave him a very bad bedroom, and Giglio, when he woke in the morning, fancying himself in the Royal Palace at home, called "John, Charles, Thomas! My chocolate—my dressing-gown—my slippers;" but nobody came. There was no bell, so he went and bawled out for the waiter at the top of the stairs.

The landlady came up, looking—looking like this—

"What are you a hollaring and bellaring for here, young man?" says she.

"There's no warm water—no servants; my boots are not even cleaned."

"He, he! Clean 'em yourself," says the landlady. "You young students give yourselves pretty airs. I never heard such impudence."

"I'll quit the house this instant," says Giglio.

"The sooner the better, young man. Pay your bill and be off. All my rooms is wanted for gentlefolks, and not for such as you."

"You may well keep the Bear Inn," said Giglio. "You should have yourself painted as the sign."

The landlady of the Bear went away *growling*. And Giglio returned to his room, where the first thing he saw was the fairy bag lying on the table, which seemed to give a little hop as he came in.

"I hope it has some breakfast in it," says 'Giglio, "for I have only a very little money left."

But on opening the bag, what do you think was there? A blacking-brush and a pot of Warren's jet, and on the pot was written,

"Poor young men their boots must black:
Use me and cork me and put me back."

So Giglio laughed and blacked his boots, and put back the brush and the bottle into the bag.

When he had done dressing himself, the bag gave another little hop, and he went to it and took out—

1. A tablecloth and a napkin.
2. A sugar-basin full of the best loaf sugar.
4, 6, 8, 10. Two forks, two teaspoons, two knives, and a pair of sugar-tongs, and a butter-knife, all marked G.
11, 12, 13. A tea-cup, saucer, and slop-basin.
14. A jug full of delicious cream.
15. A canister with black tea and green.
16. A large tea-urn and boiling water.
17. A saucepan, containing three eggs nicely done.
18. A quarter of a pound of best Epping butter.
19. A brown loaf.

And if he hadn't enough now for a good breakfast, I should like to know who ever had one?

Giglio, having had his breakfast, popped all the things back into the bag, and went out looking for lodgings. I forgot to say this celebrated university town was called Bosforo.

He took a modest lodging opposite the Schools, paid his bill at the inn, and went to his apartment with his trunk, carpet-bag, and not forgetting, we may be sure, his *other* bag.

When he opened his trunk, which the day before he had filled with his best clothes, he found it contained only books. And in the first of them which he opened there was written—

"Clothes for the back, books for the head;
Read, and remember them when they are read."

And in his bag, when Giglio looked in it, he found a student's cap and gown, a writing-book full of paper, an inkstand, pens, and a Johnson's dictionary, which was very useful to him, as his spelling had been sadly neglected.

So he sat down and worked away, very, very hard for a whole year, during which "Mr. Giles" was quite an example to all the students in the University of Bosforo. He never got into any riots or disturbances. The Professors all spoke well of him, and the students liked him too; so that, when at examinations he took all the prizes, viz.:—

The Spelling Prize	The French Prize
The Writing Prize	The Arithmetic Prize
The History Prize	The Latin Prize
The Catechism Prize	The Good Conduct Prize,

all his fellow-students said, "Hurray! Hurray for Giles! Giles is the boy—the student's joy! Hurray for Giles!" And he brought quite a quantity of medals, crowns, books, and tokens of distinction home to his lodgings.

One day after the Examinations, as he was diverting himself at a coffee-house with two friends—(Did I tell you that in his bag, every Saturday night, he found just enough to pay his bills, with a guinea over, for pocket-money? Didn't I tell you? Well, he did, as sure as twice twenty makes forty-five)—he chanced to look in the *Bosforo Chronicle*, and read off quite easily (for he could spell, read, and write the longest words now) the following—

"ROMANTIC CIRCUMSTANCE.—One of the most extraordinary adventures that we have ever heard has set the neighbouring country of Crim Tartary in a state of great excitement.

"It will be remembered that when the present revered sovereign of Crim Tartary, his Majesty King *Padella*, took possession of the throne, after having vanquished, in the terrific battle of Blunderbusco, the late King *Cavolfiore*, that Prince's only child, the Princess Rosalba, was not found in the royal palace, of which King Padella took possession, and, it was said, had strayed into the forest (being abandoned by all her attendants), where she had been eaten up by those ferocious lions, the last pair of which were captured some time since, and brought to the Tower, after killing several hundred persons.

"His Majesty King Padella, who has the kindest heart in the world, was grieved at the accident which had occurred to the harmless little Princess, for whom his Majesty's known benevolence would certainly have provided a fitting establishment. But her death seemed to be certain. The mangled remains of a cloak, and a little shoe, were found in the forest, during a hunting-party, in which the intrepid sovereign of Crim Tartary slew two of the lions' cubs with his own spear. And these interesting relics of an innocent little creature were carried home and kept by their finder, the Baron Spinachi, formerly an officer in Cavolfiore's household. The Baron was disgraced in consequence of his known legitimist opinions, and has lived for some time in the humble capacity of a woodcutter, in a forest on the outskirts of the Kingdom of Crim Tartary.

"Last Tuesday week Baron Spinachi and a number of gentlemen attached to the former dynasty, appeared in arms, crying, 'God save Rosalba, the First Queen of Crim Tartary!' and surrounding a lady whom report describes as *beautiful exceedingly*. Her history *may* be authentic, *is* certainly most romantic.

"The personage calling herself Rosalba states that she was brought out of the forest, fifteen years since, by a lady in a car drawn by dragons (this account is certainly *improbable*), that she was left in the Palace Garden of Blombodinga, where her Royal Highness the Princess Angelica, now married to his Royal Highness Bulbo, Crown Prince of Crim Tartary, found the child, and, with *that elegant benevolence* which has always distinguished the heiress of the throne of Paflagonia, gave the little outcast a *shelter and a home*! Her parentage not being known, and her garb very humble, the foundling was educated in the Palace in a menial capacity, under the name of *Betsinda*.

"She did not give satisfaction, and was dismissed, carrying with her, certainly, part of a mantle and a shoe, which she had on when first found. According to her statement she quitted Blombodinga about a year ago, since which time she has been with the Spinachi family. On the very same morning the Prince Giglio, nephew to the King of Paflagonia, a young Prince whose character for *talent* and *order* were, to say truth, *none of the highest*, also quitted Blombodinga, and has not been since heard of!"

"What an extraordinary story!" said Smith and Jones, two young students, Giglio's especial friends.

"Ha! what is this?" Giglio went on, reading:

"SECOND EDITION, EXPRESS.—We hear that the troop under Baron Spinachi has been surrounded, and utterly routed, by General Count Hogginarmo, and the *soi-disant* Princess is sent a prisoner to the capital "UNIVERSITY NEWS.—Yesterday, at the Schools, the distinguished young student, Mr. Giles, read a Latin oration, and was complimented by the Chancellor of Bosforo, Doctor Prugnaro, with the highest University honour—the wooden spoon."

"Never mind that stuff," says Giles, greatly disturbed. "Come home with me, my friends. Gallant Smith! intrepid Jones! friends of my studies—partakers of my academic toils—I have that to tell shall astonish your honest minds."

"Go it, old boy!" cried the impetuous Smith.

"Talk away, my buck!" says Jones, a lively fellow.

With an air of indescribable dignity, Giglio checked their natural, but no more seemly, familiarity. "Jones, Smith, my good friends," said the PRINCE, "disguise is henceforth useless; I am no more the humble student Giles, I am the descendent of a royal line."

"*Atavis edite regibus*, I know, old co——," cried Jones. He was going to say old cock, but a flash from THE ROYAL EYE again awed him.

"Friends," continued the Prince, "I am that Giglio, I am in fact Paflagonia. Rise, Smith, and kneel not in the public street. Jones, thou true heart! My faithless uncle, when I was a baby, filched from me that brave crown my father left me, bred me, all young and careless of my rights, like unto hapless Hamlet, Prince of Denmark; and had I any thoughts about my wrongs, soothed me with promises of near redress. I should espouse his daughter, young Angelica; we two indeed should reign in Paflagonia. His words were false—false as Angelica's heart!—false as Angelica's hair, colour, front teeth! She looked with her skew eyes upon young Bulbo, Crim Tartary's stupid heir, and she preferred him. 'Twas then I turned my eyes upon Betsinda—Rosalba, as she now is. And I saw in her the blushing sum of all perfection; the pink of maiden modesty; the nymph that my fond heart had ever woo'd in dreams," &c., &c.

(I don't give this speech, which was very fine, but very long; and though Smith and Jones knew nothing about the circumstances, my dear reader does, so I go on.)

The Prince and his young friends hastened home to his apartment, highly excited by the intelligence, as no doubt by the *royal narrator's* admirable manner of recounting it; and they ran up to his room where he had worked so hard at his books.

On his writing-table was his bag, grown so long that the Prince could not help remarking it. He went to it, opened it, and what do you think he found in it?

A splendid long, gold-handled, red-velvet-scabbarded, cut-and-thrust sword, and on the sheath was embroidered "ROSALBA FOR EVER!"

He drew out the sword, which flashed and illuminated the whole room, and called out "Rosalba for ever!" Smith and Jones following him, but quite respectfully this time, and taking the time from his Royal Highness.

And now his trunk opened with a sudden pong, and out there came three ostrich feathers in a gold crown, surrounding a beautiful shining steel helmet, a cuirass, a pair of spurs, finally a complete suit of armour.

The books on Giglio's shelves were all gone. Where there had been some great dictionaries, Giglio's friends found two pairs of jack-boots labelled, "Lieutenant Smith," "—— Jones, Esq.," which fitted them to a nicety. Besides, there were helmets, back- and breast-plates, swords, &c., just like in Mr. G. P. R. James's novels; and that evening three cavaliers might have been seen issuing from the gates of Bosforo, in whom the porters, proctors, &c., never thought of recognizing the young Prince and his friends.

They got horses at a livery-stable-keeper's, and never drew bridle until they reached the last town on the frontier before you come to Crim Tartary. Here, as their animals were tired, and the cavaliers hungry, they stopped and refreshed at an hostel. I could make a chapter of this if I were like some writers, but I like to cram my measure tight down, you see, and give you a great deal for your money, and in a word, they had some bread-and-cheese and ale upstairs on the balcony of the inn. As they were drinking, drums and trumpets sounded nearer and nearer, the market-place was filled with soldiers, and his Royal Highness looking forth, recognized the Paflagonian banners, and the Paflagonian national air which the bands were playing.

The troops all made for the tavern at once, and as they came up Giglio exclaimed, on beholding their leader, "Whom do I see? Yes! No! It is, it is! Phoo! No, it can't be! Yes! it is my friend my gallant faithful veteran, Captain Hedzoff! Ho! Hedzoff! Knowest thou not thy Prince, thy Giglio? Good Corporal, methinks we once were friends. Ha, sergeant, an my memory serves me right, we have had many a bout at singlestick."

"I' faith, we have, a many, good my lord," says the sergeant.

"Tell me, what means this mighty armament," continued his Royal Highness from the balcony, "and whither march my Paflagonians?"

Hedzoff's head fell. "My lord," he said, "we march as the allies of great Padella, Crim Tartary's monarch."

"Crim Tartary's usurper, gallant Hedzoff! Crim Tartary's grim tyrant, honest Hedzoff!" said the Prince, on the balcony, quite sarcastically.

"A soldier, Prince, must needs obey his orders: mine are to help his

Majesty Padella. And also (though alack that I should say it!) to seize wherever I should light upon him—"

"First catch your hare! ha, Hedzoff!" exclaimed his Royal Highness.

"—on the body of *Giglio*, whilom Prince of Paflagonia," Hedzoff went on, with indescribable emotion. "My Prince, give up your sword without ado. Look! we are thirty thousand men to one!"

"Give up my sword! Giglio give up his sword!" cried the Prince; and stepping well forward on to the balcony, the royal youth, *without preparation*, delivered a speech so magnificent, that no report can do justice to it. It was all in blank verse (in which, from this time, he invariably spoke, as more becoming his majestic station). It lasted for three days and three nights, during which not a single person who heard him was tired, or remarked the difference betweem daylight and dark. The soldiers only cheering tremendously, when occasionally, once in nine hours, the Prince paused to suck an orange, which Jones took out of the bag. He explained, in terms which we say we shall not attempt to convey, the whole history of the previous transaction, and his determination not only not to give up his sword, but to assume his righful crown; and at the end of this extraordinary, this truly *gigantic* effort, Captain Hedzoff flung up his helmet, and cried, "Hurray! Hurray! Long live King Giglio!"

Such were the consequences of having employed his time well at College!

When the excitement had ceased, beer was ordered out for the army, and their sovereign himself did not disdain a little! And now it was with some alarm that Captain Hedzoff told him his division was only the advanced guard of the Paflagonian contingent, hastening to King Padella's aid. The main force being a day's march in the rear under his Royal Highness Prince Bulbo.

"We will wait here, good friend, to beat the Prince," his Majesty said, "and *then* will make his royal father wince."

X V

We Return to Rosalba

King Padella made very similar proposals to Rosalba to those which she had received from the various princes who, as we have seen, had fallen in love with her. His Majesty was a widower, and offered to marry his fair captive that instant, but she declined his invitation in her usual polite gentle manner, stating that Prince Giglio was her love, and that any other union was out of the question. Having tried tears and supplications in vain, this violent-tempered monarch menaced her with threats and tortures; but she declared she would rather suffer all these than accept the hand of her father's murderer, who left her finally, uttering the most awful imprecations, and bidding her prepare for death on the following morning.

All night long the King spent in advising how he should get rid of this obdurate young creature. Cutting off her head was much too easy a death for her; hanging was so common in his Majesty's dominions that it no longer afforded him any sport: finally, he bethought himself of a pair of fierce lions which had lately been sent to him as presents, and he determined, with these ferocious brutes, to hunt poor Rosalba down. Adjoining his castle was an amphitheatre where the Prince indulged in bull-baiting, rat-hunting, and other ferocious sports. The two lions were kept in a cage under this place; their roaring might be heard over the whole city, the inhabitants of which, I am sorry to say, thronged in numbers to see a poor young lady gobbled up by two wild beasts.

The King took his place in the royal box, having the officers of the Court around and the Court Hogginarmo by his side, upon whom his Majesty was observed to look very fiercely; the fact is, royal spies had told the monarch of Hogginarmo's behaviour, his proposals to Rosalba, and his offer to fight for the crown. Black as thunder looked King Padella at this proud noble, as they sat in the front seats of the theatre waiting to see the tragedy whereof poor Rosalba was to be the heroine.

At length that Princess was brought out in her nightgown, with all her beautiful hair falling down her back, and looking so pretty that even the beef-eaters and keepers of the wild animals wept plentifully at seeing her. And she walked with her poor little feet (only luckily the arena was covered with sawdust), and went and leaned up against a great stone in the centre of the amphitheatre, round which the Court and the people were seated in boxes, with bars before them, for fear of the great, fierce, red-maned, black-throated, long-tailed, roaring, bellowing, rushing lions. And now the gates were opened, and with a wurrawarrurawarar two great lean, hungry, roaring lions rushed out of their den, where they had been kept for three weeks on nothing but a little toast-and-water, and dashed straight up to the stone where poor Rosalba was waiting. Commend her to your patron saints, all you kind people, for she is in a dreadful state.

There was a hum and a buzz all through the circus, and the fierce King Padella even felt a little compassion. But Count Hogginarmo, seated by his Majesty, roared out, "Hurray! Now for it! Soo-soo-soo!" that nobleman being uncommonly angry still at Rosalba's refusal of him.

But O strange event! O remarkable circumstance! O extraordinary coincidence, which I am sure none of you could *by any possibility* have divined! When the lions came to Rosalba, instead of devouring her with their great teeth, it was with kisses they gobbled her up! They licked her pretty feet, they nuzzled their noses in her lap, they moo'd, they seemed to say, "Dear, dear sister, don't you recollect your brothers in the forest?" And she put her pretty white arms round their tawny necks, and kissed them.

King Padella was immensely astonished. The Count Hogginarmo was extremely disgusted. "Pooh!" the Count cried. "Gammon!" exclaimed his lordship. "These lions are tame beasts come from Wombwell's or Astley's. It is a shame to put people off in this way. I believe they are little boys dressed up in door-mats. They are no lions at all."

"Ha!" said the King, "you dare to say 'gammon' to your sovereign, do you? These lions are no lions at all, aren't they? Ho, my beef-eaters! Ho! my body-guard! Take this Count Hogginarmo and fling him into the circus! Give him a sword and buckler, let him keep his armour on, and his weather-eye out, and fight these lions."

The haughty Hogginarmo laid down his opera-glass, and looked scowling round at the King and his attendants. "Touch me not, dogs!" he said, "or by St. Nicholas the Elder, I will gore you! Your Majesty thinks Hogginarmo is afraid? No, not of a hundred thousand lions! Follow me down into the circus, King Padella, and match thyself against one of yon brutes. Thou darest not. Let them both come on, then!"

And opening a grating of the box, he jumped lightly down into the circus.

Wurra wurra wurra wur-aw-aw-aw!!!
In about two minutes
The Count Hogginarmo was
GOBBLED UP
by
Those lions,
Bones, boots, and all,
and
There was an
End of him.

At this, the King said, "Serve him right, the rebellious ruffian! And now, as those lions won't eat that young woman—"

"Let her off!—let her off!" cried the crowd.

"NO!" roared the King. "Let the beef-eaters go down and chop her into small pieces. If the lions defend her, let the archers shoot them to death. That hussy shall die in tortures!"

"A-a-ah!" cried the crowd. "Shame! shame!"

"Who dares cry out shame?" cried the furious potentate (so little can tyrants command their passions). "Fling any scoundrel who says a word down among the lions!"

I warrant you there was a dead silence then, which was broken by a Pang arang pang pangkarangpang; and a Knight and a Herald rode in at the farther end of the circus. The Knight, in full armour, with his vizor up, and bearing a letter on the point of his lance.

"Ha!" exclaimed the King, "by my fay, 'tis Elephant and Castle, pursuivant of my brother of Paflagonia; and the Knight, an my memory serves me, is the gallant Captain Hedzoff! What news from Paflagonia, gallant Hedzoff? Elephant and Castle, beshrew me, thy trumpeting must have made thee thirsty. What will my trusty herald like to drink?"

"Bespeaking first safe-conduct, from your lordship," said Captain Hedzoff, "before we take a drink of anything, permit us to deliver our King's message."

"My lordship, ha!" said Crim Tartary, frowning terrifically. "That title soundeth strange in the anointed ears of a crowned King. Straightway speak out your message, Knight and Herald!"

Reining up his charger in a most elegant manner close under the King's balcony, Hedzoff turned to the herald, and bade him begin.

Elephant and Castle, dropping his trumpet over his shoulder, took a large sheet of paper out of his hat, and began to read:—

"O Yes! O Yes! O Yes! Know all men by these presents, that we, Giglio, King of Paflagonia, Grand Duke of Cappadocia, Sovereign Prince of Turkey and the Sausage Islands, having assumed our rightful throne and title, long time falsely borne by our usurping Uncle, styling himself King of Paflagonia—"

"Ha!" growled Padella.

"—hereby summon the false traitor, Padella, calling himself King of Crim Tartary—"

The King's curses were dreadful. "Go on, Elephant and Castle!" said the intrepid Hedzoff.

"—to release from cowardly imprisonment his liege lady and rightful Sovereign, ROSALBA, Queen of Crim Tartary, and restore her to her royal throne: in default of which, I, Giglio, proclaim the said Padella, sneak, traitor, humbug, usurper, and coward. I challenge him to meet me, with fists or with pistols, with battle-axe or sword, with blunderbuss or singlestick, alone or at the head of his army, on foot or on horseback; and will prove my words upon his wicked ugly body!"

"God save the King!" said Captain Hedzoff, executing a demivolte, two semilunes, and three caracols.

"Is that all?" said Padella, with the terrific calm of concentrated fury.

"That, sir, is all my royal master's message. Here is his Majesty's letter in autograph, and here is his glove, and if any gentleman of Crim Tartary chooses to find fault with his Majesty's expressions, I, Kutasoff Hedzoff, Captain of the Guard, am very much at his service," and he waved his lance, and looked at the assembly all round.

"And what says my good brother of Paflagonia, my dear son's father-in-law, to this rubbish?" asked the King.

"The King's uncle hath been deprived of the crown he unjustly wore," said Hedzoff gravely. "He and his ex-minister, Glumboso, are now in prison waiting the sentence of my royal master. After the battle of Bombardaro—"

"Of what?" asked the surprised Padella.

"Of Bombardaro, where my liege, his present Majesty, would have performed prodigies of valour, but that the whole of his uncle's army came over to our side, with the exception of Prince Bulbo."

"Ah! my boy, my boy, my Bulbo was no traitor!" cried Padella.

"Prince Bulbo, far from coming over to us, ran away, sir; but I caught him. The Prince is a prisoner in our army, and the most terrifc tortures await him if a hair of the Princess Rosalba's head is injured."

"Do they?" exclaimed the furious Padella, who was now perfectly *livid* with rage. "Do they indeed? So much the worse for Bulbo. I've twenty sons as lovely each as Bulbo. Not one but is as fit to reign as Bulbo. Whip, whack, flog, starve, rack, punish, torture Bulbo—break all his bones—roast him or flay him alive—pull all his pretty teeth out one by one! but justly dear as Bulbo is to me—Joy of my eyes, fond treasure of my soul!—Ha, ha, ha, ha! revenge is dearer still. Ho! torturers, rack-men, executioners—light up the fires and make the pincers hot! get lots of boiling lead!—Bring out ROSALBA!"

XVI

How Hedzoff Rode Back Again to King Giglio

Captain Hedzoff rode away when King Padella uttered this cruel command, having done his duty in delivering the message with which his royal master had intrusted him. Of course he was very sorry for Rosalba, but what could he do?

So he returned to King Giglio's camp, and found the young monarch in a disturbed state of mind, smoking cigars in the royal tent. His Majesty's agitation was not appeased by the news that was brought by his ambassador. "The brutal ruthless ruffian royal wretch!" Giglio exclaimed. "As England's poesy has well remarked, 'The man that lays his hand upon a woman, save in the way of kindness, is a villain.' Ha, Hedzoff?"

"That he is, your Majesty," said the attendant.

"And didst thou see her flung into the oil? and didn't the soothing oil—the emollient oil, refuse to boil, good Hedzoff—and to spoil the fairest lady ever eyes did look on?"

"Faith, good my liege, I had no heart to look and see a beauteous lady boiling down; I took your royal message to Padella, and bore his back to you. I told him you would hold Prince Bulbo answerable. He only said that he had twenty sons as good as Bulbo, and forthwith he bade the ruthless executioners proceed."

"O cruel father—O unhappy son!" cried the King. "Go, some of you, and bring Prince Bulbo hither."

Bulbo was brought in chains, looking very uncomfortable. Though a prisoner, he had been tolerably happy, perhaps because his mind was at rest, and all the fighting was over, and he was playing at marbles with his guards, when the King sent for him.

"O, my poor Bulbo," said his Majesty, with looks of infinite compassion, "hast thou heard the news?" (for you see Giglio wanted to break the thing gently to the Prince). "Thy brutal father has condemned Rosalba—p-p-p-ut her to death, P-p-p-prince Bulbo!"

"What, killed Betsinda! Boo-hoo-hoo," cried out Bulbo. "Besinda! pretty Betsinda! dear Betsinda! She was the dearest little girl in the world. I love her better twenty thousand times even than Angelica," and he went on expressing his grief in so hearty and unaffected a manner, that the King was quite touched by it, and said, shaking Bulbo's hand, that he wished he had known Bulbo sooner.

Bulbo, quite unconsciously, and meaning for the best, offered to come and sit with his Majesty, and smoke a cigar with him, and console him. The *royal kindness* supplied Bulbo with a cigar; he had not had one, he said, since he was taken prisoner.

And now think what must have been the feelings of the most *merciful of monarchs*, when he informed his prisoner that, in consequence of King Padella's *cruel and dastardly behaviour* to Rosalba, Prince Bulbo must instantly be executed! The noble Giglio could not restrain his tears, nor could the Grenadiers, nor the officers, nor could Bulbo himself, when the matter was explained to him, and he was brought to understand that his Majesty's promise, of course, was *above every* thing, and Bulbo must submit. So poor Bulbo was led out, Hedzoff trying to console him, by pointing out that if he had won the battle of Bombardaro, he might have hanged Prince Giglio. "Yes! But that is no comfort to me now!" said poor Bulbo; nor indeed was it, poor fellow!

He was told the business would be done the next morning at eight, and was taken back to his dungeon, where every attention was paid to him. The gaoler's wife sent him tea, and the turnkey's daughter begged him to write his name in her album, where a many gentlemen had wrote it on like occasions! "Bother your album!" says Bulbo. The undertaker came and measured him for the handsomest coffin which money could buy: even this didn't console Bulbo. The cook brought him dishes which he once used to like; but he wouldn't touch them: he sat down and began writing an adieu to Angelica, as the clock kept always ticking, and the hands drawing nearer to next morning. The barber came in at night, and offered to shave him for the next day. Prince Bulbo kicked him away, and went on writing a few words to Princess Angelica, as the clock kept always ticking, and the hands hopping nearer and nearer to next morning. He got up on the top of a hatbox, on the top of a chair, on the top of his bed, on the top of his table, and looked out to see whether he might escape as the clock kept always ticking and the hands drawing nearer, and nearer, and nearer.

But looking out of the window was one thing, and jumping another: and the town clock struck seven. So he got into bed for a little sleep, but the gaoler came and woke him, and said, "Git up, your Royal Ighness, if you please, it's *ten minutes to eight*."

So poor Bulbo got up: he had gone to bed in his clothes (the lazy boy), and he shook himself, and said he didn't mind about dressing, or having any breakfast, thank you; and he saw the soldiers who had come for him.

"Lead on!" he said; and they led the way, deeply affected; and they came into the courtyard, and out into the square, and there was King Giglio come to take leave of him, and his Majesty most kindly shook hands with him, and the *gloomy procession* marched on:—when hark!

Haw—wurraw—wurraw—aworr!

A roar of wild beasts was heard. And who should come riding into the town, frightening away the boys, and even the beadle and policemen, but ROSALBA!

The fact is, that when Captain Hedzoff entered into the court of Snap-dragon Castle, and was discoursing with King Padella, the lions made a dash at the open gate, gobbled up the six beef-eaters in a jiffy, and away they went with Rosalba on the back of one of them, and they carried her, turn and turn about, till they came to the city where Prince Giglio's army was encamped.

When the KING heard of the QUEEN'S arrival, you may think how he rushed out of his breakfast-room to hand her Majesty off her lion! The lions were grown as fat as pigs now, having eaten Hogginarmo and all those beef-eaters, and were so tame, anybody might pat them.

While Giglio knelt (most gracefully) and helped the Princess, Bulbo, for his part, rushed up and kissed the lion. He flung his arms round the forest monarch; he hugged him, and laughed and cried for joy. "O you darling old beast, oh, how glad I am to see you, and the dear, dear Bets—that is, Rosalba."

"What, is it you? poor Bulbo!" said the Queen. "O, how glad *I* am to see you!" and she gave him her hand to kiss. King Giglio slapped him most kindly on the back, and said, "Bulbo, my boy, I am delighted, for your sake, that her Majesty has arrived."

"So am I," said Bulbo; "and *you know why*." Captain Hedzoff here came up. "Sire, it is half-past eight: shall we proceed with the execution?"

"Execution! what for?" asked Bulbo.

"An officer only knows his orders," replied Captain Hedzoff, showing his warrant, on which his Majesty King Giglio smilingly said Prince Bulbo was reprieved this time, and most graciously invited him to breakfast.

X V I I

How a Tremendous Battle Took Place, and Who Won It

As soon as King Padella heard, what we know already, that his victim, the lovely Rosalba, had escaped him, his Majesty's fury knew no bounds, and he pitched the Lord Chancellor, Lord Chamberlain, and every officer of the Crown whom he could set eyes on, into the cauldron of boiling oil prepared for the Princess. Then he ordered out his whole army, horse, foot, and artillery; and set forth at the head of an innumerable host, and I should think twenty thousand drummers, trumpeters, and fifers.

King Giglio's advanced guard, you may be sure, kept that monarch acquainted with the enemy's dealings, and he was in no wise disconcerted. He was much too polite to alarm the Princess, his lovely guest, with any unnecessary rumours of battles impending; on the contrary, he did everything to amuse and divert her; gave her a most elegant breakfast, dinner, lunch, and got up a ball for her that evening, when he danced with her every single dance.

Poor Bulbo was taken into favour again, and allowed to go quite free now. He had new clothes given him, was called "My good cousin" by his Majesty, and was treated with the greatest distinction by everybody. But it was easy to see he was very melancholy. The fact is, the sight of Betsinda, who looked perfectly lovely in an elegant new dress, set poor Bulbo frantic in love with her again. And he never thought about Angelica, now Princess Bulbo, whom he had left at home, and who, as we know, did not care much about him.

The King, dancing the twenty-fifth polka with Rosalba, remarked with wonder the ring she wore; and then Rosalba told him how she had got it from Gruffanuff, who no doubt had picked it up when Angelica flung it away.

"Yes," says the Fairy Blackstick, who had come to see the young people, and who had very likely certain plans regarding them. "That ring I gave the Queen, Giglio's mother, who was not, saving your presence, a very wise woman; it is enchanted, and whoever wears it looks beautiful in the eyes of the world. I made poor Prince Bulbo, when he was christened, the present of a rose which made him look handsome while he had it; but he gave it to Angelica, who instantly looked beautiful again, whilst Bulbo relapsed into his natural plainness."

"Rosalba needs no ring, I'm sure," says Giglio, with a low bow. "She is beautiful enough, in my eyes, without any enchanted aid."

"O, sir!" said Rosalba.

"Take off the ring and try," said the King, and resolutely drew the ring off her finger. In *his* eyes she looked just as handsome as before!

The King was thinking of throwing the ring away, as it was so dangerous and made all the people so mad about Rosalba; but being a Prince of great humour, and good-humour too, he cast eyes upon a poor youth who happened to be looking on very disconsolately, and said:

"Bulbo, my poor lad! come and try on this ring. The Princess Rosalba makes it a present to you."

The magic properties of this ring were uncommonly strong, for no sooner had Bulbo put it on, but lo and behold, he appeared a personable, agreeable young Prince enough—with a fine complexion, fair hair, rather stout, and with bandy legs; but these were encased in such a beautiful pair of yellow morocco boots that nobody remarked them. And Bulbo's spirits rose up almost immediately after he had looked in the glass, and he talked to their Majesties in the most lively, agreeable manner, and danced opposite the Queen with one of the prettiest maids of honour, and after looking at her Majesty, could not help saying:

"How very odd! she is very pretty, but not so *extraordinarily* handsome."

"Oh no, by no means!" says the Maid of Honour.

"But what care I, dear sir," says the Queen, who overheard them, "if *you* think I am good-looking enough?"

His Majesty's glance in reply to this affectionate speech was such that no painter could draw it.

And the Fairy Blackstick said, "Bless you, my darling children! Now you are united and happy; and now you see what I said from the first, that a little misfortune has done you both good. *You*, Giglio, had you been bred in prosperity, would scarcely have learned to read or write—you would have been idle and extravagant, and could not have been a good King, as you now will be. You, Rosalba, would have been so flattered, that your little head might have been turned like Angelica's, who thought herself too good for Giglio."

"As if anybody could be good enough for *him*," cried Rosalba.

"Oh, you, you darling!" says Giglio. And so she was; and he was just holding out his arms in order to give her a hug before the whole company, when a messenger came rushing in, and said, "My lord, the enemy!"

"To arms!" cries Giglio.

"Oh, mercy!" says Rosalba, and fainted of course.

He snatched one kiss from her lips, and rushed *forth to the field* of battle!

The Rose and the Ring

. . .

The Fairy had provided King Giglio with a suit of armour, which was not only embroidered all over with jewels, and blinding to your eyes to look at, but was water-proof, gun-proof, and sword-proof; so that in the midst of the very hottest battles his Majesty rode about as calmly as if he had been a British Grenadier at Alma. Were I engaged in fighting for my country, *I* should like such a suit of armour as Prince Giglio wore; but, you know, he was a prince of a fairy tale, and they always have these wonderful things.

Besides the fairy armour, the Prince had a fairy horse, which would gallop at any pace you please; and a fairy sword, which would lengthen and run through a whole regiment of enemies at once. With such a weapon at command, I wonder, for my part, he thought of ordering his army out; but forth they all came, in magnificent new uniforms; Hedzoff and the Prince's two college friends each commanding a division, and his Majesty prancing in person at the head of them all.

Ah! if I had the pen of a Sir Archibald Alison, my dear friends, would I not now entertain you with the account of a most tremendous shindy? Should not fine blows be struck? dreadful wounds be delivered? arrows darken the air? cannon-balls crash through the battalions? cavalry charge infantry? infantry pitch into cavalry? bugles blow; drums beat; horses neigh; fifes sing; soldiers roar, swear, hurray; officers shout out "Forward, my men!" "This way, lads!" "Give it 'em, boys!" "Fight for King Giglio, and the cause of right!" "King Padella for ever!" Would I not describe all this, I say, and in the very finest language too? But this humble pen does not possess the skill necessary for the description of combats. In a word, the overthrow of King Padella's army was so complete, that if they had been Russians you could not have wished them to be more utterly smashed and confounded.

As for that usurping monarch, having performed acts of valour much more considerable than could be expected of a royal ruffian and usurper, who had such a bad cause, and who was so cruel to women,—as for King Padella, I say, when his army ran away, the King ran away too, kicking his first general, Prince Punchikoff, from his saddle, and galloping away on the Prince's horse, having, indeed, had twenty-five or twenty-six of his own shot under him. Hedzoff coming up, and finding Punchikoff down, as you may imagine, very speedily disposed of *him*.

Meanwhile King Padella was scampering off as hard as his horse could lay legs to ground. Fast as he scampered, I promise you somebody else galloped faster; and that individual, as no doubt you are aware, was the royal Giglio, who kept bawling out, "Stay, traitor! Turn, miscreant, and defend thyself! Stand, tyrant, coward, ruffian, royal wretch, till I cut thy ugly head from thy usurping shoulders!"

And, with his fairy sword, which elongated itself at will, his Majesty kept poking and prodding Padella in the back, until that wicked monarch roared with anguish.

When he was fairly brought to bay, Padella turned and dealt Prince Giglio a prodigious crack over the sconce with his battle-axe, a most enormous weapon, which had cut down I don't know how many regiments in the course of the afternoon. But, law bless you! though the blow fell right down on his Majesty's helmet, it made no more impression than if Padella had struck him with a pat of butter: his battle-axe crumpled up in Padella's hand, and the royal Giglio laughed for very scorn at the impotent efforts of that atrocious usurper.

At the ill success of his blow the Crim Tartar monarch was justly irritated.

"If," says he to Giglio, "you ride a fairy horse, and wear fairy armour, what on earth is the use of my hitting you? I may as well give myself up a prisoner at once. Your Majesty won't, I suppose, be so mean as to strike a poor fellow who can't strike again?"

The justice of Padella's remark struck the magnanimous Giglio. "Do you yield yourself a prisoner, Padella?" says he.

"Of course I do," says Padella.

"Do you acknowledge Rosalba as your rightful Queen, and give up the crown and all your treasures to your rightful mistress?"

"If I must I must," says Padella, who was naturally very sulky.

By this time King Giglio's aides-de-camp had come up, whom his Majesty ordered to bind the prisoner. And they tied his hands behind him, and bound his legs tight under his horse, having set him with his face to the tail; and in this fashion he was led back to King Giglio's quarters, and thrust into the very dungeon where young Bulbo had been confined.

Padella (who was a very different person in the depth of his distress, to Padella, the proud wearer of the Crim Tartar crown) now most affectionately and earnestly asked to see his son—his dear eldest boy—his darling Bulbo; and that good-natured young man never once reproached his haughty parent for his unkind conduct the day before, when he would have left Bulbo to be shot without any pity, but came to see his father, and spoke to him through the grating of the door, beyond which he was not allowed to go; and brought him some sandwiches from the grand supper which his Majesty was giving above stairs, in honour of the brilliant victory which had just been achieved.

"I cannot stay with you long, sir," says Bulbo, who was in his best ball dress, as he handed his father in the prog, "I am engaged to dance the next quadrille with her Majesty Queen Rosalba, and I hear the fiddles playing at this very moment."

So Bulbo went back to the ball-room, and the wretched Padella ate his solitary supper in silence and tears.

All was now joy in King Giglio's circle. Dancing, feasting, fun, illuminations, and jollifications of all sorts ensued. The people through whose villages they passed were ordered to illuminate their cottages at night, and scatter flowers on the roads during the day. They were requested, and I promise you they did not like to refuse, to serve the troops liberally with eatables and wine; besides, the army was enriched by the immense quantity of plunder which was found in King Padella's camp, and taken from his soldiers; who (after they had given up everything) were allowed to fraternize with the conquerors; and the united forces marched back by easy stages towards King Giglio's capital, his royal banner and that of Queen Rosalba being carried in front of the troops. Hedzoff was made a Duke and a Field Marshal. Smith and Jones were promoted to be Earls; the Crim Tartar Order of the Pumpkin and the Paflagonian decoration of the Cucumber were freely distributed by their Majesties to the army. Queen Rosalba wore the Paflagonian Ribbon of the Cucumber across her riding-habit, whilst King Giglio never appeared without the grand Cordon of the Pumpkin. How the people cheered them as they rode along side by side! They were pronounced to be the handsomest couple ever seen: that was a matter of course; but they really *were* very handsome, and, had they been otherwise, would have looked so, they were so happy! Their Majesties were never separated during the whole day, but breakfasted, dined, and supped together always, and rode side by side, interchanging elegant compliments, and indulging in the most delightful conversation. At night, her Majesty's ladies of honour (who had all rallied round her the day after King Padella's defeat) came and conducted her to the apartments prepared for her; whilst King Giglio, surrounded by his gentlemen, withdrew to his own royal quarters. It was agreed they should be married as soon as they reached the capital, and orders were despatched to the Archbishop of Blombodinga, to hold himself in readiness to perform the interesting ceremony. Duke Hedzoff carried the message, and gave instructions to have the Royal Castle splendidly refurnished and painted afresh. The Duke seized Glumboso the ex-Prime Minister, and made him refund that considerable sum of money which the old scoundrel had secreted out of the late King's treasure. He also clapped Valoroso into prison (who, by the way, had been dethroned for some considerable period past), and when the ex-monarch weakly remonstrated, Hedzoff said, "A soldier, sir, knows but his duty; my orders are to lock you up along with the ex-king Padella, whom I have brought hither a prisoner under guard." So these two ex-royal personages were sent for a year to the House of Correction, and thereafter were obliged to become monks of the severest Order of Flagellants, in which state, by fasting, by vigils, by flogging (which they administered to one another, humbly but resolutely), no doubt they exhibited a repentance for their past misdeeds, usurpations, and private and public crimes.

As for Glumboso, that rogue was sent to the galleys, and never had an opportunity to steal any more.

XVIII

How They All Journeyed Back to the Capital

The Fairy Blackstick, by whose means this young King and Queen had certainly won their respective crowns back, would come not unfrequently, to pay them a little visit—as they were riding in their triumphal progress towards Giglio's capital—change her wand into a pony, and travel by their Majesties' side, giving them the very best advice. I am not sure that King Giglio did not think the Fairy and her advice rather a bore, fancying it was his own valour and merits which had put him on his throne, and conquered Padella: and, in fine, I fear he rather gave himself airs toward his best friend and patroness. She exhorted him to deal justly by his subjects, to draw mildly on the taxes, never to break his promise when he had once given it—and in all respects to be a good king.

"A good King, my dear Fairy!" cries Rosalba. "Of course he will. Break his promise! can you fancy my Giglio would ever do anything so improper, so unlike him? No! never!" And she looked fondly towards Giglio, whom she thought a pattern of perfection.

"Why is Fairy Blackstick always advising me, and telling me how to manage my government, and warning me to keep my word? Does she suppose that I am not a man of sense, and a man of honour?" asks Giglio, testily. "Methinks she rather presumes upon her position."

"Hush! dear Giglio," says Rosalba. "You know Blackstick has been very kind to us, and we must not offend her." But the Fairy was not listening to Giglio's testy observations; she had fallen back, and was trotting on her pony now, by Master Bulbo's side—who rode a donkey, and made himself generally beloved in the army by his cheerfulness, kindness, and good-humour to everybody. He was eager to see his darling Angelica. He thought there never was such a charming being. Blackstick did not tell him it was the possession of the magic rose that made Angelica so lovely in his eyes. She brought him the very best accounts of his little wife, whose misfortunes and humiliations had indeed very greatly improved her; and you see, she could whisk off on her wand a hundred miles in a minute, and be back in no time, and so carry polite messages from Bulbo to Angelica, and from Angelica to Bulbo, and comfort that young man upon his journey.

When the royal party arrived at the last stage before you reach Blombodinga, who should be in waiting, in her carriage there with her lady of honour by her side, but the Princess Angelica. She rushed into her husband's arms, scarcely stopping to make a passing curtsey to the King and Queen. She had no eyes but for Bulbo, who appeared perfectly lovely to her on account of the fairy ring which he wore; whilst she herself, wearing the magic rose in her bonnet, seemed entirely beautiful to the enraptured Bulbo.

A splendid luncheon was served to the royal party, of which the Archbishop, the Chancellor, the Duke Hedzoff, Countess Gruffanuff, and all our friends partook. The Fairy Blackstick being seated on the left of King Giglio, with Bulbo and Angelica beside. You could hear the joy-bells ringing in the capital, and the guns which the citizens were firing off in honour of their Majesties.

"What can have induced that hideous old Gruffanuff to dress herself up in such an absurd way? Did you ask her to be your bridesmaid, my dear?" says Giglio to Rosalba. "What a figure of fun Gruffy is!"

Gruffy was seated opposite their Majesties, between the Archbishop and the Lord Chancellor, and a figure of fun she certainly was, for she was dressed in a low white silk dress, with lace over, a wreath of white roses on her wig, a splendid lace veil, and her yellow old neck was covered with diamonds. She ogled the King in such a manner, that his Majesty burst out laughing.

"Eleven o'clock!" cries Giglio, as the great Cathedral bell of Blombodinga tolled that hour. "Gentlemen and ladies, we must be starting. Archbishop, you must be at church I think before twelve?"

"We must be at church before twelve," sighs out Gruffanuff in a languishing voice, hiding her old face behind her fan.

"And then I shall be the happiest man in my dominions," cries Giglio, with an elegant bow to the blushing Rosalba.

"O, my Giglio! O, my dear Majesty!" exclaims Gruffanuff; "and can it be that this happy moment at length has arrived—"

"Of course it has arrived," says the King.

—"and that I am about to become the enraptured bride of my adored Giglio!" continues Gruffanuff. "Lend me a smelling-bottle, somebody. I certainly shall faint with joy."

"*You* my bride?" roars out Giglio.

"*You* marry my Prince?" cries poor little Rosalba.

"Pooh! Nonsense! The woman's mad!" exclaims the King. And all the courtiers exhibited by their countenances and expressions, marks of surprise, or ridicule, or incredulity, or wonder.

"I should like to know who else is going to be married, if I am not?" shrieks out Gruffanuff. "I should like to know if King Giglio is a gentleman, and if there is such a thing as justice in Paflagonia? Lord Chancellor! my Lord Archbishop! will your lordships sit by and see a poor, fond, confiding, tender creature put upon? Has not Prince Giglio promised to marry his Barbara? Is not this Giglio's signature? Does not this paper declare that he is mine, and only mine?" And she handed to his Grace the Archbishop the document which the Prince signed that evening when she wore the magic ring, and Giglio drank so much champagne. And the old Archbishop, taking out his eye-glasses, read:

"This is to give notice, that I, Giglio, only son of Savio, King of Paflagonia, hereby promise to marry the charming Barbara Griselda Countess Gruffanuff, and widow of the late Jenkins Gruffanuff, Esq."

"H'm," says the Archbishop, "the document is certainly a—a document."

"Phoo!" says the Lord Chancellor, "the signature is not in his Majesty's handwriting."

Indeed, since his studies at Bosforo, Giglio had made an immense improvement in calligraphy.

"Is it your handwriting, Giglio?" cries the Fairy Blackstick, with an awful severity of countenance.

"Y—y—y—es," poor Giglio gasps out, "I had quite forgotten the confounded paper: she can't mean to hold me by it. You old wretch, what will you take to let me off? Help the Queen, some one—her Majesty has fainted."

"Chop her head off!"

"Smother the old witch!" } exclaim the impetuous Hedzoff, the ardent

"Pitch her into the river!"

Smith, and the faithful Jones.

But Gruffanuff flung her arms round the Archbishop's neck, and bellowed out, "Justice, justice, my Lord Chancellor!" so loudly, that her piercing shrieks caused everybody to pause. As for Rosalba, she was borne away lifeless by her ladies; and you may imagine the look of agony which Giglio cast towards that lovely being, as his hope, his joy, his darling, his all in all, was thus removed, and in her place the horrid old Gruffanuff rushed up to his side, and once more shrieked out, "Justice, justice!"

"Won't you take that sum of money which Glumboso hid?" says Giglio: "two hundred and eighteen thousand millions, or thereabouts. It's a handsome sum."

"I will have that and you too!" says Gruffanuff.

"Let us throw the crown jewels into the bargain," gasps out Giglio.

"I will wear them by my Giglio's side!" says Gruffanuff.

"Will half, three-quarters, five-sixths, nineteen-twentieths, of my kingdom do, Countess?" asks the trembling monarch.

"What were all Europe to me without *you*, my Giglio?" cries Guff, kissing his hand.

"I won't, I can't, I sha'n't—I'll resign the crown first," shouts Giglio, tearing away his hand; but Gruff clung to it.

"I have a competency, my love," she says, "and with thee and a cottage thy Barbara will be happy."

Giglio was half mad with rage by this time. "I will not marry her," says he. "Oh, Fairy, Fairy, give me counsel!" And as he spoke he looked wildly round at the severe face of the Fairy Blackstick.

" 'Why is Fairy Blackstick always advising me, and warning me to keep my word? Does she suppose that I am not a man of honour?' " said the Fairy, quoting Giglio's own haughty words. He quailed under the brightness of her eyes; he felt that there was no escape for him from that awful inquisition.

"Well, Archbishop," said he, in a dreadful voice that made his Grace start, "since this Fairy has led me to the height of happiness but to dash me down into the depths of despair, since I am to lose Rosalba, let me at least keep my honour. Get up, Countess, and let us be married; I can keep my word, but I can die afterwards."

"O dear Giglio," cries Gruffanuff, skipping up, "I knew, I knew I could trust thee—I knew that my prince was the soul of honour. Jump into your carriages, ladies and gentlemen, and let us go to church at once; and as for dying, dear Giglio, no, no—thou wilt forget that insignificant little chambermaid of a queen—thou wilt live to be consoled by thy Barbara! She wishes to be a Queen, and not a Queen Dowager, my gracious Lord!" And hanging upon poor Giglio's arm, and leering and grinning in his face in the most disgusting manner, this old wretch tripped off in her white satin shoes, and jumped into the very carriage which had been got ready to convey Giglio and Rosalba to church. The cannons roared again, the bells pealed triple-bobmajors, the people came out flinging flowers upon the path of the royal bride and bridegroom, and Gruff looked out of the gilt coach window and bowed and grinned to them. Phoo! the horrid old wretch!

XIX

And Now We Come to the Last Scene in the Pantomime

The many ups and downs of her life had given the Princess Rosalba prodigious strength of mind, and that highly principled young woman presently recovered from her fainting-fit, out of which Fairy Blackstick, by a precious essence which the Fairy always carried in her pocket, awakened her.

Instead of tearing her hair, crying, and bemoaning herself, and fainting again, as many young women would have done, Rosalba remembered that she owed an example of firmness to her subjects; and though she loved Giglio more than her life, was determined, as she told the Fairy, not to interfere between him and justice, or to cause him to break his royal word.

"I cannot marry him, but I shall love him always," says she to Blackstick; "I will go and be present at his marriage with the Countess, and sign the book, and wish them happy with all my heart. I will see, when I get home, whether I cannot make the new Queen some handsome presents. The Crim Tartary crown diamonds are uncommonly fine, and I shall never have any use for them. I will live and die unmarried like Queen Elizabeth, and, of course, I shall leave my crown to Giglio when I quit this world. Let us go and see them married, my dear Fairy, let me say one last farewell to him; and then, if you please, I will return to my own dominions."

So the Fairy kissed Rosalba with peculiar tenderness, and at once changed her wand into a very comfortable coach-and-four, with a steady coachman, and two respectable footmen behind, and the Fairy and Rosalba got into the coach, which Angelica and Bulbo entered after them.

As for honest Bulbo, he was blubbering in the most pathetic manner, quite overcome by Rosalba's misfortune. She was touched by the honest fellow's sympathy, promised to restore to him the confiscated estates of Duke Padella his father, and created him, as he sat there in the coach, Prince, Highness, and First Grandee of the Crim Tartar Empire.

The coach moved on, and, being a fairy coach, soon came up with the bridal procession.

Before the ceremony at church it was the custom in Paflagonia, as it is in other countries, for the bride and bridegroom to sign the Contract of Marriage, which was to be witnessed by the Chancellor, Minister, Lord Mayor, and principal officers of state.

Now, as the royal palace was being painted and furnished anew, it was not ready for the reception of the King and his bride, who proposed at first to take up their residence at the Prince's palace, that one which Valoroso occupied when Angelica was born, and before he usurped the throne.

So the marriage-party drove up to the palace: the dignitaries got out of their carriages and stood aside: poor Rosalba stepped out of her coach, supported by Bulbo, and stood almost fainting up against the railings so as to have a last look of her dear Giglio.

As for Blackstick, she, according to her custom, had flown out of the coach window in some inscrutable manner, and was now standing at the palace door.

Giglio came up the steps with his horrible bride on his arm, looking as pale as if he was going to execution. He only frowned at the Fairy Blackstick—he was angry with her, and thought she came to insult his misery.

"Get out of the way, pray," says Gruffanuff, haughtily. "I wonder why you are always poking your nose into other people's affairs?"

"Are you determined to make this poor young man unhappy?" says Blackstick.

"To marry him, yes! What business is it of yours? Pray, madam, don't say 'you' to a queen," cries Gruffanuff.

"You won't take the money he offered you?"

"No."

"You won't let him off his bargain, though you know you cheated him when you made him sign the paper?"

"Impudence! Policemen, remove this woman!" cries Gruffanuff. And the policemen were rushing forward, but with a wave of her wand the Fairy struck them all like so many statues in their places.

"You won't take anything in exchange for your bond, Mrs. Gruffanuff?" cries the Fairy, with awful severity. "I speak for the last time."

"No!" shrieks Gruffanuff, stamping with her foot. "I'll have my husband, my husband, my husband!"

"YOU SHALL HAVE YOUR HUSBAND!" the Fairy Blackstick cried; and advancing a step, laid her hand upon the nose of the KNOCKER.

As she touched it, the brass nose seemed to elongate, the open mouth opened still wider, and uttered a roar which made everybody start. The eyes rolled wildly; the arms and legs uncurled themselves, writhed about, and seemed to lengthen with each twist; the knocker expanded into a figure in yellow livery, six feet high; the screws by which it was fixed to the door unloosed themselves, and JENKINS GRUFFANUFF once more trod the threshold off which he had been lifted more than twenty years ago!

"Master's not at home," says Jenkins, just in his old voice; and Mrs. Jenkins, giving a dreadful *youp*, fell down in a fit, in which nobody minded her.

For everybody was shouting, "Huzzay! huzzay!" "Hip, hip, hurray!" "Long live the King and Queen!" "Were such things ever seen?" "No, never, never, never!" "The Fairy Blackstick for ever!"

The bells were ringing double peals, the guns roaring and banging most prodigiously.

Bulbo was embracing everybody; the Lord Chancellor was flinging up his wig and shouting like a madman; Hedzoff had got the Archbishop round the waist, and they were dancing a jig for joy; and as for Giglio, I leave you to imagine what *he* was doing, and if he kissed Rosalba once, twice— twenty thousand times, I'm sure I don't think he was wrong.

So Gruffanuff opened the hall-door with a low bow, just as he had been accustomed to do, and they all went in and signed the book, and then they went to church and were married, and the Fairy Blackstick sailed away on her cane, and was never more heard of in Paflagonia.

1855

The Magic Fish-Bone

CHARLES DICKENS

There was once a King, and he had a Queen, and he was the manliest of his sex, and she was the loveliest of hers. The King was, in his private profession, Under Government. The Queen's father had been a medical man out of town.

They had nineteen children, and were always having more. Seventeen of these children took care of the baby, and Alicia, the eldest, took care of them all. Their ages varied from seven years to seven months.

Let us now resume our story.

One day the King was going to the Office, when he stopped at the fishmonger's to buy a pound and a half of salmon not too near the tail, which the Queen (who was a careful housekeeper) had requested him to send home. Mr. Pickles, the fishmonger, said, "Certainly, sir, is there any other article, good-morning."

The King went on towards the Office in a melancholy mood, for Quarter-Day was such a long way off, and several of the dear children were growing out of their clothes. He had not proceeded far, when Mr. Pickles's errand-boy came running after him, and said, "Sir, you didn't notice the old lady in our shop."

"What old lady?" inquired the King. "I saw none."

Now, the King had not seen any old lady, because this old lady had been invisible to him, though visible to Mr. Pickles's boy. Probably because he messed and splashed the water about to that degree, and flopped the pairs of soles down in that violent manner, that, if she had not been visible to him, he would have spoilt her clothes.

Just then the old lady came trotting up. She was dressed in shot-silk of the richest quality, smelling of dried lavender.

"King Watkins the First, I believe?" said the old lady.

"Watkins," replied the King, "is my name."

"Papa, if I am not mistaken, of the beautiful Princess Alicia?" said the old lady.

"And of eighteen other darlings," replied the King.

"Listen. You are going to the Office," said the old lady.

It instantly flashed upon the King that she must be a Fairy, or how could she know that?

"You are right," said the old lady, answering his thoughts, "I am the Good Fairy Grandmarina. Attend. When you return home to dinner, politely invite the Princess Alicia to have some of the salmon you bought just now."

"It may disagree with her," said the King.

The old lady became so very angry at this absurd idea, that the King was quite alarmed, and humbly begged her pardon.

"We hear a great deal too much about this thing disagreeing and that thing disagreeing," said the old lady, with the greatest contempt it was possible to express. "Don't be greedy. I think you want it all yourself."

The King hung his head under this reproof, and said he wouldn't talk about things disagreeing, any more.

"Be good then," said the Fairy Grandmarina, "and don't! When the beautiful Princess Alicia consents to partake of the salmon—as I think she will—you will find she will leave a fish-bone on her plate. Tell her to dry it, and to rub it, and to polish it till it shines like mother-of-pearl, and to take care of it as a present from me."

"Is that all?" asked the King.

"Don't be impatient, sir," returned the Fairy Grandmarina, scolding him severely. "Don't catch people short, before they have done speaking. Just the way with you grown-up persons. You are always doing it."

The King again hung his head, and said he wouldn't do so any more.

"Be good then," said the Fairy Grandmarina, "and don't! Tell the Princess Alicia, with my love, that the fish-bone is a magic present which can only be used once; but that it will bring her, that once, whatever she wishes for, PROVIDED SHE WISHES FOR IT AT THE RIGHT TIME. That is the message. Take care of it."

The King was beginning, "Might I ask the reason—?" when the Fairy became absolutely furious.

"*Will* you be good, sir?" she exclaimed, stamping her foot on the ground. "The reason for this, and the reason for that, indeed! You are always wanting the reason. No reason. There! Hoity toity me! I am sick of your grown-up reasons."

The King was extremely frightened by the old lady's flying into such a passion, and said he was very sorry to have offended her, and he wouldn't ask for reasons any more.

"Be good then," said the old lady, "and don't!"

With those words, Grandmarina vanished, and the King went on and on and on, till he came to the Office. There he wrote and wrote and wrote, till it was time to go home again. Then he politely invited the Princess Alicia, as the Fairy had directed him, to partake of the salmon. And when she had enjoyed it very much, he saw the fish-bone on her plate, as the Fairy had told him he would, and he delivered the Fairy's message, and the Princess Alicia took care to dry the bone, and to rub it, and to polish it till it shone like mother-of-pearl.

And so when the Queen was going to get up in the morning, she said, "O dear me, dear me, my head, my head!" And then she fainted away.

The Princess Alicia, who happened to be looking in at the chamber door, asking about breakfast, was very much alarmed when she saw her royal mamma in this state, and she rang the bell for Peggy—which was the name of the Lord Chamberlain. But remembering where the smelling-bottle was, she climbed on a chair and got it, and after that she climbed on another chair by the bedside and held the smelling bottle to the Queen's nose, and after that she jumped down and got some water, and after that she jumped up again and wetted the Queen's forehead, and, in short, when the Lord Chamberlain came in, that dear old woman said to the little Princess, "What a Trot you are! I couldn't have done it better myself!"

But that was not the worst of the good Queen's illness. O no! She was very ill indeed, for a long time. The Princess Alicia kept the seventeen young Princes and Princesses quiet, and dressed and undressed and danced the baby, and made the kettle boil, and heated the soup, and swept the hearth, and poured out the medicine, and nursed the Queen, and did all that ever she could, and was as busy busy busy, as busy could be. For there were not many servants at that Palace, for three reasons: because the King was short of money, because a rise in his office never seemed to come, and because Quarter-Day was so far off that it looked almost as far off and as little as one of the stars.

But on the morning when the Queen fainted away, where was the magic fish-bone? Why, there it was in the Princess Alicia's pocket. She had almost taken it out to bring the Queen to life again, when she put it back, and looked for the smelling-bottle.

After the Queen had come out of her swoon that morning, and was dozing, the Princess Alicia hurried up stairs to tell a most particular secret to a most particularly confidential friend of hers, who was a Duchess. People did suppose her to be a doll, but she was really a Duchess, though nobody knew it except the Princess.

This most particular secret was the secret about the magic fish-bone, the history of which was well known to the Duchess, because the Princess told her everything. The Princess kneeled down by the bed on which the Duchess was lying, full dressed and wide-awake, and whispered the secret to her. The Duchess smiled and nodded. People might have supposed that she never smiled and nodded, but she often did, though nobody knew it except the Princess.

Then the Princess Alicia hurried down stairs again, to keep watch in the Queen's room. She often kept watch by herself in the Queen's room; but every evening, while the illness lasted, she sat there watching with the King. And every evening the King sat looking at her with a cross look, wondering why she never brought out the magic fish-bone. As often as she noticed this, she ran up stairs, whispered the secret to the Duchess over again, and said to the Duchess besides, "They think we children never have a reason or a meaning!" And the Duchess, though the most fashionable Duchess that ever was heard of, winked her eye.

"Alicia," said the King, one evening when she wished him good-night.

"Yes, papa."

"What is become of the magic fish-bone?"

"In my pocket, papa."

"I thought you had lost it?"

"O no, papa!"

"Or forgotten it?"

"No, indeed, papa!"

And so another time the dreadful little snapping pug-dog next door made a rush at one of the young Princes as he stood on the steps coming home from school, and terrified him out of his wits, and he put his hand through a pane of glass, and bled bled bled. When the seventeen other young Princes and Princesses saw him bleed bleed bleed, they were terrified out of their wits too, and screamed themselves black in their seventeen faces all at once. But the Princess Alicia put her hands over all their seventeen mouths, one after another, and persuaded them to be quiet because of the sick Queen. And then she put the wounded Prince's hand in a basin of fresh cold water, while they stared with their twice seventeen are thirty-four put down four and carry three eyes, and then she looked in the hand for bits of glass, and there were fortunately no bits of glass there. And then she said to two chubby-legged Princes who were sturdy though small, "Bring me in the royal rag-bag; I must snip and stitch and cut and contrive." So those two young Princes tugged at the royal rag-bag and lugged it in, and the Princess Alicia sat down on the floor with a large pair of scissors and a needle and thread, and snipped and stitched and cut and contrived, and made a bandage and put it on, and it fitted beautifully, and so when it was all done she saw the King her papa looking on by the door.

"Alicia."

"Yes, papa."

"What have you been doing?"

"Snipping, stitching, cutting, and contriving, papa."

"Where is the magic fish-bone?"

"In my pocket, papa."

"I thought you had lost it?"

"O no, papa!"

"Or forgotten it?"

"No, indeed, papa!"

After that, she ran up stairs to the Duchess and told her what had passed, and told her the secret over again, and the Duchess shook her flaxen curls and laughed with her rosy lips.

Well! and so another time the baby fell under the grate. The seventeen young Princes and Princesses were used to it, for they were almost always falling under the grate or down the stairs, but the baby was not used to it yet, and it gave him a swelled face and a black eye. The way the poor little darling came to tumble was, that he slid out of the Princess Alicia's lap just as she was sitting, in a great coarse apron that quite smothered her, in front of the kitchen fire, beginning to peel the turnips for the broth for dinner; and the way she came to be doing that was, that the King's cook had run away that morning with her own true love, who was a very tall but very tipsy soldier. Then, the seventeen young Princes and Princesses, who cried at everything that happened, cried and roared. But the Princess Alicia (who couldn't help crying a little herself) quietly called to them to be still, on account of not throwing back the Queen up stairs, who was fast getting well, and said, "Hold your tongues, you wicked little monkeys, every one of you, while I examine baby!" Then she examined baby, and found that he hadn't broken anything, and she held cold iron to his poor dear eye, and smoothed his poor dear face, and he presently fell asleep in her arms. Then she said to the seventeen Princes and Princesses, "I am afraid to lay him down yet, lest he should wake and feel pain, be good and you shall all be cooks." They jumped for joy when they heard that, and began making themselves cooks' caps out of old newspapers. So to one she gave the salt-box, and to one she gave the barley, and to one she gave the herbs, and to one she gave the turnips, and to one she gave the carrots, and to one she gave the onions, and to one she gave the spice-box, till they were all cooks, and all running about at work, she sitting in the middle, smothered in the great coarse apron, nursing baby. By and by the broth was done, and the baby woke up, smiling like an angel, and was trusted to the sedatest Princess to hold, while the other Princes and Princesses were squeezed into a far-off corner to look at the Princess Alicia turning out the saucepan-full of broth, for fear (as they were always getting into trouble) they should get splashed and scalded. When the broth came tumbling out, steaming beautifully, and smelling like a nosegay good to eat, they clapped their hands. That made the baby clap his hands; and that, and his looking as if he had a comic toothache, made all the Princes and Princesses laugh. So the Princess Alicia said, "Laugh and be good, and after dinner we will make him a nest on the floor in a corner, and he shall sit in his nest and see a dance of eighteen cooks." That delighted the young Princes and Princesses, and they ate up all the broth, and washed up all the plates and dishes, and cleared away, and pushed the table into a corner, and then they in their cooks' caps, and the Princess Alicia in the smothering coarse apron that belonged to the cook that had run away with her own true love that was the very tall but very tipsy soldier, danced a dance of eighteen cooks before the angelic baby, who forgot his swelled face and his black eye, and crowed with joy.

And so then, once more the Princess Alicia saw King Watkins the First, her father, standing in the doorway looking on, and he said, "What have you been doing, Alicia?"

"Cooking and contriving, papa."

"What else have you been doing, Alicia?"

"Keeping the children light-hearted, papa."

"Where is the magic fish-bone, Alicia?"

"In my pocket, papa."

"I thought you had lost it?"

"O no, papa."

"Or forgotten it?"

"No, indeed, papa."

The King then sighed so heavily, and seemed so low-spirited, and sat down so miserably, leaning his head upon his hand, and his elbow upon the kitchen table pushed away in the corner, that the seventeen Princes and Princesses crept softly out of the kitchen, and left him alone with the Princess Alicia and the angelic baby.

"What is the matter, papa?"

"I am dreadfully poor, my child."

"Have you no money at all, papa?"

"None, my child."

"Is there no way left of getting any, papa?"

"No way," said the King. "I have tried very hard, and I have tried all ways."

When she heard those last words, the Princess Alicia began to put her hand into the pocket where she kept the magic fish-bone.

"Papa," said she, "when we have tried very hard, and tried all ways, we must have done our very very best?"

"No doubt, Alicia."

"When we have done our very very best, papa, and that is not enough, then I think the right time must have come for asking help of others." This was the very secret connected with the magic fish-bone, which she had found out for herself from the Good Fairy Grandmarina's words, and which she had so often whispered to her beautiful and fashionable friend the Duchess.

So she took out of her pocket the magic fish-bone that had been dried and rubbed and polished till it shone like mother-of-pearl, and she gave it one little kiss and wished it was Quarter-Day. And immediately it *was* Quarter-Day, and the King's quarter's salary came rattling down the chimney, and bounced into the middle of the floor.

But this was not half of what happened, no not a quarter, for immediately afterwards the Good Fairy Grandmarina came riding in, in a carriage-and-four (peacocks), with Mr. Pickles's boy up behind, dressed in silver and gold, with a cocked hat, powdered hair, pink silk stockings, a jewelled cane, and a nosegay. Down jumped Mr. Pickles's boy with his cocked hat in his hand and wonderfully polite (being entirely changed by enchantment), and handed Grandmarina out, and there she stood, in her rich shot-silk smelling of dried lavender, fanning herself with a sparkling fan.

"Alicia, my dear," said this charming old Fairy, "how do you do, I hope I see you pretty well, give me a kiss."

The Princess Alicia embraced her, and then Grandmarina turned to the King, and said rather sharply, "Are you good?"

The King said he hoped so.

"I suppose you know the reason, *now*, why my goddaughter here," kissing the Princess again, "did not apply to the fish-bone sooner?" said the Fairy.

The King made her a shy bow.

"Ah! But you didn't *then!*" said the Fairy.

The King made her a shyer bow.

"Any more reasons to ask for?" said the Fairy.

The King said no, and he was very sorry.

"Be good then," said the Fairy, "and live happy ever afterwards."

Then, Grandmarina waved her fan, and the Queen came in most splendidly dressed, and the seventeen young Princes and Princesses, no longer grown out of their clothes, came in, newly fitted out from top to toe, with tucks in everything to admit of its being let out. After that, the Fairy tapped the Princess Alicia with her fan, and the smothering coarse apron flew away, and she appeared exquisitely dressed, like a little bride, with a wreath of orange-flowers, and a silver veil. After that, the kitchen dresser changed of itself into a wardrobe, made of beautiful woods and gold and looking-glass, which was full of dresses of all sorts, all for her and all exactly fitting her. After that, the angelic baby came in, running alone, with his face and eye not a bit the worse but much the better. Then, Grandmarina begged to be introduced to the Duchess, and when the Duchess was brought down many compliments passed between them.

A little whispering took place between the Fairy and the Duchess, and then the Fairy said out loud, "Yes. I thought she would have told you." Grandmarina then turned to the King and Queen, and said, "We are going in search of Prince Certainpersonio. The pleasure of your company is requested at church in half-an-hour precisely." So she and the Princess Alicia got into the carriage, and Mr. Pickles's boy handed in the Duchess, who sat by herself on the opposite seat, and then Mr. Pickles's boy put up the steps and got up behind, and the peacocks flew away with their tails spread.

Prince Certainpersonio was sitting by himself, eating barley-sugar and waiting to be ninety. When he saw the peacocks, followed by the carriage, coming in at the window, it immediately occurred to him that something uncommon was going to happen.

"Prince," said Grandmarina, "I bring you your bride."

The moment the Fairy said those words, Prince Certainpersonio's face left off being sticky, and his jacket and corduroys changed to peach-bloom velvet, and his hair curled, and a cap and feather flew in like a bird and settled on his head. He got into the carriage by the Fairy's invitation, and there he renewed his acquaintance with the Duchess, whom he had seen before.

In the church were the Prince's relations and friends, and the Princess Alicia's relations and friends, and the seventeen Princes and Princesses, and the baby, and a crowd of the neighbours. The marriage was beautiful beyond expression. The Duchess was bridesmaid, and beheld the ceremony from the pulpit where she was supported by the cushion of the desk.

Grandmarina gave a magnificent wedding feast afterwards, in which there was everything and more to eat, and everything and more to drink. The wedding cake was delicately ornamented with white satin ribbons, frosted silver and white lilies, and was forty-two yards round.

When Grandmarina had drunk her love to the young couple, and Prince Certainpersonio had made a speech, and everybody had cried Hip Hip Hip

Hurrah! Grandmarina announced to the King and Queen that in future there would be eight Quarter-Days in every year, except in leap-year, when there would be ten. She then turned to Certainpersonio and Alicia, and said, "My dears, you will have thirty-five children, and they will all be good and beautiful. Seventeen of your children will be boys, and eighteen will be girls. The hair of the whole of your children will curl naturally. They will never have the measles, and will have recovered from the whooping-cough before being born."

On hearing such good news, everybody cried out Hip Hip Hip Hurrah! again.

"It only remains," said Grandmarina in conclusion, "to make an end of the fish-bone."

So she took it from the hand of the Princess Alicia, and it instantly flew down the throat of the dreadful little snapping pug-dog next door and choked him, and he expired in convulsions.

1868

Melilot

HENRY MORLEY

I

The Three Neighbours of Melilot

It had been raining for ten months, and everybody felt as if it had been raining for ten years. In the driest part of the country, in the driest corners of the driest houses, there was damp. Whoever came near a fire began to steam; whoever left the fire began to moisten as the damp entered the clothes. There was a breath of wet on everything in-doors, and Melilot was wet through when she came to the door of a broken-roofed cottage that stood in a marsh between two lakes.

Melilot was a pretty girl of twelve, who had lived in a cottage up the mountains, as the only child of hard-working parents, who taught her all that was good, and whose one worldly good she was; for they had nothing to eat but what they could force to grow out of a stony patch of ground upon the mountain-side. They had loved Melilot, and they loved each other. To feed their little one they had deprived themselves, till when the rain running down the mountain-side had washed away their little garden crops, first the mother died—for she it was who had denied herself the most—and then the father also died in a long passion of weeping. The nearest neighbours occupied the cottage in the valley on the marsh between the lakes. In hunger and grief, therefore, Melilot went down to them to ask for human help.

From Melilot's home it was a long way up to the peak of the mountains, and a long way down to the marshy valley in which lay the two lakes with a narrow spit of earth between them, and a black rocky mountain overhanging them upon the other side. A gloomy defile, between high rocks, led out of the valley on the one side, and on the other side it opened upon a waste of bog, over which the thick mist brooded, and the rain now fell with never-ending plash.

The runlets on the mountain formed a waterfall that, dashing over a smooth wall of rock, broke into foam on the ragged floor of a great rocky basin near Melilot's cottage door. Then after a short rush, seething and foaming down a slope rugged with granite boulders, the great cataract fell with a mighty roar over another precipice upon the stream that, swollen by the rains almost into a river, carried its flood into one of the lakes. It was partly by this waterfall that the path down into the valley ran.

Melilot knew that her father, when alive, had avoided the people in the lake cottage, and had forbidden her, although they were the only neighbours, to go near their dwelling. But her father now was dead, and her mother was dead, and there was need of human help if she would bury them. Her father, too, had told her that when she was left helpless she would have to go out and serve others for her daily bread. To what others than these could the child look? So by the stony side of the stream, and by the edge of the lake, her only path in the marsh, Melilot came down shivering and weeping through the pitiless rain, and knocked at the door of the lake cottage.

"Who's that?" asked a hoarse voice inside.

"That's Melilot from up above us," said a hoarser voice.

"Come in then, little Melilot," another voice said, that was the hoarsest of the three.

The child flinched before opening the door, but she did open it, and set one foot over the threshold; then she stopped. There was nothing in the cottage but a muddy puddle on the floor, into which rain ran from the broken roof. Three men sat together in the puddle, squatted like frogs. They had broad noses and spotted faces, and the brightest of bright eyes, which were all turned to look at Melilot when she came in.

"We are glad to see you, Melilot," said the one who sat in the middle, holding out a hand that had all its fingers webbed together. He was the one who had the hoarsest voice. "My friend on the right is Dock, Dodder sits on my left, and I am Squill. Come in and shut the door behind you."

Melilot had to choose between the dreary, empty world outside, and trust in these three creatures—who were more horrible to look at than I care to tell. She hesitated only for an instant, then went in and shut the door behind her.

"A long time ago your father came to us, and he went out and shut the door upon us. You are wiser than your father, little girl."

"My father, oh, my dear father!" began Melilot, and fell to weeping bitterly.

"Her father is dead," said Dock, who was the least hoarse.

"And her mother too," said Dodder, who was hoarser.

"And she wants us to help her to bury them," croaked Squill.

"She is fainting with hunger," said Dock.

"She is dying of hunger and grief," said Dodder.

"And we have nothing to offer her but tadpoles, which she cannot eat," said Squill.

"Dear neighbours, I am nothing," said the child. "I do not know that I am hungry. But if you would come with me and help me."

"She asks us to her house," said Dock.

"We may go," said Dodder, "if we are invited."

"Little Melilot," said Squill then, in his hoarsest tone of all, "we will all follow you to the mountain hut." Then the three ugly creatures splashed out of their pool, and moved, web-footed too, about their cottage with ungainly hopping. Melilot all the while only thanked them, frankly looking up into their bright eyes, that were eager, very eager, but not cruel.

I I

The Mountain Hut

Melilot, with her three wonderful neighbours, Dock, Dodder, and Squill, hopping arm in arm behind her, and getting a good hold on the stones with their web feet, began to climb the mountain. Rain still poured out of the sky; runlets flooded their path, and the great cataract roared by their side. The faint and hungry child had climbed but half the way to her desolate home when she swooned, and was caught in the arms of Squill.

"Sprinkle water," said Dock.

"No need of that," said Dodder.

"It will not be right for us to carry her," said Squill.

Either because there was more than a sprinkling of water, or because of her own stout young heart, Melilot recovered and climbed on. They reached the hut, and when there, the three neighbours at once bestirred themselves. Because of the flood outside, they dug the graves under the roof, one on each side of the hearth, for Melilot's dead father and mother, and so buried them. Then the child made her friends sit down to rest; one in her father's chair, one in her mother's, and one on her own little stool. She raked the embers of the fire and put on fresh wood until a blaze leapt up that was strong enough to warm them before she would turn aside. Then standing in a corner by the morsel of window that looked out towards the waterfall, she gave way to her sobbing. But again—brave little heart—conquering herself, she came forward to where the monsters were sitting, with their legs crossed, basking in the firelight, and said, "I am sorry, dear, kind neighbours, that I have no supper to offer you."

"Nay, but you have," said Dock.

The child followed the glance of his eyes, and saw that on her father's grave there stood a loaf of bread, and on her mother's grave a cup of milk.

"They are for you, from the good angels." She said, "Oh, I am thankful!" Then Melilot broke the bread into three pieces, and gave a piece to each, and held the milk for them when they would drink.

"She is famished herself," said Dodder.

"We must eat all of it up," said Squill.

So they ate all of it up; and while they ate, there was no thought in the child's heart but of pleasure that she had this bread to give.

When they had eaten all, there was another loaf upon the father's grave, and on the mother's grave another and a larger cup of milk.

"See there!" Dock said.

"Whose supper is that?" asked Dodder.

"It must be for the pious little daughter Melilot, and no one else," said Squill.

The three neighbours refused to take another crumb; they had eaten so much tadpole, they said, for their dinners. Melilot, therefore, supped, but left much bread and milk, secretly thinking that her friends would require breakfast, if they should consent to stay with her throughout the night. It was long since the sun set, reddening the mists of the plain, and now the mountain path beside the torrent was all dark and very perilous. The monsters eagerly watched their little hostess with their brilliant eyes, and assented, as it seemed, with exultation, to her wish that they would sleep in the hut. There were but two beds under its roof—Melilot's own little straw pallet, and that on which her parents were to sleep no more, on which she was no more to kneel beside them in the humble morning prayer. With sacred thoughts of hospitality the child gave up to the use of those who had smoothed for her dear parents a new bed, the bed that was no longer theirs; and the three monsters, after looking at her gratefully, lay down on it together and went to sleep on it, with their arms twisted about each other's necks. The child looked down upon them, clinging together in their sleep as in their talk, and saw a weariness of pain defined in many a kindly-turned line of their half frog-like faces. If one stirred in sleep, it was to nestle closer to the other two. "How strange," she said to herself, "that I should at first have thought them ugly!" Then she knelt in prayer by her little nest of straw, and did not forget them in her prayers. There was a blessing on them in her heart as she lay down to sleep.

But when Melilot lay down with her face towards the hearth, the dying embers shone with a red light on the two solemn graves. She turned her face to the wall, and the rush of the torrent on the other side was louder than the passion of her weeping. But the noise of the waterfall first soothed her, and then, fixing her attention, drew her from her bed towards the little window, from which she was able to look out into the black night through which it roared. A night not altogether black, for there was a short lull in the rain, though the wind howled round the mountain, and through a chance break in the scurrying night-clouds the full moon now and then flashed, lighting the lakes in the valley far below, and causing the torrent outside the window to gleam through the night-shadows of the great rocks among which it fell. Could it be the song of busy Fairies that came thence to the child's ear?

"Up to the moon and cut down that ray!
In and out the foam-wreaths plaiting;
Spin the froth and weave the spray!
Melilot is watching! Melilot is waiting!
Pick the moonbeam into shreds,
Twist it, twist it into threads!
Threads of the moonlight, yarn of the bubble,
Weave into muslin, double and double!
Fold all and carry it, tarry ye not,
To the chamber of gentle and true Melilot."

Almost at the same moment the door of the hut opened, and Melilot, turning round, saw two beautiful youths enter, bright as the moonlight, who laid a white bale at her feet, and said that it came from the Fairy Muslin Works. Having done that, they flew out in the shape of fire-flies, and Melilot herself closed the door after them. It was her first act to shut the door, because she was bred to be a careful little housewife, and she thought the night-air would not be good for the sleepers.

Then the child looked again at the three monsters cuddled together on her father's and mother's bed. "The Fairies have done this for me," she considered to herself, "that I might not have to send away kind helpers without a gift. White muslin is not quite the dress that will suit lodging such as theirs, but it is all I have! If I could make them, by the time they wake, three dresses, they would see, at any rate, that I was glad to work for them as they had worked for me."

So Melilot began measuring her neighbours with the string of her poor little apron; and when she had measured them all, shrank, with her scissors and thread and the bale of fairy muslin, into the farthest corner of her hut, and set to work by the light of a pine-stick, shaded from the eyes of her guests with a screen made of her own ragged old frock.

While the child stitched, the Fairies sang, and it was a marvel to her that her needle never wanted threading. Keeping time with her fingers to the fairy song, she worked with a speed that almost surpassed her desire, and altogether surpassed understanding. One needleful of thread made the three coats, and the thread, when the coats were made, was as long as it had been when they were begun.

Very soon after dawn the white dresses were made, and all the muslin had been used in making them, except what was left in the small litter of fragments round the stool upon which Melilot had been at work. Three coats of white muslin, daintily folded, were laid by the bed of the three guests, and each was folded with that corner uppermost on which there had been written in thread its owner's name. Dock was worked in the corner of one; Dodder in the corner of another; and in the corner of the third coat, Squill.

Then Melilot lay down for an hour's sleep, and, weary with grief as with toil, slept heavily. Dock, Dodder, and Squill were awake before her, and the first thing that each of them did upon waking was to look upon his new coat. The next thing that each of them did was to put on his new coat; and after this the next thing they all did was to change into three beautiful Fairy youths—Dock with yellow hair, Dodder with brown, and Squill with black. Thus they stood hand in hand by the little girl's bed.

"She has freed us, the dear child!" said Dock.

"She," said Dodder, "she, our darling, and our brothers of the waterfall."

"She has saved nothing for herself," said Squill. "Did not the child once wish to wear muslin in the place of these poor rags? I kiss them, brothers, for her sake," But Squill's kiss on the girl's ragged frock made it a treasure for an empire.

"And I kiss the walls that sheltered us," said Dodder. But Dodder's kiss upon the walls changed them into a close network of fragrant blossoms.

"And I kiss the lips that bade us hither," Dock said; and at his kiss the child smiled, and her eyes opened upon the three Fairies in the muslin dresses she had made.

"Ah, Fairies," she said, "those are the dresses I made for my three dear neighbours. Do not take back your gift, although the muslin is indeed yours, and the thread too, I know, and—and the work too, for surely it was you who made the needle run. I have done nothing, and am but a poor little child; only I thought you meant to give me something to be grateful with."

"We did not give you your good heart, dear little Melilot," the Fairies said; and now their speaking was in softest unison. "That has done more for us than all our love and service will repay. We were your neighbours, but we are your servants now."

"No, no, no," said the child. "I was afraid to ask to be your servant, because I thought last night you were too poor to feed me, as I am too poor and weak to feed myself. The angels themselves gave me bread yesterday, and

I have some yet. But all is changed about me. Why do the walls flower, and why is my dress covered with glittering stones? Ah, yes, I am at home," she said, for her eyes fell on the two graves.

Then, as she rose to her knees, with quivering lips, the three Fairies went out into the sun, and stood at the door to see how all the rains were gone, and the bright morning beams played in the spray of the cataract.

"Do you see anything between us and the sun?" Dock asked of the other two.

"A speck," said Dodder.

"Frogbit herself," said Squill.

I I I

Sir Crucifer

Presently Melilot bade the three Fairies come in to share her breakfast. She had saved bread from last night, and while she took it from its place among the blossoms that last night were mud, again the loaf of bread stood on her father's, and the cup of milk upon her mother's grave. "The angels of my father and mother feed me still," she said; "I must abide under the shelter of their wings."

The Fairies came at her bidding to eat with her; but Squill, excusing himself, went to the stool about which were the chips and shreds of Fairy muslin. There, joining each to each with a stroke of his finger, he was shaping them into a little net, when Melilot, who had been sent out to feel the sunshine, came in, saying that there was a chill wind; and though it was foolishness to think so, it did really seem to have come with a black raven that was sitting on the roof.

"You had better strike through the roof, Frogbit," Squill cried, looking up. The bird croaked as if in defiance, and at once began to beat a way in through the flowers. As it did so, the leaves of the bower withered, and the blossoms all began to stink.

But Squill leapt up, and holding the net he had made under the hole Frogbit was making, caught her as she fell through, and held her captured in the folds of Fairy muslin that seemed to stand like iron against the beating of her wings.

"Poor bird!" said Melilot.

"Our enemy, who came on a bad errand, is our prisoner," said Dock.

"Cleverly done," said Dodder. "Very cleverly done, brother Squill."

But Melilot, who loved man, beast, and bird, bent over the fluttering raven, and was not hindered from taking it, net and all, to her bosom, though it struck at her fiercely with its great bill that, strong as it was, could not tear through the muslin net.

"Poor bird!" said the child; "how can a raven be your enemy?"

"Theirs and yours!" the raven herself shrieked. "Theirs and yours!"

"And mine, bird! I would do you no hurt. See, I kiss you." When Melilot stooped to kiss through the thin muslin the raven's head, the bird struggled to escape from the kiss with an agony of terror.

"Nay," said the gentle child, "no evil can come of a true kiss."

Good came of it; for at the touch of her kiss, the wicked Fairy Frogbit dropped out of the form of a raven into a black, shapeless lump of earth.

"What have I done?" the child cried, weeping.

Then the three Fairies threw the lump of earth into the waterfall, and told her all that she had done. They told her how of old they had lived with their brother Fairies of the Torrent till the wicked Frogbit came and turned the land below into a marshy wilderness, in which she ruled over her own evil race. One day she and her people had contrived to seize Titania herself, as she flew over the marsh on the way to her subjects of the mountain. They could not change her beauty, or stain her bright nature, but they held her prisoner for a time among their stagnant pools, till she was rescued in a moonlight attack by the Fairies of the waterfall, who left three prisoners, Dock, Dodder, and Squill, in the hands of the enemy. Those prisoners Frogbit had shut up in loathsome frog-like bodies, and set in the cottage between the lakes, while she brought down never-ending rain over the whole district, to make their prison more gloomy. The Fairies of the bright running and leaping water were condemned to sit in stagnant puddles, and eat tadpoles, having their own bright natures shut up in forms so detestable, that Frogbit hoped to make their case more wretched by a mockery of hope.

"Live there," she said, "till a mortal child can look at you without being afraid: till there is a little girl in the world bold enough to seek you out, and trust you with all that she holds most sacred; to shut herself up with you, and believe in you entirely; to give up to you her own supper, and of her own free thought make white muslin dresses to your filthy shapes."

She spoke mockingly of white muslin, because she knew of the old Fairy trade that had been carried on for ages on the mountains. There the Fairies weave after their own fashion into muslin the white sheets of foam; and when the three prisoners had heard their doom they were not in despair. For although Frogbit, who had never been up the mountain, knew nothing of the one little hut there was upon it, yet all the Fairies knew it, and they knew well the little Melilot.

"Then I have really been a friend to you," the child said.

"Ay," they replied, "and to Frogbit a friend. An innocent kiss is the charm that breaks all evil spells, and you have with a kiss broken the spell that raised in her a clod of earth into a creature of mischief. We of the torrent will direct the waters that they wash that clod of earth from which evil is banned to a place where it may yield lilies and violets, of which good Fairies shall be born."

The three Fairies returning to their own race, were still Melilot's neighbours and friends, and the child grew up to womanhood, the favourite of all the Fairies of the waterfall. Her bower blossomed, and the ground about it was made into a delicious garden. Her dress of precious stones was thrown into a corner, and she was arrayed by the Fairies in their shining muslin that would take no soil. But still she found, morning and night, the only bread she ate upon her father's grave, and upon her mother's grave the milk that nourished her.

Whether the bad Fairies over whom Frogbit had ruled left the marsh, Melilot did not know, but the marsh dried and became a great plain, which men tilled, and upon which at last men fought.

Sobbing and panting, Melilot ran down the hill-side when she saw men cased in iron galloping to and fro, and falling wounded to lie bleeding and uncared for on the quaking ground. Every fear was mastered by her sacred pity, and her Fairy muslin was unstained, though she knelt on the red mud of the battlefield and laid the wounded soldier's head upon her lap. None, even in the direst madness of the strife, could strike upon the frail white girl, who saw only the suffering about her, and thought only of wounds that she might bind. Had any struck, her muslin was an armour firmer than all steel; and there was no rent in her dress, as she tore from it strip after strip, to bind rents in the flesh of men who lay in their death-agonies about her.

In the tumult of flight, the defeated host parted before her, and sped on, still leaving her untrampled and untouched. But once, reaching a white arm into the crowd, she caught from it a wounded soldier as he fell, and with the other hand seized the shaft of the spear that a fierce youth, hot in pursuit, thrust on his falling enemy. She fainted as she did so; and the youth, letting his spear drop, knelt beside her, and looked down into her face. His tears presently were falling on her lifeless cheek. The flight and the pursuit rushed by, and he was still kneeling beside her, when the moon rose, and three youths, dressed in white, stood near.

"Are you her brothers?" he asked. "Who is this, with a dress that has passed unstained through blood and mire, and with a face so holy?"

"Take her up in your arms," they said, "and we will show you where to carry her."

The young soldier lifted her with reverence, and took her up the mountain to the bower by the waterfall. The scent of the flowers, when they came into its garden, gave fresh life to her. The soldier gently laid her down upon a bank of wild thyme, and looked up for the three youths, but they were gone. He went into the bower, and saw therein scanty furniture, a dress of jewels worth an empire thrown into a corner, and two graves, on one of which stood bread, and on the other milk. He brought the food out to the girl, and, at her bidding, broke bread with her.

Now Dock, Dodder, and Squill were match-makers. They had made up their minds that Melilot should be to Sir Crucifer—that was the soldier's name—as near in trust and in love as her mother had been to her father. So they put the cottage between the two lakes into repair, and made him a home out of the place in which they had been imprisoned. There he dreamt, all the night through, sacred dreams of her by whose side he spent all his days.

Much the girl heard, as she sat with the soldier by the waterfall, of the high struggle for all that makes man good and glorious, that bred the strife out of which she had drawn him for a little time. Much the soldier learnt as he sat with the girl, from a companion whose thoughts purified his zeal, and made his aspirations happier and more unbounded. One day there were words said that made the girl a woman; and when she awoke on the next morning, her father's grave was overgrown with laurel bushes, and her mother's grave was lost under a wealth of flowering myrtle.

But there was no food provided.

When Sir Crucifer came to her that sunny morning, "I have a sign," she said. "It is time that I also take my part in the struggle of which you have told me. Let us go down together to the plains."

She gathered for him a branch of laurel, and she plucked a sprig of myrtle for herself. These never faded; they remained green as the daughter's memory of those two dear ones from whose grave they came. But in all their long after-lives of love and labour, neither of them remembered the worth of an empire in stones that they left unguarded in a corner of the hut.

The spray was radiant, and the foam was white as her bright Fairy muslin, as it floated over the strength of the waterfall, when Melilot and her soldier, hand in hand, went down the mountain. They passed out of her bower, she in the full flood of the sunshine, with an arm raised upward and a calm face turned towards him, as he, walking in her shadow, pointed to the plains below.

1861

The Fairies

WILLIAM ALLINGHAM

Up the airy mountain,
    Down the rushy glen,
We daren't go a-hunting
    For fear of little men;
Wee folk, good folk,
    Trooping all together;
Green jacket, red cap,
    And grey-cock's feather!

Down along the rocky shore
    Some make their home,
They live on crispy pancakes
    Of yellow tide-foam;
Some in the reeds
    Of the black mountain-lake,
With frogs for their watch-dogs,
    All night awake.

High on the hill-top
    The old King sits;
He is now so old and grey
    He's nigh lost his wits.
With a bridge of white mist
    Columbkill he crosses,
On his stately journeys
    From Slieveleague to Rosses;

Or going up with music
    On cold starry nights,
To sup with the Queen
    Of the gay Northern Lights.

They stole little Bridget
    For seven years long;
When she came down again
    Her friends were all gone.
They took her lightly back,
    Between the night and morrow,
They thought that she was fast asleep,
    But she was dead with sorrow.
They have kept her ever since
    Deep within the lakes,
On a bed of flagon-leaves,
    Watching till she wakes.

By the craggy hill-side,
    Through the mosses bare,
They have planted thorn-trees
    For pleasure here and there.
Is any man so daring
    To dig up one in spite,
He shall find the thornies set
    In his bed at night.

Up the airy mountain,
    Down the rushy glen,
We daren't go a-hunting
    For fear of little men;
Wee folk, good folk,
    Trooping all together;
Green jacket, red cap,
    And grey-cock's feather!

                    1850

The Little Lame Prince and his Travelling-Cloak

DINAH MARIA MULOCK CRAIK

I

Yes, he was the most beautiful Prince that ever was born.

Of course, being a prince, people said this; but it was true besides. When he looked at the candle, his eyes had an expression of earnest inquiry quite startling in a newborn baby. His nose—there was not much of it certainly, but what there was seemed an aquiline shape. His complexion was a charming, healthy purple. He was round and fat, straight-limbed and long—in fact, a splendid baby. Everybody was exceedingly proud of him, especially his father and mother, the King and Queen of Nomansland, who had waited for him during their happy reign of ten years—now made happier than ever, to themselves and their subjects, by the appearance of a son and heir.

The only person who was not quite happy was the King's brother, the heir-presumptive, who would have been king one day had the baby not been born. But as his Majesty was very kind to him, and even rather sorry for him—insomuch that at the Queen's request he gave him a dukedom almost as big as a county—the Crown Prince, as he was called, tried to seem pleased also; and let us hope he succeeded.

The Prince's christening was to be a grand affair. According to the custom of the country, there were chosen for him four-and-twenty godfathers and godmothers, who each had to give him a name, and promise to do their utmost for him. When he came of age, he himself had to choose the name—and the godfather or godmother—that he liked the best, for the rest of his days.

Meantime, all was rejoicing. Subscriptions were made among the rich to give pleasure to the poor: dinners in town halls for the working-men; tea-parties in the streets for their wives; and milk-and-bun feasts for the children in the schoolrooms. For Nomansland, though I cannot point it out on any map or read of it in any history, was, I believe, much like our own or many another country.

As for the palace—which was no different from other palaces—it was clean "turned out of the windows," as people say, with the preparations going on. The only quiet place in it was the room which, though the Prince was six weeks old, his mother the Queen had never quitted. Nobody said she was ill, however—it would have been so inconvenient. And as she said nothing about it herself, but lay pale and placid, giving no trouble to anybody, nobody thought much about her. All the world was absorbed in admiring the baby.

The christening-day came at last, and it was as lovely as the Prince himself. All the people in the palace were lovely too—or thought themselves so— in the elegant new clothes which the Queen, who thought of everybody, had taken care to give them, from the ladies-in-waiting down to the poor little kitchen-maid, who looked at herself in her pink cotton gown, and thought, doubtless, that there never was such a pretty girl as she.

By six in the morning all the royal household had dressed itself in its very best. And then the little Prince was dressed in his best—his magnificent christening robe; which proceeding his Royal Highness did not like at all, but kicked and screamed like any common baby. When he had calmed down a little, they carried him to be looked at by the Queen his mother, who, though her royal robes had been brought and laid upon the bed, was, as everybody well knew, quite unable to rise and put them on.

She admired her baby very much; kissed and blessed him, and lay looking at him, as she did for hours sometimes, when he was placed beside her fast asleep. Then she gave him up with a gentle smile, and, saying she hoped he would be very good, that it would be a very nice christening, and all the guests would enjoy themselves, turned peacefully over on her bed, saying nothing more to anybody. She was a very uncomplaining person, the Queen—and her name was Dolorez.

Everything went on exactly as if she had been present. All, even the King himself, had grown used to her absence; for she was not strong, and for years had not joined in any gaieties. She always did her royal duties, but as to pleasures, they could go on quite well without her, or it seemed so. The company arrived: great and notable persons in this and neighbouring countries; also the four-and-twenty godfathers and godmothers, who had been chosen with care, as the people who would be most useful to his Royal Highness should he ever want friends, which did not seem likely. What such want could possibly happen to the heir of the powerful monarch of Nomansland?

They came, walking two and two, with their coronets on their heads—being dukes and duchesses, princes and princesses, or the like. They all kissed the child and pronounced the name each had given him. Then the four-and-twenty names were shouted out with great energy by six heralds, one after the other, and afterwards written down, to be preserved in the state records, in readiness for the next time they were wanted, which would be either on his Royal Highness's coronation or his funeral.

Soon the ceremony was over, and everybody satisfied; except, perhaps, the little Prince himself, who moaned faintly under his christening robes, which nearly smothered him.

In truth, though very few knew, the Prince in coming to the chapel had met with a slight disaster. His nurse—not his ordinary one, but the state nursemaid, an elegant and fashionable young lady of rank, whose duty it was to carry him to and from the chapel—had been so occupied in arranging her train with one hand, while she held the baby with the other, that she stumbled and let him fall, just at the foot of the marble staircase.

To be sure, she contrived to pick him up again the next minute; and the accident was so slight it seemed hardly worth speaking of. Consequently, nobody did speak of it. The baby had turned deadly pale, but did not cry, so no person a step or two behind could discover anything wrong. Afterwards, even if he had moaned, the silver trumpets were loud enough to drown his voice. It would have been a pity to let anything trouble such a day of felicity.

So, after a minute's pause, the procession had moved on. Such a procession! Heralds in blue and silver; pages in crimson and gold; and a troop of little girls in dazzling white, carrying baskets of flowers, which they strewed all the way before the nurse and child. Finally the four-and-twenty godfathers and godmothers, as proud as possible, and so splendid to look at that they would have quite extinguished their small godson—merely a heap of lace and muslin with a baby face inside—had it not been for a canopy of white satin and ostrich feathers which was held over him wherever he was carried.

Thus, with the sun shining on them through the painted windows, they stood; the King and his train on one side, the Prince and his attendants on the other, as pretty a sight as ever was seen out of Fairyland.

"It's just like Fairyland," whispered the eldest little girl to the next eldest, as she shook the last rose out of her basket; "and I think the only thing the Prince wants now is a fairy godmother."

"Does he?" said a shrill but soft and not unpleasant voice behind; and there was seen among the group of children somebody—not a child, yet no bigger than a child—somebody whom nobody had seen before, and who certainly had not been invited, for she had no christening clothes on.

She was a little old woman dressed all in grey: grey gown; grey hooded cloak, of a material excessively fine, and a tint that seemed perpetually changing, like the grey of an evening sky. Her hair was grey, and her eyes also; even her complexion had a soft grey shadow over it. But there was nothing unpleasantly old about her, and her smile was as sweet and child-like as the Prince's own, which stole over his pale little face the instant she came near enough to touch him.

"Take care! Don't let the baby fall again."

The grand young lady nurse started, flushing angrily.

"Who spoke to me? How did anybody know?—I mean, what business has anybody—" Then, frightened, but still speaking in a much sharper tone than I hope young ladies of rank are in the habit of speaking—"Old woman, you will be kind enough not to say 'the baby,' but 'the Prince.' Keep away; his Royal Highness is just going to sleep."

"Nevertheless I must kiss him. I am his godmother."

"You!" cried the elegant lady nurse.

"You!!" repeated all the gentleman- and ladies-in-waiting.

"You!!!" echoed the heralds and pages—and they began to blow the silver trumpets in order to stop all further conversation.

The Prince's procession formed itself for returning—the King and his train having already moved off towards the palace—but on the topmost step of the marble stairs stood, right in front of all, the little old woman clothed in grey.

She stretched herself on tiptoe by the help of her stick, and gave the little Prince three kisses.

"This is intolerable!" cried the young lady nurse, wiping the kisses off rapidly with her lace handkerchief. "Such an insult to his Royal Highness! Take yourself out of the way, old woman, or the King shall be informed immediately."

"The King knows nothing of me, more's the pity," replied the old woman, with an indifferent air, as if she thought the loss was more on his Majesty's side than hers. "My friend in the palace is the King's wife."

"Kings have not wives, but queens," said the lady nurse, with a contemptuous air.

"You are right," replied the old woman. "Nevertheless, I know her Majesty well, and I love her and her child. And—since you dropped him on the marble stairs" (this she said in a mysterious whisper, which made the young lady tremble in spite of her anger)—"I choose to take him for my own, and be his godmother, ready to help him whenever he wants me."

"You help him!" cried all the group, breaking into shouts of laughter, to which the little old woman paid not the slightest attention. Her soft grey eyes were fixed on the Prince, who seemed to answer to the look, smiling again and again in the causeless, aimless fashion that babies do smile.

"His Majesty must hear of this," said a gentleman-in-waiting.

"His Majesty will hear quite enough news in a minute or two," said the old woman sadly. And again stretching up to the little Prince, she kissed him on the forehead solemnly.

"Be called by a new name which nobody has ever thought of. Be Prince Dolor, in memory of your mother Dolorez."

"In memory of!" Everybody started at the ominous phrase, and also at a most terrible breach of etiquette which the old woman had committed. In Nomansland, neither the King nor the Queen was supposed to have any Christian name at all. They dropped it on their coronation-day, and it never was mentioned again till it was engraved on their coffins when they died.

"Old woman, you are exceedingly ill-bred," cried the eldest lady-in-waiting, much horrified. "How you could know the fact passes my comprehension. But even if you did know it, how dared you presume to hint that her most gracious Majesty is called Dolorez?"

"*Was* called Dolorez," said the old woman, with a tender solemnity.

The first gentleman, called the Gold-stick-in-waiting, raised it to strike her, and all the rest stretched out their hands to seize her; but the grey mantle melted from between their fingers like air. And, before anybody had time to do anything more, there came a heavy, muffled, startling sound.

The great bell of the palace—the bell which was heard only on the death of some one of the royal family, and for as many times as he or she was years old—began to toll. They listened, mute and horror-stricken. Someone counted: One—two—three—four—up to nine-and-twenty—just the Queen's age.

It was, indeed, the Queen. Her Majesty was dead! In the midst of the festivities she had slipped away out of her new happiness and her old sufferings, not few nor small. Sending away all her women to see the grand sight—at least they said afterwards, in excuse, that she had done so, and it was very like her to do it—she had turned with her face to the window, whence one could just see the tops of the distant mountains—the Beautiful Mountains, as they were called—where she was born. So gazing, she had quietly passed away.

When the little Prince was carried back to his mother's room, there was no mother to kiss him. And, though he did not know it, there would be for him no mother's kiss any more.

As for his godmother—the little old woman in grey who called herself so—whether she melted into air, like her gown when they touched it, or whether she flew out of the chapel window, or slipped through the doorway among the bewildered crowd, nobody knew—nobody ever thought about her.

Only the nurse, the ordinary homely one, coming out of the Prince's nursery in the middle of the night in search of a cordial to quiet his continual moans, saw, sitting in the doorway, something which she would have thought a mere shadow had she not seen shining out of it two eyes, grey and soft and sweet. She put her hands before her own, screaming loudly. When she took them away the old woman was gone.

I I

Everybody was very kind to the poor little Prince. I think people generally are kind to motherless children, whether princes or peasants. He had a magnificent nursery and a regular suite of attendants, and was treated with the greatest respect and state. Nobody was allowed to talk to him in silly baby language, or dandle him, or above all to kiss him, though perhaps some people did it surreptitiously, for he was such a sweet baby that it was difficult to help it.

It could not be said that the Prince missed his mother—children of his age cannot do that; but somehow after she died everything seemed to go wrong with him. From a beautiful baby he became sickly and pale, seeming to have almost ceased growing, especially in his legs, which had been so fat and strong. But after the day of his christening they withered and shrank. He no longer kicked them out in either passion or play, and when, as he got to be nearly a year old, his nurse tried to make him stand upon them, he only tumbled down.

This happened so many times that at last people began to talk about it. A prince, and not able to stand on his own legs! What a dreadful thing! What a misfortune for the country!

Rather a misfortune to him also, poor little boy! but nobody seemed to think of that. And when, after a while, his health revived, and the old bright look came back to his sweet little face, and his body grew larger and stronger, though still his legs remained the same, people continued to speak of him in whispers, and with graves shakes of the head. Everybody knew, though nobody said it, that something, it was impossible to guess what, was not quite right with the poor little Prince.

Of course, nobody hinted this to the King his father. It does not do to tell great people anything unpleasant. And besides, his Majesty took very little notice of his son, or of his other affairs, beyond the necessary duties of his kingdom.

People had said he would not miss the Queen at all, she having been so long an invalid, but he did. After her death he never was quite the same. He established himself in her empty rooms, the only rooms in the palace whence one could see the Beautiful Mountains, and was often observed looking at them as if he thought she had flown away thither, and that his longing could bring her back again. And by a curious coincidence, which nobody dared inquire into, he desired that the Prince might be called, not by any of the four-and-twenty grand names given him by his godfathers and godmothers, but by the identical name mentioned by the little old woman in grey—Dolor, after his mother Dolorez.

Once a week, according to established state custom, the Prince, dressed in his very best, was brought to the King his father for half-an-hour, but his Majesty was generally too ill and too melancholy to pay much heed to the child.

Only once, when he and the Crown Prince, who was exceedingly attentive to his royal brother, were sitting together, with Prince Dolor playing in a corner of the room, dragging himself about with his arms rather than his legs, and sometimes trying feebly to crawl from one chair to another, it seemed to strike the father that all was not right with his son.

"How old is his Royal Highness?" said he suddenly to the nurse.

"Two years, three months and five days, please your Majesty."

"It does not please me," said the King, with a sigh. "He ought to be far more forward than he is now—ought he not, brother? You, who have so many children, must know. Is there not something wrong about him?"

"Oh, no," said the Crown Prince, exchanging meaning looks with the nurse, who did not understand at all, but stood frightened and trembling with the tears in her eyes. "Nothing to make your Majesty at all uneasy. No doubt his Royal Highness will outgrow it in time."

"Outgrow—what?"

"A slight delicacy—ahem!—in the spine; something inherited, perhaps, from his dear mother."

"Ah, she was always delicate; but she was the sweetest woman that ever lived. Come here, my little son."

And as the Prince turned round upon his father a small, sweet, grave face—so like his mother's—his Majesty the King smiled and held out his arms. But when the boy came to him, not running like a boy, but wriggling awkwardly along the floor, the royal countenance clouded over.

"I ought to have been told of this. It is terrible—terrible! And for a prince, too! Send for all the doctors in my kingdom immediately."

They came, and each gave a different opinion and ordered a different mode of treatment. The only thing they agreed in was what had been pretty well known before: that the Prince must have been hurt when he was an infant—let fall, perhaps, so as to injure his spine and lower limbs. Did nobody remember?

No, nobody. Indignantly, all the nurses denied that any such accident had happened, was possible to have happened, until the faithful country nurse recollected that it really had happened, on the day of the christening. For which unluckily good memory all the others scolded her so severely that she had no peace of her life, and soon after, by the influence of the young lady nurse who had carried the baby that fatal day, and who was a sort of connection of the Crown Prince—being his wife's second cousin once removed—the poor woman was pensioned off and sent to the Beautiful Mountains from whence she came, with orders to remain there for the rest of her days.

But of all this the King knew nothing, for, indeed, after the first shock of finding out that his son could not walk, and seemed never likely to walk, he interfered very little concerning him. The whole thing was too painful, and his Majesty never liked painful things. Sometimes he inquired after Prince Dolor, and they told him his Royal Highness was going on as well as could be expected, which really was the case. For, after worrying the poor child and perplexing themselves with one remedy after another, the Crown Prince, not wishing to offend any of the differing doctors, had proposed leaving him to Nature; and Nature, the safest doctor of all, had come to his help and done her best. He could not walk, it is true. His limbs were mere useless appendages to his body; but the body itself was strong and sound. And his face was the same as ever—just his mother's face, one of the sweetest in the world.

Even the King, indifferent as he was, sometimes looked at the little fellow with sad tenderness, noticing how cleverly he learned to crawl and swing himself about by his arms, so that in his own awkward way he was as active in motion as most children of his age.

"Poor little man! he does his best, and he is not unhappy—not half so unhappy as I, brother," addressing the Crown Prince, who was more constant than ever in his attendance upon the sick monarch. "If anything should befall me, I have appointed you Regent. In case of my death, you will take care of my poor little boy?"

"Certainly, certainly; but do not let us imagine any such misfortune. I assure your Majesty—everybody will assure you—that it is not in the least likely."

He knew, however, and everybody knew, that it was likely, and soon after it actually did happen. The King died as suddenly and quietly as the Queen had done—indeed, in her very room and bed; and Prince Dolor was left without either father or mother—as sad a thing as could happen, even to a prince.

He was more than that now, though. He was a king. In Nomansland, as in other countries, the people were struck with grief one day and revived the next. "The King is dead—long live the King!" was the cry that rang through the nation, and almost before his late Majesty had been laid beside the Queen in their splendid mausoleum, crowds came thronging from all parts to the royal palace, eager to see the new monarch.

They did see him—the Prince Regent took care they should—sitting on the floor of the council-chamber, sucking his thumb! And when one of the gentlemen-in-waiting lifted him up and carried him—fancy carrying a king!—to the chair of state, and put the crown on his head, he shook it off again, it was so heavy and uncomfortable. Sliding down to the foot of the throne, he began playing with the golden lions that supported it, stroking their paws and putting his tiny fingers into their eyes, and laughing— laughing as if he had at last found something to amuse him.

"There's a fine king for you!" said the first lord-in-waiting, a friend of the Prince Regent's (the Crown Prince that used to be, who, in the deepest mourning, stood silently beside the throne of his young nephew; he was a handsome man, very grand and clever-looking). "What a king! who can never stand to receive his subjects, never walk in processions, who to the last day of his life will have to be carried about like a baby. Very unfortunate!"

"Exceedingly unfortunate," repeated the second lord. "It is always bad for a nation when its king is a child; but such a child—a permanent cripple, if not worse."

"Let us hope not worse," said the first lord in a very hopeless tone, and looking toward the Regent, who stood erect and pretended to hear nothing. "I have heard that these children with very large heads, and great broad foreheads and staring eyes, are—well, well, let us hope for the best and be prepared for the worst. In the meantime—"

"I swear," said the Crown Prince, coming forward and kissing the hilt of his sword—"I swear to perform my duties as Regent, to take all care of his Royal Highness—his Majesty, I mean," with a grand bow to the little child, who laughed innocently back again. "And I will do my humble best to govern the country, Still, if the country has the slightest objection—"

But the Crown Prince being generalissimo, having the whole army at his beck and call, so that he could have begun a civil war in no time, the country had, of course, not the slightest objection.

So the King and Queen slept in their tomb in peace, and Prince Dolor reigned over the land—that is, his uncle did; and everybody said what a fortunate thing it was for the poor little Prince to have such a clever uncle to take care of him.

All things went on as usual. Indeed, after the Regent had brought his wife and her seven sons, and established them in the palace, they went on rather better than usual. For they gave such splendid entertainments and made the capital so lively that trade revived, and the country was said to be more flourishing than it had been for a century.

Whenever the Regent and his sons appeared, they were received with shouts: "Long live the Crown Prince!" Long live the royal family!" And, in truth, they were very fine children, the whole seven of them, and made a great show when they rode out together on seven beautiful horses, one height above another, down to the youngest, on his tiny black pony, no bigger than a large dog.

As for the other child, his Royal Highness Prince Dolor—for somehow people soon ceased to call him his Majesty, which seemed such a ridiculous title for a poor little fellow, a helpless cripple with only head and trunk, and no legs to speak of—he was seen very seldom by anybody.

Sometimes people daring enough to peer over the high wall of the palace garden noticed there, carried in a footman's arms, or drawn in a chair, or left to play on the grass, often with nobody to mind him, a pretty little boy, with a bright, intelligent face and large, melancholy eyes—no, not exactly melancholy, for they were his mother's, and she was by no means sad-minded, but thoughtful and dreamy. They rather perplexed people, those childish eyes; they were so exceedingly innocent and yet so penetrating. If anybody did a wrong thing—told a lie, for instance—they would turn around with such a grave, silent surprise—the child never talked much—that every naughty person in the palace was rather afraid of Prince Dolor.

He could not help it, and perhaps he did not even know it, being no better a child than many other children, but there was something about him which made bad people sorry, and grumbling people ashamed of themselves, and ill-natured people gentle and kind. I suppose, because they were touched to see a poor little fellow who did not in the least know what had befallen him or what lay before him, living his baby life as happy as the day is long. Thus, whether or not he was good himself, the sight of him and his affliction made other people good, and, above all, made everybody love him—so much so that his uncle the Regent began to feel a little uncomfortable.

Now, I having nothing to say against uncles in general. They are usually very excellent people, and very convenient to little boys and girls. Even the "cruel uncle" of the *Babes in the Wood* I believe to be quite an exceptional character. And this "cruel uncle" of whom I am telling was, I hope, an exception, too.

He did not mean to be cruel. If anybody had called him so, he would have resented it extremely. He would have said that what he did was done entirely for the good of the country. But he was a man who had always been accustomed to consider himself first and foremost, believing that whatever he wanted was sure to be right, and therefore he ought to have it. So he tried to get it, and got it too, as people like him very often do. Whether they enjoy it when they have it is another question.

Therefore he went one day to the council-chamber, determined on making a speech and informing the ministers and the country at large that the young King was in failing health, and that it would be advisable to send him for a time to the Beautiful Mountains. Whether he really meant to do this, or whether it occurred to him afterwards that there would be an easier way of attaining his great desire, the crown of Nomansland, is a point which I cannot decide.

But soon after, when he had obtained an order in council to send the King away—which was done in great state, with a guard of honour composed of two whole regiments of soldiers—the nation learned, without much surprise, that the poor little Prince—nobody ever called him king now—had gone a much longer journey than to the Beautiful Mountains.

He had fallen ill on the road and died within a few hours; at least, so declared the physician in attendance and the nurse who had been sent to take care of him. They brought his coffin back in great state, and buried it in the mausoleum with his parents.

So Prince Dolor was seen no more. The country went into deep mourning for him, and then forgot him, and his uncle reigned in his stead. That illustrious personage accepted his crown with great decorum, and wore it with great dignity to the last. But whether he enjoyed it or not, there is no evidence to show.

I I I

And what of the little lame Prince, whom everybody seemed so easily to have forgotten?

Not everybody. There were a few kind souls, mothers of families, who had heard his sad story, and some servants about the palace, who had been familiar with his sweet ways—these many a time sighed and said, "Poor Prince Dolor!" Or, looking at the Beautiful Mountains, which were visible all over Nomansland, though few people ever visited them, "Well, perhaps his Royal Highness is better where he is than even there."

They did not know—indeed, hardly anybody did know—that beyond the mountains, between them and the sea, lay a tract of country, barren, level, bare, except for short, stunted grass, and here and there a patch of tiny flowers. Not a bush—not a tree—not a resting-place for bird or beast was in that dreary plain. In summer the sunshine fell upon it hour after hour with a blinding glare. In winter the winds and rains swept over it unhindered, and the snow came down steadily, noiselessly, covering it from end to end in one great white sheet, which lay for days and weeks unmarked by a single footprint.

Not a pleasant place to live in—and nobody did live there, apparently. The only sign that human creatures had ever been near the spot was one large round tower which rose up in the centre of the plain, and might be seen from every part of it—if there had been anybody to see, which there never was. Rose right up out of the ground, as if it had grown of itself, like a mushroom. But it was not at all mushroom-like; on the contrary, it was very solidly built. In form it resembled the Irish round towers, which have puzzled people for so long, nobody being able to find out when, or by whom, or for what purpose they were made; seemingly for no use at all, like this tower. It was circular, of very firm brickwork, with neither doors nor windows, until near the top, when you could perceive some slits in the wall through which one might possibly creep in or look out. Its height was nearly a hundred feet, and it had a battlemented parapet showing sharp against the sky.

As the plain was quite desolate—almost like a desert, only without sand, and led to nowhere except the still more desolate sea-coast—nobody ever crossed it. Whatever mystery there was about the tower, it and the sky and the plain kept their secret to themselves.

It was a very great secret indeed—a state secret—which none but so clever a man as the present King of Nomansland would ever have thought of. How he carried it out, undiscovered, I cannot tell. People said, long afterwards, that it was by means of a gang of condemned criminals, who were set to work, and executed immediately after they had finished, so that nobody knew anything, or in the least suspected the real fact.

And what was the fact? Why, that this tower, which seemed a mere mass of masonry, utterly forsaken and uninhabited, was not so at all. Within twenty feet of the top some ingenious architect had planned a perfect little house, divided into four rooms—as by drawing a cross within a circle you will see might easily be done. By making skylights, and a few slits in the walls for windows, and raising a peaked roof which was hidden by the parapet, here was a dwelling complete, eighty feet from the ground, and as inaccessible as a rook's nest on the top of a tree.

A charming place to live in! if you once got up there—and never wanted to come down again.

Inside—though nobody could have looked inside except a bird, and hardly even a bird flew past that lonely tower—inside it was furnished with all the comfort and elegance imaginable; with lots of books and toys, and everything that the heart of a child could desire. For its only inhabitant, except a nurse of course, was a poor solitary child.

One winter's night, when all the plain was white with moonlight, there was seen crossing it a great tall black horse, ridden by a man also big and equally black, carrying before him on the saddle a woman and a child. The woman—she had a sad, fierce look, and no wonder, for she was a criminal under sentence of death, but her sentence had been changed to almost as severe a punishment. She was to inhabit the lonely tower with the child, and was allowed to live as long as the child lived—no longer. This, in order that she might take the utmost care of him; for those who put him there were equally afraid of his dying and of his living.

Yet he was only a little, gentle boy, with a sweet sleepy smile—he had been very tired from his long journey—and with clinging arms, which held tight to the man's neck, for he was rather frightened, and the face, black as it was, looked kindly at him. And he was very helpless, with his poor, small, shrivelled legs, which could neither stand nor run away—for the little forlorn boy was Prince Dolor.

He had not been dead at all—or buried either. His grand funeral had been a mere pretence: a wax figure having been put in his place, while he himself was spirited away under charge of these two, the condemned woman and the black man. The latter was deaf and dumb, so could neither tell nor repeat anything.

When they reached the foot of the tower, there was light enough to see a huge chain dangling from the parapet, but dangling only half-way. The deaf-mute took from his saddle-wallet a sort of ladder, arranged in pieces like a puzzle, fitted it together, and lifted it up to meet the chain. Then he mounted to the top of the tower, and slung from it a sort of chair, in which the woman and the child placed themselves and were drawn up, never to come down again as long as they lived. Leaving them there, the man descended the ladder, took it to pieces again and packed it in his pack, mounted the horse, and disappeared across the plain.

Every month they used to watch for him, appearing like a speck in the distance. He fastened his horse to the foot of the tower, and climbed it, as before, laden with provisions and many other things. He always saw the Prince, so as to make sure that the chid was alive and well, and then went away until the following month.

While his first childhood lasted, Prince Dolor was happy enough. He had every luxury that even a prince could need, and the one thing wanting— love—never having known, he did not miss. His nurse was very kind to him though she was a wicked woman. But either she had not been quite so wicked as people said, or she grew better through being shut up continually with a little innocent child who was dependent upon her for every comfort and pleasure of his life.

It was not an unhappy life. There was nobody to tease or ill-use him, and he was never ill. He played about from room to room—there were four rooms, parlour, kitchen, his nurse's bedroom, and his own; learned to crawl like a fly, and to jump like a frog, and to run about on all fours almost as fast as a puppy. In fact, he was very much like a puppy or a kitten, as thoughtless and as merry—scarcely ever cross, though sometimes a little weary.

As he grew older, he occasionally liked to be quiet for a while, and then he would sit at the slits of windows—which were, however, much bigger than they looked from the bottom of the tower—and watch the sky above and the ground below, with the storms sweeping over and the sunshine coming and going, and the shadows of the clouds running races across the blank plain.

By-and-by he began to learn lessons—not that his nurse had been ordered to teach him, but she did it partly to amuse herself. She was not a stupid woman, and Prince Dolor was by no means a stupid boy; so they got on very well, and his continual entreaty, "What can I do? what can you find me to do?" was stopped, at least for an hour or two in the day.

It was a dull life, but he had never known any other; anyhow, he re-membered no other, and he did not pity himself at all. Not for a long time, till he grew quite a big little boy, and could read quite easily. Then he suddenly took to books, which the deaf-mute brought him from time to time—books which, not being acquainted with the literature of Nomansland, I cannot describe, but no doubt they were very interesting; and they informed him of everything in the outside world, and filled him with an intense longing to see it.

From this time a change came over the boy. He began to look sad and thin, and to shut himself up for hours without speaking. For his nurse hardly spoke, and whatever questions he asked beyond their ordinary daily life she never answered. She had, indeed, been forbidden, on pain of death, to tell him anything about himself, who he was, or what he might have been.

He knew he was Prince Dolor, because she always addressed him as "my Prince" and "your Royal Highness," but what a prince was he had not the least idea. He had no idea of anything in the world, except what he found in his books.

He sat one day surrounded by them, having built them up round him like a little castle wall, He had been reading them half the day, but feeling all the while that to read about things which you never can see is like hearing about a beautiful dinner while you are starving. For almost the first time in his life he grew melancholy; his hands fell on his lap; he sat gazing out of the window slit upon the view outside—the view he had looked at every day of his life, and might look at for endless days more.

Not a very cheerful view—just the plain and the sky—but he liked it. He used to think, if he could only fly out of that window, up to the sky or down to the plain, how nice it would be! Perhaps when he died—his nurse had told him once in anger that he would never leave the tower till he died—he might be able to do this. Not that he understood much what dying meant, but it must be a change, and any change seemed to him a blessing.

"And I wish I had somebody to tell me all about it—about that and many other things; somebody that would be fond of me, like my poor white kitten."

Here the tears came into his eyes, for the boy's one friend, the one interest of his life, had been a little white kitten, which the deaf-mute, kindly smiling, once took out of his pocket and gave him—the only living creature Prince Dolor had ever seen.

For four weeks it was his constant plaything and companion, till one moonlight night it took a fancy for wandering, climbed onto the parapet of the tower, dropped over and disappeared. It was not killed, he hoped, for cats had nine lives; indeed, he almost fancied he saw it pick itself up and scamper away; but he never caught sight of it again.

"Yes, I wish I had something better than a kitten—a person, a real live person, who would be fond of me and kind to me. Oh, I want somebody—dreadfully, dreadfully!"

As he spoke, there sounded behind him a slight tap-tap-tap, as of a stick or a cane, and twisting himself round, he saw—what do you think he saw?

Nothing either frightening or ugly, but still exceedingly curious. A little woman, no bigger than he might himself have been had his legs grown like those of other children; but she was not a child—she was an old woman. Her hair was grey, and her dress was grey, and there was a grey shadow over her wherever she moved. But she had the sweetest smile, the prettiest hands, and when she spoke it was in the softest voice imaginable.

"My dear little boy"—and dropping her cane, the only bright and rich thing about her, she laid those two tiny hands on his shoulder—"my own little boy, I could not come to you until you had said you wanted me; but now you do want me, here I am."

"And you are very welcome, madam," replied the Prince, trying to speak politely, as princes always did in books; "and I am exceedingly obliged to you. May I ask who you are? Perhaps my mother?" For he knew that little boys usually had a mother, and had occasionally wondered what had become of his own.

"No," said the vistor, with a tender, half-smile, putting back the hair from his forehead, and looking right into his eyes—"no, I am not your mother, though she was a dear friend of mine; and you are as like her as ever you can be."

"Will you tell her to come and see me, then?"

"She cannot; but I dare say she knows all about you. And she loves you very much—and so do I; and I want to help you all I can, my poor little boy."

"Why do you call me poor?" asked Prince Dolor, in surprise.

The little old woman glanced down on his legs and feet, which he did not know were different from those of other children, and then at his sweet, bright face, which, though he knew not that either, was exceedingly different from many children's faces, which are often so fretful, cross, sullen. Looking at him, instead of sighing, she smiled. "I beg your pardon, my Prince," said she.

"Yes, I am a prince, and my name is Dolor; will you tell me yours, madam?"

The little old woman laughed like a chime of silver bells.

"I have not got a name—or rather, I have so many names that I don't know which to choose. However, it was I who gave you yours, and you will belong to me all your days. I am your godmother."

"Hurrah!" cried the little Prince; "I am glad I belong to you, for I like you very much. Will you come and play with me?"

So they sat down together and played. By and by they began to talk.

"Are you very dull here?" asked the little old woman.

"Not particularly, thank you, godmother. I have plenty to eat and drink, and my lessons to do, and my books to read—lots of books."

"And you want nothing?"

"Nothing. Yes—perhaps—If you please, godmother, could you bring me just one more thing?"

"What sort of thing?"

"A little boy to play with."

The old woman looked very sad. "Just the thing, alas! which I cannot give you. My child, I cannot alter your lot in any way, but I can help you to bear it."

"Thank you. But why do you talk of bearing it? I have nothing to bear."

"My poor little man!" said the old woman in the very tenderest tone of her tender voice. "Kiss me!"

"What is kissing?" asked the wondering child.

His godmother took him in her arms and embraced him many times. By-and-by he kissed her back again—at first awkwardly and shyly, then with all the strength of his warm little heart.

"You are better to cuddle than even my white kitten, I think. Promise me that you will never go away."

"I must; but I will leave a present behind me—something as good as myself to amuse you—something that will take you wherever you want to go, and show you all that you wish to see."

"What is it?"

"A travelling-cloak."

The Prince's countenance fell. "I don't want a cloak, for I never go out. Sometimes nurse hoists me onto the roof, and carries me round by the parapet; but that is all. I can't walk, you know, as she does."

"The more reason why you should ride; and besides, this travelling-cloak—"

"Hush!—she's coming."

There sounded outside the room door a heavy step and a grumpy voice, and a rattle of plates and dishes.

"It's my nurse, and she is bringing my dinner; but I don't want dinner at all—I only want you. Will her coming drive you away, godmother?"

"Perhaps: but only for a little while. Never mind; all the bolts and bars in the world couldn't keep me out. I'd fly in at the window, or down through the chimney. Only wish for me, and I come."

"Thank you," said Prince Dolor, but almost in a whisper, for he was very uneasy at what might happen next. His nurse and his godmother—what would they say to one another? how would they look at one another?—two such different faces: one harsh-lined, sullen, cross, and sad; the other sweet and bright and calm as a summer evening before the dark begins.

When the door was flung open, Prince Dolor shut his eyes, trembling all over. Opening them again, he saw he need fear nothing—his lovely old godmother had melted away just like the rainbow out of the sky, as he had watched it many a time. Nobody but his nurse was in the room.

"What a muddle your Royal Highness is sitting in," said she sharply. "Such a heap of untidy books; and what's this rubbish?" knocking a little bundle that lay beside them.

"Oh, nothing, nothing—give it me!" cried the Prince, and, darting after it, he hid it under his pinafore, and then pushed it quickly into his pocket. Rubbish as it was, it was left in the place where she sat, and might be something belonging to her—his dear, kind godmother, whom already he loved with all his lonely, tender, passionate heart.

It was, though he did not know this, his wonderful travelling-cloak.

I V

And what of the travelling-cloak? What sort of cloak was it, and what good did it do the Prince?

Stay, and I'll tell you about it.

Outside it was the commonest-looking bundle imaginable—shabby and small; and the instant Prince Dolor touched it, it grew smaller still, dwindling down till he could put it in his trousers-pocket, like a handkerchief rolled up into a ball. He did this at once, for fear his nurse should see it, and kept it there all day—all night, too. Till after his next morning's lessons he had no opportunity of examining his treasure.

When he did, it seemed no treasure at all; but a mere piece of cloth—circular in form, dark green in colour—that is, if it had any colour at all, being so worn and shabby, though not dirty. It had a split cut to the centre, forming a round hole for the neck—and that was all its shape; the shape, in fact, of those cloaks which in South America are called ponchos—very simple, but most graceful and convenient.

Prince Dolor had never seen anything like it. In spite of his disappointment, he examined it curiously. He spread it out on the floor, then arranged it on his shoulders. It felt very warm and comfortable; but it was so exceedingly shabby—the only shabby thing that the Prince had ever seen in his life.

"And what use will it be to me?" said he sadly. "I have no need of outdoor clothes, as I never go out. Why was this given me? I wonder. And what in the world am I to do with it? She must be a rather funny person, this dear godmother of mine."

Nevertheless, because she was his godmother, and had given him the cloak, he folded it carefully and put it away, poor and shabby as it was, hiding it in a safe corner of his toy cupboard, which his nurse never meddled with. He did not want her to find it, or to laugh at it or at his godmother—as he felt sure she would, if she knew all.

There it lay, and by-and-by he forgot all about it. Nay, I am sorry to say that, being but a child, and not seeing her again, he almost forgot his sweet old godmother, or thought of her only as he did of the angels or fairies that he read of in his books, and of her visit as if it had been a mere dream of the night.

There were times, certainly, when he recalled her: of early mornings, like that morning when she appeared beside him, and late evenings, when the grey twilight reminded him of the colour of her hair and her pretty soft garments; above all, when, waking in the middle of the night, with the stars peering in at his window, or the moonlight shining across his little bed, he would not have been surprised to see her standing beside it, looking at him with those beautiful tender eyes, which seemed to have a pleasantness and comfort in them different from anything he had ever known.

But she never came, and gradually she slipped out of his memory—only a boy's memory, after all; until something happened which made him remember her, and want her as he had never wanted anything before.

Prince Dolor fell ill. He caught—his nurse could not tell how—a complaint common to the people of Nomansland, called the doldrums, as unpleasant as measles or any other of our complaints; and it made him restless, cross, and disagreeable. Even when a little better, he was too weak to enjoy anything, but lay all day long on his sofa, fidgetting his nurse extremely—while, in her intense terror lest he might die, she fidgetted him still more. At last, seeing he really was getting well, she left him to himself—which he was most glad of, in spite of his dullness and dreariness. There he lay, alone, quite alone.

Now and then an irritable fit came over him, in which he longed to get up and do something, or to go somewhere. He would have liked to imitate his white kitten—jump down from the tower and run away, taking the chance of whatever might happen.

Only one thing, alas! was likely to happen; for the kitten, he remembered, had four active legs, while he—

"I wonder what my godmother meant when she looked at my legs and sighed so bitterly? I wonder why I can't walk straight and steady like my nurse—only I wouldn't like to have her great, noisy, clumping shoes. Still it would be very nice to move about quickly—perhaps to fly, like a bird, like that string of birds I saw the other day skimming across the sky, one after the other."

These were the passage-birds—the only living creatures that ever crossed the lonely plain; and he had been much interested in them, wondering whence they came and whither they were going.

"How nice it must be to be a bird! If legs are no good, why cannot one have wings? People have wings when they die—perhaps. I wish I were dead, that I do. I am so tired, so tired; and nobody cares for me. Nobody ever did care for me, except perhaps my godmother. Godmother, dear, have you quite forsaken me?"

He stretched himself wearily, gathered himself up, and dropped his head upon his hands; as he did so, he felt somebody kiss him at the back of his neck, and, turning, found that he was resting, not on the sofa-pillows, but on a warm shoulder—that of the little old woman clothed in grey.

How glad he was to see her! How he looked into her kind eyes and felt her hands, to see if she were all real and alive! Then he put both his arms round her neck, and kissed her as if he would never have done kissing.

"Stop, stop!" cried she, pretending to be smothered. "I see you have not forgotten my teachings. Kissing is a good thing—in moderation. Only just let me have breath to speak one word."

"A dozen!" he said.

"Well, then, tell me all that has happened to you since I saw you—or rather, since you saw me, which is quite a different thing."

"Nothing has happened—nothing ever does happen to me," answered the Prince dolefully.

"And are you very dull, my boy?"

"So dull that I was just thinking whether I could not jump down to the bottom of the tower, like my white kitten."

"Don't do that, not being a white kitten."

"I wish I were—I wish I were anything but what I am."

"And you can't make yourself any different, nor can I do it either. You must be content to stay just what you are."

The little old woman said this—very firmly, but gently, too—with her arms round his neck and her lips on his forehead. It was the first time the boy had ever heard anyone talk like this, and he looked up in surprise—but not in pain, for her sweet manner softened the hardness of her words.

"Now, my Prince—for you are a prince, and must behave as such—let us see what we can do; how much I can do for you, or show you how to do for yourself. Where is your travelling-cloak?"

Prince Dolor blushed extremely. "I—I put it away in the cupboard. I suppose it is there still."

"You have never used it; you dislike it?"

He hesitated, not wishing to be impolite. "Don't you think it's—just a little old and shabby for a prince?"

The old woman laughed—long and loud, though very sweetly.

"Prince, indeed! Why, if all the princes in the world craved for it, they couldn't get it, unless I gave it them. Old and shabby! It's the most valuable thing imaginable! Very few ever have it; but I thought I would give it to you, because—because you are different from other people."

"Am I?" said the Prince, and looked first with curiosity, then with a sort of anxiety, into his godmother's face, which was sad and grave, with slow tears beginning to steal down.

She touched his poor little legs. "These are not like those of other little boys."

"Indeed!—my nurse never told me that."

"Very likely not. But it is time you were told; and I tell you, because I love you."

"Tell me what, dear godmother?"

"That you will never be able to walk or run or jump or play—that your life will be quite different from most people's lives; but it may be a very happy life for all that. Do not be afraid."

"I am not afraid," said the boy. But he turned very pale, and his lips began to quiver, though he did not actually cry—he was too old for that, and, perhaps, too proud.

Though not wholly comprehending, he began dimly to guess what his godmother meant. He had never seen any real live boys, but he had seen pictures of them running and jumping; which he had admired and tried hard to imitate, but always failed. Now he began to understand why he failed, and that he always should fail—that, in fact, he was not like other little boys; and it was of no use his wishing to do as they did, and play as they played, even if he had had them to play with. His was a separate life, in which he must find out new work and new pleasures for himself.

The sense of *the inevitable*, as grown-up people call it—that we cannot have things as we want them to be, but as they are, and that we must learn to bear them and make the best of them—this lesson, which everybody has to learn soon or late—came, alas! sadly soon to the poor boy. He fought against it for a while, and then, quite overcome, turned and sobbed bitterly in his godmother's arms.

She comforted him—I do not know how, except that love always comforts. And then she whispered to him, in her sweet, strong, cheerful voice, "Never mind!"

"No, I don't think I do mind—that is, I *won't* mind," replied he, catching the courage of her tone and speaking like a man, though he was still such a mere boy.

"That is right, my Prince!—that is being like a prince. Now we know exactly where we are; let us put our shoulders to the wheel and—"

"We are in Hopeless Tower" (this was its name, if it had a name), "and there is no wheel to put our shoulders to," said the child sadly.

"You little matter-of-fact goose! Well for you that you have a godmother called—"

"What?" he eagerly asked.

"Stuff-and-Nonsense."

"Stuff-and-Nonsense! What a funny name!"

"Some people give it me, but they are not my most intimate friends. These call me—never mind what," added the old woman, with a soft twinkle in her eyes. "So as you know me, and know me well, you may give me any name you please; it doesn't matter. But I am your godmother, child. I have few godchildren. Those I have love me dearly, and find me the greatest blessing in all the world."

"I can well believe it," cried the little lame Prince, and forgot his troubles in looking at her—as her figure dilated, her eyes grew lustrous as stars, her very raiment brightened, and the whole room seemed filled with her beautiful and beneficent presence like light.

He could have looked at her for ever—half in love, half in awe; but she suddenly dwindled down into the little old woman all in grey, and, with a malicious twinkle in her eyes, asked for the travelling-cloak.

"Bring it out of the rubbish-cupboard, and shake the dust off it, quick!" said she to Prince Dolor, who hung his head, rather ashamed. "Spread it out on the floor, and wait till the split closes and the edges turn up like a rim all round. Then go and open the skylight—mind, I say *open the skylight*— set yourself down in the middle of it, like a frog on a water-lily leaf; say 'Abracadabra, dum dum dum,' and—see what will happen!"

The Prince burst into a fit of laughing. It all seemed so exceedingly silly; he wondered that a wise old woman like his godmother should talk such nonsense.

"Stuff-and-nonsense, you mean," said she, answering, to his great alarm, his unspoken thoughts. "Did I not tell you some people called me by that name? Never mind; it doesn't harm me."

And she laughed—her merry laugh—as child-like as if she were the Prince's age instead of her own, whatever that might be. She certainly was a most extraordinary old woman.

"Believe me or not, it doesn't matter," said she. "Here is the cloak. When you want to go traveling on it, say 'Abracadabra, dum dum dum'; when you want to come back again, say 'Abracadabra, tum tum ti.' That's all; good-bye."

A puff of most pleasant air passing by him, making him feel for the moment quite strong and well, was all the Prince was conscious of. His most extraordinary godmother was gone.

"Really now, how rosy your Royal Highness's cheeks have grown! You seem to have got well already," said the nurse, entering the room.

"I think I have," replied the Prince very gently—he felt gentle and kind even to his grim nurse. "And now let me have my dinner, and go you to your sewing as usual."

The instant she was gone, however, taking with her the plate and dishes, which for the first time since his illness he had satisfactorily cleared, Prince Dolor hopped down from his sofa, and with one or two of his frog-like jumps reached the cupboard where he kept his toys, and looked everywhere for his travelling-cloak.

Alas! it was not there.

While he was ill of the doldrums, his nurse, thinking it a good opportunity for putting things to rights, had made a grand clearance of all his "rubbish"—as she considered it. His beloved headless horses, broken carts, sheep without feet, and birds without wings—all the treasures of his baby days, which he could not bear to part with, were gone. Though he seldom played with them now, he liked just to feel they were there.

They were all gone and with them the travelling-cloak. He sat down on the floor, looking at the empty shelves, so beautifully clean and tidy, then burst out sobbing as if his heart would break.

But quietly—always quietly. He never let his nurse hear him cry. She only laughed at him, as he felt she would laugh now.

"And it is all my own fault!" he cried. "I ought to have taken better care of my godmother's gift. Oh, godmother, forgive me! I'll never be so careless again. I don't know what the cloak is exactly, but I am sure it is something precious. Help me to find it again. Oh, don't let it be stolen from me—don't, please!"

"Ha, ha, ha!" laughed a silvery voice. "Why, that travelling-cloak is the one thing in the world which nobody can steal. It is of no use to anybody except the owner. Open your eyes, my Prince, and see what you shall see."

His dear old godmother, he thought, and turned eagerly round. But no; he beheld, lying in a corner of the room, all dust and cobwebs, his precious travelling-cloak.

Prince Dolor darted toward it, tumbling several times on the way, as he often did tumble, poor boy! and pick himself up again, never complaining. Snatching it to his breast, he hugged and kissed it, cobwebs and all, as if it had been something alive. Then he began unrolling it, wondering each minute what would happen. What did happen was so curious that I must leave it for another chapter.

V

If any reader, big or little, should wonder whether there is a meaning in this story deeper than that of an ordinary fairy tale, I will own that there is. But I have hidden it so carefully that the smaller people, and many larger folk, will never find it out, and meantime the book may be read straight on, like *Cinderella*, or *Bluebeard*, or *Hop-o'-My-Thumb*, for what interest it has or what amusement it may bring.

Having said this, I return to Prince Dolor, that little lame boy whom many may think so exceedingly to be pitied. But if you had seen him as he sat patiently untying his wonderful cloak, which was done up in a very tight and perplexing parcel, using skillfully his deft little hands, and knitting his brows with firm determination, while his eyes glistened with pleasure and energy and eager anticipation—if you had beheld him thus, you might have changed your opinion.

When we see people suffering or unfortunate, we feel very sorry for them. But when we see them bravely bearing their sufferings and making the best of their misfortunes, it is quite a different thing. We respect, we admire them. One can respect and admire even a little child.

When Prince Dolor had patiently untied all the knots, a remarkable thing happened. The cloak began to undo itself. Slowly unfolding, it laid itself down on the carpet, as flat as if it had been ironed. The split joined with a little sharp crick-crack, and the rim turned up all round till it was breast-high. Meantime the cloak had grown and grown, and become quite large enough for one person to sit in it as comfortably as if in a boat.

The Prince watched it rather anxiously; it was such an extraordinary, not to say a frightening, thing. However, he was no coward, but a thorough boy, who, if he had been like other boys, would doubtless have grown up daring and adventurous—a soldier, a sailor, or the like. As it was, he could only show his courage morally, not physically, by being afraid of nothing, and by doing boldly all that it was in his narrow powers to do. And I am not sure but that in this way he showed more real valour than if he had had six pairs of proper legs.

He said to himself, "What a goose I am! As if my dear godmother would ever have given me anything to hurt me. Here goes!"

So, with one of his active leaps, he sprang right into the middle of the cloak, where he squatted down, wrapping his arms tight round his knees, for they shook a little and his heart beat fast. But there he sat, steady and silent, waiting for what might happen next.

Nothing did happen, and he began to think nothing would, and to feel rather disappointed, when he recollected the words he had been told to repeat—"Abracadabra, dum dum dum!"

He repeated them, laughing all the while, they seemed such nonsense. And then—and then—

Now I don't expect anybody to believe what I am going to relate, though a good many wise people have believed a good many sillier things. And as seeing's believing, and I never saw it, I cannot be expected implicitly to believe it myself, except in a sort of way. And yet there is truth in it—for some people.

The cloak rose, slowly and steadily, at first only a few inches, then gradually higher and higher, till it nearly touched the skylight. Prince Dolor's head actually bumped against the glass, or would have done so had he not crouched down, crying, "Oh, please don't hurt me!" in a most melancholy voice.

Then he suddenly remembered his godmother's express command—"Open the skylight!"

Regaining his courage at once, without a moment's delay he lifted up his head and began searching for the bolt—the cloak meanwhile remaining perfectly still, balanced in the air. But the minute the window was opened, out it sailed—right out into the clear, fresh air, with nothing between it and the cloudless blue.

Prince Dolor had never felt any such delicious sensation before. I can understand it. Cannot you? Did you never think, in watching the rooks going home singly or in pairs, soaring their way across the calm evening sky till they vanish like black dots in the misty gray, how pleasant it must feel to be up there, quite out of the noise and din of the world, able to hear and see everything down below, yet troubled by nothing and teased by no one—all alone, but perfectly content?

Something like this was the happiness of the little lame Prince when he got out of Hopeless Tower, and found himself for the first time in the pure open air, with the sky above him and the earth below.

True, there was nothing but earth and sky; no houses, no trees, no rivers, mountains, seas—not a beast on the ground or a bird in the air. But to him even the level plain looked beautiful. And then there was the glorious arch of the sky, with a little young moon sitting in the west like a baby queen. And the evening breeze was so sweet and fresh—it kissed him like his godmother's kisses. And by-and-by a few stars came out—first two or three, and then quantities—quantities! so that when he began to count them he was utterly bewildered.

By this time, however, the cool breeze had become cold. The mist gathered; and as he had, as he said, no outdoor clothes, poor Prince Dolor was not very comfortable. The dews fell damp on his curls. He began to shiver.

"Perhaps I had better go home," thought he.

But how? For in his excitement the other words which his godmother had told him to use had slipped his memory. They were only a little different from the first, but in that slight difference all the importance lay. As he repeated his "Abracadabra," trying ever so many other syllables after it, the cloak only went faster and faster, skimming on through the dusky, empty air.

The poor little Prince began to feel frightened. What if his wonderful travelling-cloak should keep on thus travelling, perhaps to the world's end, carrying with it a poor, tired, hungry boy, who, after all, was beginning to think there was something very pleasant in supper and bed!

"Dear godmother," he cried pitifully, "do help me! Tell me just this once and I'll never forget again."

Instantly the words came rushing into his head—"Abracadabra, tum tum ti!" Was that it? Ah! yes—for the cloak began to turn slowly. He repeated the charm again, more distinctly and firmly, when it gave a gentle dip, like a nod of satisfaction, and immediately started back, as fast as ever, in the direction of the tower.

He reached the skylight, which he found exactly as he had left it, and slipped in, cloak and all, as easily as he had got out. He had scarcely reached the floor, and was still sitting in the middle of his travelling-cloak—like a frog on a water-lily leaf, as his godmother had expressed it—when he heard his nurse's voice outside.

"Bless us! what has become of your Royal Highness all this time? To sit stupidly here at the window till it is quite dark, and leave the skylight open, too. Prince! what can you be thinking of? You are the silliest boy I ever knew."

"Am I?" said he absently, and never heeding her crossness; for his only anxiety was lest she might find out what he had been doing.

She would have been a very clever person to have done so. The instant Prince Dolor got off it, the cloak folded itself up into the tiniest possible parcel, tied all its own knots, and rolled itself on its own accord into the farthest and darkest corner of the room. If the nurse had seen it, which she didn't, she would have taken it for a mere bundle of rubbish not worth noticing.

Shutting the skylight with an angry bang, she brought in the supper and lit the candles with her usual unhappy expression of countenance. But Prince Dolor hardly saw it. He saw only, hid in the corner where nobody else would see it, his wonderful travelling-cloak. And though his supper was not particularly nice, he ate it heartily, scarcely hearing a word of his nurse's grumbling, which to-night seemed to have taken the place of her sullen silence.

"Poor woman!" he thought, when he paused a minute to listen and look at her with those quiet, happy eyes, so like his mother's. "Poor woman! she hasn't got a travelling-cloak!"

And when he was left alone at last, and crept into his little bed, where he lay awake a good while, watching what he called his "sky-garden," all planted with stars, like flowers, his chief thought was—"I must be up very early to-morrow morning, and get my lessons done, and then I'll go travelling all over the world on my beautiful cloak."

So next day he opened his eyes with the sun, and went with a good heart to his lessons. They had hitherto been the chief amusement of his dull life. Now, I am afraid, he found them also a little dull. But he tried to be good— I don't say Prince Dolor always was good, but he generally tried to be— and when his mind went wandering after the dark, dusty corner where lay his precious treasure, he resolutely called it back again.

"For," he said, "how ashamed my godmother would be of me if I grew up a stupid boy!"

But the instant lessons were done, and he was alone in the empty room, he crept across the floor, undid the shabby little bundle, his fingers trembling with eagerness, climbed on the chair, and thence to the table, so as to unbar the skylight—he forgot nothing now—said his magic charm, and was away out the window, as children say, "in a few minutes less than no time."

Nobody missed him. He was accustomed to sit so quietly always that his nurse, though only in the next room, perceived no difference. And besides, she might have gone in and out a dozen times, and it would have been just the same; she never could have found out his absence.

For what do you think the clever godmother did? She took a quantity of moonshine, or some equally convenient material, and made an image, which she set on the window-sill reading, or by the table drawing, where it looked so like Prince Dolor that any common observer would never have guessed the deception. And even the boy would have been puzzled to know which was the image and which was himself.

And all this while the happy little fellow was away, floating in the air on his magic cloak, and seeing all sorts of wonderful things—or they seemed wonderful to him, who had hitherto seen nothing at all.

First, there were the flowers that grew on the plain, which, whenever the cloak came near enough, he strained his eyes to look at. They were very tiny, but very beautiful—white saxifrage, and yellow lotus, and ground-thistles, purple and bright, with many others the names of which I do not know. No more did Prince Dolor, though he tried to find them out by recalling any pictures he had seen of them. But he was too far off; and though it was pleasant enough to admire them as brilliant patches of colour, still he would have liked to examine them all. He was, as a little girl I know once said of a playfellow, "a very *examining* boy."

"I wonder," he thought, "whether I could see better through a pair of glasses like those my nurse reads with, and takes such care of. How I would take care of them, too, if I only had a pair!"

Immediately he felt something queer and hard fixing itself to the bridge of his nose. It was a pair of the prettiest gold spectacles ever seen. Looking downwards, he found that, though ever so high above the ground, he could see every minute blade of grass, every tiny bud and flower—nay, even the insects that walked over them.

"Thank you, thank you!" he cried, in a gush of gratitude—to anybody or everybody, but especially to his dear godmother, who he felt sure had given him this new present. He amused himself with it for ever so long, with his chin pressed on the rim of the cloak, gazing down upon the grass, every square foot of which was a mine of wonders.

Then, just to rest his eyes, he turned them up to the sky—the blue, bright, empty sky, which he had looked at so often and seen nothing.

Now surely there was something. A long, black, wavy line, moving on in the distance, not by chance, as the clouds move apparently, but delib-erately, as if it were alive. He might have seen it before—he almost thought he had; but then he could not tell what it was. Looking at it through his spectacles, he discovered that it really was alive; being a long string of birds, flying one after the other, their wings moving steadily and their heads pointed in one direction, as steadily as if each were a little ship, guided invisibly by an unerring helm.

"They must be the passage-birds flying seawards!" cried the boy, who had read a little about them, and had a great talent for putting two and two together and finding out all he could. "Oh, how I should like to see them quite close, and to know where they come from and whither they are going! How I wish I knew everything in all the world!"

A silly speech for even an "examining" little boy to make; because, as we grow older, the more we know the more we find out there is to know. And

Prince Dolor blushed when he had said it, and hoped nobody had heard him.

Apparently somebody had, however. For the cloak gave a sudden bound forward, and presently he found himself high in the air, in the very middle of that band of aerial travellers, who had no magic cloak to travel on— nothing except their wings. Yet there they were, making their fearless way through the sky.

Prince Dolor looked at them as one after the other they glided past him; and they looked at him—those pretty swallows with their changing necks and bright eyes—as if wondering to meet in mid-air such an extraordinary sort of bird.

"Oh, I wish I were going with you, you lovely creatures! I'm getting so tired of this dull plain, and the dreary and lonely tower. I do so want to see the world! Pretty swallows, dear swallows! tell me what it looks like— the beautiful, wonderful world!"

But the swallows flew past him—steadily, slowly pursuing their course as if inside each little head had been a mariner's compass, to guide him safe over land and sea, direct to the place where he wished to go.

The boy looked after them with envy. For a long time he followed with his eyes the faint, wavy black line as it floated away, sometimes changing its curves a little, but never deviating from its settled course, till it vanished entirely out of sight.

Then he settled himself down in the centre of the cloak, feeling quite sad and lonely.

"I think I'll go home," said he, and repeated his "Abracadabra, tum tum ti!" with a rather heavy heart. The more he had, the more he wanted. It is not always one can have everything one wants—at least, at the exact minute one craves for it; not even though one is a prince, and has a powerful and beneficent godmother.

He did not like to vex her by calling for her and telling her how unhappy he was, in spite of all her goodness. So he just kept his trouble to himself, went back to his lonely tower, and spent three days in silent melancholy, without even attempting another journey on his travelling-cloak.

V I

The fourth day it happened that the deaf-mute paid his accustomed visit, after which Prince Dolor's spirits rose. They always did when he got the new books which, just to relieve his conscience, the King of Nomansland regularly sent to his nephew; with many new toys also, though the latter were disregarded now.

"Toys, indeed! when I'm a big boy," said the Prince, with disdain, and would scarcely condescend to mount a rocking-horse which had come, some-how or other—I can't be expected to explain things very exactly—packed on the back of the other, the great black horse, which stood and fed contentedly at the bottom of the tower.

Prince Dolor leaned over and looked at it, and thought how grand it must be to get upon its back—this grand live steed—and ride away, like the pictures of knights.

"Suppose I were a knight," he said to himself; "then I should be obliged to ride out and see the world."

But he kept all these thoughts to himself, and just sat still, devouring his new books till he had come to the end of them all. It was a repast not unlike the Barmecide feast which you read of in the *Arabian Nights*, which consisted of very elegant but empty dishes, or that supper of Sancho Panza in *Don Quixote*, where, the minute the smoking dishes came on the table, the physician waved his hand and they were all taken away.

Thus almost all the ordinary delights of boy-life had been taken away from, or rather never given to, this poor little prince.

"I wonder," he would sometimes think—"I wonder what it feels like to be on the back of a horse, galloping away, or holding the reins in a carriage, and tearing across the country, or jumping a ditch, or running a race, such as I read of or see in pictures. What a lot of things there are that I should like to do! But first I should like to go and see the world. I'll try."

Apparently it was his godmother's plan always to let him try, and try hard, before he gained anything. This day the knots that tied up his travelling-cloak were more than usually troublesome, and he was a full half-hour before he got out into the open air, and found himself floating merrily over the top of the tower.

Hitherto, in all his journeys, he had never let himself go out of sight of home, for the dreary building, after all, was home—he remembered no other. But now he felt sick of the very look of his tower, with its round smooth walls and level battlements.

"Off we go!" cried he, when the cloak stirred itself with a slight, slow motion, as if awaiting his orders. "Anywhere—anywhere, so that I am away from here, and out into the world."

As he spoke, the cloak, as if seized suddenly with a new idea, bounded forward and went skimming through the air, faster than the very fastest railway train.

"Gee-up! gee-up!" cried Prince Dolor in great excitement. "This is as good as riding a race."

And he patted the cloak as if it had been a horse—that is, in the way he supposed horses ought to be patted—and tossed his head back to meet the fresh breeze, and pulled his coat-collar up and his hat down as he felt the wind grow keener and colder—colder than anything he had ever known.

"What does it matter, though?" said he. "I'm a boy, and boys ought not to mind anything."

Still, for all his good-will, by-and-by he began to shiver exceedingly. Also, he had come away without his dinner, and he grew frightfully hungry. And to add to everything, the sunshiny day changed into rain, and being high up, in the very midst of the clouds, he got soaked through and through in a very few minutes.

"Shall I turn back?" meditated he. "Suppose I say 'Abracadabra'?"

Here he stopped, for already the cloak gave an obedient lurch, as if it were expecting to be sent home immediately.

"No—I can't—I can't go back! I must go forward and see the world. But oh! if I had but the shabbiest old rug to shelter me from the rain, or the driest morsel of bread-and-cheese, just to keep me from starving! Still, I don't much mind. I'm a prince, and ought to be able to stand anything. Hold on, cloak, we'll make the best of it."

It was a most curious circumstance, but no sooner had he said this than he felt stealing over his knees something warm and soft; in fact, a most beautiful bearskin, which folded itself round him quite naturally, and cuddled him up as closely as if he had been the cub of the kind old mother-bear that once owned it. Then feeling in his pocket, which suddenly stuck out in a marvellous way, he found, not exactly bread-and-cheese, nor even sandwiches, but a packet of the most delicious food he had ever tasted. It was not meat, nor pudding, but a combination of both, and it served him excellently for both. He ate his dinner with the greatest gusto imaginable, till he grew so thirsty he did not know what to do.

"Couldn't I have just one drop of water, if it didn't trouble you too much, kindest of godmothers?"

For he really thought this want was beyond her power to supply. All the water which supplied Hopeless Tower was pumped up with difficulty from a deep artesian well—there were such things known in Nomansland—which had been drilled at the foot of it. But around, for miles upon miles, the desolate plain was perfectly dry. And above it, high in the air, how could he expect to find a well, or to get even a drop of water?

He forgot one thing—the rain. While he spoke, it came on in another wild burst, as if the clouds had poured themselves out in a passion of crying, wetting him certainly, but leaving behind, in a large glass vessel which he had never noticed before, enough water to quench the thirst of two or three boys at least. And it was so fresh, so pure—as water from the clouds always is when it does not catch the soot from city chimneys and other defilements— that he drank it, every drop, with the greatest delight and content.

Also, as soon as it was empty the rain filled it again, so that he was able to wash his face and hands and refresh himself exceedingly. Then the sun came out and dried him in no time. After that he curled himself up under the bearskin rug, and though he determined to be the most wide-awake boy imaginable, being so snug and warm and comfortable, Prince Dolor condescended to shut his eyes just for one minute. The next minute he was sound asleep.

When he awoke, he found himself floating over a country quite unlike anything he had ever seen before.

Yet it was nothing but what most of you children see every day and never notice it—a pretty country landscape, like England, Scotland, France, or any other land you choose to name. It had no particular features—nothing in it was grand or lovely. It was simply pretty, nothing more. Yet to Prince Dolor, who had never gone beyond his lonely tower and level plain, it appeared the most charming sight imaginable.

First, there was a river. It came tumbling down the hillside, frothing and foaming, playing at hide-and-seek among the rocks, then bursting out in noisy fun like a child, to bury itself in deep, still pools. Afterwards it went steadily on for a while, like a good grown-up person, till it came to another big rock, where it misbehaved itself extremely. It turned into a cataract, and went tumbling over and over, after a fashion that made the Prince— who had never seen water before, except in his bath or his drinking-cup— clap his hands with delight.

"It is so active, so alive! I like things active and alive!" cried he, and watched it shimmering and dancing, whirling and leaping, till, after a few windings and vagaries, it settled into a respectable stream. After that it went along, deep and quiet, but flowing steadily on, till it reached a large lake, into which it slipped and so ended its course.

All this the boy saw, either with his own naked eyes or through his gold spectacles. He saw also as in a picture, beautiful but silent, many other things which struck him with wonder, especially a grove of trees.

Only think, to have lived to his age (which he himself did not know, as he did not know his own birthday) and never to have seen trees! As he floated over these oaks, they seemed to him—trunk, branches, and leaves—the most curious sight imaginable.

"If I could only get nearer, so as to touch them," said he, and immediately the obedient cloak ducked down. Prince Dolor made a snatch at the topmost twig of the tallest tree, and caught a bunch of leaves in his hand.

Just a bunch of green leaves—such as we see in myriads; watching them bud, grow, fall, and then kicking them along on the ground as if they were worth nothing. Yet how wonderful they are—every one of them a little different. I don't suppose you could ever find two leaves exactly alike in form, colour, and size—no more than you could find two faces alike, or two characters exactly the same. The plan of this world is infinite similarity and yet infinite variety.

Prince Dolor examined his leaves with the greatest curiosity—and also a little caterpillar that he found walking over one of them. He coaxed it to take an additional walk over his finger, which it did with the greatest dignity and decorum, as if it, Mr. Caterpillar, were the most important individual in existence. It amused him for a long time; when a sudden gust of wind blew it overboard, leaves and all, he felt quite disconsolate.

"Still there must be many live creatures in the world besides caterpillars. I should like to see a few of them."

The cloak gave a little dip down, as if to say "All right, my Prince," and bore him across the oak forest to a long fertile valley—called in Scotland a strath and in England a weald, but what they call it in the tongue of Nomansland I do not know. It was made up of cornfields, pasturefields, lanes, hedges, brooks, and ponds. Also, in it were what the Prince desired to see—a quantity of living creatures, wild and tame. Cows and horses, lambs and sheep, fed in the meadows; pigs and fowls walked about the farmyards; and in lonelier places hares scudded, rabbits burrowed, and pheasants and partridges, with many other smaller birds, inhabited the fields and woods.

Through his wonderful spectacles the Prince could see everything. But, as I said, it was a silent picture; he was too high up to catch anything except a faint murmur, which only aroused his anxiety to hear more.

"I have as good as two pairs of eyes," he thought. "I wonder if my godmother would give me a second pair of ears."

Scarcely had he spoken than he found lying on his lap the most curious little parcel, all done up in silvery paper. And it contained—what do you think? Actually, a pair of silver ears, which, when he tried them on, fitted so exactly over his own that he hardly felt them, except for the difference they made in his hearing.

There is something which we listen to daily and never notice. I mean the sounds of the visible world, animate and inanimate. Winds blowing, waters flowing, trees stirring, insects whirring (dear me! I am quite unconsciously writing rhyme), with the various cries of birds and beasts—lowing cattle, bleating sheep, grunting pigs, and cackling hens—all the infinite discords that somehow or other make a beautiful harmony.

We hear this, and are so accustomed to it that we think nothing of it. But Prince Dolor, who had lived all his days in the dead silence of Hopeless Tower, heard it for the first time. And oh! if you had seen his face.

He listened, listened, as if he could never have done listening. And he looked and looked, as if he could not gaze enough. Above all, the motion of the animals delighted him: cows walking, horses galloping, little lambs and calves running races across the meadows, were such a treat for him to watch—he that was always so quiet. But, these creatures having four legs, and he only two, the difference did not strike him painfully.

Still, by-and-by, after the fashion of children—and, I fear, of many big people too—he began to want something more than he had, something fresh and new.

"Godmother," he said, having now begun to believe that, whether he saw her or not, he could always speak to her with full confidence that she would hear him—"godmother, all these creatures I like exceedingly; but I should like better to see a creature like myself. Couldn't you show me just one little boy?"

There was a sigh behind him—it might have been only the wind—and the cloak remained so long balanced motionless in air that he was half afraid his godmother had forgotten him, or was offended with him for asking too much. Suddenly a shrill whistle startled him, even through his silver ears, and looking downwards, he saw start up from behind a bush on a common, something—

Neither a sheep nor a horse nor a cow—nothing upon four legs. This creature had only two; but they were long, straight, and strong. And it had a lithe, active body, and a curly head of black hair set upon its shoulders. It was a boy, a shepherd boy, about the Prince's own age—but, oh! so different.

Not that he was an ugly boy—though his face was almost as red as his hands, and his shaggy hair matted like the backs of his own sheep. He was rather a nice-looking lad; and seemed so bright and healthy and good-tempered—"jolly" would be the word, only I am not sure if they have such a one in the elegant language of Nomansland—that the little Prince watched him with great admiration.

"Might he come and play with me? I would drop down to the ground to him, or fetch him up to me here. Oh, how nice it would be if I only had a little boy to play with me."

But the cloak, usually so obedient to his wishes, disobeyed him now. There were evidently some things which his godmother either could not or would not give. The cloak hung stationary, high in air, never attempting to descend. The shepherd lad evidently took it for a large bird, and, shading his eyes, looked up at it, making the Prince's heart beat fast.

However, nothing ensued. The boy turned round, with a long, loud whistle—seemingly his usual and only way of expressing his feelings. He could not make the thing out exactly—it was a rather mysterious affair, but it did not trouble him much—he was not an "examining" boy.

Then, stretching himself, for he had been evidently half asleep, he began flopping his shoulders with his arms to wake and warm himself; while his dog, a rough collie, who had been guarding the sheep meanwhile, began to jump upon him, barking with delight.

"Down, Snap, down! Stop that, or I'll thrash you," the Prince heard him say; though with such a rough, hard voice and queer pronunciation that it was difficult to make the words out. "Hollo! Let's warm ourselves by a race."

They started off together, boy and dog—barking and shouting, till it was doubtful which made the more noise or ran the faster. A regular steeplechase it was: first across the level common, greatly disturbing the quiet sheep; and then tearing away across country, scrambling through hedges and leaping ditches, and tumbling up and down over ploughed fields. They did not seem to have anything to run for—but they ran as if they did it, both of them, for the mere pleasure of motion.

And what a pleasure that seemed! To the dog of course, but scarcely less so to the boy. How he skimmed along over the ground—his cheeks glowing, and his hair flying, and his legs—oh, what a pair of legs he had!

Prince Dolor watched him with great intentness, and in a state of excitement almost equal to that of the runner himself—for a while. Then the sweet, pale face grew a trifle paler, the lips began to quiver, and the eyes to fill.

"How nice it must be to run like that!" he said softly, thinking that never—no, never in this world—would he be able to do the same.

Now he understood what his godmother had meant when she gave him his travelling-cloak, and why he had heard that sigh—he was sure it was hers—when he had asked to see "just one little boy."

"I think I had rather not look at him again," said the poor little Prince, drawing himself back into the centre of his cloak, and resuming his favourite posture, sitting like a Turk, with his arms wrapped round his feeble, useless legs.

"You're no good to me," he said, patting them mournfully. "You never will be any good to me. I wonder why I had you at all. I wonder why I was born at all, since I was not to grow up like other boys. *Why* not?"

A question so strange, so sad, yet so often occurring in some form or other in this world—as you will find, my children, when you are older—that even if he had put it to his mother she could only have answered it, as we have to answer many as difficult things, by simply saying, "I don't know." There is much that we do not know and cannot understand—we big folks any more than you little ones. We have to accept it all just as you have to accept anything which your parents may tell you, even though you don't as yet see the reason of it. You may some time, if you do exactly as they tell you, and are content to wait.

Prince Dolor sat a good while thus, or it appeared to him a good while, so many thoughts came and went through his poor young mind—thoughts of great bitterness, which, little though he was, seemed to make him grow years older in a few minutes.

Then he fancied the cloak began to rock gently to and fro, with a soothing kind of motion, as if he were in somebody's arms, somebody who did not speak, but loved him and comforted him without need of words. Not by deceiving him with false encouragement or hope, but by making him see the plain, hard truth in all its hardness, and thus letting him quietly face it, till it became softened, and did not seem nearly so dreadful after all.

Through the dreary silence and blankness, for he had placed himself so that he could see nothing but the sky, and had taken off his silver ears as well as his gold spectacles—what was the use of either when he had no legs with which to walk or run?—up from below there rose a delicious sound.

You have heard it hundreds of times, my children, and so have I. When I was a child I thought there was nothing so sweet; and I think so still. It was just the song of a skylark, mounting higher and higher from the ground, till it came so close that Prince Dolor could distinguish its quivering wings and tiny body, almost too tiny to contain such a gush of music.

"Oh, you beautiful, beautiful bird!" cried he; "I should dearly like to take you in and cuddle you. That is, if I could—if I dared."

But he hesitated. The little brown creature with its loud heavenly voice almost made him afraid. Nevertheless, it also made him happy. And he watched and listened—so absorbed that he forgot all regret and pain, forgot everything in the world except the little lark.

It soared and soared, and he was just wondering if it would soar out of sight, and what in the world he should do when it was gone, when it suddenly closed its wings, as larks do when they mean to drop to the ground. But, instead of dropping to the ground, it dropped right into the little boy's breast.

What felicity! If it would only stay! A tiny, soft thing to fondle and kiss, to sing to him all day long, and be his playfellow and companion, tame and tender, while to the rest of the world it was a wild bird of the air. What a pride, what a delight! To have something that nobody else had—something all his own. As the travelling-cloak travelled on, he little heeded where, and the lark still stayed, nestled down in his bosom, hopped from his hand to his shoulder, and kissed him with its dainty beak, as if it loved him, Prince Dolor forgot all his grief, and was entirely happy.

But when he got in sight of Hopeless Tower a painful thought struck him.

"My pretty bird, what am I to do with you? If I take you into my room and shut you up there, you, a wild skylark of the air, what will become of you? I am used to this, but you are not. You will be so miserable. And suppose my nurse should find you—she who can't bear the sound of singing? Besides, I remember her once telling me that the nicest thing she ever ate in her life was lark-pie!"

The little boy shivered all over at the thought. And, though the merry lark immediately broke into the loudest carol, as if saying derisively that he defied anybody to eat *him*, still Prince Dolor was very uneasy. In another minute he had made up his mind.

"No, my bird, nothing so dreadful shall happen to you if I can help it. I would rather do without you altogether. Yes, I'll try. Fly away, my darling, my beautiful! Good-bye, my merry, merry bird."

Opening his two caressing hands, in which, as if for protection, he had folded it, he let the lark go. It lingered a minute, perching on the rim of the cloak, and looking at him with eyes of almost human tenderness. Then away it flew, far up into the blue sky. It was only a bird.

But some time after, when Prince Dolor had eaten his supper—somewhat drearily, except for the thought that he could not possibly sup off lark-pie now—and gone quietly to bed, the old familiar little bed, where he was accustomed to sleep, or lie awake contentedly thinking—suddenly he heard outside the window a little faint carol—faint but cheerful—cheerful even though it was the middle of the night.

The dear little lark! it had not flown away, after all. And it was truly the most extraordinary bird, for, unlike ordinary larks, it kept hovering about the tower in the silence and darkness of the night, outside the window or over the roof. Whenever he listened for a moment, he heard it singing still.

He went to sleep as happy as a king.

VII

"Happy as a king." How far kings are happy I cannot say, no more than could Prince Dolor, though he had once been a king himself. But he remembered nothing about it, and there was nobody to tell him, except his nurse, who had been forbidden upon pain of death to let him know anything about his dead parents, or the King his uncle, or indeed any part of his own history.

Sometimes he speculated about himself, whether he had had a father and mother as other little boys had, what they had been like, and why he had never seen them. But, knowing nothing about them, he did not miss them—only once or twice, reading pretty stories about little children and their mothers, who helped them when they were in difficulty and comforted them when they were sick, he, feeling ill and dull and lonely, wondered what had become of his mother and why she never came to see him.

Then, in his history lessons, of course, he read about kings and princes, and the governments of different countries, and the events that happened there. And though he but faintly took in all this, still he did take it in a little, and worried his young brain about it, and perplexed his nurse with questions, to which she returned sharp and mysterious answers, which only set him thinking the more.

He had plenty of time for thinking. After his last journey in the travelling-cloak, the journey which had given him so much pain, his desire to see the world somehow faded away. He contented himself with reading his books, and looking out the tower windows, and listening to his beloved little lark, which had come home with him that day, and had never left him again.

True, it kept out of the way; and though his nurse sometimes dimly heard it, and said, "What is that horrid noise outside?" she never got the faintest chance of making it into a lark-pie. Prince Dolor had his pet all to himself, and though he seldom saw it, he knew it was near him, and he caught continually, at odd hours of the day, and even in the night, fragments of its delicious song.

All during the winter—so far as there ever was any difference between summer and winter in Hopeless Tower—the little bird cheered and amused him. He scarcely needed anything more—not even his travelling-cloak, which lay bundled up unnoticed in a corner, tied up in its innumerable knots.

Nor did his godmother come near him. It seemed as if she had given these treasures and left him alone—to use them or lose them, apply them or misapply them, according to his own choice. That is all we can do with children when they grow into big children old enough to distinguish between right and wrong, and too old to be forced to do either.

Prince Dolor was now quite a big boy. Not tall—alas! he never could be that, with his poor little shrunken legs, which were of no use, only an encumbrance. But he was stout and strong, with great sturdy shoulders, and muscular arms, upon which he could swing himself about almost like a monkey. As if in compensation for his useless lower limbs, Nature had given to these extra strength and activity. His face, too, was very handsome. It was thinner, firmer, more manly; but still the sweet face of his childhood— his mother's own face.

How his mother would have liked to look at him! Perhaps she did—who knows?

The boy was not a stupid boy either. He could learn almost anything he chose—and he did choose, which was more than half the battle. He never gave up his lessons till he had learned them all—never thought it a punishment that he had to work at them, and that they cost him a deal of trouble sometimes.

"But," thought he, "men work, and it must be so grand to be a man— a prince too; and I fancy princes work harder than anybody—except kings. The princes I read about generally turn into kings. I wonder—" the boy was always wondering. "Nurse"—and one day he startled her with a sudden question—"tell me—shall I ever be a king?"

The woman stood, perplexed beyond expression. So long a time had passed by since her crime—if it were a crime—and her sentence that she now seldom thought of either. Even her punishment—to be shut up for life in Hopeless Tower—she had gradually got used to. Used also to the little lame Prince, her charge—whom at first she had hated, though she carefully did everything to keep him alive, since upon him her own life hung.

But latterly she had ceased to hate him, and, in a sort of way, almost loved him—at least, enough to be sorry for him—an innocent child, imprisoned here till he grew into an old man, and became a dull, worn-out creature like herself. Sometimes, watching him, she felt more sorry for him than even for herself; and then, seeing she looked a less miserable and ugly woman, he did not shrink from her as usual.

He did not now. "Nurse—dear nurse," said he, "I don't mean to vex you, but tell me—what is a king? Shall I ever be one?"

When she began to think less of herself and more of the child, the woman's courage increased. The idea came to her—what harm would it be, even if he did know his own history? Perhaps he ought to know it—for there had been various ups and downs, usurpations, revolutions, and restorations in Nomansland, as in most other countries. Something might happen—who could tell? Changes might occur. Possibly a crown would even yet be set upon those pretty, fair curls—which she began to think prettier than ever when she saw the imaginary coronet upon them.

She sat down, considering whether her oath, never to "say a word" to Prince Dolor about himself, would be broken if she were to take a pencil and write what was to be told. A mere quibble—a mean, miserable quibble. But then she was a miserable woman, more to be pitied than scorned.

After long doubt, and with great trepidation, she put her fingers to her lips, and taking the Prince's slate—with the sponge tied to it, ready to rub out the writing in a minute—she wrote:

"You are a king."

Prince Dolor started. His face grew pale, and then flushed all over; he held himself erect. Lame as he was, anybody could see he was born to be a king.

"Hush!" said the nurse, as he was beginning to speak. And then, terribly frightened all the while—people who have done wrong always are frightened—she wrote down in a few hurried sentences his history. How his parents had died—his uncle had usurped his throne, and sent him to end his days in this lonely tower.

"I, too," added she, bursting into tears. "Unless, indeed, you could get out into the world, and fight for your rights like a man. And fight for me also, my Prince, that I may not die in this desolate place."

"Poor old nurse!" said the boy compassionately. For somehow, boy as he was, when he heard he was born to be a king, he felt like a man—like a king—who could afford to be tender because he was strong.

He scarcely slept that night, and even though he heard his little lark singing in the sunrise, he barely listened to it. Things more serious and important had taken possession of his mind.

"Suppose," thought he, "I were to do as she says, and go out in the world, no matter how it hurts me—the world of people, active people, as active as that boy I saw. They might only laugh at me—poor helpless creature that I am. But still I might show them I could do something. At any rate, I might go and see if there were anything for me to do. Godmother, help me!"

It was so long since he had asked her help that he was hardly surprised when he got no answer—only the little lark outside the window sang louder and louder, and the sun rose, flooding the room with light.

Prince Dolor sprang out of bed, and began dressing himself, which was hard work, for he was not used to it—he had always been accustomed to depend upon his nurse for everything.

"But I must now learn to be independent," thought he. "Fancy a king being dressed like a baby!"

So he did the best he could—awkwardly but cheerily—and then he leaped to the corner where lay his travelling-cloak, untied it as before, and watched it unrolling itself—which it did rapidly, with a hearty good-will, as if quite tired of idleness. So was Prince Dolor—or felt as if he were. He jumped into the middle of it, said his charm, and was out through the skylight immediately.

"Good-bye, pretty lark!" he shouted, as he passed it on the wing, still warbling its carol to the newly-risen sun. "You have been my pleasure, my delight; now I must go and work. Sing to old nurse till I come back again. Perhaps she'll hear you—perhaps she won't—but it will do her good all the same. Good-bye!"

But, as the cloak hung irresolute in air, he suddenly remembered that he had not determined where to go—indeed, he did not know, and there was nobody to tell him.

"Godmother," he cried, in much perplexity, "you know what I want—at least, I hope you do, for I hardly do myself—take me where I ought to go. Show me whatever I ought to see—never mind what I like to see," as a sudden idea came into his mind that he might see many painful and disagreeable things. But this journey was not for pleasure—as before. He was not a baby now, to do nothing but play—big boys do not always play. Nor men neither—they work. Thus much Prince Dolor knew—though very little more.

As the cloak started off, travelling faster than he had ever known it to do—through sky-land and cloud-land, over freezing mountain-tops, and desolate stretches of forest, and smiling cultivated plains, and great lakes that seemed to him almost as shoreless as the sea—he was often rather frightened. But he crouched down, silent and quiet; what was the use of making a fuss? And, wrapping himself up in his bearskin, he waited for what was to happen.

After some time he heard a murmur in the distance, increasing more and more till it grew like the hum of a gigantic hive of bees. And, stretching his chin over the rim of his cloak, Prince Dolor saw—far, far below him, yet, with his gold spectacles and silver ears on, he could distinctly hear and see—what?

Most of us have some time or other visited a great metropolis—have wandered through its network of streets—lost ourselves in its crowds of people—looked up at its tall rows of houses, its grand public buildings, churches, and squares. Also, perhaps, we have peeped into its miserable little back-alleys, where dirty children play in gutters all day and half the night—where even young boys go about picking pockets, with nobody to tell them it is wrong except the policeman, and he simply takes them off to prison. And all this wretchedness is close behind the grandeur—like the two sides of the leaf of a book.

An awful sight is a large city, seen anyhow, from anywhere. But, suppose you were to see it from the upper air, where, with your eyes and ears open, you could take in everything at once? What would it look like? How would you feel about it? I hardly know myself. Do you?

Prince Dolor had need to be a king—that is, a boy with a kingly nature—to be able to stand such a sight without being utterly overcome. But he was very much bewildered—as bewildered as a blind person who is suddenly made to see.

He gazed down on the city below him, and then put his hand over his eyes.

"I can't bear to look at it, it is so beautiful—so dreadful. And I don't understand it—not one bit. There is nobody to tell me about it. I wish I had somebody to speak to."

"Do you? Then pray speak to me. I was always considered good at conversation."

The voice that squeaked out this reply was an excellent imitation of the human one, though it came only from a bird. No lark this time, however, but a great black-and-white creature that flew into the cloak, and began walking round and round on the edge of it with a dignified stride, one foot before the other, like any unfeathered biped you could name.

"I haven't the honour of your acquaintance, sir," said the boy politely.

"Ma'am, if you please. I am a mother-bird, and my name is Mag, and I shall be happy to tell you everything you want to know. For I know a great deal; and I enjoy talking. My family is of great antiquity. We have built in this palace for hundreds—that is to say, dozens of years. I am intimately acquainted with the King, the Queen, and the little Princes and Princesses—also the maids of honour, and all the inhabitants of the city. I talk a good deal, but I always talk sense, and I dare say I should be exceedingly useful to a poor little ignorant boy like you."

"I am a prince," said the other gently.

"All right. And I am a magpie. You will find me a most respectable bird."

"I have no doubt of it," was the polite answer—though he thought in his own mind that Mag must have a very good opinion of herself. But she was a lady and a stranger, so of course he was civil to her.

She settled herself at his elbow, and began to chatter away, pointing out with one skinny claw, while she balanced herself on the other, every object of interest, evidently believing, as no doubt all its inhabitants did, that there was no capital in the world like the great metropolis of Nomansland.

I have not seen it, and therefore cannot describe it, so we will just take it upon trust, and suppose it to be, like every other fine city, the finest city that ever was built. Mag said so—and of course she knew.

Nevertheless, there were a few things in it which surprised Prince Dolor— and, as he had said, he could not understand them at all. One half the people seemed so happy and busy—hurrying up and down the full streets, or driving lazily along the parks in their grand carriages, while the other half were so wretched and miserable.

"Can't the world be made a little more equal? I would try to do it if I were a king."

"But you're not the King: only a little goose of a boy," returned the magpie loftily. "And I'm here not to explain things, only to show them. Shall I show you the royal palace?"

It was a very magnificent palace. It had terraces and gardens, battlements and towers. It extended over acres of ground, and had in it rooms enough to accommodate half the city. Its windows looked in all directions, but none of them had any particular view—except a small one, high up towards the roof, which looked out on the Beautiful Mountains. But since the Queen died there it had been closed, boarded up, indeed, the magpie said. It was so little and inconvenient that nobody cared to live in it. Besides, the lower apartments, which had no view, were magnificent—worthy of being inhabited by the King.

"I should like to see the King," said Prince Dolor.

VIII

What, I wonder, would be most people's idea of a king? What was Prince Dolor's?

Perhaps a very splendid personage, with a crown on his head and a sceptre in his hand, sitting on a throne and judging the people. Always doing right, and never wrong—"The king can do no wrong" was a law laid down in olden times. Never cross, or tired, or sick, or suffering; perfectly handsome and well-dressed, calm and good-tempered, ready to see and hear everybody, and discourteous to nobody; all things always going well with him, and nothing unpleasant ever happening.

This, probably, was what Prince Dolor expected to see. And what did he see? But I must tell you how he saw it.

"Ah," said the magpie, "no levée to-day. The King is ill, though his Majesty does not wish it to be generally known—it would be so very inconvenient. He can't see you, but perhaps you might like to go and take a look at him in a way I often do? It is so very amusing."

Amusing, indeed!

The Prince was just now too much excited to talk much. Was he not going to see the King his uncle, who had succeeded his father and dethroned himself; had stepped into all the pleasant things that he, Prince Dolor, ought to have had, and shut him up in a desolate tower? What was he like, this great, bad, clever man? Had he got all the things he wanted, which another ought to have had? And did he enjoy them?

"Nobody knows," answered the magpie, just as if she had been sitting inside the Prince's heart, instead of on the top of his shoulder. "He is a king, and that's enough. For the rest, nobody knows."

As she spoke, Mag flew down on to the palace roof, where the cloak had rested, settling down between the great stacks of chimneys as comfortably as if on the ground. She pecked at the tiles with her beak—truly she was a wonderful bird—and immediately a little hole opened, a sort of door, through which could be seen distinctly the chamber below.

"Now look in, my Prince. Make haste, for I must soon shut it up again."

But the boy hesitated. "Isn't it rude?—won't they think us intruding?"

"Oh, dear, no! There's a hole like this in every palace; dozens of holes, indeed. Everybody knows it, but nobody speaks of it. Intrusion! Why, though the royal family are supposed to live shut up behind stone walls ever so thick, all the world knows that they live in a glass house where everybody can see them and throw a stone at them. Now pop down on your knees, and take a peep at his Majesty!"

His Majesty!

The Prince gazed eagerly down into the large room, the largest room he had ever beheld, with furniture and hangings grander than anything he could have ever imagined. A stray sunbeam, coming through a crevice of the darkened windows, struck across the carpet, and it was the loveliest carpet ever woven—just like a bed of flowers to walk over; only nobody walked over it, the room being perfectly empty and silent.

"Where is the King?" asked the puzzled boy.

"There," said Mag, pointing with one wrinkled claw to a magnificent bed, large enough to contain six people. In the centre of it, just visible under the silken counterpane—quite straight and still, with its head on the lace pillow—lay a small figure, something like waxwork, fast asleep—very fast asleep! There were a number of sparkling rings on the tiny yellow hands, that were curled a little, helplessly, like a baby's, outside the coverlet. The eyes were shut, the nose looked sharp and thin, and the long grey beard hid the mouth and lay over the breast. A sight not ugly nor frightening, only solemn and quiet. And so very silent—two little flies buzzing about the curtains of the bed being the only audible sound.

"Is that the King?" whispered Prince Dolor.

"Yes," replied the bird.

He had been angry—furiously angry—ever since he knew how his uncle had taken the crown, and sent him, a poor little helpless child, to be shut up for life, just as if he had been dead. Many times the boy had felt as if, king as he was, he should like to strike him, this great, strong, wicked man.

Why, you might as well have struck a baby! How helpless he lay, with his eyes shut, and his idle hands folded: they had no more work to do, bad or good.

"What is the matter with him?" asked the Prince.

"He is dead," said the magpie, with a croak.

No, there was not the least use in being angry with him now. On the contrary, the Prince felt almost sorry for him, except that he looked so peaceful with all his cares at rest. And this was being dead? So even kings died?

"Well, well, he hadn't an easy life, folk say, for all his grandeur. Perhaps he is glad it is over. Good-bye, your Majesty."

With another cheerful tap of her beak, Mistress Mag shut down the little door in the tiles, and Prince Dolor's first and last sight of his uncle was ended.

He sat in the centre of his travelling-cloak, silent and thoughtful.

"What shall we do now?" said the magpie. "There's nothing much more to be done with his Majesty, except a fine funeral, which I shall certainly go and see. All the world will. He interested the world exceedingly when he was alive, and he ought to do it now he's dead—just once more. And since he can't hear me, I may as well say that, on the whole, his Majesty is much better dead than alive—if we can only get somebody in his place. There'll be such a row in the city presently. Suppose we float up again and see it all—at a safe distance, though. It will be such fun!"

"What will be fun?"

"A revolution."

Whether anybody except a magpie would have called it "fun" I don't know, but it certainly was a remarkable scene.

As soon as the cathedral bell began to toll and the minute guns to fire, announcing to the kingdom that it was without a king, the people gathered in crowds, stopping at street-corners to talk together. The murmur now and then rose into a shout, and the shout into a roar. When Prince Dolor, quietly floating in upper air, caught the sound of their different and opposite cries, it seemed to him as if the whole city had gone mad together.

"Long live the King!" "The King is dead—down with the King!" "Down with the crown, and the King too!" "Hurrah for the republic!" "Hurrah for no government at all!"

Such were the shouts which travelled up to the travelling-cloak. And then began—oh, what a scene!

When you children are grown men and women—or before—you will hear and read in books about what are called revolutions—earnestly I trust that neither I nor you may ever see one. But they have happened, and may happen again, in other countries besides Nomansland, when wicked kings have helped to make their people wicked too, or out of an unrighteous nation have sprung rulers equally bad; or, without either of these causes, when a restless country has fancied any change better than no change at all.

For me, I don't like changes, unless I am pretty sure that they are for good. And how good can come out of absolute evil—the horrible evil that went on this night under Prince Dolor's very eyes—soldiers shooting down people by hundreds in the streets, scaffolds erected, and heads dropping off—houses burnt, and women and children murdered—this is more than I can understand.

But all these things you will find in history, my children, and must by-and-by judge for yourselves the right and wrong of them, as far as anybody ever can judge.

Prince Dolor saw it all. Things happened so fast one after another that they quite confused his faculties.

"Oh, let me go home," he cried at last, stopping his ears and shutting his eyes; "only let me go home!" For even his lonely tower seemed home, and its dreariness and silence absolute paradise after all this.

"Good-bye, then," said the magpie, flapping her wings. She had been chatting incessantly all day and all night, for it was actually thus long that Prince Dolor had been hovering over the city, neither eating nor sleeping, with all these terrible things happening under his very eyes. "You've had enough, I suppose, of seeing the world?"

"Oh, I have—I have!" cried the Prince, with a shudder.

"That is, till next time. All right, your Royal Highness. You don't know me, but I know you. We may meet again sometime."

She looked at him with her clear, piercing eyes, sharp enough to see through everything, and it seemed as if they changed from bird's eyes to human eyes—the very eyes of his godmother, whom he had not seen for ever so long. But the minute afterwards she became only a bird, and with a screech and a chatter, spread her wings and flew away.

Prince Dolor fell into a kind of swoon of utter misery, bewilderment, and exhaustion, and when he awoke he found himself in his own room—alone and quiet—with the dawn just breaking, and the long rim of yellow light in the horizon glimmering through the window-panes.

I X

When Prince Dolor sat up in bed, trying to remember where he was, whither he had been, and what he had seen the day before, he perceived that his room was empty.

Generally his nurse rather worried him by breaking his slumbers, coming in and "setting things to rights," as she called it. Now the dust lay thick upon chairs and tables. There was no harsh voice heard to scold him for not getting up immediately—which, I am sorry to say, this boy did not always do. For he so enjoyed lying still, and thinking lazily about everything or nothing, that, if he had not tried hard to avoid it, he would certainly have become like those celebrated

> Two little men
> Who lay in their bed till the clock struck ten.

It was striking ten now, and still no nurse was to be seen. He was rather relieved at first, for he felt so tired. And besides, when he stretched out his arm, he found to his dismay that he had gone to bed in his clothes.

Very uncomfortable he felt, of course; and just a little frightened. Especially when he began to call and call again, but nobody answered. Often he used to think how nice it would be to get rid of his nurse and live in this tower all by himself—like a sort of monarch, able to do everything he liked, and leave undone all that he did not want to do. But now that this seemed really to have happened, he did not like it at all.

"Nurse—dear nurse—please come back!" he called out. "Come back, and I will be the best boy in all the land."

And when she did not come back, and nothing but silence answered his lamentable call, he very nearly began to cry.

"This won't do," he said at last, dashing the tears from his eyes. "It's just like a baby, and I'm a big boy—shall be a man some day. What has happened? I wonder. I'll go and see."

He sprang out of bed—not to his feet, alas! but to his poor little weak knees, and crawled on them from room to room. All the four chambers were deserted—not forlorn or untidy, for everything seemed to have been done for his comfort—the breakfast and dinner things were laid, the food spread in order. He might live "like a prince," as the proverb is, for several days. But the place was entirely forsaken—there was evidently not a creature but himself in the solitary tower.

A great fear came over the poor boy. Lonely as his life had been, he had never known what it was to be absolutely alone. A kind of despair seized him—no violent anger or terror, but a sort of patient desolation.

"What in the world am I to do?" thought he, and sat down in the middle of the floor, half inclined to believe that it would be better to give up entirely, lay himself down, and die.

This feeling, however, did not last long, for he was young and strong, and, I said before, by nature a very courageous boy. There came into his head, somehow or other, a proverb that his nurse had taught him—the people of Nomansland were very fond of proverbs—

> For every evil under the sun
> There is a remedy, or there's none;
> If there is one, try to find it—
> If there isn't, never mind it.

"I wonder—is there a remedy now, and could I find it?" cried the Prince, jumping up and looking out of the window.

No help there. He saw only the broad, bleak, sunshiny plain—that is, at first. But by-and-by, in the circle of mud that surrounded the base of the tower, he perceived distinctly the marks of a horse's feet, and just in the spot where the deaf-mute was accustomed to tie up his great black charger, while he himself ascended, there lay the remains of a bundle of hay and a feed of corn.

"Yes, that's it. He has come and gone, taking nurse away with him. Poor nurse! how glad she would be to go!"

That was Prince Dolor's first thought. His second—wasn't it natural?—

was a passionate indignation at her cruelty—at the cruelty of all the world towards him, a poor little helpless boy. Then he determined, forsaken as he was, to try and hold on to the last, and not to die as long as he could possibly help it.

Anyhow, it would be easier to die here than out in the world, among the terrible doings which he had just beheld—from the midst of which, it suddenly struck him, the deaf-mute had come, contriving somehow to make the nurse understand that the King was dead, and she need have no fear in going back to the capital, where there was a grand revolution, and everything turned upside down. So, of course, she had gone.

"I hope she'll enjoy it, miserable woman—if they don't cut off her head, too."

And then a kind of remorse smote him for feeling so bitterly towards her, after all the years she had taken care of him—grudgingly, perhaps, and coldly; still she had taken care of him, and that even to the last. For, as I have said, all his four rooms were as tidy as possible, and his meals laid out, that he might have no more trouble than could be helped.

"Possibly she did not mean to be cruel. I won't judge her," said he. And afterwards he was very glad that he had so determined.

For the second time he tried to dress himself, and then to do everything he could for himself—even to sweeping up the hearth and putting on more coals. "It's a funny thing for a prince to have to do," said he, laughing. "But my godmother once said princes need never mind doing anything."

And then he thought a little of his godmother. Not of summoning her, or asking her to help him—she had evidently left him to help himself, and he was determined to try his best to do it, being a very proud and independent boy—but he remembered her tenderly and regretfully, as if even she had been a little hard upon him—poor, forlorn boy that he was. But he seemed to have seen and learned so much within the last few days that he scarcely felt like a boy, but a man—until he went to bed at night.

When I was a child, I used often to think how nice it would be to live in a little house all by my own self—a house built high up in a tree, or far away in a forest, or half-way up a hill-side—so deliciously alone and independent. Not a lesson to learn—but no! I always liked learning my lessons. Anyhow, to choose the lessons I liked best, to have as many books to read and dolls to play with as ever I wanted: above all, to be free and at rest, with nobody to tease or trouble or scold me, would be charming. For I was a lonely little thing, who liked quietness—as many children do; which other children, and sometimes grown-up people even, cannot always understand. And so I can understand Prince Dolor.

After his first despair, he was not merely comfortable, but actually happy in his solitude, doing everything for himself, and enjoying everything by himself—until bedtime. Then he did not like it at all. No more, I suppose, than other children would have liked my imaginary house in a tree when they had had sufficient of their own company.

But the Prince had to bear it—and he did bear it, like a prince—for fully five days. All that time he got up in the morning and went to bed at night without having spoken to a creature, or, indeed, having heard a single sound. For even his little lark was silent. And as for his travelling-cloak, either he never thought about it, or else it had been spirited away—for he made no use of it, nor attempted to do so.

A very strange existence it was, those five lonely days. He never entirely forgot it. It threw him back upon himself, and into himself—in a way that all of us have to learn when we grow up, and are the better for it; but it is somewhat hard learning.

On the sixth day Prince Dolor had a strange composure in his look, but he was very grave and thin and white. He had nearly come to the end of his provisions—and what was to happen next? Get out of the tower he could not. The ladder the deaf-mute used was always carried away again; and if it had not been, how could the poor boy have used it? And even if he slung or flung himself down, and by miraculous chance came alive to the foot of the tower, how could he run away?

Fate had been very hard on him, or so it seemed.

He made up his mind to die. Not that he wished to die. On the contrary, there was a great deal that he wished to live to do; but if he must die, he must. Dying did not seem so very dreadful; not even to lie quiet like his uncle, whom he had entirely forgiven now, and never be miserable or naughty any more, and escape all those horrible things that he had seen going on outside the palace, in that awful place which was called "the world."

"It's a great deal nicer here," said the poor little Prince, and collected all his pretty things round him: his favourite pictures, which he thought he should like to have near him when he died; his books and toys—no, he had ceased to care for toys now; he only liked them because he had done so as a child. And there he sat very calm and patient, like a king in his castle, waiting for the end.

"Still, I wish I had done something first—something worth doing, that someody might remember me by," thought he. "Suppose I had grown a man, and had had work to do, and people to care for, and was so useful and busy that they liked me, and perhaps even forgot I was lame? Then it would have been nice to live, I think."

A tear came into the little fellow's eyes, and he listened intently through the dead silence for some hopeful sound.

Was there one?—was it his little lark, whom he had almost forgotten? No, nothing half so sweet. But it really was something—something which came nearer and nearer, so that there was no mistaking it. It was the sound of a trumpet, one of the great silver trumpets so admired in Nomansland. Not pleasant music, but very bold, grand, and inspiring.

As he listened to it the boy seemed to recall many things which had slipped his memory for years, and to nerve himself for whatever might be going to happen.

What had happened was this.

The poor condemned woman had not been such a wicked woman after all. Perhaps her courage was not wholly disinterested, but she had done a very heroic thing. As soon as she heard of the death and burial of the King and of the changes that were taking place in the country, a daring idea came into her head—to set upon the throne of Nomansland its rightful heir. Thereupon she persuaded the deaf-mute to take her away with him, and they galloped like the wind from city to city, spreading everywhere the news that Prince Dolor's death and burial had been an invention concocted by his wicked uncle—that he was alive and well, and the noblest young Prince that ever was born.

It was a bold stroke, but it succeeded. The country, weary perhaps of the late King's harsh rule, and yet glad to save itself from the horrors of the last few days, and the still further horrors of no rule at all, and having no particular interest in the other young Princes, jumped at the idea of this Prince, who was the son of their late good King and the beloved Queen Dolorez.

"Hurrah for Prince Dolor! Let Prince Dolor be our sovereign!" rang from end to end of the kingdom. Everybody tried to remember what a dear baby he once was—how like his mother, who had been so sweet and kind, and his father, the finest-looking king that ever reigned. Nobody remembered his lameness—or, if they did, they passed it over as a matter of no consequence. They were determined to have him reign over them, boy as he was—perhaps just because he was a boy, since in that case the great nobles thought they should be able to do as they liked with the country.

Accordingly, with a fickleness not confined to the people of Nomansland, no sooner was the late King laid in his grave than they pronounced him to have been a usurper; turned all his family out of the palace, and left it empty for the reception of the new sovereign, whom they went to fetch with great rejoicing, a select body of lords, gentlemen, and soldiers travelling night and day in solemn procession through the country until they reached Hopeless Tower.

There they found the Prince, sitting calmly on the floor—deadly pale, indeed, for he expected a quite different end from this, and was resolved, if he had to die, to die courageously, like a prince and a king.

But when they hailed him as Prince and King, and explained to him how matters stood, and went down on their knees before him, offering the crown (on a velvet cushion, with four golden tassels, each nearly as big as his head)—small though he was and lame, which lameness the courtiers pretended not to notice—there came such a glow into his face, such a dignity into his demeanour, that he became beautiful, king-like.

"Yes," he said, "if you desire it, I will be your king. And I will do my best to make my people happy."

Then there arose, from inside and outside the tower, such a shout as never yet was heard across the lonely plain.

Prince Dolor shrank a little from the deafening sound. "How shall I be able to rule all this great people? You forget, my lords, that I am only a little boy still."

"Not so very little," was the respectful answer. "We have searched in the records, and found that your Royal Highness—your Majesty, I mean—is fifteen years old."

"Am I?" said Prince Dolor; and his first thought was a thoroughly childish pleasure that he should now have a birthday, with a whole nation to keep it. Then he remembered that his childish days were done. He was a monarch now. Even his nurse, to whom, the moment he saw her, he had held out his hand, kissed it reverently, and called him ceremoniously "his Majesty the King."

"A king must be always a king, I suppose," said he half sadly, when, the ceremonies over, he had been left to himself for just ten minutes, to put off his boy's clothes and be reattired in magnificent robes, before he was conveyed away from his tower to the royal palace.

He could take nothing with him; indeed, he soon saw that, however politely they spoke, they would not allow him to take anything. If he was to be their king, he must give up his old life for ever. So he looked with tender farewell on his old books, old toys, the furniture he knew so well, and the familiar plain in all its levelness—ugly yet pleasant, simply because it was familiar.

"It will be a new life in a new world," said he to himself; "but I'll remember the old things still. And, oh! if before I go I could but once see my dear old godmother."

While he spoke he had laid himself down on the bed for a minute or two, rather tired with his grandeur, and confused by the noise of the trumpets which kept playing incessantly down below. He gazed, half sadly, up to the skylight, whence there came pouring a stream of sun-rays, with innumerable motes floating there, like a bridge thrown between heaven and earth. Sliding down it, as if she had been made of air, came the little old woman in grey.

So beautiful looked she—old as she was—that Prince Dolor was at first quite startled by the apparition. Then he held out his arms in eager delight.

"Oh, godmother, you have not forsaken me!"

"Not at all, my son. You may not have seen me, but I have seen you many a time."

"How?"

"Oh, never mind. I can turn into anything I please, you know. And I have been a bear-skin rug, and a crystal goblet—and sometimes I have changed from inanimate to animate nature, put on feathers, and made myself very comfortable as a bird."

"Ha!" laughed the Prince, a new light breaking in upon him as he caught the infection of her tone, lively and mischievous. "Ha! ha! a lark, for instance?"

"Or a magpie," answered she, with a capital imitation of Mistress Mag's croaky voice. "Do you suppose I am always sentimental, and never funny? If anything makes you happy, gay, or grave, don't you think it is more than likely to come through your old godmother?"

"I believe that," said the boy tenderly, holding out his arms. They clasped one another in a close embrace.

Suddenly Prince Dolor looked very anxious. "You will not leave me now that I am a king? Otherwise I had rather not be a king at all. Promise never to forsake me!"

The little old woman laughed gaily. "Forsake you? that is impossible. But it is just possible you may forsake me. Not probable though. Your mother never did, and she was a queen. The sweetest queen in all the world was the Lady Dolorez."

"Tell me about her," said the boy eagerly. "As I get older I think I can understand more. Do tell me."

"Not now. You couldn't hear me for the trumpets and the shouting. But when you are come to the palace, ask for a long-closed upper room, which looks out upon the Beautiful Mountains. Open it and take it for your own. Whenever you go there you will always find me, and we will talk together about all sorts of things."

"And about my mother?"

The little old woman nodded—and kept nodding and smiling to herself many times, as the boy repeated over and over again the sweet words he had never known or understood—"my mother—my mother."

"Now I must go," said she, as the trumpets blared louder and louder, and the shouts of the people showed that they would not endure any delay. "Good-bye, good-bye! Open the window and out I fly."

Prince Dolor repeated gaily the musical rhyme—but all the while tried to hold his godmother fast.

Vain, vain! for the moment that a knocking was heard at his door the sun went behind a cloud, the bright stream of dancing motes vanished, and the little old woman with them—he knew not where.

So Prince Dolor quitted his tower—which he had entered so mournfully and ignominiously as a little helpless baby carried in the deaf-mute's arms—quitted it as the great King of Nomansland.

The only thing he took away with him was something so insignificant that none of the lords, gentlemen, and soldiers who escorted him with such triumphant splendour could possibly notice it—a tiny bundle, which he had found lying on the floor just where the bridge of sunbeams had rested. At once he had pounced upon it, and thrust it secretly into his bosom, where it dwindled into such small proportions that it might have been taken for a mere chest-comforter—a bit of flannel—or an old pocket-handkerchief.

It was his travelling-cloak!

X

Did Prince Dolor become a great king? Was he, though little more than a boy, "the father of his people," as all kings ought to be? Did his reign last long—long and happy? And what were the principal events of it, as chronicled in the history of Nomansland?

Why, if I were to answer all these questions I should have to write another book. And I'm tired, children; tired—as grown-up people sometimes are, though not always with play. (Besides, I have a small person belonging to me, who, though she likes extremely to listen to the word-of-mouth story of this book, grumbles much at the writing of it, and has run about the house clapping her hands with joy when mamma told her that it was nearly finished. But that is neither here nor there.)

I have related as well as I could the history of Prince Dolor, but with the history of Nomansland I am as yet unacquainted. If anybody knows it, perhaps he or she will kindly write it all down in another book. But mine is done.

However, of this I am sure, that Prince Dolor made an excellent king.

Nobody ever does anything less well, not even the commonest duty of common daily life, for having such a godmother as the little old woman clothed in grey, whose name is—well, I leave you to guess. Nor, I think, is anybody less good, less capable of both work and enjoyment in after life, for having been a little unhappy in his youth, as the Prince had been.

I cannot take upon myself to say that he was always happy now—who is?—or that he had no cares; just show me the person who is quite free from them! But whenever people worried and bothered him—as they did sometimes, with state etiquette, state squabbles, and the like, setting up themselves and pulling down their neighbours—he would take refuge in that upper room which looked out on the Beautiful Mountains, and, laying his head on his godmother's shoulder, become calmed and at rest.

Also, she helped him out of any difficulty which now and then occurred—for there never was such a wise old woman. When the people of Nomansland raised the alarm—as sometimes they did—for what people can exist without a little fault-finding?—and began to cry out, "Unhappy is the nation whose king is a child," she would say to him gently, "You are a child. Accept the fact. Be humble—be teachable. Lean upon the wisdom of others till you have gained your own."

He did so. He learned how to take advice before attempting to give it, to obey before he could righteously command. He assembled round him all the good and wise of his kingdom—laid all its affairs before them, and was guided by their opinions until he had maturely formed his own.

This he did, sooner than anybody would have imagined who did not know of his godmother and his travelling-cloak—two secret blessings, which, though many guessed at, nobody quite understood. Nor did they understand why he loved so the little upper room, except that it had been his mother's room, in the window of which, as people remembered now, she had used to sit for hours watching the Beautiful Mountains.

Out of that window he used to fly—not very often. As he grew older, the labours of state prevented the frequent use of his travelling-cloak; still he did use it sometimes. Only now it was less for his own pleasure and amusement than to see something or investigate something for the good of the country. But he prized his godmother's gift as dearly as ever. It was a comfort to him in all his vexations, an enhancement of all his joys. It made him almost forget his lameness—which was never cured.

However, the cruel things which had been once foreboded of him did not happen. His misfortune was not such a heavy one, after all. It proved to be of much less inconvenience, even to himself, than had been feared. A council of eminent surgeons and mechanicians invented for him a wonderful pair of

crutches, with the help of which, though he never walked easily or gracefully, he did manage to walk so as to be quite independent. And such was the love his people bore him that they never heard the sound of his crutches on the marble palace floors without a leap of the heart, for they knew that good was coming to them whenever he approached.

Thus, though he never walked in processions, never reviewed his troops mounted on a magnificent charger, nor did any of the things which make a show monarch so much appreciated, he was able to perform all the duties and to enjoy a great many of the pleasures of his rank. When he held his levees, not standing, but seated on a throne ingeniously contrived to hide his infirmity, the people thronged to greet him. When he drove out through the city streets, shouts followed him wherever he went—every countenance brightened as he passed, and his own, perhaps, was the brightest of all.

First, because, accepting his affliction as inevitable, he took it patiently; second, because, being a brave man, he bore it bravely, trying to forget himself, and live out of himself, and in and for other people. Therefore other people grew to love him so well that I think hundreds of his subjects might have been found who were almost ready to die for their poor lame King.

He never gave them a queen. When they implored him to choose one, he replied that his country was his bride, and he desired no other. But perhaps the real reason was that he shrank from any change; and that no wife in all the world would have been found so perfect, so lovable, so tender to him in all his weaknesses, as his beautiful old godmother.

His four-and-twenty other godfathers and godmothers, or as many of them as were still alive, crowded round him as soon as he ascended the throne. He was very civil to them all, but adopted none of the names they had given him, keeping to the one by which he had been always known, though it had now almost lost its meaning; for King Dolor was one of the happiest and cheerfullest men alive.

He did a good many things, however, unlike most men and most kings, which a little astonished his subjects. First, he pardoned the condemned woman who had been his nurse, and ordained that from henceforth there should be no such thing as the punishment of death in Nomansland. All capital criminals were to be sent to perpetual imprisonment in Hopeless Tower and the plain round about it, where they could do no harm to anybody, and might in time do a little good, as the woman had done.

Another surprise he shortly afterwards gave the nation. He recalled his uncle's family, who had fled away in terror to another country, and restored them to all their honours. By-and-by he chose the eldest son of his eldest cousin (who had been dead a year), and had him educated in the royal palace, as the heir to the throne. This little prince was a quiet, unobtrusive boy, so that everybody wondered at the King's choosing him when there were so many more. But as he grew into a fine young fellow, good and brave, they agreed that the King had judged more wisely than they.

"Not a lame prince, either," his Majesty observed one day, watching him affectionately. For he was the best runner, the highest leaper, the keenest and most active sportsman in the country. "One cannot make oneself, but one can sometimes help a little in the making of somebody else. It is well."

This was said, not to any of his great lords and ladies, but to a good old woman—his first homely nurse—whom he had sought for far and wide, and at last found in her cottage among the Beautiful Mountains. He sent for her to visit him once a year, and treated her with great honour until she died. He was equally kind, though somewhat less tender, to his other nurse, who, after receiving his pardon, returned to her native town and grew into a great lady, and I hope a good one. But as she was so grand a personage now, any little faults she had did not show.

Thus King Dolor's reign passed year after year, long and prosperous. Whether he was happy—"as happy as a king"—is a question no human being can decide. But I think he was, because he had the power of making everybody about him happy, and did it too; also because he was his god-mother's godson, and could shut himself up with her whenever he liked, in that quiet little room in view of the Beautiful Mountains, which nobody else ever saw or cared to see. They were too far-off, and the city lay so low. But there they were, all the time. No change ever came to them; and I think, at any day throughout his long reign, the King would sooner have lost his crown than have lost sight of the Beautiful Mountains.

In course of time, when the little Prince his cousin was grown into a tall young man, capable of all the duties of a man, his Majesty did one of the most extraordinary acts ever known in a sovereign beloved by his people and prosperous in his reign. He announced that he wished to invest his heir with the royal purple—at any rate, for a time—while he himself went away on a distant journey, whither he had long desired to go.

Everybody marvelled, but nobody opposed him. Who could oppose the good King, who was not a young king now? And besides, the nation had a great admiration for the young Regent—and possibly, a lurking pleasure in change.

So there was fixed a day when all the people whom it would hold assembled in the great square of the capital, to see the young Prince installed solemnly in his new duties, and undertaking his new vows. He was a very fine young fellow; tall and straight as a poplar-tree, with a frank, handsome face—a great deal handsomer than the King's, some people said, but others thought differently. However, as his Majesty sat on his throne, with his grey hair falling from underneath his crown, and a few wrinkles showing in spite of his smile, there was something about his countenance which made his people, even while they shouted, regard him with a tenderness mixed with awe.

He lifted up his thin, slender hand, and there came a silence over the vast crowd immediately. Then he spoke, in his own accustomed way, using no grand words, but saying what he had to say in the simplest fashion, though with a clearness that struck their ears like the first song of a bird in the dusk of the morning.

"My people, I am tired; I want to rest. I have had a long reign, and done much work—at least, as much as I was able to do. Many might have done it better than I—but none with a better will. Now I leave it to others; I am tired, very tired. Let me go home."

There arose a murmur—of content or discontent none could well tell; then it died down again, and the assembly listened silently once more.

"I am not anxious about you, my people—my children," continued the King. "You are prosperous and at peace. I leave you in good hands. The Prince Regent will be a fitter king for you than I."

"No, no, no!" rose the universal shout—and those who had sometimes found fault with him shouted louder than anybody. But he seemed as if he heard them not.

"Yes, yes," said he, as soon as the tumult had a little subsided; and his voice sounded firm and clear. Some very old people, who boasted of having seen him as a child, declared that his face took a sudden change, and grew as young and sweet as that of the little Prince Dolor. "Yes, I must go. It is time for me to go. Remember me sometimes, my people, for I have loved you well. And I am going a long way, and I do not think I shall come back any more."

He drew a little bundle out of his breast-pocket—a bundle that nobody had ever seen before. It was small and shabby-looking, and tied up with many knots, which untied themselves in an instant. With a joyful countenance, he muttered over it a few half-intelligible words. Then, so suddenly that even those nearest to his Majesty could not tell how it came about, the King was away—away—floating right up in the air—upon something, they knew not what, except that it appeared to be as safe and pleasant as the wings of a bird.

And after him sprang a bird—a dear little lark, rising from whence no one could say, since larks do not usually build their nests on the pavement of city squares. But there is was, a real lark, singing far over their heads, louder and clearer and more joyful as it vanished farther into the blue sky.

Shading their eyes, and straining their ears, the astonished people stood until the whole vision disappeared like a speck in the clouds—the rosy clouds that overhung the Beautiful Mountains.

King Dolor was never again beheld or heard of in his own country. But the good he had done there lasted for years and years. He was long missed and deeply mourned—at least, so far as anybody could mourn one who was gone on such a happy journey.

Whither he went, or who went with him, it is impossible to say. But I myself believe that his godmother took him, on his travelling-cloak, to the Beautiful Mountains. What he did there, or where he is now, who can tell? I cannot. But one thing I am quite sure of, that, wherever he is, he is perfectly happy.

And so, when I think of him, am I.

1875

Goblin Market

CHRISTINA ROSSETTI

Morning and evening
Maids heard the goblins cry:
"Come buy our orchard fruits,
Come buy, come buy:
Apples and quinces,
Lemons and oranges,
Plump unpecked cherries,
Melons and raspberries,
Bloom-down-cheeked peaches,
Swart-headed mulberries,
Wild free-born cranberries,
Crab-apples, dewberries,
Pine-apples, blackberries,
Apricots, strawberries;—
All ripe together
In summer weather,—
Morns that pass by,
Fair eves that fly;
Come buy, come buy:
Our grapes fresh from the vine,
Pomegranates full and fine,
Dates and sharp bullaces,
Rare pears and greengages,
Damsons and bilberries,
Taste them and try:
Currants and gooseberries,
Bright-fire-like barberries,
Figs to fill your mouth,

Citrons from the South
Sweet to tongue and sound to eye;
Come buy, come buy."

Evening by evening
Among the brookside rushes,
Laura bowed her head to hear,
Lizzie veiled her blushes:
Crouching close together
In the cooling weather,
With clasping arms and cautioning lips,
With tingling cheeks and finger tips.
"Lie close," Laura said,
Pricking up her golden head:
"We must not look at goblin men,
We must not buy their fruits:
Who knows upon what soil they fed
Their hungry thirsty roots?"
"Come buy," call the goblins
Hobbling down the glen.
"Oh," cried Lizzie, "Laura, Laura,
You should not peep at goblin men."
Lizzie covered up her eyes,
Covered close lest they should look;
Laura reared her glossy head,
And whispered like the restless brook:
"Look, Lizzie, look, Lizzie,
Down the glen tramp little men.
One hauls a basket,
One bears a plate,
One lugs a golden dish
Of many pounds weight.
How fair the vine must grow
Whose grapes are so luscious;
How warm the wind must blow
Through those fruit bushes."
"No," said Lizzie: "No, no, no;
Their offers should not charm us,
Their evil gifts would harm us."
She thrust a dimpled finger

In each ear, shut eyes and ran:
Curious Laura chose to linger
Wondering at each merchant man.
One had a cat's face,
One whisked a tail,
One tramped at a rat's pace,
One crawled like a snail,
One like a wombat prowled obtuse and furry,
One like a ratel tumbled hurry skurry.
She heard a voice like voice of doves
Cooing all together:
They sounded kind and full of loves
In the pleasant weather.

Laura stretched her gleaming neck
Like a rush-imbedded swan,
Like a lily from the beck,
Like a moonlit poplar branch,
Like a vessel at the launch
When its last restraint is gone.

Backwards up the mossy glen
Turned and trooped the goblin men,
With their shrill repeated cry,
"Come buy, come buy."
When they reached where Laura was
They stood stock still upon the moss,
Leering at each other,
Brother with queer brother;
Signalling each other,
Brother with sly brother.
One set his basket down,
One reared his plate;
One began to weave a crown
Of tendrils, leaves, and rough nuts brown
(Men sell not such in any town);
One heaved the golden weight
Of dish and fruit to offer her:
"Come buy, come buy," was still their cry.
Laura stared but did not stir,

Longed but had no money:
The whisk-tailed merchant bade her taste
In tones as smooth as honey,
The cat-faced purr'd,
The rat-paced spoke a word
Of welcome, and the snail-paced even was heard;
One parrot-voiced and jolly
Cried "Pretty Goblin" still for "Pretty Polly";—
One whistled like a bird.

But sweet-tooth Laura spoke in haste:
"Good folk, I have no coin;
To take were to purloin:
I have no copper in my purse,
I have no silver either,
And all my gold is on the furze
That shakes in windy weather
Above the rusty heather."
"You have much gold upon your head,"
They answered all together:
"Buy from us with a golden curl."
She clipped a precious golden lock,
She dropped a tear more rare than pearl,
Then sucked their fruit globes fair or red:
Sweeter than honey from the rock,
Stronger than man-rejoicing wine,
Clearer than water flowed that juice;
She never tasted such before,
How should it cloy with length of use?
She sucked and sucked and sucked the more
Fruits which that unknown orchard bore;
She sucked until her lips were sore;
Then flung the emptied rinds away
But gathered up one kernel-stone,
And knew not was it night or day
As she turned home alone.

Lizzie met her at the gate
Full of wise upbraidings:
"Dear, you should not stay so late,

Goblin Market

Twilight is not good for maidens;
Should not loiter in the glen
In the haunts of goblin men.
Do you not remember Jeanie,
How she met them in the moonlight,
Took their gifts both choice and many,
Ate their fruits and wore their flowers
Plucked from bowers
Where summer ripens at all hours?
But ever in the moonlight
She pined and pined away;
Sought them by night and day,
Found them no more but dwindled and grew grey;
Then fell with the first snow,
While to this day no grass will grow
Where she lies low:
I planted daisies there a year ago
That never blow.
You should not loiter so."
"Nay, hush," said Laura.
"Nay, hush, my sister:
I ate and ate my fill,
Yet my mouth waters still;
To-morrow night I will
Buy more": and kissed her:
"Have done with sorrow;
I'll bring you plums to-morrow
Fresh on their mother twigs,
Cherries worth getting;
You cannot think what figs
My teeth have met in,
What melons icy-cold
Piled on a dish of gold
Too huge for me to hold,
What peaches with a velvet nap,
Pellucid grapes without one seed:
Odorous indeed must be the mead
Whereon they grow, and pure the wave they drink
With lilies at the brink,
And sugar-sweet their sap."

Golden head by golden head,
Like two pigeons in one nest
Folded in each other's wings,
They lay down in their curtained bed:
Like two blossoms on one stem,
Like two flakes of new-fall's snow,
Like two wands of ivory
Tipped with gold for awful kings.
Moon and stars gazed in at them,
Wind sang to them lullaby,
Lumbering owls forbore to fly,
Not a bat flapped to and fro
Round their rest:
Cheek to cheek and breast to breast
Locked together in one nest.

Early in the morning
When the first cock crowed his warning,
Neat like bees, as sweet and busy,
Laura rose with Lizzie:
Fetched in honey, milked the cows,
Aired and set to rights the house,
Kneaded cakes of whitest wheat,
Cakes for dainty mouths to eat,
Next churned butter, whipped up cream,

Fed their poultry, sat and sewed;
Talked as modest maidens should:
Lizzie with an open heart,
Laura in an absent dream,
One content, one sick in part;
One warbling for the mere bright day's delight,
One longing for the night.

At length slow evening came:
They went with pitchers to the reedy brook;
Lizzie most placid in her look,
Laura most like a leaping flame.
They drew the gurgling water from its deep;
Lizzie plucked purple and rich golden flags,
Then turning homeward said: "The sunset flushes
Those furthest loftiest crags;
Come, Laura, not another maiden lags,
No wilful squirrel wags,
The beasts and birds are fast asleep."

But Laura loitered still among the rushes
And said the bank was steep,
And said the hour was early still,
The dew not fall'n, the wind not chill:
Listening ever, but not catching
The customary cry,
"Come buy, come buy,"
With its iterated jingle
Of sugar-baited words:
Not for all her watching
Once discerning even one goblin
Racing, whisking, tumbling, hobbling;
Let alone the herds
That used to tramp along the glen,
In groups or single,
Of brisk fruit-merchant men.

Till Lizzie urged, "O Laura, come;
I hear the fruit-call but I dare not look:
You should not loiter longer at this brook:
Come with me home

The stars rise, the moon bends her arc,
Each glow-worm winks her spark,
Let us get home before the night grows dark:
For clouds may gather
Though this is summer weather,
Put out the lights and drench us through;
Then if we lost our way what should we do?"

   Laura turned cold as stone
To find her sister heard that cry alone,
That goblin cry,
"Come buy our fruits, come buy."
Must she then buy no more such dainty fruits?
Must she no more that succous pasture find,
Gone deaf and blind?
Her tree of life drooped from the root:
She said not one word in her heart's sore ache;
But peering thro' the dimness, nought discerning,
Trudged home, her pitcher dripping all the way;
So crept to bed, and lay
Silent till Lizzie slept;
Then sat up in a passionate yearning,
And gnashed her teeth for baulked desire, and wept
As if her heart would break.

   Day after day, night after night,
Laura kept watch in vain
In sullen silence of exceeding pain.
She never caught again the goblin cry:
"Come buy, come buy";—
She never spied the goblin men
Hawking their fruits along the glen:
But when the noon waxed bright
Her hair grew thin and grey;
She dwindled, as the fair full moon doth turn
To swift decay and burn
Her fire away.

   One day remembering her kernel-stone
She set it by a wall that faced the south;
Dewed it with tears, hoped for a root,

Watched for a waxing shoot,
But there came none;
It never saw the sun,
It never felt the trickling moisture run:
While with sunk eyes and faded mouth
She dreamed of melons, as a traveller sees
False waves in desert drouth
With shade of leaf-crowned trees,
And burns the thirstier in the sandful breeze.

She no more swept the house,
Tended the fowls or cows,
Fetched honey, kneaded cakes of wheat,
Brought water from the brook:
But sat down listless in the chimney-nook
And would not eat.

Tender Lizzie could not bear
To watch her sister's cankerous care
Yet not to share.
She night and morning
Caught the goblins' cry:
"Come buy our orchard fruits,
Come buy, come buy":—
Beside the brook, along the glen,
She heard the tramp of goblin men,
The voice and stir
Poor Laura could not hear;
Longed to buy fruit to comfort her,
But feared to pay too dear.
She thought of Jeanie in her grave,
Who should have been a bride;
But who for joys brides hope to have
Fell sick and died
In her gay prime,
In earliest Winter time,
With the first glazing rime,
With the first snow-fall of crisp Winter time.

Till Laura dwindling
Seemed knocking at Death's door:

Then Lizzie weighed no more
Better and worse;
But put a silver penny in her purse,
Kissed Laura, crossed the heath with clumps of furze
At twilight, halted by the brook:
And for the first time in her life
Began to listen and look.

Laughed every goblin
When they spied her peeping:
Came towards her hobbling,
Flying, running, leaping,
Puffing and blowing,
Chuckling, clapping, crowing,
Clucking and gobbling,
Mopping and mowing,
Full of airs and graces,
Pulling wry faces,
Demure grimaces,
Cat-like and rat-like,
Ratel- and wombat-like,
Snail-paced in a hurry,
Parrot-voiced and whistler,
Helter skelter, hurry skurry,
Chattering like magpies,
Fluttering like pigeons,
Gliding like fishes—
Hugged her and kissed her,
Squeezed and caressed her:
Stretched up their dishes,
Panniers, and plates:
"Look at our apples
Russet and dun,
Bob at our cherries,
Bite at our peaches,
Citrons and dates,
Grapes for the asking,
Pears red with basking
Out in the sun,
Plums on their twigs;

Pluck them and suck them,
Pomegranates, figs."—

  "Good folk," said Lizzie,
Mindful of Jeanie:
"Give me much and many":—
Held out her apron,
Tossed them her penny.
"Nay, take a seat with us,
Honour and eat with us,"
They answered grinning:
"Our feast is but beginning.
Night yet is early,
Warm and dew-pearly,
Wakeful and starry:
Such fruits as these
No man can carry;
Half their bloom would fly,
Half their dew would dry,
Half their flavour would pass by.
Sit down and feast with us,
Be welcome guest with us,
Cheer you and rest with us."—
"Thank you," said Lizzie: "But one waits
At home alone for me:
So without further parleying,
If you will not sell me any
Of your fruits though much and many,
Give me back my silver penny
I tossed you for a fee."—
They began to scratch their pates,
No longer wagging, purring,
But visibly demurring,
Grunting and snarling.
One called her proud,
Cross-grained, uncivil;
Their tones waxed loud,
Their looks were evil.
Lashing their tails
They trod and hustled her,

Elbowed and jostled her,
Clawed with their nails,
Barking, mewing, hissing, mocking,
Tore her gown and soiled her stocking,
Twitched her hair out by the roots,
Stamped upon her tender feet,
Held her hands and squeezed their fruits
Against her mouth to make her eat.

White and golden Lizzie stood,
Like a lily in a flood,—
Like a rock of blue-veined stone
Lashed by tides obstreperously,—
Like a beacon left alone
In a hoary roaring sea,
Sending up a golden fire,—
Like a fruit-crowned orange-tree
White with blossoms honey-sweet
Sore beset by wasp and bee,—
Like a royal virgin town
Topped with gilded dome and spire
Close beleaguered by a fleet
Mad to tug her standard down.

One may lead a horse to water,
Twenty cannot make him drink.
Though the goblins cuffed and caught her,
Coaxed and fought her,
Bullied and besought her,
Scratched her, pinched her black as ink,
Kicked and knocked her,
Mauled and mocked her,
Lizzie uttered not a word;
Would not open lip from lip
Lest they should cram a mouthful in:
But laughed in heart to feel the drip
Of juice that syrupped all her face,
And lodged in dimples of her chin,
And streaked her neck which quaked like curd.
At last the evil people
Worn out by her resistance

Flung back her penny, kicked their fruit
Along whichever road they took,
Not leaving root or stone or shoot;
Some writhed into the ground,
Some dived into the brook
With ring and ripple,
Some scudded on the gale without a sound,
Some vanished in the distance.

   In a smart, ache, tingle,
Lizzie went her way;
Knew not was it night or day;
Sprang up the bank, tore thro' the furze,
Threaded copse and dingle,
And heard her penny jingle
Bouncing in her purse,—
Its bounce was music to her ear.
She ran and ran
As if she feared some goblin man
Dogged her with gibe or curse
Or something worse:
But not one goblin skurried after,
Nor was she pricked by fear;
The kind heart made her windy-paced
That urged her home quite out of breath with haste
And inward laughter.

   She cried "Laura," up the garden,
"Did you miss me?
Come and kiss me.
Never mind my bruises,
Hug me, kiss me, suck my juices
Squeezed from goblin fruits for you,
Goblin pulp and goblin dew.
Eat me, drink me, love me;
Laura, make much of me:
For your sake I have braved the glen
And had to do with goblin merchant men."

   Laura started from her chair,
flung her arms up in the air,

Clutched her hair:
"Lizzie, Lizzie, have you tasted
For my sake the fruit forbidden?
Must your light like mine be hidden,
Your young life like mine be wasted,
Undone in mine undoing
And ruined in my ruin,
Thirsty, cankered, goblin-ridden?"—
She clung about her sister,
Kissed and kissed and kissed her:
Tears once again
Refreshed her shrunken eyes,
Dropping like rain
After long sultry drouth;
Shaking with aguish fear, and pain,
She kissed and kissed her with a hungry mouth.

Her lips began to scorch,
The juice was wormwood to her tongue,
She loathed the feast:
Writhing as one possessed she leaped and sung,
Rent all her robe, and wrung
Her hands in lamentable haste,
And beat her breast.
Her locks streamed like the torch
Borne by a racer at full speed,
Or like the mane of horses in their flight,
Or like an eagle when she stems the light
Straight toward the sun,
Or like a caged thing freed,
Or like a flying flag when armies run.

Swift fire spread through her veins, knocked at her heart.
Met the fire smouldering there
And overbore its lesser flame;
She gorged on bitterness without a name:
Ah! fool, to choose such part
Of soul-consuming care!
Sense failed in the mortal strife:
Like the watch-tower of a town

Which an earthquake shatters down,
Like a lightning-stricken mast,
Like a wind-uprooted tree
Spun about,
Like a foam-topped waterspout
Cast down headlong in the sea,
She fell at last;
Pleasure past and anguish past,
Is it death or is it life?

Life out of death.
That night long Lizzie watched by her,
Counted her pulse's flagging stir,
Felt for her breath,
Held water to her lips, and cooled her face
With tears and fanning leaves:
But when the first birds chirped about their eaves,
And early reapers plodded to the place
Of golden sheaves,
And dew-wet grasss
Bowed in the morning winds so brisk to pass,
And new buds with new day
Opened of cup-like lilies on the stream,
Laura awoke as from a dream,
Laughed in the innocent old way,
Hugged Lizzie but not twice or thrice;
Her gleaming locks showed not one thread of grey,
Her breath was sweet as May
And light danced in her eyes.

Days, weeks, months, years,
Afterwards, when both were wives
With children of their own;
Their mother-hearts beset with fears,
Their lives bound up in tender lives;
Laura would call the little ones
And tell them of her early prime,
Those pleasant days long gone
Of not-returning time:
Would talk about the haunted glen,

The wicked, quaint fruit-merchant men,
Their fruits like honey to the throat
But poison in the blood
(Men sell not such in any town):
Would tell them how her sister stood
In deadly peril to do her good,
And win the fiery antidote:
Then joining hands to little hands
Would bid them cling together,
"For there is no friend like a sister
In calm or stormy weather;
To cheer one on the tedious way,
To fetch one if one goes astray,
To lift one if one totters down,
To strengthen whilst one stands."

1862

The Necklace of
Princess Fiorimonde

MARY DE MORGAN

Once there lived a King, whose wife was dead, but who had a most beautiful daughter—so beautiful that every one thought she must be good as well, instead of which the Princess was really very wicked, and practised witchcraft and black magic, which she had learned from an old witch who lived in a hut on the side of a lonely mountain. This old witch was wicked and hideous, and no one but the King's daughter knew that she lived there; but at night, when every one else was asleep, the Princess, whose name was Fiorimonde, used to visit her by stealth to learn sorcery. It was only the witch's arts which had made Fiorimonde so beautiful that there was no one like her in the world, and in return the Princess helped her with all her tricks, and never told any one she was there.

The time came when the King began to think he should like his daughter to marry, so he summoned his council and said, "We have no son to reign after our death, so we had best seek for a suitable prince to marry to our royal daughter, and then, when we are too old, he shall be king in our stead." And all the council said he was very wise, and it would be well for the Princess to marry. So heralds were sent to all the neighbouring kings and princes to say that the King would choose a husband for the Princess, who should be king after him. But when Fiorimonde heard this she wept with rage, for she knew quite well that if she had a husband he would find out how she went to visit the old witch, and would stop her practising magic, and then she would lose her beauty.

When night came, and every one in the palace was fast asleep, the Princess went to her bedroom window and softly opened it. Then she took from her pocket a handful of peas and held them out of the window and chirruped low, and there flew down from the roof a small brown bird and sat upon her wrist and began to eat the peas. No sooner had it swallowed them than it began to grow and grow and grow till it was so big that the Princess could not hold it, but let it stand on the window-sill, and still it grew and grew and grew till it was as large as an ostrich. Then the Princess climbed out of the window and seated herself on the bird's back, and at once it flew straight away over the tops of the trees till it came to the mountain where the old witch dwelt, and stopped in front of the door of her hut.

The Princess jumped off, and muttered some words through the keyhole, when a croaking voice from within called:

"Why do you come to-night? Have I not told you I wished to be left alone for thirteen nights; why do you disturb me?"

"But I beg of you to let me in," said the Princess, "for I am in trouble and want your help."

"Come in then," said the voice; and the door flew open, and the Princess trod into the hut, in the middle of which, wrapped in a grey cloak which almost hid her, sat the witch. Princess Fiorimonde sat down near her, and told her, her story. How the King wished her to marry, and had sent word to the neighbouring princes, that they might make offers for her.

"This is truly bad hearing," croaked the witch, "but we shall beat them yet; and you must deal with each Prince as he comes. Would you like them to become dogs, to come at your call, or birds, to fly in the air, and sing of your beauty, or will you make them all into beads, the beads of such a necklace as never woman wore before, so that they may rest upon your neck, and you may take them with you always."

"The necklace! the necklace!" cried the Princess, clapping her hands with joy. "That will be best of all, to sling them upon a string and wear them round my throat. Little will the courtiers know whence come my new jewels."

"But this is a dangerous play," quoth the witch, "for, unless you are very careful, you yourself may become a bead and hang upon the string with the others, and there you will remain till some one cuts the string, and draws you off."

"Nay, never fear," said the Princess, "I will be careful, only tell me what to do, and I will have great princes and kings to adorn me, and all their greatness shall not help them."

Then the witch dipped her hand into a black bag which stood on the ground beside her, and drew out a long gold thread.

The ends were joined together, but no one could see the joins, and however much you pulled, it would not break. It would easily go over Fiorimonde's head, and the witch slipped it on her neck saying:

"Now mind, while this hangs here you are safe enough, but if once you join your fingers around the string you too will meet the fate of your lovers, and hang upon it yourself. As for the kings and princes who would marry you, all you have to do is to make them close their fingers around the chain, and at once they will be strung upon it as bright hard beads, and there they shall remain, till it is cut and they drop off."

"This is really delightful," cried the Princess; "and I am already quite impatient for the first to come that I may try."

"And now," said the witch, "since you are here, and there is yet time, we will have a dance, and I will summon the guests." So saying, she took from a corner a drum and a pair of drum-sticks, and going to the door, began to beat upon it. It made a terrible rattling. In a moment came flying through the air all sorts of forms. There were little dark elves with long tails, and goblins who chattered and laughed, and other witches who rode on broom-sticks. There was one wicked fairy in the form of a large cat, with bright green eyes, and another came sliding in like a long shining viper.

Then, when all had arrived, the witch stopped drumming, and, going to the middle of the hut, stamped on the floor, and a trap-door opened in the ground. The old witch stepped through it, and led the way down a narrow dark passage, to a large underground chamber, and all her strange guests followed, and here they all danced and made merry in a terrible way, but at first sound of cock-crow all the guests disappeared with a whiff, and the Princess hastened up the dark passage again, and out of the hut to where her big bird still waited for her, and mounting its back she flew home in a trice. Then, when she had stepped in at her bedroom window, she poured into a cup from a small black bottle, a few drops of magic water, and gave it to the bird to drink, and as it sipped it grew smaller, and smaller, till at last it had quite regained its natural size, and hopped on to the roof as before, and the Princess shut her window, and got into bed, and fell asleep, and no one knew of her strange journey, or where she had been.

Next day Fiorimonde declared to her father the King, that she was quite willing to wed any prince he should fix upon as a husband for her, at which he was much pleased, and soon after informed her, that a young king was coming from over the sea to be her husband. He was king of a large rich country, and would take back his bride with him to his home. He was called King Pierrot. Great preparations were made for his arrival, and the Princess was decked in her finest array to greet him, and when he came all the courtiers said, "This is truly a proper husband for our beautiful Princess," for he was strong and handsome, with black hair, and eyes like sloes. King Pierrot was delighted with Fiorimonde's beauty, and was happy as the day is long; and all things went merrily till the evening before the marriage. A great feast was held, at which the Princess looked lovelier than ever dressed in a red gown, the colour of the inside of a rose, but she wore no jewels or ornaments of any kind, save one shining gold string round her milk-white throat.

When the feast was done, the Princess stepped from her golden chair at her father's side, and walked softly into the garden, and stood under an elm-tree looking at the shining moon. In a few moments King Pierrot followed her, and stood beside her, looking at her and wondering at her beauty.

"To-morrow, then, my sweet Princess, you will be my Queen, and share all I possess. What gift would you wish me to give you on our wedding day?"

"I would have a necklace wrought of the finest gold and jewels to be found, and just the length of this gold cord which I wear around my throat," answered Princess Fiorimonde.

"Why do you wear that cord?" asked King Pierrot; "it has no jewel nor ornament about it."

"Nay, but there is no cord like mine in all the world," cried Fiorimonde, and her eyes sparkled wickedly as she spoke; "it is as light as a feather, but stronger than an iron chain. Take it in both hands and try to break it, that you may see how strong it is"; and King Pierrot took the cord in both hands to pull it hard; but no sooner were his fingers closed around it than he vanished like a puff of smoke, and on the cord appeared a bright, beautiful bead—so bright and beautiful as was never bead before—clear as crystal, but shining with all colours—green, blue, and gold.

Princess Fiorimonde gazed down at it and laughed aloud.

"Aha, my proud lover! are you there?" she cried with glee; "my necklace bids fair to beat all others in the world," and she caressed the bead with the tips of her soft, white fingers, but was careful that they did not close around the string. Then she returned into the banqueting-hall, and spoke to the King.

"Pray, sire," said she, "send some one at once to find King Pierrot, for, as he was talking to me a minute ago, he suddenly left me, and I am afraid lest I may have given him offence, or perhaps he is ill."

The King desired that the servants should seek for King Pierrot all over the grounds, and seek him they did, but nowhere was he to be found, and the old King looked offended.

"Doubtless he will be ready to-morrow in time for the wedding," quoth he, "but we are not best pleased that he should treat us in this way."

Princess Fiorimonde had a little maid called Yolande. She was a bright-faced girl with merry brown eyes, but she was not beautiful like Fiorimonde, and she did not love her mistress, for she was afraid of her, and suspected her of her wicked ways. When she undressed her that night she noticed the gold cord, and the one bright bead upon it, and as she combed the Princess's hair she looked over her shoulder into the looking-glass, and saw how she laughed, and how fondly she looked at the cord, and caressed the bead again and again with her fingers.

"That is a wonderful bead on your Highness's cord," said Yolande, looking at its reflection in the mirror; "surely it must be a bridal gift from King Pierrot."

"And so it is, little Yolande," cried Fiorimonde, laughing merrily; "and the best gift he could give me. But I think one bead alone looks ugly and ungainly; soon I hope I shall have another, and another, and another, all as beautiful as the first."

Then Yolande shook her head, and said to herself, "This bodes no good."

Next morning all was prepared for the marriage, and the Princess was dressed in white satin and pearls with a long white lace veil over her, and a bridal wreath on her head, and she stood waiting among her grandly dressed ladies, who all said that such a beautiful bride had never been seen in the world before. But just as they were preparing to go down to the fine company in the hall, a messenger came in great haste summoning the Princess at once to her father the King, as he was much perplexed.

"My daughter," cried he, as Fiorimonde in all her bridal array entered the room where he sat alone, "what can we do? King Pierrot is nowhere to be found; I fear lest he may have been seized by robbers and basely murdered for his rich clothes, or carried away to some mountain and left there to starve. My soldiers are gone far and wide to seek him—and we shall hear of him ere day is done—but where there is no bridegroom there can be no bridal."

"Then let it be put off, my father," cried the Princess, "and to-morrow we shall know if it is for a wedding, or a funeral, we must dress"; and she pretended to weep, but even then could hardly keep from laughing.

So the wedding guests went away, and the Princess laid aside her bridal dress, and all waited anxiously for news of King Pierrot; and no news came. So at last every one gave him up for dead, and mourned for him, and wondered how he had met his fate.

Princess Fiorimonde put on a black gown, and begged to be allowed to live in seclusion for one month in which to grieve for King Pierrot; but when she was again alone in her bedroom she sat before her looking-glass and laughed till tears ran down her cheeks; and Yolande watched her, and trembled, when she heard her laughter. She noticed, too, that beneath her black gown, the Princess still wore her gold cord, and did not move it night or day.

The month had barely passed away when the King came to his daughter, and announced that another suitor had presented himself, whom he should much like to be her husband. The Princess agreed quite obediently to all her father said; and it was arranged that the marriage should take place. This new prince was called Prince Hildebrandt. He came from a country far north, of which one day he would be king. He was tall, and fair, and strong, with flaxen hair and bright blue eyes. When Princess Fiorimonde saw his portrait she was much pleased, and said, "By all means let him come, and the sooner the better." So she put off her black clothes, and again great preparations were made for a wedding; and King Pierrot was quite forgotten.

Prince Hildebrandt came, and with him many fine gentlemen, and they brought beautiful gifts for the bride. The evening of his arrival all went well, and again there was a grand feast, and Fiorimonde looked so beautiful that Prince Hildebrandt was delighted; and this time she did not leave her father's side, but sat by him all the evening.

Early next morning at sunrise, when every one was still sleeping, the Princess rose, and dressed herself in a plain white gown, and brushed all her hair over her shoulders, and crept quietly down stairs into the palace gardens; then she walked on till she came beneath the window of Prince Hildebrandt's room, and here she paused and began to sing a little song as sweet and joyous as a lark's. When Prince Hildebrandt heard it he got up and went to the window and looked out to see who sang, and when he saw Fiorimonde standing in the red sunrise-light, which made her hair look gold, and her face rosy, he made haste to dress himself and go down to meet her.

"How, my Princess," cried he, as he stepped into the garden beside her. "This is indeed great happiness to meet you here so early. Tell me, why do you come out at sunrise to sing by yourself?"

"I come that I may see the colours of the sky—red, blue, and gold," answered the Princess. "Look, there are no such colours to be seen anywhere, unless, indeed, it be in this bead which I wear here on my golden cord."

"What is that bead, and where did it come from?" asked Hildebrandt.

"It came from over the sea, where it shall never return again," answered the Princess. And again her eyes began to sparkle with eagerness, and she could scarcely conceal her mirth. "Lift the cord off my neck and look at it near, and tell me if you ever saw one like it."

Hildebrandt put out his hands and took hold of the cord, but no sooner were his fingers closed around it than he vanished, and a new bright bead was slung next to the first one on Fiorimonde's chain, and this one was even more beautiful than the other.

The Princess gave a long low laugh, quite terrible to hear.

"Oh, my sweet necklace," cried she, "how beautiful you are growing! I think I love you more than anything in the world besides." Then she went softly back to bed, without any one hearing her, and fell sound asleep, and slept till Yolande came to tell her it was time for her to get up and dress for the wedding.

The Princess was dressed in gorgeous clothes, and only Yolande noticed that beneath her satin gown, she wore the golden cord, but now there were two beads upon it instead of one. Scarcely was she ready when the King burst into her room in a towering rage.

"My daughter," cried he, "there is a plot against us. Lay aside your bridal attire and think no more of Prince Hildebrandt, for he too has disappeared, and is nowhere to be found."

At this the Princess wept, and entreated that Hildebrandt should be sought for far and near, but she laughed to herself, and said, "Search where you will, yet you shall not find him"; and so again a great search was made, and when no trace of the Prince was found, all the palace was in an uproar.

The Princess again put off her bride's dress and clad herself in black, and sat alone, and pretended to weep, but Yolande, who watched her, shook her head, and said, "More will come and go before the wicked Princess has done her worst."

A month passed, in which Fiorimonde pretended to mourn for Hildebrandt, then she went to the King and said:

"Sire, I pray that you will not let people say that when any bridegroom comes to marry me, as soon as he has seen me he flies rather than be my husband. I beg that suitors may be summoned from far and near that I may not be left alone unwed."

The King agreed, and envoys were sent all the world over to bid any who would come and be the husband of Princess Fiorimonde. And come they did, kings and princes from south and north, east, and west—King Adrian, Prince Sigbert, Prince Algar, and many more—but though all went well till the wedding morning, when it was time to go to church, no bridegroom was to be found. The old King was sadly frightened, and would fain have given up all hope of finding a husband for the Princess, but now she implored him, with tears in her eyes, not to let her be disgraced in this way. And so suitor after suitor continued to come, and now it was known, far and wide, that whoever came to ask for the hand of Princess Fiorimonde vanished, and was seen no more of men. The courtiers were afraid and whispered under their breath, "It is not all right, it cannot be"; but only Yolande noticed how the beads came upon the golden thread, till it was well-nigh covered, yet there always was room for one bead more.

So the years passed, and every year Princess Fiorimonde grew lovelier and lovelier, so that no one who saw her could guess how wicked she was.

In a far-off country lived a young prince whose name was Florestan. He had a dear friend named Gervaise, whom he loved better than any one in the world. Gervaise was tall, and broad, and stout of limb, and he loved Prince Florestan so well, that he would gladly have died to serve him.

It chanced that Prince Florestan saw a portrait of Princess Fiorimonde, and at once swore he would go to her father's court, and beg that he might have her for his wife, and Gervaise in vain tried to dissuade him.

"There is an evil fate about the Princess Fiorimonde," quoth he; "many have gone to marry her, but where are they now?"

"I don't know or care," answered Florestan, "but this is sure, that I will wed her and return here, and bring my bride with me."

So he set out for Fiorimonde's home, and Gervaise went with him with a heavy heart.

When they reached the court, the old King received them and welcomed them warmly, and he said to his courtiers, "Here is a fine young prince to whom we would gladly see our daughter wed. Let us hope that this time all will be well." But now Fiorimonde had grown so bold, that she scarcely tried to conceal her mirth.

"I will gladly marry him to-morrow, if he comes to the church," she said; "but if he is not there, what can I do," and she laughed long and merrily, till those who heard her shuddered.

When the Princess's ladies came to tell her that Prince Florestan was arrived, she was in the garden, lying on the marble edge of a fountain, feeding the gold-fish who swam in the water.

"Bid him come to me," she said, "for I will not go any more in state to meet any suitors, neither will I put on grand attire for them. Let him come and find me as I am, since all find it so easy to come and go." So her ladies told the prince that Fiorimonde waited for him near the fountain.

She did not rise when he came to where she lay, but his heart bounded with joy, for he had never in his life beheld such a beautiful woman.

She wore a thin soft white dress, which clung to her lithe figure. Her beautiful arms and hands were bare, and she dabbled with them in the water, and played with the fish. Her great blue eyes were sparkling with mirth, and were so beautiful, that no one noticed the wicked look hid in them; and on her neck lay the marvellous many-coloured necklace, which was itself a wonder to behold.

"You have my best greetings, Prince Florestan," she said. "And you, too, would be my suitor. Have you thought well of what you would do, since so many princes who have seen me have fled for ever, rather than marry me?" and as she spoke, she raised her white hand from the water, and held it out to the Prince, who stooped and kissed it, and scarcely knew how to answer her for bewilderment at her great loveliness.

Gervaise followed his master at a short distance, but he was ill at ease, and trembled for fear of what should come.

"Come, bid your friend leave us," said Fiorimonde, looking at Gervaise, "and sit beside me, and tell me of your home, and why you wish to marry me, and all pleasant things."

Florestan begged that Gervaise would leave them for a little, and he walked slowly away, in a very mournful mood.

He went on down the walks, not heeding where he was going, till he met Yolande, who stood beneath a tree laden with rosy apples, picking the fruit, and throwing it into a basket at her feet. He would have passed her in silence, but she stopped him, and said:

"Have you come with the new Prince? Do you love your master?"

"Ay, better than any one else on the earth," answered Gervaise. "Why do you ask?"

"And where is he now," said Yolande, not heeding Gervaise's question.

"He sits by the fountain with the beautiful Princess," said Gervaise.

"Then, I hope you have said good-bye to him well, for be assured you shall never see him again," said Yolande, nodding her head.

"Why not, and who are you to talk like this?" asked Gervaise.

"My name is Yolande," answered she, "and I am Princess Fiorimonde's maid. Do you not know that Prince Florestan is the eleventh lover who has come to marry her, and one by one they have disappeared, and only I know where they are gone."

"And where are they gone?" cried Gervaise, "and why do you not tell the world, and prevent good men being lost like this?"

"Because I fear my mistress," said Yolande, speaking low and drawing near to him; "she is a sorceress, and she wears the brave kings and princes who come to woo her, strung upon a cord round her neck. Each one forms the bead of a necklace which she wears, both day and night. I have watched that necklace growing; first it was only an empty gold thread; then came King Pierrot, and when he disappeared the first bead appeared upon it. Then came Hildebrandt, and two beads were on the string instead of one; then followed Adrian, Sigbert, and Algar, and Cenred, and Pharamond, and Baldwyn, and Leofric, and Raoul, and all are gone, and ten beads hang upon the string, and to-night there will be eleven, and the eleventh will be your Prince Florestan."

"If this be so," cried Gervaise, "I will never rest till I have plunged my sword into Fiorimonde's heart"; but Yolande shook her head.

"She is a sorceress," she said, "and it might be hard to kill her; besides, that might not break the spell, and bring back the princes to life. I wish I could show you the necklace, and you might count the beads, and see if I do not speak truth, but it is always about her neck, both night and day, so it is impossible."

"Take me to her room to-night when she is asleep, and let me see it there," said Gervaise.

"Very well, we will try," said Yolande; "but you must be very still, and make no noise, for if she wakes, remember it will be worse for us both."

When night came and all in the palace were fast asleep, Gervaise and Yolande met in the great hall, and Yolande told him that the Princess slumbered soundly.

"So now let us go," said she, "and I will show you the necklace on which Fiorimonde wears her lovers strung like beads, though how she transforms them I know not."

"Stay one instant, Yolande," said Gervaise, holding her back, as she would have tripped up stairs. "Perhaps, try how I may, I shall be beaten, and either die or become a bead like those who have come before me. But if I succeed and rid the land of your wicked Princess, what will you promise me for a reward?"

"What would you have?" asked Yolande.

"I would have you say you will be my wife, and come back with me to my own land," said Gervaise.

"That I will promise gladly," said Yolande, kissing him, "but we must not speak or think of this till we have cut the cord from Fiorimonde's neck, and all her lovers are set free."

So they went softly up to the Princess's room, Yolande holding a small lantern, which gave only a dim light. There, in her grand bed, lay Princess Fiorimonde. They could just see her by the lantern's light, and she looked so beautiful that Gervaise began to think Yolande spoke falsely, when she said she was so wicked.

Her face was calm and sweet as a baby's; her hair fell in ruddy waves on the pillow; her rosy lips smiled, and little dimples showed in her cheeks; her white soft hands were folded amidst the scented lace and linen of which the bed was made. Gervaise almost forgot to look at the glittering beads hung round her throat, in wondering at her loveliness, but Yolande pulled him by the arm.

"Do not look at her," she whispered softly, "since her beauty has cost dear already; look rather at what remains of those who thought her as fair as you do now; see here," and she pointed with her finger to each bead in turn.

"This was Pierrot, and this Hildebrandt, and these are Adrian, and Sigbert, and Algar, and Cenred, and that is Pharamond, and that Raoul, and last of all here is your own master Prince Florestan. Seek him now where you will and you will not find him, and you shall never see him again till the cord is cut and the charm broken."

"Of what is the cord made?" whispered Gervaise.

"It is of the finest gold," she answered. "Nay, do not you touch her lest she wake. I will show it to you." And Yolande put down the lantern and softly put out her hands to slip the beads aside, but as she did so, her fingers closed around the golden string, and directly she was gone. Another bead was added to the necklace, and Gervaise was alone with the sleeping Princess. He gazed about him in sore amazement and fear. He dared not call lest Fiorimonde should wake.

"Yolande," he whispered as loud as he dared, "Yolande, where are you?" but no Yolande answered.

Then he bent down over the Princess and gazed at the necklace. Another bead was strung upon it next to the one to which Yolande had pointed as Prince Florestan. Again he counted them. "Eleven before, now there are twelve. Oh hateful Princess! I know now where go the brave kings and princes who came to woo you, and where, too, is my Yolande," and as he looked at the last bead, tears filled his eyes. It was brighter and clearer than the others, and of a warm red hue, like the red dress Yolande had worn. The Princess turned and laughed in her sleep, and at the sound of her laughter Gervaise was filled with horror and loathing. He crept shuddering from the room, and all night long sat up alone, plotting how he might defeat Fiorimonde, and set Florestan and Yolande free.

Next morning when Fiorimonde dressed she looked at her necklace and counted its beads, but she was much perplexed, for a new bead was added to the string.

"Who can have come and grasped my chain unknown to me?" she said to herself, and she sat and pondered for a long time. At last she broke into weird laughter.

"At any rate, whoever it was, is fitly punished," quoth she. "My brave necklace, you can take care of yourself, and if any one tries to steal you, they will get their reward, and add to my glory. In truth I may sleep in peace, and fear nothing."

The day passed away and no one missed Yolande. Towards sunset the rain

began to pour in torrents, and there was such a terrible thunderstorm that every one was frightened. The thunder roared, the lightning gleamed flash after flash, every moment it grew fiercer and fiercer. The sky was so dark that, save for the lightning's light, nothing could be seen, but Princess Fiorimonde loved the thunder and lightning.

She sat in a room high up in one of the towers, clad in a black velvet dress, and she watched the lightning from the window, and laughed at each peal of thunder. In the midst of the storm a stranger, wrapped in a cloak, rode to the palace door, and the ladies ran to tell the Princess that a new prince had come to be her suitor. "And he will not tell his name," said they, "but says he hears that all are bidden to ask for the hand of Princess Fiorimonde, and he too would try his good fortune."

"Let him come at once," cried the Princess. "Be he prince or knave, what care I? If princes all fly from me it may be better to marry a peasant."

So they led the new-comer up to the room where Fiorimonde sat. He was wrapped in a thick cloak, but he flung it aside as he came in, and showed how rich was his silken clothing underneath; and so well was he disguised, that Fiorimonde never saw that it was Gervaise, but looked at him, and thought she had never seen him before.

"You are most welcome, stranger prince, who has come through such lightning and thunder to find me," said she. "Is it true, then, that you wish to be my suitor? What have you heard of me?"

"It is quite true, Princess," said Gervaise. "And I have heard that you are the most beautiful woman in the world."

"And is that true also?" asked the Princess. "Look at me now, and see."

Gervaise looked at her and in his heart he said, "It is quite true, oh wicked Princess! There never was woman as beautiful as you, and never before did I hate a woman as I hate you now"; but aloud he said:

"No, Princess, that is not true; you are very beautiful, but I have seen a woman who is fairer than you for all that your skin looks ivory against your velvet dress, and your hair is like gold."

"A woman who is fairer than I?" cried Fiorimonde, and her breast began to heave and her eyes to sparkle with rage, for never before had she heard such a thing said. "Who are you who dares come and tell me of women more beautiful than I am?"

"I am a suitor who asks to be your husband, Princess," answered Gervaise, "but still I say I have seen a woman who was fairer than you."

"Who is she—where is she?" cried Fiorimonde, who could scarcely contain her anger. "Bring her here at once that I may see if you speak the truth."

"What will you give me to bring her to you?" said Gervaise. "Give me that necklace you wear on your neck, and then I will summon her in an instant"; but Fiorimonde shook her head.

"You have asked," said she, "for the only thing from which I cannot part," and then she bade her maids bring her her jewel-casket, and she drew out diamonds, and rubies, and pearls, and offered them, all or any, to Gervaise. The lightning shone on them and made them shine and flash, but he shook his head.

"No, none of these will do," quoth he. "You can see her for the necklace, but for nothing else."

"Take it off for yourself then," cried Fiorimonde, who now was so angry that she only wished to be rid of Gervaise in any way.

"No, indeed," said Gervaise, "I am no tire-woman, and should not know how to clasp and unclasp it"; and in spite of all Fiorimonde could say or do, he would not touch either her or the magic chain.

At night the storm grew even fiercer, but it did not trouble the Princess. She waited till all were asleep, and then she opened her bedroom window and chirruped softly to the little brown bird, who flew down from the roof at her call. Then she gave him a handful of seeds as before, and he grew and grew and grew till he was as large as an ostrich, and she sat upon his back and flew out through the air, laughing at the lightning and thunder which flashed and roared around her. Away they flew till they came to the old witch's cave, and here they found the witch sitting at her open door catching the lightning to make charms with.

"Welcome, my dear," croaked she, as Fiorimonde stepped from the bird; "here is a night we both love well. And how goes the necklace?—right merrily I see. Twelve beads already—but what is that twelfth?" and she looked at it closely.

"Nay, that is one thing I want you to tell me," said Fiorimonde, drying the rain from her golden hair. "Last night when I slept there were eleven, and this morning there are twelve; and I know not from whence comes the twelfth."

"It is no suitor," said the witch, "but from some young maid, that that bead is made. But why should you mind? It looks well with the others."

"Some young maid," said the Princess. "Then it must be Cicely or Marybel, or Yolande, who would have robbed me of my necklace as I slept. But what care I? The silly wench is punished now, and so may all others be, who would do the same."

"And when will you get the thirteenth bead, and where will he come from?" asked the witch.

"He waits at the palace now," said Fiorimonde, chuckling. "And this is why I have to speak to you"; and then she told the witch of the stranger who had come in the storm, and of how he would not touch her necklace, nor take the cord in his hand, and how he said also that he knew a woman fairer than she.

"Beware, Princess, beware," cried the witch in a warning voice, as she listened. "Why should you heed tales of other women fairer than you? Have I not made you the most beautiful woman in the world, and can any others do more than I? Give no ear to what this stranger says or you shall rue it." But still the Princess murmured, and said she did not love to hear any one speak of others as beautiful as she.

"Be warned in time," cried the witch, "or you will have cause to repeat it. Are you so silly or so vain as to be troubled because a prince says idly what you know is not true? I tell you do not listen to him, but let him be slung to your chain as soon as may be, and then he will speak no more." And then they talked together of how Fiorimonde could make Gervaise grasp the fatal string.

Next morning when the sun rose, Gervaise started off into the woods, and there he plucked acorns and haws, and hips, and strung them on to a string to form a rude necklace. This he hid in his bosom *then*, and went back to the palace without telling any one.

When the Princess rose, she dressed herself as beautifully as she could, and braided her golden locks with great care, for this morning she meant her new suitor to meet his fate. After breakfast, she stepped into the garden, where the sun shone brightly, and all looked fresh after the storm. Here from the grass she picked up a golden ball, and began to play with it.

"Go to our new guest," cried she to her ladies, "and ask him to come here and play at ball with me." So they went, and soon they returned bringing Gervaise with them.

"Good morrow, Prince," cried she. "Pray, come and try your skill at this game with me; and you," she said to her ladies, "do not wait to watch our play, but each go your way, and do what pleases you best." So they all went away, and left her alone with Gervaise.

"Well, Prince," cried she as they began to play, "what do you think of me by morning light? Yesterday when you came it was so dark, with thunder and clouds, that you could scarcely see my face, but now that there is bright sunshine, pray look well at me, and see if you do not think me as beautiful as any woman on earth," and she smiled at Gervaise, and looked so lovely as she spoke, that he scarce knew how to answer her; but he remembered Yolande, and said:

"Doubtless you are very beautiful; then why should you mind my telling you that I have seen a woman lovelier than you?"

At this the Princess again began to be angry, but she thought of the witch's words and said:

"Then, if you think there is a woman fairer than I, look at my beads, and now, that you see their colours in the sun, say if you ever saw such jewels before."

"It is true I have never seen beads like yours, but I have a necklace here, which pleases me better"; and from his pocket he drew the haws and acorns, which he had strung together.

"What is that necklace, and where did you get it? Show it to me!" cried Fiorimonde; but Gervaise held it out of her reach, and said:

"I like my necklace better than yours, Princess; and, believe me, there is no necklace like mine in all the world."

"Why; is it a fairy necklace? What does it do? Pray give it to me!" cried Fiorimonde, trembling with anger and curiosity, for she thought, "Perhaps it has power to make the wearer beautiful; perhaps it was worn by the woman whom he thought more beautiful than I, and that is why she looked so fair."

"Come, I will make a fair exchange," said Gervaise. "Give me your necklace and you shall have mine, and when it is round your throat I will truthfully say that you are the fairest woman in the world; but first I must have your necklace."

"Take it, then," cried the Princess, who, in her rage and eagerness, forgot all else, and she seized the string of beads to lift it from her neck, but no sooner had she taken it in her hands than they fell with a rattle to the earth, and Fiorimonde herself was nowhere to be seen. Gervaise bent down over the necklace as it lay upon the grass, and, with a smile, counted thirteen beads; and he knew the thirteenth was the wicked Princess, who had herself met the evil fate she had prepared for so many others.

"Oh, clever Princess!" cried he, laughing aloud, "you are not so very clever, I think, to be so easily outwitted." Then he picked up the necklace on the point of the sword and carried it, slung thereon, into the council-chamber, where sat the King surrounded by statesmen and courtiers busy with state affairs.

"Pray, King," said Gervaise, "send some one to seek for Princess Fiorimonde. A moment ago she played with me at ball in the garden, and now she is nowhere to be seen."

The King desired that servants should seek her Royal Highness; but they came back saying she was not to be found.

"Then let me see if I cannot bring her to you; but first let those who have been longer lost than she, come and tell their own tale." And, so saying, Gervaise let the necklace slip from his sword on to the floor, and taking from his breast a sharp dagger, proceeded to cut the golden thread on which the beads were strung, and as he clave it in two there came a mighty noise like a clap of thunder.

"Now," cried he, "look, and see King Pierrot who was lost," and as he spoke he drew from the cord a bead, and King Pierrot, in his royal clothes, with his sword at his side, stood before them.

"Treachery!" he cried, but ere he could say more Gervaise had drawn off another bead, and King Hildebrandt appeared, and after him came Adrian, and Sigbert, and Algar, and Cenred, and Pharamond, and Raoul, and last of the princes, Gervaise's own dear master Florestan, and they all denounced Princess Fiorimonde and her wickedness.

"And now," cried Gervaise, "here is she who has helped to save you all," and he drew off the twelfth bead, and there stood Yolande in her red dress; and when he saw her Gervaise flung away his dagger and took her in his arms, and they wept for joy.

The King and all the courtiers sat pale and trembling, unable to speak for fear and shame. At length the King said with a deep groan:

"We owe you deep amends, O noble kings and princes! What punishment do you wish to prepare for our most guilty daughter?" but here Gervaise stopped him, and said:

"Give her no other punishment than what she has chosen for herself. See, here she is, the thirteenth bead upon the string; let no one dare to draw it off, but let this string be hung up where all people can see it and see the one bead, and know the wicked Princess is punished for her sorcery, so it will be a warning to others who would do like her."

So they lifted the golden thread with great care and hung it up outside the town hall, and there the one bead glittered and gleamed in the sunlight, and all who saw it knew that it was the wicked Princess Fiorimonde who had justly met her fate.

Then all the kings and princes thanked Gervaise and Yolande, and loaded them with presents, and each went to his own land.

And Gervaise married Yolande, and they went back with Prince Florestan to their home, and all lived happily to the end of their lives.

1880

The Golden Key

GEORGE MACDONALD

There was a boy who used to sit in the twilight and listen to his great-aunt's stories.

She told him that if he could reach the place where the end of the rainbow stands he would find there a golden key.

"And what is the key for?" the boy would ask. "What is it the key of? What will it open?"

"That nobody knows," his aunt would reply. "He has to find that out."

"I suppose, being gold," the boy once said, thoughtfully, "that I could get a good deal of money for it if I sold it."

"Better never find it than sell it," returned his aunt.

And then the boy went to bed and dreamed about the golden key.

Now all that his great-aunt told the boy about the golden key would have been nonsense, had it not been that their little house stood on the borders of Fairyland. For it is perfectly well known that out of Fairyland nobody ever can find where the rainbow stands. The creature takes such good care of its golden key, always flitting from place to place, lest any one should find it! But in Fairyland it is quite different. Things that look real in this country look very thin indeed in Fairyland, while some of the things that here cannot stand still for a moment, will not move there. So it was not in the least absurd of the old lady to tell her nephew such things about the golden key.

"Did you ever know anybody find it?" he asked, one evening.

"Yes. Your father, I believe, found it."

"And what did he do with it, can you tell me?"

"He never told me."

"What was it like?"

"He never showed it to me."

"How does a new key come there always?"

"I don't know. There it is."

"Perhaps it is the rainbow's egg."

"Perhaps it is. You will be a happy boy if you find the nest."

"Perhaps it comes tumbling down the rainbow from the sky."

"Perhaps it does."

One evening, in summer, he went into his own room, and stood at the lattice-window, and gazed into the forest which fringed the outskirts of Fairyland. It came close up to his great-aunt's garden, and, indeed, sent some straggling trees into it. The forest lay to the east, and the sun, which was setting behind the cottage, looked straight into the dark wood with his level red eye. The trees were all old, and had few branches below, so that the sun could see a great way into the forest; and the boy, being keen-sighted, could see almost as far as the sun. The trunks stood like rows of red columns in the shine of the red sun, and he could see down aisle after aisle in the vanishing distance. And as he gazed into the forest he began to feel as if the trees were all waiting for him, and had something they could not go on with till he came to them. But he was hungry, and wanted his supper. So he lingered.

Suddenly, far among the trees, as far as the sun could shine, he saw a glorious thing. It was the end of a rainbow, large and brilliant. He could count all the seven colours, and could see shade after shade beyond the violet; while before the red stood a colour more gorgeous and mysterious still. It was a colour he had never seen before. Only the spring of the rainbow-arch was visible. He could see nothing of it above the trees.

"The golden key!" he said to himself, and darted out of the house, and into the wood.

He had not gone far before the sun set. But the rainbow only glowed the brighter. For the rainbow of Fairyland is not dependent upon the sun as ours is. The trees welcomed him. The bushes made way for him. The rainbow grew larger and brighter; and at length he found himself within two trees of it.

It was a grand sight, burning away there in silence, with its gorgeous, its lovely, its delicate colours, each distinct, all combining. He could now see a great deal more of it. It rose high into the blue heavens, but bent so little that he could not tell how high the crown of the arch must reach. It was still only a small portion of a huge bow.

He stood gazing at it till he forgot himself with delight—even forgot the key which he had come to seek. And as he stood it grew more wonderful still. For in each of the colours, which was as large as the column of a church, he could faintly see beautiful forms slowly ascending as if by the steps of a winding stair. The forms appeared irregularly—now one, now many, now several, now none—men and women and children—all different, all beautiful.

He drew nearer to the rainbow. It vanished. He started back a step in dismay. It was there again, as beautiful as ever. So he contented himself with standing as near it as he might, and watching the forms that ascended the glorious colours towards the unknown height of the arch, which did not end abruptly, but faded away in the blue air, so gradually that he could not say where it ceased.

When the thought of the golden key returned, the boy very wisely proceeded to mark out in his mind the space covered by the foundation of the rainbow, in order that he might know where to search, should the rainbow disappear. It was based chiefly upon a bed of moss.

Meantime it had grown quite dark in the wood. The rainbow alone was visible by its own light. But the moment the moon rose the rainbow vanished. Nor could any change of place restore the vision to the boy's eyes. So he threw himself down upon the mossy bed, to wait till the sunlight would give him a chance of finding the key. There he fell fast asleep.

When he woke in the morning the sun was looking straight into his eyes. He turned away from it, and the same moment saw a brilliant little thing lying on the moss within a foot of his face. It was the golden key. The pipe of it was plain gold, as bright as gold could be. The handle was curiously wrought and set with sapphires. In a terror of delight he put out his hand and took it, and had it.

He lay for a while, turning over and over, and feeding his eyes upon its beauty. Then he jumped to his feet, remembering that the pretty thing was of no use to him yet. Where was the lock to which the key belonged? It must be somewhere, for how could anybody be so silly as make a key for which there was no lock? Where should he go to look for it? He gazed about him, up into the air, down to the earth, but saw no keyhole in the clouds, in the grass, or in the trees.

Just as he began to grow disconsolate, however, he saw something glimmering in the wood. It was a mere glimmer that he saw, but he took it for a glimmer of rainbow, and went towards it.—And now I will go back to the borders of the forest.

Not far from the house where the boy had lived, there was another house, the owner of which was a merchant, who was much away from home. He had lost his wife some years before, and had only one child, a little girl, whom he left to the charge of two servants, who were very idle and careless. So she was neglected and left untidy, and was sometimes ill-used besides.

Now it is well known that the little creatures commonly called fairies, though there are many different kinds of fairies in Fairyland, have an exceeding dislike to untidiness. Indeed, they are quite spiteful to slovenly people. Being used to all the lovely ways of the trees and flowers, and to the neatness of the birds and all woodland creatures, it makes them feel miserable, even in their deep woods and on their grassy carpets, to think that within the same moonlight lies a dirty, uncomfortable, slovenly house. And this makes them angry with the people that live in it, and they would gladly drive them out of the world if they could. They want the whole earth nice and clean. So they pinch the maids black and blue, and play them all manner of uncomfortable tricks.

But this house was quite a shame, and the fairies in the forest could not endure it. They tried everything on the maids without effect, and at last resolved upon making a clean riddance, beginning with the child. They ought to have known that it was not her fault, but they have little principle and much mischief in them, and they thought that if they got rid of her the maids would be sure to be turned away.

So one evening, the poor little girl having been put to bed early, before the sun was down, the servants went off to the village, locking the door behind them. The child did not know she was alone, and lay contentedly looking out of her window towards the forest, of which, however, she could not see much, because of the ivy and other creeping plants which had straggled across her window. All at once she saw an ape making faces at her out of the mirror, and the heads carved upon a great old wardrobe grinning fearfully. Then two old spider-legged chairs came forward into the middle of the room, and began to dance a queer, old-fashioned dance. This set her laughing, and she forgot the ape and the grinning heads. So the fairies saw they had made a mistake, and sent the chairs back to their places. But they knew that she had been reading the story of Silverhair all day. So the next moment she heard the voices of the three bears upon the stair, big voice, middle voice, and little voice, and she heard their soft, heavy tread, as if they had had stockings over their boots, coming nearer and nearer to the door of her room, till she could bear it no longer. She did just as Silverhair did, and as the fairies wanted her to do: she darted to the window, pulled it open, got upon the ivy, and so scrambled to the ground. She then fled to the forest as fast as she could run.

Now, although she did not know it, this was the very best way she could have gone; for nothing is ever so mischievous in its own place as it is out of it; and, besides, these mischievous creatures were only the children of Fairyland, as it were, and there are many other beings there as well; and if a wanderer gets in among them, the good ones will always help him more than the evil ones will be able to hurt him.

The sun was now set, and the darkness coming on, but the child thought of no danger but the bears behind her. If she had looked round, however, she would have seen that she was followed by a very different creature from a bear. It was a curious creature, made like a fish, but covered, instead of scales, with feathers of all colours, sparkling like those of a humming-bird. It had fins, not wings, and swam through the air as a fish does through the water. Its head was like the head of a small owl.

After running a long way, and as the last of the light was disappearing, she passed under a tree with drooping branches. It dropped its branches to the ground all about her, and caught her as in a trap. She struggled to get out, but the branches pressed her closer and closer to the trunk. She was in great terror and distress, when the air-fish, swimming into the thicket of branches, began tearing them with its beak. They loosened their hold at once, and the creature went on attacking them, till at length they let the child go. Then the air-fish came from behind her, and swam on in front, glittering and sparkling all lovely colours; and she followed.

It led her gently along till all at once it swam in at a cottage-door. The child followed still. There was a bright fire in the middle of the floor, upon which stood a pot without a lid, full of water that boiled and bubbled furiously. The air-fish swam straight to the pot and into the boiling water, where it lay quiet. A beautiful woman rose from the opposite side of the fire and came to meet the girl. She took her up in her arms, and said:

"Ah, you are come at last! I have been looking for you a long time."

She sat down with her on her lap, and there the girl sat staring at her. She had never seen anything so beautiful. She was tall and strong, with white arms and neck, and a delicate flush on her face. The child could not tell what was the colour of her hair, but could not help thinking it had a tinge of dark green. She had not one ornament upon her, but she looked as if she had just put off quantities of diamonds and emeralds. Yet here she was in the simplest, poorest little cottage, where she was evidently at home. She was dressed in shining green.

The girl looked at the lady, and the lady looked at the girl.

"What is your name?" asked the lady.

"The servants always called me Tangle."

"Ah, that was because your hair was so untidy. But that was their fault, the naughty women! Still it is a pretty name, and I will call you Tangle too. You must not mind me asking you questions, for you may ask me the same questions, every one of them, and any others that you like. How old are you?"

"Ten," answered Tangle.

"You don't look like it," said the lady.

"How old are you, please?" returned Tangle.

"Thousands of years old," answered the lady.

"You don't look like it," said Tangle.

"Don't I? I think I do. Don't you see how beautiful I am?"

And her great blue eyes looked down on the little Tangle, as if all the stars in the sky were melted in them to make their brightness.

"Ah! but," said Tangle, "when people live long they grow old. At least I always thought so."

"I have no time to grow old," said the lady. "I am too busy for that. It is very idle to grow old.—But I cannot have my little girl so untidy. Do you know I can't find a clean spot on your face to kiss?"

"Perhaps," suggested Tangle, feeling ashamed, but not too much so to say a word for herself—"perhaps that is because the tree made me cry so."

"My poor darling!" said the lady, looking now as if the moon were melted in her eyes, and kissing her little face, dirty as it was, "the naughty tree must suffer for making a girl cry."

"And what is your name, please?" asked Tangle.

"Grandmother," answered the lady.

"Is it really?"

"Yes, indeed. I never tell stories, even in fun."

"How good of you!"

"I couldn't if I tried. It would come true if I said it, and then I should be punished enough."

And she smiled like the sun through a summer-shower.

"But now," she went on, "I must get you washed and dressed, and then we shall have some supper."

"Oh! I had supper long ago," said Tangle.

"Yes, indeed you had," answered the lady—"three years ago. You don't know that it is three years since you ran away from the bears. You are thirteen and more now."

Tangle could only stare. She felt quite sure it was true.

"You will not be afraid of anything I do with you—will you?" said the lady.

"I will try very hard not to be; but I can't be certain, you know," replied Tangle.

"I like your saying so, and I shall be quite satisfied," answered the lady.

She took off the girl's nightgown, rose with her in her arms, and going to the wall of the cottage, opened a door. Then Tangle saw a deep tank, the sides of which were filled with green plants, which had flowers of all colours. There was a roof over it like the roof of the cottage. It was filled with beautiful clear water, in which swam a multitude of such fishes as the one that had led her to the cottage. It was the light their colours gave that showed the place in which they were.

The lady spoke some words Tangle could not understand, and threw her into the tank.

The fishes came crowding about her. Two or three of them got under her head and kept it up. The rest of them rubbed themselves all over her, and with their wet feathers washed her quite clean. Then the lady, who had been looking on all the time, spoke again; whereupon some thirty or forty of the fishes rose out of the water underneath Tangle, and so bore her up to the arms the lady held out to her. She carried her back to the fire, and, having dried her well, opened a chest, and taking out the finest linen garments, smelling of grass and lavender, put them upon her, and over all a green dress, just like her own, shining like hers, and soft like hers, and going into just such lovely folds from the waist, where it was tied with a brown cord, to her bare feet.

"Won't you give me a pair of shoes too, Grandmother?" said Tangle.

"No, my dear; no shoes. Look here. I wear no shoes."

So saying, she lifted her dress a little, and there were the loveliest white feet, but no shoes. Then Tangle was content to go without shoes too. And the lady sat down with her again, and combed her hair, and brushed it, and then left it to dry while she got the supper.

First she got bread out of one hole in the wall; then milk out of another; then several kinds of fruit out of a third; and then she went to the pot on the fire, and took out the fish, now nicely cooked, and, as soon as she had pulled off its feathered skin, ready to be eaten.

"But," exclaimed Tangle. And she stared at the fish, and could say no more.

"I know what you mean," returned the lady. "You do not like to eat the messenger that brought you home. But it is the kindest return you can make. The creature was afraid to go until it saw me put the pot on, and heard me promise it should be boiled the moment it returned with you. Then it darted out of the door at once. You saw it go into the pot of itself the moment it entered, did you not?"

"I did," answered Tangle, "and I thought it very strange; but then I saw you, and forgot all about the fish."

"In Fairyland," resumed the lady, as they sat down to the table, "the ambition of the animals is to be eaten by the people; for that is their highest end in that condition. But they are not therefore destroyed. Out of that pot comes something more than the dead fish, you will see."

Tangle now remarked that the lid was on the pot. But the lady took no further notice of it till they had eaten the fish, which Tangle found nicer than any fish she had ever tasted before. It was as white as snow, and as delicate as cream. And the moment she had swallowed a mouthful of it, a change she could not describe began to take place in her. She heard a murmuring all about her, which became more and more articulate, and at length, as she went on eating, grew intelligible. By the time she had finished her share, the sounds of all the animals in the forest came crowding through the door to her ears; for the door still stood wide open, though it was pitch-dark outside; and they were no longer sounds only; they were speech, and speech that she could understand. She could tell what the insects in the cottage were saying to each other too. She had even a suspicion that the trees and flowers all about the cottage were holding midnight communications with each other; but what they said she could not hear.

As soon as the fish was eaten, the lady went to the fire and took the lid off the pot. A lovely little creature in human shape, with large white wings, rose out of it, and flew round and round the roof of the cottage; then dropped, fluttering, and nestled in the lap of the lady. She spoke to it some strange words, carried it to the door, and threw it out into the darkness. Tangle heard the flapping of its wings die away in the distance.

"Now have we done the fish any harm?" she said, returning.

"No," answered Tangle, "I do not think we have. I should not mind eating one every day."

"They must wait their time, like you and me too, my little Tangle."

And she smiled a smile which the sadness in it made more lovely.

"But," she continued, "I think we may have one for supper to-morrow."

So saying she went to the door of the tank, and spoke; and now Tangle understood her perfectly.

"I want one of you," she said, "—the wisest."

Thereupon the fishes got together in the middle of the tank, with their heads forming a circle above the water, and their tails a larger circle beneath it. They were holding a council, in which their relative wisdom should be determined. At length one of them flew up into the lady's hand, looking lively and ready.

"You know where the rainbow stands?" she asked.

"Yes, mother, quite well," answered the fish.

"Bring home a young man you will find there, who does not know where to go."

The fish was out of the door in a moment. Then the lady told Tangle it was time to go to bed; and, opening another door in the side of the cottage, showed her a little arbour, cool and green, with a bed of purple heath growing in it, upon which she threw a large wrapper made of the feathered skins of the wise fishes, shining gorgeous in the firelight. Tangle was soon lost in the strangest, loveliest dreams. And the beautiful lady was in every one of her dreams.

In the morning she awoke to the rustling of leaves over her head, and the sound of running water. But, to her surprise, she could find no door— nothing but the moss-grown wall of the cottage. So she crept through an opening in the arbour, and stood in the forest. Then she bathed in a stream that ran merrily through the trees, and felt happier; for having once been in her grandmother's pond, she must be clean and tidy ever after; and, having put on her green dress, felt like a lady.

She spent that day in the wood, listening to the birds and beasts and creeping things. She understood all that they said, though she could not repeat a word of it; and every kind had a different language, while there was a common though more limited understanding between all the inhabitants of the forest. She saw nothing of the beautiful lady, but she felt that she was near her all the time; and she took care not to go out of sight of the cottage. It was round, like a snow-hut or a wigwam; and she could see neither door nor window in it. The fact was, it had no windows; and though it was full of doors, they all opened from the inside, and could not even be seen from the outside.

She was standing at the foot of a tree in the twilight, listening to a quarrel between a mole and a squirrel, in which the mole told the squirrel that the tail was the best of him, and the squirrel called the mole Spade-fists, when, the darkness having deepened around her, she became aware of something shining in her face, and looking round, saw that the door of the cottage was open, and the red light of the fire flowing from it like a river through the darkness. She left Mole and Squirrel to settle matters as they might, and darted off to the cottage. Entering, she found the pot boiling on the fire, and the grand, lovely lady sitting on the other side of it.

"I've been watching you all day," said the lady. "You shall have something to eat by-and-by, but we must wait till our supper comes home."

She took Tangle on her knee, and began to sing to her—such songs as made her wish she could listen to them for ever. But at length in rushed the shining fish, and snuggled down in the pot. It was followed by a youth who had outgrown his worn garments. His face was ruddy with health, and in his hand he carried a little jewel, which sparkled in the firelight.

The first words the lady said were:

"What is that in your hand, Mossy?"

Now Mossy was the name his companions had given him, because he had a favorite stone covered with moss, on which he used to sit whole days reading; and they said the moss had begun to grow upon him too.

Mossy held out his hand. The moment the lady saw that it was the golden key, she rose from her chair, kissed Mossy on the forehead, made him sit down on her seat, and stood before him like a servant. Mossy could not bear this, and rose at once. But the lady begged him, with tears in her beautiful eyes, to sit, and let her wait on him.

"But you are a great, splendid, beautiful lady," said Mossy.

"Yes, I am. But I work all day long—that is my pleasure; and you will have to leave me so soon!"

"How do you know that, if you please, madam?" asked Mossy.

"Because you have got the golden key."

"But I don't know what it is for. I can't find the keyhole. Will you tell me what to do?"

"You must look for the keyhole. That is your work. I cannot help you. I can only tell you that if you look for it you will find it."

"What kind of box will it open? What is there inside?"

"I do not know. I dream about it, but I know nothing."

"Must I go at once?"

"You may stop here to-night, and have some of my supper. But you must go in the morning. All I can do for you is to give you clothes. Here is a girl called Tangle, whom you must take with you."

"That *will* be nice," said Mossy.

"No, no!" said Tangle. "I don't want to leave you, please, Grandmother."

"You must go with him, Tangle. I am sorry to lose you, but it will be the best thing for you. Even the fishes, you see, have to go into the pot, and then out into the dark. If you fall in with the Old Man of the Sea, mind you ask him whether he has not got some more fishes ready for me. My tank is getting thin."

So saying, she took the fish from the pot, and put the lid on as before. They sat down and ate the fish, and then the winged creature rose from the pot, circled the roof, and settled on the lady's lap. She talked to it, carried it to the door, and threw it out into the dark. They heard the flap of its wings die away in the distance.

The lady then showed Mossy into just another chamber as that of Tangle; and in the morning he found a suit of clothes laid beside him. He looked very handsome in them. But the wearer of Grandmother's clothes never thinks about how he or she looks, but thinks always how handsome other people are.

Tangle was very unwilling to go.

"Why should I leave you? I don't know the young man," she said to the lady.

"I am never allowed to keep my children long. You need not go with him except you please, but you must go some day; and I should like you to go with him, for he has the golden key. No girl need be afraid to go with a youth that has the golden key. You will take care of her, Mossy, will you not?"

"That I will," said Mossy.

And Tangle cast a glance at him, and thought she should like to go with him.

"And," said the lady, "if you should lose each other as you go through the—the—I never can remember the name of that country—do not be afraid, but go on and on."

She kissed Tangle on the mouth and Mossy on the forehead, led them to the door, and waved her hand eastward. Mossy and Tangle took each other's hand and walked away into the depth of the forest. In his right hand Mossy held the golden key.

They wandered thus a long way, with endless amusement from the talk of the animals. They soon learned enough of their language to ask them necessary questions. The squirrels were always friendly, and gave them nuts out of their own hoards; but the bees were selfish and rude, justifying themselves on the ground that Tangle and Mossy were not subjects of their queen, and charity must begin at home, though indeed they had not one drone in their poorhouse at the time. Even the blinking moles would fetch them an earth-nut or a truffle now and then, talking as if their mouths, as well as their eyes and ears, were full of cotton wool, or their own velvety fur. By the time they got out of the forest they were very fond of each other, and Tangle was not in the least sorry that her grandmother had sent her away with Mossy.

At length the trees grew smaller, and stood farther apart, and the ground began to rise, and it got more and more steep, till the trees were all left behind, and the two were climbing a narrow path with rocks on each side. Suddenly they came upon a rude doorway, by which they entered a narrow gallery cut in the rock. It grew darker and darker, till it was pitch-dark, and they had to feel their way. At length the light began to return, and at last they came out upon a narrow path on the face of a lofty precipice. This path went winding down the rock to a wide plain, circular in shape, and surrounded on all sides by mountains. Those opposite to them were a great way off, and towered to an awful height, shooting up sharp, blue, ice-enamelled pinnacles. An utter silence reigned where they stood. Not even the sound of water reached them.

Looking down, they could not tell whether the valley below was a grassy plain or a great still lake. They had never seen any space look like it. The way to it was difficult and dangerous, but down the narrow path they went, and reached the bottom in safety. They found it composed of smooth, light-coloured sandstone, undulating in parts, but mostly level. It was no wonder to them now that they had not been able to tell what it was, for this surface was everywhere crowded with shadows. It was a sea of shadows. The mass was chiefly made up of the shadows of leaves innumerable, of all lovely and imaginative forms, waving to and fro, floating and quivering in the breath of a breeze whose motion was unfelt, whose sound was unheard. No forests clothed the mountain-sides, no trees were anywhere to be seen, and yet the shadows of the leaves, branches, and stems of all various trees covered the valley as far as their eyes could reach. They soon spied the shadows of flowers mingled with those of the leaves, and now and then the shadow of a bird with open beak, and throat distended with song. At times would appear the forms of strange, graceful creatures, running up and down the shadow-boles and along the branches, to disappear in the wind-tossed foliage. As they walked they waded knee-deep in the lovely lake. For the shadows were not merely lying on the surface of the ground, but heaped up above it like substantial forms of darkness, as if they had been cast upon a thousand different planes of the air. Tangle and Mossy often lifted their heads and gazed upwards to descry whence the shadows came; but they could see nothing more than a bright mist spread above them, higher than the tops of the mountains, which stood clear against it. No forests, no leaves, no birds were visible.

After a while, they reached more open spaces, where the shadows were thinner; and came even to portions over which shadows only flitted, leaving them clear for such as might follow. Now a wonderful form, half bird-like half human, would float across on outspread sailing pinions. Anon an exquisite shadow-group of gambolling children would be followed by the loveliest female form, and that again by the grand stride of a Titanic shape, each disappearing in the surrounding press of shadowy foliage. Sometimes a profile of unspeakable beauty or grandeur would appear for a moment and vanish. Sometimes they seemed lovers that passed linked arm in arm, sometimes father and son, sometimes brothers in loving contest, sometimes sisters entwined in gracefullest community of complex form. Sometimes wild horses would tear across, free, or bestrode by noble shadows of ruling men. But some of the things which pleased them most they never knew how to describe.

About the middle of the plain they sat down to rest in the heart of a heap of shadows. After sitting for a while, each, looking up, saw the other in tears: they were each longing after the country whence the shadows fell.

"We *must* find the country from which the shadows come," said Mossy.

"We must, dear Mossy," responded Tangle. "What if your golden key should be the key to *it*?"

"Ah! that would be grand," returned Mossy.—"But we must rest here for a little, and then we shall be able to cross the plain before night."

So he lay down on the ground, and about him on every side, and over his head, was the constant play of the wonderful shadows. He could look through them, and see the one behind the other, till they mixed in a mass of darkness. Tangle, too, lay admiring, and wondering, and longing after the country whence the shadows came. When they were rested they rose and pursued their journey.

How long they were in crossing this plain I cannot tell; but before night Mossy's hair was streaked with grey, and Tangle had got wrinkles on her forehead.

As evening drew on, the shadows fell deeper and rose higher. At length they reached a place where they rose above their heads, and made all dark around them. Then they took hold of each other's hand, and walked on in silence and in some dismay. They felt the gathering darkness, and something strangely solemn besides, and the beauty of the shadows ceased to delight them. All at once Tangle found that she had not a hold of Mossy's hand, though when she lost it she could not tell.

"Mossy, Mossy!" she cried aloud in terror.

But no Mossy replied.

A moment after, the shadows sank to her feet, and down under her feet, and the mountains rose before her. She turned towards the gloomy region she had left, and called once more upon Mossy. There the gloom lay tossing and heaving, a dark, stormy, foamless sea of shadows, but no Mossy rose out of it, or came climbing up the hill on which she stood. She threw herself down and wept in despair.

Suddenly she remembered that the beautiful lady had told them, if they lost each other in a country of which she could not remember the name, they were not to be afraid, but to go straight on.

"And besides," she said to herself, "Mossy has the golden key, and so no harm will come to him, I do believe."

She rose from the ground, and went on.

Before long she arrived at a precipice, in the face of which a stair was cut. When she had ascended half-way, the stair ceased, and the path led straight into the mountain. She was afraid to enter, and turning again towards the stair, grew giddy at the sight of the depth beneath her, and was forced to throw herself down in the mouth of the cave.

When she opened her eyes, she saw a beautiful little creature with wings standing beside her, waiting.

"I know you," said Tangle. "You are my fish."

"Yes. But I am a fish no longer. I am an aëranth now."

"What is that?" asked Tangle.

"What you see I am," answered the shape. "And I am come to lead you through the mountain."

"Oh! thank you, dear fish—aëranth, I mean," returned Tangle, rising.

Thereupon the aëranth took to his wings, and flew on through the long, narrow passage, reminding Tangle very much of the way he had swum on before when he was a fish. And the moment his white wings moved, they began to throw off a continuous shower of sparks of all colours, which lighted up the passage before them.—All at once he vanished, and Tangle heard a low, sweet sound, quite different from the rush and crackle of his wings. Before her was an open arch, and through it came light, mixed with the sound of sea-waves.

She hurried out, and fell, tired and happy, upon the yellow sand of the shore. There she lay, half asleep with weariness and rest, listening to the low plash and retreat of the tiny waves, which seemed ever enticing the land to leave off being land, and become sea. And as she lay, her eyes were fixed upon the foot of a great rainbow standing far away against the sky on the other side of the sea. At length she fell fast asleep.

When she awoke, she saw an old man with long white hair down to his shoulders, leaning upon a stick covered with green buds, and so bending over her.

"What do you want here, beautiful woman?" he said.

"Am I beautiful? I am so glad!" answered Tangle, rising. "My grandmother is beautiful."

"Yes. But what do you want?" he repeated, kindly.

"I think I want you. Are not you the Old Man of the Sea?"

"I am."

"Then Grandmother says, have you any more fishes ready for her?"

"We will go and see, my dear," answered the old man, speaking yet more kindly than before. "And I can do something for you, can I not?"

"Yes—show me the way up to the country from which the shadows fall," said Tangle.

For there she hoped to find Mossy again.

"Ah! indeed, that would be worth doing," said the old man. "But I cannot, for I do not know the way myself. But I will send you to the Old Man of the Earth. Perhaps he can tell you. He is much older than I am."

Leaning on his staff, he conducted her along the shore to a steep rock, that looked like a petrified ship turned upside down. The door of it was the rudder of a great vessel, ages ago at the bottom of the sea. Immediately within the door was a stair in the rock, down which the old man went, and Tangle followed. At the bottom the old man had his house, and there he lived.

As soon as she entered it, Tangle heard a strange noise, unlike anything she had ever heard before. She soon found that it was the fishes talking. She tried to understand what they said; but their speech was so old-fashioned, and rude, and undefined, that she could not make much of it.

"I will go and see about those fishes for my daughter," said the Old Man of the Sea.

And moving a slide in the wall of his house, he first looked out, and then tapped upon a thick piece of crystal that filled the round opening. Tangle came up behind him, and peeping through the window into the heart of the great deep green ocean, saw the most curious creatures, some very ugly, all very odd, and with especially queer mouths, swimming about everywhere, above and below, but all coming towards the window in answer to the tap of the Old Man of the Sea. Only a few could get their mouths against the glass; but those who were floating miles away yet turned their heads towards it. The Old Man looked through the whole flock carefully for some minutes, and then turning to Tangle, said:

"I am sorry I have not got one ready yet. I want more time than she does. But I will send some as soon as I can."

He then shut the slide.

Presently a great noise arose in the sea. The Old Man opened the slide again, and tapped on the glass, whereupon the fishes were all as still as asleep.

"They were only talking about you," he said. "And they do speak such nonsense!—To-morrow," he continued, "I must show you the way to the Old Man of the Earth. He lives a long way from here."

"Do let me go at once," said Tangle.

"No. That is not possible. You must come this way first."

He led her to a hole in the wall, which she had not observed before. It was covered with the green leaves and white blossoms of a creeping plant.

"Only white-blossoming plants can grow under the sea," said the Old Man. "In there you will find a bath, in which you must lie till I call you."

Tangle went in, and found a smaller room or cave, in the further corner of which was a great basin hollowed out of rock, and half-full of the clearest sea-water. Little streams were constantly running into it from cracks in the wall of the cavern. It was polished quite smooth inside, and had a carpet of yellow sand in the bottom of it. Large green leaves and white flowers of various plants crowded up and over it, draping and covering it almost entirely.

No sooner was she undressed and lying in the bath, than she began to feel as if the water were sinking into her, and she were receiving all the good of sleep without undergoing its forgetfulness. She felt the good coming all the time. And she grew happier and more hopeful than she had been since she lost Mossy. But she could not help thinking how very sad it was for a poor old man to live there all alone, and have to take care of a whole seaful of stupid and riotous fishes.

After about an hour, as she thought, she heard his voice calling her, and rose out of the bath. All the fatigue and aching of her long journey had vanished. She was as whole, and strong, and well as if she had slept for seven days.

Returning to the opening that led into the other part of the house, she started back with amazement, for through it she saw the form of a grand man, with a majestic and beautiful face, waiting for her.

"Come," he said; "I see you are ready."

She entered with reverence.

"Where is the Old Man of the Sea?" she asked, humbly.

"There is no one here but me," he answered, smiling. "Some people call me the Old Man of the Sea. Others have another name for me, and are terribly frightened when they meet me taking a walk by the shore. Therefore I avoid being seen by them, for they are so afraid, that they never see what I really am. You see me now.—But I must show you the way to the Old Man of the Earth."

He led her into the cave where the bath was, and there she saw, in the opposite corner, a second opening in the rock.

"Go down that stair, and it will bring you to him," said the Old Man of the Sea.

With humble thanks Tangle took her leave. She went down the winding stair, till she began to fear there was no end to it. Still down and down it went, rough and broken, with springs of water bursting out of the rocks and running down the steps beside her. It was quite dark about her, and yet she could see. For after being in that bath, people's eyes always give out a light they can see by. There were no creeping things in the way. All was safe and pleasant, though so dark and damp and deep.

At last there was not one step more, and she found herself in a glimmering cave. On a stone in the middle of it sat a figure with its back towards her— the figure of an old man bent double with age. From behind she could see his white beard spread out on the rocky floor in front of him. He did not move as she entered, so she passed round that she might stand before him and speak to him.

The moment she looked in his face, she saw that he was a youth of marvellous beauty. He sat entranced with the delight of what he beheld in a mirror of something like silver, which lay on the floor at his feet, and which from behind she had taken for his white beard. He sat on, heedless of her presence, pale with the joy of his vision. She stood and watched him. At length, all trembling, she spoke. But her voice made no sound. Yet the youth lifted up his head. He showed no surprise, however, at seeing her— only smiled a welcome.

"Are you the Old Man of the Earth?" Tangle had said.

And the youth answered, and Tangle heard him, though not with her ears:

"I am. What can I do for you?"

"Tell me the way to the country whence the shadows fall."

"Ah! that I do not know. I only dream about it myself. I see its shadows sometimes in my mirror: the way to it I do not know. But I think the Old Man of the Fire must know. He is much older than I am. He is the oldest man of all."

"Where does he live?"

"I will show you the way to his place. I never saw him myself."

So saying, the young man rose, and then stood for a while gazing at Tangle.

"I wish I could see that country too," he said. "But I must mind my work."

He led her to the side of the cave, and told her to lay her ear against the wall.

"What do you hear?" he asked.

"I hear," answered Tangle, "the sound of a great water running inside the rock."

"That river runs down to the dwelling of the oldest man of all—the Old Man of the Fire. I wish I could go to see him. But I must mind my work. That river is the only way to him."

Then the Old Man of the Earth stooped over the floor of the cave, raised a huge stone from it, and left it leaning. It disclosed a great hole that went plumb-down.

"That is the way," he said.

"But there are no stairs."

"You must throw yourself in. There is no other way."

She turned and looked him full in the face—stood so for a whole minute, as she thought: it was a whole year—then threw herself headlong into the hole.

When she came to herself, she found herself gliding down fast and deep. Her head was under water, but that did not signify, for, when she thought about it, she could not remember that she had breathed once since her bath in the cave of the Old Man of the Sea. When she lifted up her head a sudden and fierce heat struck her, and she sank it again instantly, and went sweeping on.

Gradually the stream grew shallower. At length she could hardly keep her head under. Then the water could carry her no farther. She rose from the channel, and went step for step down the burning descent. The water ceased altogether. The heat was terrible. She felt scorched to the bone, but it did not touch her strength. It grew hotter and hotter. She said, "I can bear it no longer." Yet she went on.

At the long last, the stair ended at a rude archway in an all but glowing rock. Through this archway Tangle fell exhausted into a cool mossy cave. The floor and walls were covered with moss—green, soft, and damp. A little stream spouted from a rent in the rock and fell into a basin of moss. She plunged her face into it and drank. Then she lifted her head and looked around. Then she rose and looked again. She saw no one in the cave. But the moment she stood upright she had a marvellous sense that she was in the secret of the earth and all its ways. Everything she had seen, or learned from books; all that her grandmother had said or sung to her; all the talk of the beasts, birds, and fishes; all that happened to her on her journey with Mossy, and since then in the heart of the earth with the old man and the older man—all was plain: she understood it all, and saw that everything meant the same thing, though she could not have put it into words again.

The next moment she descried, in a corner of the cave, a little naked child, sitting on the moss. He was playing with balls of various colours and sizes, which he disposed in strange figures upon the floor beside him. And now Tangle felt that there was something in her knowledge which was not in her understanding. For she knew there must be an infinite meaning in the change and sequence and individual forms of the figures into which the child arranged the balls, as well as in the varied harmonies of their colours, but what it all meant she could not tell.* He went on busily, tirelessly, playing his solitary game, without looking up, or seeming to know that there was a stranger in his deep-withdrawn cell. Diligently as a lace-maker shifts her bobbins, he shifted and arranged his balls. Flashes of meaning would now pass from them to Tangle, and now again all would be not

* I think I must be indebted to Novalis for these geometrical figures.

merely obscure, but utterly dark. She stood looking for a long time, for there was fascination in the sight; and the longer she looked the more an indescribable vague intelligence went on rousing itself in her mind. For seven years she had stood there watching the naked child with his coloured balls, and it seemed to her like seven hours, when all at once the shape the balls took, she knew not why, reminded her of the Valley of Shadows, and she spoke:

"Where is the Old Man of the Fire?" she said.

"Here I am," answered the child, rising and leaving his balls on the moss. "What can I do for you?"

There was such an awfulness of absolute repose on the face of the child that Tangle stood dumb before him. He had no smile, but the love in his large grey eyes was deep as the centre. And with the repose there lay on his face a shimmer as of moonlight, which seemed as if any moment it might break into such a ravishing smile as would cause the beholder to weep himself to death. But the smile never came, and the moonlight lay there unbroken. For the heart of the child was too deep for any smile to reach from it to his face.

"Are you the oldest man of all?" Tangle at length, although filled with awe, ventured to ask.

"Yes, I am. I am very, very old. I am able to help you, I know. I can help everybody."

And the child drew near and looked up in her face so that she burst into tears.

"Can you tell me the way to the country the shadows fall from?" she sobbed.

"Yes. I know the way quite well. I go there myself sometimes. But you could not go my way; you are not old enough. I will show you how you can go."

"Do not send me out into the great heat again," prayed Tangle.

"I will not," answered the child.

And he reached up, and put his little cool hand on her heart.

"Now," he said, "you can go. The fire will not burn you. Come."

He led her from the cave, and following him through another archway, she found herself in a vast desert of sand and rock. The sky of it was of rock, lowering over them like solid thunderclouds; and the whole place was so hot that she saw, in bright rivulets, the yellow gold and white silver and red copper trickling molten from the rocks. But the heat never came near her.

When they had gone some distance, the child turned up a great stone, and took something like an egg from under it. He next drew a long curved line in the sand with his finger, and laid the egg in it. He then spoke something Tangle could not understand. The egg broke, a small snake came out, and, lying in the line in the sand, grew and grew till he filled it. The moment he was thus full-grown, he began to glide away, undulating like a sea-wave.

"Follow that serpent," said the child. "He will lead you the right way."

Tangle followed the serpent. But she could not go far without looking back at the marvellous Child. He stood alone in the midst of the glowing desert, beside a fountain of red flame that had burst forth at his feet, his naked whiteness glimmering a pale rosy red in the torrid fire. There he stood, looking after her, till, from the lengthening distance, she could see him no more. The serpent went straight on, turning neither to the right nor left.

Meantime Mossy had got out of the lake of shadows, and, following his mournful, lonely way, had reached the sea-shore. It was a dark, stormy evening. The sun had set. The wind was blowing from the sea. The waves had surrounded the rock within which lay the Old Man's house. A deep water rolled between it and the shore, upon which a majestic figure was walking alone.

Mossy went up to him and said:

"Will you tell me where to find the Old Man of the Sea?"

"I am the Old Man of the Sea," the figure answered.

"I see a strong kingly man of middle age," returned Mossy.

Then the Old Man looked at him more intently, and said:

"Your sight, young man, is better than that of most who take this way. The night is stormy: come to my house and tell me what I can do for you."

Mossy followed him. The waves flew from before the footsteps of the Old Man of the Sea, and Mossy followed upon dry sand.

When they had reached the cave, they sat down and gazed at each other.

Now Mossy was an old man by this time. He looked much older than the Old Man of the Sea, and his feet were very weary.

After looking at him for a moment, the Old Man took him by the hand and led him into his inner cave. There he helped him to undress, and laid him in the bath. And he saw that one of his hands Mossy did not open.

"What have you in that hand?" he asked.

Mossy opened his hand, and there lay the golden key.

"Ah!" said the Old Man, "that accounts for your knowing me. And I know the way you have to go."

"I want to find the country whence the shadows fall," said Mossy.

"I dare say you do. So do I. But meantime, one thing is certain.—What is the key for, do you think?"

"For a keyhole somewhere. But I don't know why I keep it. I never could find the keyhole. And I have lived a good while, I believe," said Mossy, sadly. "I'm not sure that I'm not old. I know my feet ache."

"Do they?" said the Old Man, as if he really meant to ask the question; and Mossy, who was still lying in the bath, watched his feet for a moment before he replied.

"No, they do not," he answered. "Perhaps I am not old either."

"Get up and look at yourself in the water."

He rose and looked at himself in the water, and there was not a grey hair on his head or a wrinkle on his skin.

"You have tasted of death now," said the Old Man. "Is it good?"

"It is good," said Mossy. "It is better than life."

"No," said the Old Man; "it is only more life.—Your feet will make no holes in the water now."

"What do you mean?"

"I will show you that presently."

They returned to the outer cave, and sat and talked together for a long time. At length the Old Man of the Sea rose, and said to Mossy:

"Follow me."

He led him up the stair again, and opened another door. They stood on the level of the raging sea, looking towards the east. Across the waste of waters, against the bosom of a fierce black cloud, stood the foot of a rainbow, glowing in the dark.

"This indeed is my way," said Mossy, as soon as he saw the rainbow, and stepped out upon the sea. His feet made no holes in the water. He fought the wind, and clomb the waves, and went on towards the rainbow.

The storm died away. A lovely day and a lovelier night followed. A cool wind blew over the wide plain of the quiet ocean. And still Mossy journeyed eastward. But the rainbow had vanished with the storm.

Day after day he held on, and he thought he had no guide. He did not see how a shining fish under the waters directed his steps. He crossed the sea, and came to a great precipice of rock, up which he could discover but one path. Nor did this lead him farther than half-way up the rock, where it ended on a platform. Here he stood and pondered.—It could not be that the way stopped here, else what was the path for? It was a rough path, not very plain, yet certainly a path.—He examined the face of the rock. It was smooth as glass. But as his eyes kept roving hopelessly over it, something glittered, and he caught sight of a row of small sapphires. They bordered a little hole in the rock.

"The keyhole!" he cried.

He tried the key. It fitted. It turned. A great clang and clash, as of iron bolts on huge brazen cauldrons, echoed thunderously within. He drew out the key. The rock in front of him began to fall. He retreated from it as far as the breadth of the platform would allow. A great slab fell at his feet. In front was still the solid rock, with this one slab fallen forward out of it. But the moment he stepped upon it, a second fell, just short of the edge of the first, making the next step of a stair, which thus kept dropping itself before him as he ascended into the heart of the precipice. It led him into a hall fit for such an approach—irregular and rude in formation, but floor, sides, pillars, and vaulted roof, all one mass of shining stones of every colour that light can show. In the centre stood seven columns, ranged from red to violet. And on the pedestal of one of them sat a woman, motionless, with her face bowed upon her knees. Seven years had she sat there waiting. She lifted her head as Mossy drew near. It was Tangle. Her hair had grown to her feet, and was rippled like the windless sea on broad sands. Her face was beautiful, like her grandmother's, and as still and peaceful as that of the Old Man of the Fire. Her form was tall and noble. Yet Mossy knew her at once.

"How beautiful you are, Tangle!" he said, in delight and astonishment.

"Am I?" she returned. "Oh, I have waited for you so long! But you, you are like the Old Man of the Sea. No. You are like the Old Man of the Earth. No, no. You are like the oldest man of all. You are like them all. And yet you are my own old Mossy! How did you come here? What did you do after I lost you? Did you find the keyhole? Have you got the key still?"

She had a hundred questions to ask him, and he a hundred more to ask her. They told each other all their adventures, and were as happy as man and woman could be. For they were younger and better, and stronger and wiser, than they had ever been before.

It began to grow dark. And they wanted more than ever to reach the country whence the shadows fall. So they looked about them for a way out of the cave. The door by which Mossy entered had closed again, and there was half a mile of rock between them and the sea. Neither could Tangle find the opening in the floor by which the serpent had led her thither. They searched till it grew so dark that they could see nothing, and gave it up.

After a while, however, the cave began to glimmer again. The light came from the moon, but it did not look like moonlight, for it gleamed through those seven pillars in the middle, and filled the place with all colours. And now Mossy saw that there was a pillar beside the red one, which he had not observed before. And it was of the same new colour that he had seen in the rainbow when he saw it first in the fairy forest. And on it he saw a sparkle of blue. It was the sapphires round the keyhole.

He took his key. It turned in the lock to the sound of Aeolian music. A door opened upon slow hinges, and disclosed a winding stair within. The key vanished from his fingers. Tangle went up. Mossy followed. The door closed behind them. They climbed out of the earth; and, still climbing, rose above it. They were in the rainbow. Far abroad, over ocean and land, they could see through its transparent walls the earth beneath their feet. Stairs beside stairs wound up together, and beautiful beings of all ages climbed along with them.

They knew that they were going up to the country whence the shadows fall.

And by this time I think they must have got there.

1867

The Stolen Child

WILLIAM BUTLER YEATS

Where dips the rocky highland
   Of Slewth Wood in the lake.
There lies a leafy island
   Where flapping herons wake
The drowsy water-rats;
There we've hid our fairy vats
Full of berries
And of reddest stolen cherries.
Come away, O human child!
To the woods and waters wild
With a fairy, hand in hand,
For the world's more full of weeping than you
   can understand.

Where the wave of moonlight glosses
   The dim grey sands with light,
Far off by furthest Rosses
   We foot it all the night,
Weaving olden dances,
Mingling hands and mingling glances
   Till the moon has taken flight;
To and fro we leap
   And chase the frothy bubbles.
   While the world is full of troubles
And is anxious in its sleep.

The Stolen Child

Come away, O human child!
To the woods and waters wild
With a fairy, hand in hand,
For the world's more full of weeping than you
    can understand.

Where the wandering water gushes
    From the hills above Glen-Car,
In pools among the rushes
    That scarce could bathe a star,
We seek for slumbering trout,
    And whispering in their ears
      We give them evil dreams,
Leaning softly out
    From ferns that drop their tears
      Of dew on the young streams.
Come, O human child!
To the woods and waters wild
With a fairy, hand in hand,
For the world's more full of weeping than you
    can understand.

Away with us he's going,
    The solemn-eyed—
He'll hear no more the lowing
Of the calves on the warm hill-side,
Or the kettle on the hob
Sing peace into his breast,
Or see the brown mice bob
    Round and round the oatmeal chest.
For he comes, the human child,
To the woods and waters wild
With a fairy, hand in hand,
For the world's more full of weeping than he
    can understand.

1889

The Selfish Giant

OSCAR WILDE

E very afternoon, as they were coming from school, the children used to go and play in the Giant's garden.

It was a large lovely garden, with soft green grass. Here and there over the grass stood beautiful flowers like stars, and there were twelve peach-trees that in the springtime broke out into delicate blossoms of pink and pearl, and in the autumn bore rich fruit. The birds sat on the trees and sang so sweetly that the children used to stop their games in order to listen to them. "How happy we are here!" they cried to each other.

One day the Giant came back. He had been to visit his friend the Cornish ogre, and had stayed with him for seven years. After the seven years were over he had said all that he had to say, for his conversation was limited, and he determined to return to his own castle. When he arrived he saw the children playing in the garden.

"What are you doing there?" he cried in a very gruff voice, and the children ran away.

"My own garden is my own garden," said the Giant; "anyone can understand that, and I will allow nobody to play in it but myself." So he built a high wall all around it, and put up a notice-board.

TRESPASSERS

WILL BE

PROSECUTED

He was a very selfish Giant.

The poor children had now nowhere to play. They tried to play on the road, but the road was very dusty and full of hard stones, and they did not like it. They used to wander round the high wall when their lessons were over, and talk about the beautiful garden inside. "How happy we were there," they said to each other.

Then the Spring came, and all over the country there were little blossoms and little birds. Only in the garden of the Selfish Giant it was still winter. The birds did not care to sing in it as there were no children, and the trees forgot to blossom. Once a beautiful flower put its head out from the grass, but when it saw the notice-board it was so sorry for the children that it slipped back into the ground again, and went off to sleep. The only people who were pleased were the Snow and the Frost. "Spring has forgotten this garden," they cried, "so we will live here all the year round." The Snow covered up the grass with her great white cloak, and the Frost painted all the trees silver. Then they invited the North Wind to stay with them, and he came. He was wrapped in furs, and he roared all day about the garden, and blew the chimney-pots down. "This is a delightful spot," he said, "we must ask the Hail on a visit." So the Hail came. Every day for three hours he rattled on the roof of the castle till he broke most of the slates, and then he ran round and round the garden as fast as he could go. He was dressed in grey, and his breath was like ice.

"I cannot understand why the Spring is so late in coming," said the Selfish Giant, as he sat at the window and looked out at his cold white garden; "I hope there will be a change in the weather."

But the Spring never came, nor the Summer. The Autumn gave golden fruit to every garden, but to the Giant's garden she gave none. "He is too selfish," she said. So it was always winter there, and the North Wind, and the Hail, and the Frost, and the Snow danced about through the trees.

One morning the Giant was lying awake in bed when he heard some lovely music. It sounded so sweet to his ears that he thought it must be the King's musicians passing by. It was really only a little linnet singing outside his window, but it was so long since he had heard a bird sing in his garden that it seemed to him to be the most beautiful music in the world. Then the Hail stopped dancing over his head, and the North Wind ceased roaring, and a delicious perfume came to him through the open casement. "I believe the Spring has come at last," said the Giant; and he jumped out of bed and looked out.

What did he see?

He saw a most wonderful sight. Through a little hole in the wall the children had crept in, and they were sitting in the branches of the trees. In every tree that he could see there was a little child. And the trees were so glad to have the children back again that they had covered themselves with blossoms, and were waving their arms gently above the children's heads. The birds were flying about and twittering with delight, and the flowers were looking up through the green grass and laughing. It was a lovely scene, only in one corner it was still winter. It was the farthest corner of the garden, and in it was standing a little boy. He was so small that he could not reach up to the branches of the tree, and he was wandering all round it, crying bitterly. The poor tree was still quite covered with frost and snow, and the North Wind was blowing and roaring above it. "Climb up! little boy," said the tree, and it bent its branches down as low as it could; but the boy was too tiny.

And the Giant's heart melted as he looked out. "How selfish I have been!" he said; "now I know why the Spring would not come here. I will put that poor little boy on the top of the tree, and then I will knock down the wall, and my garden shall be the children's playground for ever and ever." He was really very sorry for what he had done.

So he crept down stairs and opened the front door quite softly, and went out into the garden. But when the children saw him they were so frightened that they all ran away, and the garden became winter again. Only the little boy did not run, for his eyes were so full of tears that he did not see the Giant coming. And the Giant stole up behind him and took him gently in his hand, and put him up into the tree. And the tree broke at once into blossom, and the birds came and sang on it, and the little boy stretched out his two arms and flung them round the Giant's neck, and kissed him. And the other children, when they saw that the Giant was not wicked any longer, came running back, and with them came the Spring. "It is your garden now, little children," said the Giant, and he took a great axe and knocked down the wall. And when the people were going to market at twelve o'clock they found the Giant playing with the children in the most beautiful garden they had ever seen.

All day long they played, and in the evening they came to the Giant to bid him good-bye.

"But where is your little companion?" he said; "the boy I put into the tree." The Giant loved him the best because he had kissed him.

"We don't know," answered the children; "he has gone away."

"You must tell him to be sure and come here to-morrow," said the Giant. But the children said that they did not know where he lived, and had never seen him before; and the Giant felt very sad.

Every afternoon, when school was over, the children came and played with the Giant. But the little boy whom the Giant loved was never seen again. The Giant was very kind to all the children, yet he longed for his first little friend, and often spoke of him. "How I would like to see him!" he used to say.

Years went over, and the Giant grew very old and feeble. He could not play about any more, so he sat in a huge arm-chair, and watched the children at their games, and admired his garden. "I have many beautiful flowers," he said; "but the children are the most beautiful flowers of all."

One winter morning he looked out of his window as he was dressing. He did not hate the Winter now, for he knew that it was merely the Spring asleep, and that the flowers were resting.

Suddenly he rubbed his eyes in wonder, and looked and looked. It certainly was a marvellous sight. In the farthest corner of the garden was a tree quite covered with lovely white blossoms. Its branches were all golden, and silver fruit hung down from them, and underneath it stood the little boy he had loved.

Down stairs ran the Giant in great joy, and out into the garden. He hastened across the grass, and came near to the child. And when he came quite close his face grew red with anger, and he said, "Who hath dared to wound thee?" For on the palms of the child's hands were the prints of two nails, and the prints of two nails were on the little feet.

"Who hath dared to wound thee?" cried the Giant; "tell me, that I may take my big sword and slay him."

"Nay!" answered the child; "but these are the wounds of Love."

"Who art thou?" said the Giant, and a strange awe fell on him, and he knelt before the little child.

And the child smiled on the Giant, and said to him, "You let me play once in your garden, today you shall come with me to my garden, which is Paradise."

And when the children ran in that afternoon, they found the Giant lying dead under the tree, all covered with white blossoms.

1888

The Brown Owl

FORD MADOX FORD

Once upon a time, a long while ago—in fact long before Egypt had risen to power and before Rome or Greece had ever been heard of—and that was some time before you were born, you know—there was a king who reigned over a very large and powerful kingdom.

Now this king was rather old, he had founded his kingdom himself, and he had reigned over it nine hundred and ninety-nine and a half years already. As I have said before, it was a very large kingdom, for it contained, among other things, the whole of the western half of the world. The rest of the world was divided into smaller kingdoms, and each kingdom was ruled over by separate princes, who, however, were none of them so old as Intafernes, as he was called.

Now King Intafernes was an exceedingly powerful magician—that was why he had remained so long on the throne; for you must know that in this country the people were divided into two classes—those who were magicians, and those who weren't. The magicians called themselves Aristocrats, and the others called themselves what they liked; also in this country, as in all other countries, the rich magicians had the upper hand over the rest, but still the others did not grumble, for they were not badly treated on the whole. Now of all the magicians in the country the King was the greatest, and no one approached him in magic power but the Chancellor, who was called Merrymineral, and he even was no match for the King.

Among other things King Intafernes had a daughter, who was exceedingly beautiful—as indeed all princesses are or ought to be. She had a very fair face, and a wealth of golden hair that fell over her shoulders, like a shining waterfall falling in ripples to her waist.

Now in the thousandth year of her father's reign the Princess was eighteen, and in that country she was already of age. Three days before her nineteenth birthday, however, her father fell sick and gradually weakened, until at last he had only strength left to lie in his royal bed. Still, however, he retained his faculties, and on the Princess's birthday he made all the magicians file before his bed and swear to be faithful for ever to the Princess. Last of all came the Chancellor, the pious Merrymineral, and as he took the oath the King looked at him with a loving glance and said:

"Ah! my dear Merrymineral, in truth there was no need for thee to have taken the oath, for it is thy nature to be faithful; and it being thy nature, thou couldst not but be faithful."

To which the pious Merrymineral answered:

"To such a master and to such a mistress how could I but be faithful?" and to this noble sentiment the three hundred and forty-seven magicians could not help according unanimous applause.

When they were quiet again the King said:

"So be it, good Merrymineral, do thou always act up to thy words. But now leave, good men all, for I am near my end, and would fain spend my last moments with my daughter here."

Sorrowfully, one by one, the courtiers left, wishing him their last adieux. He had been a good king to all, all through his long reign, and they were sorry that he had to leave them at last.

Soon they were all gone except the good Merrymineral, and at last he too went, his whole frame shaking with suppressed sobs; his body seemed powerless with grief, and his limbs seemed to refuse their functions. The King looked after him, carefully noticing whether the door was shut. Then he spoke:

"My dear daughter," he said, "when I am gone be kind to every one, and, above all, cherish the Owl—do cherish the Owl—promise me to cherish the Owl."

"But how can I cherish the Owl?" cried the poor Princess; "how can I, unless I know who he is?"

But the King only answered:

"Dear Ismara, do promise to cherish the Owl!"

And he said nothing else for a long time, until at last the Princess saw that the only way to let him rest in peace was to promise, and she said:

"I promise, dear father, but still I do wish I knew who or what the Owl is that I am to cherish."

"You will see that in good time." answered the King. "Now, my dear Ismara, I shall die happy, and you will be safe. If you had not promised—however, we will let that rest unsaid. Now wheel the bed to where I can see out of the window."

The Princess did as she was told. Now from this you must not imagine that she was a very strong princess—for she was no stronger than most princesses her age; but the old King, who was a very powerful magician, as I have told you already, made the bed easy for her to move. He might have made it move of its own accord, but he knew that it would please his daughter to be of service to him, and so he let her move it.

The view from the window was very fine. A dark wood grew in the foreground, and far away over the tree-tops were the blue hills, behind which the sun was just preparing to retire. And it seemed angry, the sun, for its face was dark and clouded, and its beams smote fiercely on everything, and gilded the tops of the autumn trees with a purer gold than their natural tint. But overhead the clouds spread darkly, and they reached in a black pall to the verge of the horizon, forming a black frame to the red-gold sunset; for only the extreme west was bright with the waning light.

The Princess sat on the bed beside the King, and the dying sun lit them both and fell with a ruddy glare on the King's hard countenance, as if it knew that his work on earth for the day, and for ever, was done.

"Is it not grand?" cried the old King, as if the glorious sight warmed his blood again and made him once more young. "And is it not grand to think of the power thou hast, my daughter? If thou but raise thy little finger armies will move from world's end to world's end. Fleets come daily from every land for thee alone; all that thou seest is thine, and utterly within thy power. Think of the power, the grand power, of swaying the world."

But long before he had got thus far, the Princess was weeping bitterly— partly at the overwhelming prospect, and partly from her great grief. She seized her father's hand and kissed it passionately.

"My father, my father," she cried, "say not so; they are all thine, not mine, for thou livest still, and all is yet well."

But the old King cut her short:

"Dost thou see the sun? Look, its lower rim is already cut by the mountains. When its disc is hidden I too shall have joined the majority, and my soul will have left my body, and the power will be thine. But above all cherish the Owl. Never go out of its sight, for if thou do, some harm will happen."

As he stopped speaking a flash of lightning lit up the sky, and the sullen roar of distant thunder followed.

From every church in the land the passing bell tolled forth and the solemn sounds came swelling on the breeze. Again came the flash of lightning, and again the thunder, and now the splash of falling rain accompanied and almost drowned the thunder. The sun's rim was now almost down.

For the last time the old King kissed his daughter, as she hung weeping on his neck. Again the lightning came, but this time the thunder was drowned in a more fearful sound. Never before had the sound been heard, except at the death of the Princess's mother. It was the passing bell of the cathedral of the town. And as its sound went forth throughout the whole land men shook their heads in sorrow, for they knew that the soul of the good King had left his body. Through the whole land the news was known—to every one except to the Princess.

For she lay on the bed passionately kissing the dead face—not yet cold in death—and calling on his name in vain; for the ears of the dead are closed "to the voice of the charmer, charm he never so wisely."

Gradually the voice of the Princess died away into low sobs and her breathing came more regularly, and in spite of the tolling of the death-bell she slept, worn out by her grief. No one came near her, for at the Court no one was allowed to enter the royal presence without a command, whatever happened. So for a time the Princess slept on, clasping the still face to her warm cheek. But at last the death-cold of the face wakened her once more to the death-cold of the world. For a time her wakening dreams refused to let her believe the worst, but the stern reality forced itself on her. She raised herself on her two arms and gazed through the darkness at the white face that made her shudder when her longing eyes at last traced out its lines as a flash of lightning lit it up. She sprang off the bed with the wild impulse of calling for help.

But no sooner had she got to the door and had given the call than she once more fainted and seemed for a time lifeless.

When she came to herself again she was in bed in her own room. It was still night, and at the side of her bed a night-light was burning in a glass shade. She could not understand what it all meant; but her head did ache so, and she could not tell why they were making such a noise at the far end of the room. For you see she was lying on her back low down in the pillows, and so she could not see beyond the foot of the bed. However, she raised herself on her elbow and looked. For a short time she could see nothing, for the room was somewhat dark, as the night-light gave but little light. But at the other end of the room a large fire was burning, and by its light the Princess saw a strange scene.

For in the middle of the floor she could make out a group of three ladies-in-waiting, who were struggling with a large black object—what it was the Princess could not see, but it seemed to be attempting to attack the Court doctor, who was huddled up in a corner with his umbrella spread out before him, and he was gradually sinking down behind it, giving vent to the most horrible groans and shrieks for mercy, and calling to the ladies to keep it off. However, in spite of their efforts, the "thing" was gradually drawing them nearer and nearer to the poor doctor.

But the strangest thing of all was that the doctor's face was lit up by two distinct rounds of light. It was just as if some one had turned the light of a bull's-eye lantern on him, and this the Princess could not understand at all. However, she lay still and watched.

The doctor got farther and farther behind the umbrella until only his head appeared over the top of it. At last he shrieked:

"Send for a regiment of Lifeguards—let them shoot the Owl—it is necessary for the health of the Princess. Owls are very bad things to have in bedrooms—they bring scarlatina, and they always carry the influenza epidemic. Lifeguards, I tell you, send for them." But still the "thing" came nearer, and with an agonized shriek of "The Owl!" he sank altogether under the rim.

This loud cry of "The Owl" roused the Princess, and she remembered her promise to cherish the Owl. So she called to the ladies-in-waiting, and they, astonished, let go the thing, and the Owl immediately flew at the umbrella, underneath which the doctor was coiled up, and perched on the top. The Princess, however, thought it was rather rash to have promised to cherish the Owl if it was going to eat up her physicians in that reckless manner. However, the Owl did not seem aggressive, and only seemed as if it were waiting for further orders. The Princess determined to see if it would come when it was called, like a dog. So she called in a sweet, persuasive voice:

"Come here, good Owl."

Immediately the dark shape of the Owl flitted noiselessly to her side as she sat on the bed. The wind of its flight blew out the flickering nightlight in spite of the glass shade. But the glittering eyes of the Owl lit up the whole room, so that there was no need of light. As it alighted on the bed it turned its eyes on the Princess as much as to say, "What shall I do now?"

But the fierce light of the eyes was softened as it turned to her, as if the Owl feared to hurt her with the blinding rays.

"Cherished Owl," said the Princess, "why didst thou hurt the physician?"

The Owl shook his head; but the Princess could not understand whether he meant that he did not know why he had hurt him, or if he meant he had not hurt him. So the Princess told one of the ladies-in-waiting to remove the umbrella from over the doctor. But this was not so easy as it sounded, for the doctor held firmly on to the handle, and in spite of the united efforts of the three ladies-in-waiting he managed to hold on. At last the Princess lost patience.

"Go and help them, good Owl," she said; and the Owl, overjoyed, flew to the doctor, and seizing the top of the umbrella flew with it up to the ceiling, and as the doctor still held on, he flew round and round, until the doctor, hitting the top of a cupboard, let go, and fell in a heap in the middle of the floor, where he lay half unconscious, repeating as he sat:

"Orange juice for influenza; try a seidlitz powder and a blue pill, and keep the owls out of the room and take a warm bath, and—send for the Lifeguards."

But the Princess did not seem inclined to send for them; and in truth it would have been rather awkward for the horses to get in, as the room was on the second floor.

So the Princess told the ladies-in-waiting to drag him out of the room, and they obeyed; but as he went he said, "Sleeping in unaired sheets causes rheumatism, sciatica, pleurisy, pneumonia, and—owls"; and as the door closed they heard him say, "Gregory powder and Epsom salts."

The poor Princess, however, began to weep again, and the Owl sat perched on the bed-post at her feet, watching her with his bright eyes.

However, after she had cried thus for a long time, she thought it would be better to stop her tears, for they were all in vain, as she knew but too well.

So she rose from her bed; for you must know she had only been laid on her bed when she had fainted, and so she still had all her clothes on.

Through the window-blinds the light of dawn was already beginning to show itself. So the Princess went to the window and drew back the curtains, and let the bright sunlight shine into the room. A beautiful day was dawning after last night's rain, and the sun was rising brightly over the edge of the blue sea. For a moment, as she looked out, everything was quiet except the shrill chirp of a solitary sparrow that seemed to have awakened too early. From the chimneys of the red-roofed town below her no smoke was rising, for all in the town were asleep still.

Suddenly, with a rush, the morning breeze came from over the land behind her, and with the rustle of the wind everything seemed to wake and come to life once more. The solitary chirp of the sparrow was drowned in the flood of song that poured forth from the trees in the palace garden, and with the birds the rest of the living animals awoke, and from far inland the lowing of the cows was borne on the breeze, and now and again came the joyful bark of the shepherd's dog as it recognized its master's whistle as he called it to work again among the sheep, whose plaintive bleating came softly, as if from a distance, to the Princess's ear.

Everything seemed joyful at the sight of the beautiful morning except the Princess, and she felt oh so lonely, for it seemed as if her only friend had gone from her for ever. And at the thought her tears began to flow afresh, for she felt very lonely, while everything else seemed to rejoice. But as she leant thus against the window-sill, with a great lump in her throat and the hot tears in her eyes, she suddenly felt a weight on her shoulder and rushing wind waved her hair, and as she turned her head to see what it was, her face was covered in the soft brown feathers of the Owl, who had perched on her shoulder.

The touch of the Owl seemed to have driven away her grief, and she felt quite light and joyful in the beautiful sunshine. For it seemed as if the Owl had become a companion to her that would take the place of her father; so she leaned her head against the Owl, and her golden hair mixed with the dusky brown feathers, till each streak of golden hair shone again in the bright sunlight. And the Owl too seemed very happy. So for a time the Princess stood looking over the deep-blue sea.

Suddenly, however, a footstep sounded in the courtyard below, and the Princess drew back from the window, for a thought suddenly came into her head:

"Oh dear," she said, "I have been crying such a lot that my eyes must be quite red, and my hair is all ruffled. This will never do." And as she looked in the glass she said, "Ah, just as I thought. Come, my cherished Owl, sit there on the crown on the top of the looking-glass frame and wait while I wash my hands and face and make myself tidy."

The Owl did as he was told, and the Princess began to wash in cold water—a thing she had never done before—but she did not like to call to her ladies-in-waiting, lest they should see how red her eyes were. So she had to put up with the cold water, and very pleasant she found it, for it cleared the tear-mist out of her eyes and made her feel quite happy and cheerful again: "And I have heard," she thought to herself, "that washing in cold water is matchless for the complexion."

When she had finished washing she went and combed her hair before the glass. For she was a very artistic Princess, and liked looking at beautiful things, and so she liked sometimes to look at herself in the glass. Not that she was in the least conceited.

So she combed her hair with a gold comb, and when she had finished combing it, she put on her gold circlet as a sign of her rank, and then she said to the Owl, who had been sitting patiently on the looking-glass blinking at her as if he quite enjoyed himself:

"Now, cherished Owl, you may sit on my shoulder again."

When the Owl was again in his place he blinked in the glass at his own reflection as if the light were too strong for him, and he shut his eyes and drew in his neck and lifted up one foot into his feathers, as if he felt quite happy and comfortable, and the Princess smiled at his happy look, for she seemed quite to have forgotten her sorrow in the company of the Owl.

So she, with the Owl on her shoulder, went to the window. Here in the courtyard already a large crowd had collected to catch a glimpse of the Princess if possible, so that it fell about that when they saw her they raised a mighty shout of joy and pity:

"The King is dead," they cried. "Long live the Queen!" And throughout the city far and wide echoed and re-echoed the cry:

"Long live the Queen"; and it seemed as if the waves of the sea murmured the sound.

The Princess, however, held out her little hand to still the tumult, and as if by magic the cries stopped.

"Good people all," she said in clear ringing tones, "I thank you for your good wishes, and I will always try to be worthy of them as my father was. For to-day, however, rejoice not; remember that the great King Intrafernes, the founder of the kingdom to which we all belong, has but just left the earth—sorrow for him but a short time; joy will come soon enough for all."

So the crowd, silent and pensive for a time, dispersed in groups. More than one of them asked what had been perched on the Princess's shoulder, and those who had been near enough, said that it was an owl—though what it meant they knew not.

"To me it seemed as if the head of the old King were looking over his daughter's shoulder," said one of the listeners who stood on the outskirts of the crowd.

But she was only a little hunchback, and the rich citizens laughed at her, saying: "Tush, child—thy fancy is not sound! Or else before looking at the Princess thou didst look at the fierce sun, and the sun spots in thy eyes caused thee to see it thus. It was but an owl." But the little hunchback held to her own opnion.

But while the Princesss stood watching them depart, a tapping came at the door, and the Princess cried, "Come in." A page entered and said that the Chancellor, Merrymineral, was below and requested the audience of the Princess.

"Let him be shown into the audience-chamber to await me there."

The page bowed and departed on his errand, and the Princess went to another door in the room and down the staircase that led from it to the audience-chamber, and the Owl remained seated on her shoulder until they reached the room. When they got there the Chancellor had not yet entered, for the staircase from the Princess's bedroom to the audience-chamber was much shorter than that from the entrance-hall, and then you see the Princess was much more nimble than Merrymineral, who was an old man, and she ran quickly down stairs whilst he walked slowly up. However, at last he entered. As he came in the Princess said:

"Good morning, dear Merrymineral. How is it you are so late? I shall have to fine you if you keep me waiting like this again. And now what do you want with me?"

The good Chancellor received her laughing reproach with his head bowed down. He heaved a deep sigh, and drew his pocket-handkerchief from his pocket and applied it to his eyes. As he drew it away the tears could be seen flowing fast down his withered cheeks.

"I came," he moaned, "to console you for your great loss. I too," he continued in a voice choked with sobs, "I too am an orphan."

It seemed funny to the Princess to see him weeping thus, and she could hardly help laughing at him, but her grief soon came back.

"Poor Merrymineral," she sighed, "to you also it must be a sad blow, for you were always faithful and attached. But it was fated to happen thus, and you must really try and be comforted, for crying will not mend matters."

The Chancellor began again:

"The beloved King your father;" but his sobs choked him, and he hid his face.

"The beloved King your father," echoed a loud voice, exactly mimicking the tones of the Chancellor, but where the voice came from no one could tell. The Chancellor started.

"Did you say that?" said the Princess.

"Not the second time," answered Merrymineral.

"Who could it be?" said the Princess; "for there is no one in the room except the cherished Owl; and you can't speak, can you, Owl dear?"

The Owl shook his head dismally. But the change that came over Merrymineral was most astonishing as his eye suddenly lit upon the Owl—for since his entrance he had not raised his eyes from the floor. He jumped backwards over three rows of seats, for you see the seats in the audience-chamber were arranged in rows, and he alighted in a sitting position on the other side. As he sat on the floor he looked up at the Owl in a terrified manner, then threw up his arms and fainted. The poor Princess did not know what to do, so she rang a bell that stood on the table in front of the throne. Several pages at once came in.

"Just bring that man to," said the Princess.

The pages bowed low, and went and shook the Chancellor violently. He showed no signs of recovering, so one of the pages turned to the Princess and said:

"May it please your Majesty, but the Chancellor refuses to come to, and we can't bring him."

"So he refuses to obey my orders," said the Princess. "He must be punished for this. However, now go and get a bucketful of water and pour it on him. Perhaps that will bring him to."

Now when she said he was going to be punished, she was only joking, but she said it very gravely, so that many people might have thought it was quite in earnest. Meanwhile the pages departed to fetch the water. They soon came back and brought a large pailful.

"You had better not throw it all over him," said the Princess; "just let it trickle over his face gently."

So one of the pages began to do as he was told, but somehow—either he had a sudden push, or as he said afterwards, the Owl looked at him, and startled him—he let the pail go, and all the water and the pail too fell over the unlucky Chancellor. This really did bring him very much to—much too much to, in fact—for he sprang up in such a rage that the Princess really wished herself out of the room.

"You jackanapes," he screamed at the unfortunate page; "you ape, you boar, you cow, you clumsy monkey, I'll be revenged on you."

But the Princess, who had gained courage while he was screaming, said: "You will not be revenged on him."

"But I shall," he said.

"Indeed you will not," said the Princess, "for he did it by my orders,"

"Oh! he did it by your orders," said the Chancellor; "then I'll be revenged on you too," and he began to move uncomfortably near to the Princess. But the three pages threw themselves on him and tried to drag him back, but he turned suddenly on them.

"What," he said scornfully, "you try and stop me—ye frogs! Ah! a good idea—by virtue of my magic power I command you to turn into water-rats; then perhaps the Owl there will eat you up."

No sooner said than done, and the three pages instantly became water-rats, squattering in the water that was still in a pool on the floor.

Somehow the Princess did not seem to be frightened at this; she was only very angry.

"I thought I told you not to hurt those pages."

"Who cares what you say?"

"Dear me," thought the Princess, "he is getting excessively insolent—I shall have to be severe with him in a moment." So she said:

"Turn those pages back again."

"I shall not."

"Then leave the room."

"I shall not."

The Princess did not know what to do; he was really very rude, and he was walking towards her evidently intending to attack her. When he was within ten feet of her he stopped, and though he tried to get nearer he could not.

"Ha! ha!" he cried; "you think to keep me off by magic, but it is not so easy, I can tell you. I command you to turn into a mouse."

But the Princess, leaning her head against the soft feathers of the Owl, only smiled, and did not turn into a mouse at all.

The Chancellor seemed perplexed.

"Is that not enough for you?" he said; "I thought I told you to turn into a mouse."

But the Princess smiled calmly and said:

"Do you suppose I am going to do anything of the sort—you have forgotten your manners to speak to your Queen thus. I believe there is a fine of five shillings for any one who speaks to the King or Queen without saying 'your Majesty.' You had better pay it, Sir Chancellor, and turn those pages back again, or I shall have you turned out of the kingdom."

But the Chancellor laughed, "You can't send me out if you wanted to. Meanwhile I shall not turn those rats back, for if I am not much mistaken your Owl there will carry them off."

It really seemed as if the Owl were going to obey him, for greatly to the Princess's surprise it sprang off her shoulder and seized the three rats, one in each claw, and one in its beak—but it returned at once to her and laid them squeaking on the table in front of her—but no sooner did they touch the table than they turned into men again just as quickly as they had become rats. When Merrymineral saw this he became perfectly frantic, and tried in vain to get at the Princess—he even went back a little and tried to run at her—but it was no use, for no sooner did he reach a certain spot than he was suddenly stopped, just as if he had run against a wall. At last he became so frantic that the Princess could stand it no longer. So she said:

"Will you be quiet, you naughty old man?—leave the room or I will send for the police."

But Merrymineral answered:

"Oh, send for the police and the soldiers and sailors and candlestick-makers."

So the Princess rang the bell that stood on the table: a page at once appeared at the door.

"Send for a policeman and ask him to step this way."

The page looked astonished, but he saluted and left the room. Almost immediately a policeman came in—for you see there was one always on the palace steps. He entered the room with a low bow.

"Take the Chancellor out of the room," said the Princess, "and put him in prison for three days."

But the policeman shook his head.

"Excuse me, mum—I mean your most gracious Majesty—but it is against the law to imprison a member of Parliament, much less a chancellor."

The Chancellor laughed sarcastically.

"Oh, is it?" said the Princess; "never mind, take him into custody; I depose him—he is no longer Chancellor."

Merrymineral looked astonished but the policeman cleared his throat and said:

"Come, I say, young fellow; will you go quietly, or shall I make you?"

"Oh, make me, by all means," answered Merrymineral.

So the policeman advanced and held out his hand to take him by the collar, but had no sooner touched Merrymineral than he fell to the ground as if he had been thunderstruck.

The Chancellor smiled. "I told you so," he said.

The Princess was now thoroughly nonplussed. However, she rang the bell again. Again the page appeared.

"Summon the Lords of the Council; let them come here at once."

Almost immediately afterwards the lords appeared. As they came in each one bowed profoundly to the Princess. But in spite of their grave appearance they could not help looking astonished at the policeman who was lying on the floor, and at the three pages who were still sitting on the table—for as they had not yet been told to go they could not depart.

But each one took his seat without questioning. Last of all came the Court doctor, who looked in an alarmed manner at the Owl—nevertheless he took his seat.

When all was quiet the Princess began to speak.

"My lords," she said, "I have been obliged to assemble you on the first day of my reign; but the matter is a very grave one. I have found it necessary to dismiss the Chancellor, for these reasons: first, he attacked these three pages who were executing my bidding; next, he attacked me; and lastly, he attacked the law, in the person of the policeman there, whom he knocked down. Now I ask your advice as to how I am to get rid of him, for he refuses to leave the room at my command."

So spoke the Princess, but before any one could answer Merrymineral spoke:

"My lords," he said, "are we, we, the lords of the kingdom, to be governed by this schoolgirl, who is not even a magician as we are? What good has she ever done us? What power is to keep us from deposing her and electing as a ruler one of ourselves?"—but before he could finish a perfect uproar of shouts of rage interrupted him.

The Princess put her fingers in her ears to keep out the sound, and when the lords saw that the noise was annoying her they stopped at once. When they were quiet the Princess spoke again:

"What he has just said is right," she said; "I have no right to reign over you, for I am but a girl. Do ye therefore elect a ruler."

For a moment all was silence in the Council, but all eyes were turned on a lord who stood next to Merrymineral in rank. He was a portly man, and a great magician too, though his power was not quite so great as Merrymineral's. When therefore he saw that all eyes were turned on him, Lord Licec, for so he was called, rose.

"Your most gracious Majesty," he began, "although you had no need to command us to elect a ruler, we are of course bound to obey your commands, whatever they are. I therefore speak, giving my vote, and I believe the vote of all the rest of the assembly, that you shall be our ruler according to the oath which we sware to your father."

And then turning to the rest of the assembly he said:

"Am I not right, my lords?" and with one voice they answered:

"We will die for our Queen Ismara."

Only one voice objected, but as that was Merrymineral, no one noticed him.

So the Princess rose and thanked them for their confidence in her, though, to tell the truth, she had known all along what they would say. That done she said:

"And now what are we to do about turning this man out? for he refuses to go of his own accord."

No one could suggest anything better than to send for the Lifeguards and let them carry him off. But before this was done they decided to try to persuade him to go. But it was of no use, for he stood on the spot where he had stopped, with his arms folded and his hat on, looking down at the ground in a brown study, and he took no notice of anything they could do, even though they rang the bell close to his ear. Now he did no particular harm as he stood here, but you see no one could tell whom he might attack next. So they determined to send for the Lifeguards as a last resource.

So they were sent for, and in a short time they came, although they left their horses outside in the courtyard. Fifty of them were then marched into the hall and they were ordered to move the man out. So they divided into two parties of twenty-five each, and they put a rope around him, and each body of twenty-five took an end of the rope and pulled, but it was no good, for he took no more notice of the pulling than if he had been Samson or any other strong man. So the fifty gave up the attempt in despair; the only thing to do seemed to be to cut him to pieces. So they drew their swords and hacked at him, but it was no use: the swords bent or broke just as if they had been bulrushes or paper, and still Merrymineral took no notice in particular. So they gave up the attempt in despair when they had broken up all their swords. However, they did not give in, for they called in the best horseman in the regiment and told him to charge on horseback with his lance in rest. So the soldier rode in on his horse; this was not so difficult as it may seem, for the council chamber was on a level with the ground, and a lane was opened in between the chairs to where Merrymineral still stood with his arms folded.

At the word of command the soldier rode at full speed towards Merry-mineral, aiming his lance at the centre of his face—that is, his nose. His aim was true, and the lance hit fair, but it might just as well have been made of macaroni, for it crumbled just as a stick of that delightful eatable would do if you ran it against a wall. The horse, however, swerved just in time, although it pushed against him in going by; but even this made no difference to Merrymineral. As a last resource they suggested putting a lighted match under his nose. Whether this would have succeeded or not I can't say. But just at this moment Merrymineral seemed to wake up again.

"Ah," he said, "I see you have not yet managed to get me out of the room. However, as your soldiers have been practising on me for some time past, I think it only right that I should try my hand on them a little. I used to be thought rather strong in the arms at one time, and I have cut down a good many trees in my time. Just see how you like that," he said to the man on the horse as he swung his umbrella round his head and brought it down with a tremendous thwack on the horse's side. In fact he hit so hard that the horse and man were knocked right through the window into the courtyard below. With three more blows he knocked twenty more of the men through the same window, and the rest made their escape as fast as they could by the door.

"I see I have not quite forgotten how to clear a room yet," he said, as he once more folded his arms in the same attitude and relapsed into silence.

"What *am* I to do?" said the poor Princess, wringing her hands and almost crying with vexation.

A voice came from the far end of the room, and every one turned to see who it might be. And all saw it was the Court physician who spoke. "If I might be allowed to make a suggestion," he said, "I would say that the best thing your Majesty could do would be to request that gentleman who is sitting on your shoulder to turn him out. From my own experience I should say he was very competent to perform such a task. And if I might be allowed to add yet another suggestion it would be, 'to be well shaken before taken,' as they say in prescriptions."

As he said this an extraordinary change came over Merrymineral. He pressed his hat on his head, put his umbrella under his arm, and began to put on his gloves in such a hurry that he mistook the left for the right hand. As he did so he said:

"Do you know, I can't stop any longer; so sorry, but I have an engagement and I am rather in a hurry. Good-day." And he began to walk quickly towards the door. But the Princess had already whispered to the Owl, "Catch him, dear Owl."

And however fast he went the Owl caught him up, and taking him by the middle of his coat-tails—and I am bound to say some of his skin too— he shook him violently, and flew round and round the room, banging him violently against any high piece of furniture that was convenient.

"O-o-o-h," shrieked the wretched man, "I say, do you know you're tearing my best coat, and your beak is awfully sharp? O-o-ouch," and he filled the room with his shrieks. After they had continued like that for some minutes the Princess said:

"I think he has been punished enough now, cherished Owl, so let him down."

The Owl did as he was told, not, however, without giving him a sly tweak with his bill that must have hurt him a good deal.

"I'll be revenged on you," roared Merrymineral; "you've spoilt my Sunday coat, and I shan't be able to afford another for I don't know how long. I'll be revenged on you." And he took out a red pocket-handkerchief and began to suage the blood that was coming from the bite, all the while abusing the Owl and the Princess and threatening to be revenged.

"You had better be quiet and go," she said.

"I shall not."

"Oh, very well," she answered, "perhaps you would like to try the Owl again."

At the same time the Owl gave him such a look from its gleaming eyes that he turned first red and then white with fright. He made a dash for the window, and he was in such a hurry that he left his umbrella and one of his gloves behind him.

He jumped right through the window high into the air, and as soon as he got outside, strange to say, he began to burn furiously, and he went gradually up into the sky like a fire-balloon —just as when a piece of tissue-paper is put on the fire, if you are not careful, it will fly blazing up the chimney.

They watched him out of sight, and then the Princess said with a little sigh of relief:

"That's an end of him at last."

But the Owl shook his head—he knew better.

When he was thus at last got rid of the Princess said to the physician:

"How can we ever thank thee enough, good doctor, for thy timely suggestion!"

"Oh, your Majesty," said the blushing doctor, "experience does it; and I had plenty of that this morning. Do you know, I think I shall never be free again from pain—although I have bathed in opodeldoc and arnica, and I am clothed from head to foot in court plaster."

The Princess smiled and said:

"I am afraid the Owl is a little over-vigorous in such matters; however, I will give orders to the court apothecary to supply you with remedies at my expense until you shall be cured." She then said to the three pages who still sat on the table:

"I must ask you to depart now as Parliament cannot carry on business with strangers in the house. However, ye are, I believe, pages; I will turn over a new leaf and will advance you each a step in rank. Now, however, go."

Thanking her profusely they went. When they had gone the Princess turned to the Councillors and said:

"As there seems no further need to keep you, I will detain you no longer."

Having her permission the Councillors left the hall. Last of all was Lord Licec, and he remained as if hesitating whether to go, or to stay and speak to the Princess. She, noticing his hesitation, said:

"Ah, Lord Licec, hast thou something to ask me?"

The old lord made answer:

"I would ask your Majesty's permission to enter the room of the late King, your Majesty's father, for, as you are aware, it is against the law to enter the royal presence without royal permission."

"You have my permission of course; but ought not some preparations to be made for the funeral?"

Lord Licec answered:

"They are already made. For as the late King had announced his intention of dying yesterday at half-past six P.M., there was ample time."

"Let us then go together to the room, my lord," said the Princess.

So they went together, the Princess leaning on Licec's arm, and the Owl sitting on her shoulder.

The guards of the room saluted as they passed in, but what was their astonishment on entering to find that the King had disappeared. When they asked the guards who had come into the room during the day, they replied that no one had been near the room during their watch, and the guards of the watch before said exactly the same thing. All over the palace inquiries were made, but to no purpose, and the rumour gradually spread to the town, and throngs of anxious citizens flocked about the palace gates to ask, but neither they nor any one else ever heard what had become of him, and it is my opinion that the King himself is the only person who knew anything about it. It came out in the course of inquiries that when the attendants had rushed in on hearing the Princess's call for assistance the night before, they had not seen the King on the bed, but in his place had sat an enormous owl, and this owl had insisted on accompanying the Princess wherever she went.

This was the first time that the Princess had heard of how the Owl had come to her, but still she had known all along that the Owl was the one her father had made her promise to cherish. But there were ill-natured people who said that it was not so very unlikely that the Owl had eaten the King up, but the Princess laughed and said:

"How could the Owl eat a king up when the poor thing has so little appetite that it only eats very small pieces of meat off my golden fork at dinner?"

And so the Owl remained with the Princess: during the day it always sat on her shoulder, or took short flights round her head, and at night it slept on the foot of her bed.

So six weeks glided peacefully away, and everything prospered; but one day a terrified messenger rode into the city at full speed, and the message that he brought was this.

Merrymineral, who, as the Owl had said, was by no means done with, had been inciting the people of far-off lands such as Mesopotamia and Padan-Aram and Ireland to rebel, and he was now marching against the Princess at the head of an immense army, laying waste the country for miles around. At the rate he was coming, however, it would take him a fortnight to get near the country round. So you see there was no immediate danger; still an enemy's army could not be allowed to remain in the country unopposed. So the Princess gave Lord Licec the order to assemble the army, and, as you may imagine, it was an immense one when it did assemble. I can't say how large it was, but if you could have stood on a hill in the centre of the town you would have seen nothing for miles around but shining silk banners and glistening helmets and lances. Never before had the world held such an army, and never will again. Yet this army even was hardly as large as that of the enemy. The command of the army was given to Lord Licec, for he was well known to be the most prudent man in the kingdom.

Three days passed till the last of the army had started, and all the while the Princess stood at the window and watched them march along the winding street below, and the knights and men-at-arms were inspired with fresh courage at the sight of such a princess as they had to defend, and they cheered so loud and long that it seemed like the continual roar of the sea beating on a rocky shore, sometimes rising, sometimes falling, but always sounding.

The Princess indeed felt quite lonely when they had all gone, even though their shouts did make her head ache. However, she consoled herself by riding all day towards the army, and returning at night to the lonely town. So she occupied three days; and the Owl always flew over her head, protecting her from the sun when it was too hot, or else sitting on her shoulder, or on the horse's head, although the horse did not like it at all.

For three days no news came, but on the fourth as the Princess was riding out with her ladies-in-waiting she saw at a great distance in front of her along the straight white road a cloud of dust that was coming swiftly towards her. As it came nearer she could see the glint of armour, and soon she could plainly see the form of an armed knight galloping at full speed towards them. He came so fast that they had to rein their horses to one side that they might not be run down. At first he did not seem to know who the Princess was, or perhaps he was going so furiously that he could not see; at any rate he had almost got past them before he recognized her. As soon as he did, however, he drew up, but so sudden was the action that the horse first sank back on his haunches, and then bounded so high into the air that the marks his hoofs made when he alighted on the ground again, were a foot deep in the hard road. As soon as the plunging of the horse stopped and the Princess could make herself heard she said:

"What news, Sir Knight, from the front, that thou ridest in such haste?"

"But bad news, I fear," answered the knight.

"What say you?" said the Princess; "bad news, and with such an army as ye had? has some fresh rebellion broken out among the men?"

"No rebellion, but plain fighting has beaten us—but what can we do against such foes? This Merrymineral, alone, rides on a green dragon, and with one stroke of his sword he kills a hundred men. Myself I charged him with my lance, but as it struck his shield it broke in pieces as if it had been made of glass; and it was fortunate for me that my horse carried me past him before he could strike me, for I saw him myself cut the Knight of Pendred in half, as you would cut a radish. And if we slay a thousand men during the day he restores them in the night. So we have gradually been driven back, till after three days' fighting the army remains at Arecarp. Thence I started at eight this morning to hurry the reinforcements from Britain and Gaul."

"Alas! they are still at three days' march from here, though they are marching night and day. But thou saidst the army was at Arecarp, and that thou didst start to-day at eight in the morning. That is impossible. Arecarp is twenty-four hours' journey for a fast horse, and it is now but twelve o'clock. Not even the horse that I ride could go faster than that, though he is said to be the fastest horse in the world, except Selim, the horse of the Prince of India. However, no time is to be lost. Sir Knight, will you escort these ladies back to the town, and rest for a while?"

"But what will you do, your Majesty?"

"I must ride forward to Arecarp."

"To Arecarp! Your Majesty, what will you do there? The battlefield is no place for a girl."

"Nevertheless I must go, for my place is with the army."

"But if you are killed, what will happen to your people without their Queen?"

"What do they do now without their Queen? Besides once before the cherished Owl has defeated this man and he may do it again. If he does not, no power on earth could save me from death, for the army is gradually defeated."

"But your Majesty could send the Owl in a cage against the enemy."

"I promised my father never to go out of its sight—no, I must go."

"I beseech you then, your Majesty, to allow me to accompany you, for the road to the camp is full of danger."

"But your horse is tired, and even if he were not he could never keep up with me."

"But if you will excuse the contradiction, I think I shall."

"Well then, have your way, but mark me, if you lag behind I shall not stop. However, we are losing time. Let us go."

And they set off—the Princess ignoring the entreaties of the ladies that she should not go.

The Princess immediately started at the full speed of her horse, expecting that the knight would soon fall behind; but no, he galloped at her side as if the speed were not more than usual, and his great black charger seemed to enjoy the exercise as though he had not already galloped over a hundred miles that morning.

The Princess could not understand how it was, but she thought he would soon get tired and fall behind, but an hour passed and he showed no signs of being fatigued. So she leant over her horse and whispered softly in his ear. Instantly the horse bounded forward more swiftly than ever—so fast, indeed, that she could hardly keep her eyes open against the wind, and her golden crown was suddenly whisked away, and her beautiful golden hair streamed far out behind. Still the knight kept up, and seemed not the least distressed at the speed. The Owl meanwhile was flying far overhead, but she was not at all surprised at his keeping up, for nothing seemed impossible to him. After they had been riding thus for nearly two hours they came to a place where the path was crossed by a river, and here the Princess thought it advisable to stop and rest a moment and to let the horses drink. So she called to the knight to stop, as she was going to get off for a moment, and he at once sprang off his horse, and coming to her saddle-bow held her stirrup for her to dismount. When she was off she leaned against a tree looking at the horses as they drank eagerly from the river, and then came out to browse for a moment on the bank. Then she went to where the knight's horse stood, and patted him on the neck, for you see he was not a very fierce-looking animal, and she was not at all afraid of him.

"He's a wonderfully swift horse, Sir Knight," she said suddenly, "and I believe there is no other horse in the world as swift—not even Selim—the horse I spoke about—that belongs to the Prince of India."

The knight nodded.

"He is a good horse, but he is no better than Selim, your Majesty, for I know Selim very well."

All this while he had kept his vizor down, and the Princess had been too polite to ask him to raise it, even though it was rather rude of him to keep it down. So she could not tell who he was. She knew all the knights of her own kingdom by sight, as well as most of her allies, for you must know that a great many foreign princes had sent her troops to assist her against the rebel. She looked at the device on his shield; it was a crowned tiger, but that did not help her, for she did not know whose crest it was. So at last when she could bear her curiosity no longer, she determined to ask him. So she said:

"Sir Knight, should you think me very rude if I were to ask you whether you are under a vow of hiding your face?"

"I am bound by no such vow; but why do you ask, your Majesty?"

"Because ever since I have seen you you have kept your vizor down, and I thought perhaps it was on account of some such vow."

"Oh, I beg your pardon, a thousand times, your Majesty," said the knight. "But I did not remember that I had let it down, for you see I look through its bars without noticing the difference. But I hope your Majesty will pardon the absent-mindedness," and he raised the vizor, at the same time bowing low to her. But it was now the Princess's turn to be confused, for she saw before her Sir Alured, the Emperor of India, a prince nearly as powerful as herself. She blushed with shame and then said:

"Oh, Sir Knight, I mean your Royal Highness, it is I who should crave your pardon, for all the while I have addressed you as 'Sir Knight,' instead of as 'your Majesty.' But I am very sorry."

But Sir Alured said:

"Nay, your Majesty, you have the right to call me what you will, for I am always your humble vassal."

"My ally, you should say, your Majesty."

"I am always your servant, not your ally, your Majesty."

"Then I fear you will soon be a vassal of a queen without a kingdom; and if this Merrymineral prevail over me, I fear he will punish you for aiding me."

But the Prince said:

"All is not yet lost, your Majesty, and whatever happens your Majesty will always have a protector while I am alive."

The Princess smiled.

"Ah! you mean the cherished Owl. You will always protect me, won't you, Owl?" she said, looking up at the Owl who was seated again on her shoulder. And the Owl nodded his head.

She looked at her watch just them. "Why," she said, "we have been just ten minutes, and it is time to start again, if you are rested sufficiently."

So he helped her to mount, and they crossed the river. It was not very deep, but still she got the skirts of her dress quite wet, for the water was high enough for that.

However, the gallop in the hot sun on the other side soon dried them.

In an hour and a half they were on the top of a hill from which they could see the town of Arecarp in the valley beneath.

The sun was shining brightly on the tents of the army as it lay round the town, and at some distance the camp of the enemy looked peaceful.

The Prince gazed carefully at the armies. After a moment he said:

"There has been no fighting since I left the city this morning, nor has the position altered at all. I fancy Merrymineral has sent ambassadors to demand surrender from Lord Licec."

The Princess smiled.

"He will never surrender," she said.

"Nor will any of us, your Majesty," added the Prince. "However, let us descend the hill."

Down the hill the road lay through a deep gorge, so deep that the sun did not penetrate it, and it lay in delicious shade. The sides of the valley were lined with silver-barked birch, below which grew nodding foxgloves, and as they went slowly down the steep path, ever and anon a rabbit would scuttle out of the grassy track to a safe distance in front of them, where it sat on its haunches with its little ears pricked up, smelling at them anxiously as they came near again, and then it would scutter along into the thick rank grass to its home.

So they went slowly down the path until they came once more to the level ground, and they were again able to gallop on. Soon they reached the town, and clattered through the cobbled streets to the market-place, where Lord Licec had his headquarters. But the market-place was crowded with soldiers and knights who were bargaining for food, so that it was by no means easy to get through the crowd. However, as soon as they got near the place, the soldiers recognized the Princess and began to cheer, and immediately an avenue was formed up to the door of the council-house, and the Princess rode smiling through the throng, followed by the Prince.

The news of her arrival ran through the whole camp, and immediately such a shout went up from the men that the enemy thought they were preparing for battle, and they made ready to resist the attack. At the door of the council-hall Lord Licec was waiting with the rest of the captains of renown, and they followed the Princess upstairs to the council-chamber.

As soon as they were seated the Princess asked for the latest news. She was told all that had happened, and when she had heard it she dismissed the Lords of the Council, all except Lord Licec and the Prince of India, who were to stay and dine with her, and she gave orders that the dinner should be brought as soon as possible, for to tell the truth she felt rather hungry, as she had had nothing to eat since breakfast-time.

Now when the Princess had finished giving her orders about the dinner, Licec could not refrain from asking her why she had come.

"Was it not rather foolish," he said, "to hazard your life for nothing? for of a truth you are—"

But the Princess put her finger on his mouth.

"I will not be bullied by you, my lord, even though you are old enough to be my father. I know what you were going to say—that the battlefield is no place for girls. Now I won't be called a girl, for I'm nineteen, you know. His Majesty the Emperor of India there insulted me by calling me a girl, and I have not forgiven him yet. Besides you'll spoil my appetite for dinner if you lecture me. It always does; so do be quiet now, at any rate till after dinner."

So Licec had to be quiet, and they talked about something else till dinner-time.

Just as they finished, a frightful shouting outside made them drop their dessert-knives and run to the window, but as the window did not face on to the street they could not tell what was the matter. So the Princess rang the bell, and when the servant appeared she asked him what was the cause of the shouting.

"May it please your Majesty, ambassadors have arrived from the enemy and would speak to you."

"Show them this way and send at the same time for the Lords of the Council."

So the servant went, and in a short time a heavy stumping was heard on the stairs. Suddenly the door burst open and the ambassadors entered. They were rather a remarkable pair of ambassadors, although they could hardly be said to pair well. For the one was an enormous giant with a long beard, dressed in leaves mostly, and so tall that he could not stand upright in the room; in his hand he carried an enormous pole, from the end of which a spiked ball dangled. The other, however, was very nearly his opposite in everything. For he was very small, a dwarf in fact, and he was dressed in very tight yellow armour, and from the top of his helmet a crest of red roses hung down to his saddle—for you must know he had insisted on not getting off his horse, or rather pony, for that too was very small—in fact it just fitted the dwarf.

As soon as the Princess had recovered from her astonishment, she rose from her seat and said:

"Are you the ambassadors from the rebel Merrymineral?"

The dwarf replied:

"I don't know anything about the rebel part of the business, but we are the ambassadors from Merrymineral, whom we are bound to serve for a certain time. But who are you, I should like to know, and what right have you to speak to me in this insulting manner? D'you think I'm here to be insulted by you? If you think so, I'll tell you point-blank I'm not—so there."

And in the rage he had worked himself into he began to spur his steed till it jumped off the floor so high that it knocked his head against the ceiling.

The Princess was not used to being treated like that. However, she was not at all angry at it—she only laughed at his misfortune, which made him all the more outrageous.

"How dare you laugh at me?" he screamed; "who are you, you minx, you minx, you lynx—you—"

But the Princess did not listen to him. She turned to the giant, who at any rate was quiet, and said:

"Will you not take a chair until the Lords of the Council arrive?"

The giant looked at her in stupid astonishment.

"What shall I do with the chair when I've taken it?" he mumbled.

"I mean you to sit down on it, of course," said the Princess.

The giant growled out in reply:

"Well, I never sat on a chair before, but to please you I will."

So he sat down, but as he was not used to sitting on chairs he sat down on its back; but it was only a small cane-bottomed chair, and as he was very big, and the chair was very small, the result is easily foreseen, for the chair collapsed under him as if he had sat on a top-hat, and he reclined comfortably on the floor, where he remained for the rest of the time.

"I think I'll stop where I am," he said, when they offered him a wooden stool to sit on, "for you see I'm not used to chairs." So they let him stop where he was.

One by one the Lords of the Council began to arrive; they looked curiously at the ambassadors but said nothing. When they were all arrived the Princess said to the dwarf:

"Now if you will state your message we will listen."

So the dwarf snarled in a bad-tempered voice:

"I shan't tell you—you aren't the commander-in-chief of the army, are you?"

"No, but I am the Queen of the Western World."

"Oh! you're the Queen of the Western World, are you? Well, you won't be Queen of the Western World long, if you don't mind your P's and Q's. The king Merrymineral sent me to say that if you don't marry him and make him king, he'll kill the lot of you and make himself king in spite of you—so there; and I'm to wait for an answer."

After consulting with Council for a moment the Princess said:

"Of course I shan't marry him—how could he be so ridiculous as to think so?"

The dwarf laughed.

"That's your answer, is it?" he said. "I thought so, I say, Gog, have you got it written down?"

But Gog had gone to sleep. So the dwarf pricked him with the end of his lance.

"I say, Gog," he said, "she's given me her answer and you haven't written it down, and I've forgotten it already. Just say it over again, Queen, will you? and not too fast, or Gog here will never get it down."

The giant now drew from his pocket a very soiled and crumpled half-sheet of a copy-book and began to write from the Princess's dictation.

"Of course I should not do anything so—" Here he stopped.

"How do you spell 'ridiculous'?" he said.

"With two 'k's,' of course," said the dwarf; "even I know that, though I can't write."

When he had finished he handed it to the Princess:

"Just sign your name, will you?"

The Princess signed her name, but she could not help seeing that the writing was very bad and the spelling was awful.

"Why didn't they send some one who could write better? Why! that 'r' is more like a 'k' than an 'r'."

But the giant shook his head mournfully.

"They hadn't got any one else in the army who could write except Merrymineral, and he was afraid to come."

"But weren't you afraid to come?" she said.

The giant shook his mace round so violently that it grazed the helmet of the dwarf, and cut his crest of roses off.

"Whom am I to be afraid of?" he growled. "I could kill your whole army single-handed"; and he laughed loud and long.

But just at this moment the Owl, that had been sitting on the floor behind the Princess's chair, flew up on to her shoulder, and no sooner did the giant see the Owl than he jumped up from the floor where you remember he was sitting, and he was in such a hurry that he knocked a hole in the plaster of the ceiling with his head.

"Come, I say, you know" he said, "I can fight anything in reason—but I'm not going to tackle that, you know; besides, we're ambassadors, and you can't hurt us. I'm going"; and he rushed out of the room as fast as he could, and the dwarf followed him as fast as he could make his horse gallop, and they never stopped till they reached the camp of Merrymineral. For they were very frightened, you see.

After they had gone the Princess again dismissed the Councillors, and when they had gone, she said to Lord Licec and the Prince, who by the bye still remained:

"Now let us finish our dessert"—for the ambassadors had come in right in the middle of it.

After a moment the Princess said:

"How absurd of him to think I would marry him—why, he's old enough to be my great-grandfather."

But suddenly she became grave:

"But perhaps I ought to have thought before I gave the answer. Would it not have been better for my people if I had consented? for then he would kill no more of them."

But the Prince became quite angry at such an idea. "It's absurd," he said. "Why, as soon as he had married you and become king he would murder you and then kill just as many of your people as he will now; besides, who knows that we may not still conquer him?"

The Princess turned to Lord Licec:

"What do you say, my lord?" she said.

"I think just as the Prince of India—for even if he did not murder you he would oppress the people without mercy, and besides, your people would never allow you to marry him, so that is out of the question."

The Princess gave a sigh of relief.

"Since you say so, Lord Licec, it must be right; besides, I don't think I could ever marry him—he is such a very unpleasant sort of man."

And the Prince answered:

"You are quite right there"; and he seemed quite happy again.

Soon after it became evening, and Lord Licec had to go out to look after his army, and the Prince too went to see that his men were all prepared for any night attack—for his men were right in the very front of all, and so they were quite close to the enemy, who might at any time begin an attack.

So the Princess was left all alone with the Owl, but she did not feel lonely with him, for he was very sociable, and would do anything that he was told to do. So they played hide-and-seek till it was too dark to see any more, and then she went to bed and slept soundly till the rays of the sun falling on her face the next morning woke her up. She was soon dressed, and when she had finished she went into the next room, where she found Lord Licec already awaiting her.

"What does your Majesty intend to do this morning? for I shall not be with you, as I am going to order the army to advance to the attack, and so your Majesty had better stay within the town for the rest of the day."

"Indeed, I shall do nothing of the sort," she answered. "I am going to lead the army to-day to see if we cannot regain some ground, for I had rather die fighting than be driven back like this, so please don't say I mustn't go; besides, the Owl will protect me; he promised to; didn't you, Owl?" and the Owl nodded.

"But they may shoot the Owl with their arrows, and then—"

"But the Owl before now has conquered Merrymineral himself, and he may still do it. Oh, please don't tell me not to go. If you'll only let me go I'll promise to keep near the Prince of India, and he'll protect me, even if the Owl can't."

"But the Prince of India is always in the thickest of the fight, and you will be in much greater danger if you keep near him."

"Oh, never mind the danger; do let me go."

And she begged so hard that Lord Licec had to give in. She put on a breastplate and a sword, but she would not put on a helmet, for she said that it made her head ache, and that no one would know who she was if she covered her face up. So she only wore a gold circlet on her head, as she usually did, and besides this she carried a silver shield with the royal crest on it, and a small lance just like a knight's spear, only not so heavy, and thus mounted on her white horse she rode to the very front of the line of battle, and there she found the Prince of India at the head of his men.

They had already furled their tents and were quite ready to begin the battle as soon as the others were ready.

The Prince was very much astonished when he saw her, for it was the last place in the world he had expected to see her in.

"Do you really mean to say," he exclaimed, "that Lord Licec allowed you to come out to the field of battle? Why, he must be mad."

"Oh, no, he's not," answered the Princess; "but you see if I only beg hard enough he'll let me do whatever I like, and then I promised to keep near you, for I thought you would protect me. However, you don't seem very glad to see me—perhaps you think I shall hinder you—so I'll go and ask some one else to take care of me, as you don't seem to relish the task. Good-morning"; and she began to move off; but she knew very well that he would not let her go like that, and to tell the truth she rather hoped he wouldn't, for she thought she would like him to take care of her better than any one else in the army. Of course he did stop her and said:

"If you really insist on stopping on the field no one is more fit to take care of you than I. So *do* stop."

And she allowed herself to be persuaded to stop with him.

Just as they had managed to arrange it so, a trumpet blew in the direction of the town, and immediately troops of knights and men-at-arms began to pour out of the gates, and to form the line of battle, and as each band of men came along they cheered long and loud at the sight of the Princess, and the Princess felt very happy, for she liked to know that her people loved her. Gradually the immense army came into one long line of glistening steel, and again the trumpets sounded, and the line began to move forward like a wave of the sea as it runs up the smooth sand sweeping all before it. The smooth plain which was to form the battlefield was dotted here and there with troops of cattle which had come down in the night from the hills to feed on the long sweet grass, and they raised their heads in astonishment at the line of knights and bowmen that marched slowly down on them; so they shook their heads and galloped off straight in front of the line, with their tails high in the air, and they were in such blind haste that they charged right through the lines of the enemy who were now approaching, and not only through them they went, but also through their camp, tossing the tents into the air with their horns as they went by. However, at last they reached the hills, and did not disturb the combatants any more.

Meanwhile the armies had got quite close together—so close indeed that they could see each other's faces quite plainly—but they did not seem particularly eager to fight. So when they had got thus far they halted, and looked at one another.

As yet Merrymineral had not arrived, for to tell the truth he was never a very early riser, and he did not see why he should hurry himself—for you see he was quite sure of winning the battle without much trouble.

Just opposite the Princess was the flower of the enemy, and she recognized many of the great men of the countries that had rebelled with Merrymineral. They did not seem particularly happy where they were, and especially when the Princess looked at them they looked very red and uncomfortable, as if they did not like it at all.

"I do believe they're ashamed of themselves," she said to the Prince; and he answered:

"They certainly look like it."

"Do you think," she asked, "if I were to go over to them and offer to pardon them that they would leave Merrymineral and come to my side?"

The Prince thought a moment.

"I believe they would," he said; "only if I were you I would not go, I should send an ambassador or a herald."

But the Princess shook her head.

"That would never do," she said. "I'm sure they'd be offended at that. Why, it would look as if I thought they were not to be trusted, and besides they would not hurt me. No, I'll go to them quite alone."

But the Prince said:

"You had better let me go with you, for if they did attack you it would be awkward; besides, you know you promised to keep near me all the morning, and if you go without me you will not be keeping your promise, don't you see?"

So the Princess said:

"Well, I suppose you're right, only you must come alone."

And as he agreed to this they went forward. Her own army evidently did not understand what she meant to do, nor, for the matter of that, did the enemy, but as they had neither of them received the order to commence fighting they neither of them advanced.

So the Prince and Princess advanced at a gentle trot until they were quite close to the others, and the Owl sat on her shoulder.

When they were quite close the knights tried to get one behind the other just as if they had done something they ought not to have done, and were each afraid of being punished first.

In particular the Princess noted the giant and dwarf, the ambassadors of the evening before; they tried to hide themselves behind the others altogether. For the dwarf this was easy enough, but for the poor giant, he could not manage it at all, he was so very big.

However, she did not look at all angry, and she only said:

"Good-morning, my lords."

And they replied in chorus:

"Good morning, your Majesty."

So she went on:

"I have come to ask you why you have assisted my rebellious subject, and what grievance you have? If there is any I will try to redress it."

One of the nobles replied:

"We have no grievances."

"Then why have you fought against me?"

"Because we could not help it, your Majesty."

"But I should have thought you could have helped fighting."

"I mean, your Majesty, that Merrymineral threatened to kill us all if we did not fight."

"Then you were not very brave. But that has nothing to do with it. What I wish to know is, whether you will now submit to me again?"

"We would most willingly; only perhaps your Majesty might inflict some punishment on us for our misdeeds."

But the Princess shook her head.

"No; I will give you all a free pardon if you return to your allegiance."

So the nobles gave a shout of joy, and they seemed quite happy again. And the Princess too was overjoyed; however, she ordered them to go each knight to his own men and to tell them what had happened, and to conduct them to her own army.

So they all went and did as they were told, and soon the whole army of Merrymineral melted away, with the exception of a very few, and these were mostly the servants of Merrymineral himself, and of the giant and the dwarf, who still remained faithful to him. However, they seemed quite unhappy about it.

So the Princess turned to them and said:

"And you, sirs, will you not also join me?"

But the giant shook his head, and the dwarf said snappishly:

"Don't you know we can't?"

But the Princess answered:

"No; I do not know why you can't."

So the dwarf snarled:

"We're bound to serve him for a certain time, whether we like it or not. I'm the King of the Underground Gnomes—we live in tunnels under the earth, and never come up unless we're obliged to."

And the giant said:

"I'm the Spirit of the Woods—that's why I'm dressed in leaves like this; and I'm the King of the Foresters, and we live in trees."

But just at this moment a frightful roar came from the camp:

"Why don't you begin?" it came.

It was so sudden that it quite startled the Princess, but the giant shook his head mournfully:

"He always roars like that when he's in a temper. He'll be coming out in a moment, and won't there be a row?"

Just then the voice came again:

"Bring Popfelwuski to the door."

"Popfelwuski's his dragon that he rides on," said the giant.

And then some servants led the dragon to the door of one of the tents.

It was a most marvellous-looking creature, for it had eyes as large as tea-trays, and they twinkled awfully; and it was golden-coloured all over, and it shone so brightly in the sun that it made the Princess's eyes quite ache to look at it. And it was growling and prancing and kicking up the dust, and making more fuss than fifty horses could have done. Just then the tent opened and Merrymineral came out. He looked just as usual, and had not any armour or weapons except a huge battle-axe, which must have weighed nearly a ton, but he carried it with the greatest ease, although he was an old man—for he was over eight hundred years old. He vaulted on to his dragon's back with very great ease, and putting his spurs to its golden sides made it gallop at a great rate. As yet he had not seen what had happened to his army, for he was rather short-sighted, but when he had got within a few yards of where it ought to have been, he suddenly stopped as if he were bewildered, but then his eye fell on the Princess and he roared out:

"Oh, it's you, is it? I'll soon do for you," and he made his dragon fly towards the Princess at a very great rate. But precisely the same thing happened now as had happened once before, for the dragon came to a sudden stop as if it had hit against a wall. The Prince of India did not understand it at all.

"Had we not better retreat and join the rest of the army?" he said.

But the Princess answered:

"Oh no, we're quite safe here. He won't be able to get at us. Only you'd better come a little closer to me, because he might be able to hit you."

So the Prince came a good deal closer, and they sat watching the frantic efforts of Merrymineral to get at them, but it was no use. Suddenly, however, he changed his mode of attack. He made his dragon fly high into the air—so high indeed that it would have been invisible if its golden coat had not shone brightly in the sun. It was quite unpleasant to look at him, for he was so high up that it made them feel dizzy as it shone out against the sky, miles high. Suddenly, however, just as it was directly over them, it seemed to be growing larger.

"I do believe he's going to drop on us from above"; and so he was. The Prince put up his lance that the dragon might be spiked on it as it fell. But he might have saved himself the trouble, for suddenly, when the thing had fallen to within a few feet of their heads, it stopped as if it had fallen on to the roof of a house, and then it bounced off again like a ball.

But the Princess had shut her eyes, so she did not see this; but when she opened them she saw the dragon and Merrymineral lying on the grass in a heap where they had fallen.

But he was soon on his feet again, and again he tried to charge at the Princess; but it was no use, and he only tired himself. At last the Princess began to get tired too, so she turned to the Prince and said:

"I think we've had enough of this—don't you?"

And he replied:

"Oh, plenty; but I don't see how we're to get rid of him, unless I go out and fight him."

But the Princess answered:

"Oh, I don't think you need do that, although it's very good of you to offer—but you've forgotten all about the Owl." So she took the Owl off her shoulder, and putting it on the horse's head with its face to her she asked it:

"You can drive him away, can't you, dear Owl?"

And the Owl nodded gravely. So the Princess said:

"Then I wish you would—only don't hurt him; only drive him away."

As she said this a wonderful change came over the Owl. It began to grow bigger and bigger, until it quite covered them over as it spread its wings to fly. Merrymineral seemed to know what was coming, for he drew his steed's reins up tight and examined his stirrups and saddle. And then, as the Owl flew towards him, he tried to spur the golden dragon against him; but the dragon refused to move, and at last it turned and bolted with its tail between its legs, like a whipped dog.

Merrymineral tried hard to stop it, but he might as well have tried to stop a mad bull. As he could not stop, and the Owl was catching him up, he turned in his saddle and hurled his heavy battle-axe at the Owl; but the Owl caught it as it flew, and flung it back with such good aim and force that it hit the dragon on the back and cut it clean in half, so that it fell from under Merrymineral and left him standing on the ground.

But when he saw that the Owl was quite close to him, a wonder happened—for he suddenly caught fire at his feet and shot up into the air just as you may have seen a rocket do, and he shot right away, so that the last they saw of him was just as he disappeared over the mountains. But the Owl flew back to its mistress quite small again, and it perched once more on her shoulder as affectionately as ever. As to the golden dragon, it had disappeared altogether—and the funny part was that nothing was heard of it ever after, and no one knew how it had gone—so that the only thing that remained was the battle-axe, and that took seven men to lift it. However, the main thing was that Merrymineral had departed, and there seemed no likelihood of his returning.

So you may imagine how great the Princess's joy was.

As soon as he had quite disappeared, she said:

"That really does seem to be the last of him."

But the Prince shook his head:

"You never know when that sort of man will turn up again; and in the meantime what are we to do with the giant and the dwarf? I suppose we had better attack them at once and get rid of them."

"But why?" asked the Princess. "They don't seem to want to fight much, and why should we attack them? Let us go and ask them to go away quietly, and I should think they will."

So they went up to where the giant and the dwarf and their forces were standing.

"What are you going to do now?" she asked of them.

"I don't know," answered the dwarf, and the giant too shook his head. So the Princess said:

"Will you come and join our rejoicings?"

But the dwarf said:

"No; I must be going back to my kingdom, or I don't know what won't happen."

And the giant said:

"And I'll go too, or they might rebel there just as your subjects have done."

So he said good-day, and in three minutes he had disappeared. The dwarf too said good-day quite politely for him, and then he struck the ground with the point of his lance, and immediately the earth opened before him and he marched into the opening at the head of his troops, and with their trumpets blowing and banners waving they disappeared, and the Princess never saw them nor their master again—and to tell the truth she was not very sorry. But the Prince and Princess marched back to the town at the head of the army, and there Lord Licec met them and congratulated the Princess on her success, and the people shouted for joy, and the bells pealed gladly.

So they marched through the town to the principal city, from which you may remember she had set out on the day before. And there they were received with even greater joy, and for six days there was feasting and rejoicing throughout the whole land, but on the seventh day, after the Princess had rewarded the knights who had fought the best, the army dispersed, and the town quieted down, and everything went on just as usual.

Only the Prince of India remained of all the knights who had fought. He said he was not well, and wanted a rest before he set out for India, which was a long way off. So he stopped and rested, and the winter changed to summer, and the summer to autumn, and he was still there, and he did not seem as if he were likely to go either. The time slipped away quietly enough, and no more was heard of Merrymineral—not even a word. One day when the Lords of the Council had finished sitting for the day, and were departing, Lord Licec remained, as he always did when he had anything private to say to the Princess. So she said:

"Well, my lord, what is it that you wish to tell to me to-day?"

"I had come, your Majesty, to make a suggestion to you that it would be greatly to the good of the nation if your Majesty would condescend to think about marrying some one."

The Princess was so startled that she quite jumped:

"Marry any one! good gracious me, whom am I to marry? I don't know any one that I like at all."

Lord Licec stroken his chin:

"That is rather a drawback," he said; "but I had thought that perhaps the Prince of India might—"

But the Princess interrupted him:

"Oh, he would never do; besides he would have to ask me, and he won't do that."

But it might have been noticed that she blushed just a little as she said it, so that perhaps she was not quite sincere in what she said. Lord Licec did not notice that, so he said:

"Well, if he won't suit, the only thing to do is to have a tournament, and then you must marry the winner."

But she did not seem to like the idea at all. "Suppose the winner should turn out a hunchback, or a cripple, or a very hideous man," she said.

"Your Majesty might arrange it so that the candidates should only be allowed to tilt if they were sufficiently handsome."

She agreed to the suggestion.

"I suppose it is the only thing to do," she said; and it was arranged that in four weeks' time a grand tournament was to take place for the hand of the Princess Ismara, and that all the handsome knights in the world could come if they liked.

As to the Owl, when he was asked if he liked the arrangement, he gravely nodded his head; so the Princess felt quite safe in her choice, and the Prince of India felt contented also, for he knew he had a very good chance of winning, unless some knight of whom he had never heard should suddenly turn up. He spent the time in between in practising for the tournament, and he ordered a new set of armour to be sent to him from India in time.

So every one seemed pleased with the arrangement, except, perhaps, the ugly knights, but they kept quiet about it.

The month went away quietly, except that the town was gradually filling with knights, who were coming to take part in the contest. The lists were erected on a plain just outside the town-walls, and on the day before the tournament the free seats were already filled with people, who had come there determined to get places even if they had to wait all day long and had to sleep there all night. As you may imagine, the Princess did not get much sleep that night, for she was naturally in a great fever of excitement thinking about who the knight would be. One thing she was sure about, and that was, that if she did not like him she would not have anything to do with him, even if she had to forfeit her kingdom. However that might be, she did not sleep that night, and on the morrow she felt quite tired. She dressed herself in her most splendid robes, and drove to the lists in a little basket-work pony carriage drawn by eight little mouse-coloured ponies. It was a beautiful day, and the road to the lists was covered with people who were going to look on, or to take part in the tournament, and as she went by they drew up their horses to bow to her, for she had specially forbidden them to cheer—she said it made her head ache. So she drove down the hard, white road bowing and smiling to the people, and they smiled and looked glad too, for they were very fond of their Princess.

After she had gone along thus for about five minutes she overtook the Prince of India, who was going the same way on his famous horse. The Prince did not seem to see her—in fact he was engaged in looking very hard at his spur on the other side.

But the Princess did not mean to pass him like that, so she said cheerfully:

"Good morning, Prince,"

He looked up quite astonished:

"Good morning, your Majesty!" he said, and he took off his cap and bowed low in his saddle, for you see he had not got his armour on—he had sent it on with his page.

The Princess did not know exactly what to say next, so for a moment they were silent, and the Prince trotted quietly by her side. At last she said:

"Are you, too, going to look on at the tournament?"

The Prince answered:

"I had purposed taking part in it—that, ahem!—is if your Majesty thinks I am sufficiently handsome, and if you have no other objection."

The Princess answered quickly:

"Oh, no objection at all. I should like it very much—that is, if you are content to run the risk of your life for such a small prize."

But the Prince only answered:

"Oh, your Majesty!" and her Majesty flushed a little at his reply.

So they went on again in silence, and the road began to get fuller and fuller of people, and the Princess had her time so taken up by managing her ponies—for she was driving herself, you know—that she could not say much.

However, just as they reached the entry, she said:

"By the bye, what seat have you got?"

"I believe they've given me a seat over on the south side," he answered.

"Dear me, how careless of them. Why, you'll have the sun in your face all the time you're not tilting, and it will give you such a headache. You'd better come into the Royal Box—they've got an awning over that, and you'll be able to see much better. Do come."

So the Prince gave his horse to his page and went with the Princess and the Owl—for you must remember that the Owl was always perched on her shoulder.

The lists were very gay with horses, and knights, and heralds, and many and great were the knights that intended to tilt. They had come from the uttermost parts of the world—from Kensington, from Nubia, from—well, from everywhere, for you see they did not get the chance of fighting for a princess every day. So you may imagine how many suitors there were. Nearly a thousand came, but a good many of them were not considered handsome enough, so they either went away in a tiff or else they stayed to look on. Still it would take a good three days before the last man had tilted.

The entrance of the Princess was the signal for the music to begin, and the procession of knights filed past, each one bowing to the Princess and making his horse perform feats of skill. And then the tournament began and the knights charged each other, each in their turn. The way they managed it was for each knight to throw lots for the order of their fighting, and then they were to be divided into two bodies—the challengers and those to be challenged; and as it came to the turn of each challenger, he rode out and touched the shield of the knight on the other side with whom he wished to fight, and then the victors were to fight it out among themselves until they were all finished except one.

The Prince of India happened to be one of the challengers, and his turn did not come until the afternoon. So during the morning he sat in the Royal Box talking to the Princess or to the lords- and maids-in-waiting.

But the Princess did not seem to enjoy the gentle and joyous passages of arms at all, for you see she was very soft-hearted, and did not like to see the knights knocked off their horses so very roughly. So, on the whole, she was not nearly so gay as the Prince, and indeed, she seemed very unhappy when he went to put on his panoply as his turn came near.

However, he soon afterwards came into the lists dressed in his full armour, and you may be sure he looked very splendid, mounted on his black horse—for his armour was entirely of silver, and his shield shone so brightly that it hurt one's eyes to look at it, and his long plumes floated in the wind a great many yards behind him.

The spectators cheered him very much as he caracoled from one end of the lists to the other, and the Princess quite brightened up as she saw him.

"I wonder whose shield he's going to touch?" she said to herself; and when she saw who it was she said:

"Good gracious me! he's challenged the Knight of Sarragos; why, he's the greatest knight in the world. Oh dear, I'm sure the Prince will be beaten."

However, the knights were now going each to his own station at different ends of the lists. The horses seemed quite as excited as the knights, and they champed their bits and foamed and pawed up the ground, while the heralds read the challenge from the Prince of India to the Knight of Sarragos.

It seemed as if the Princess was right about the strength of the Knight, for he was of enormous size, and he looked a veritable pillar of steel as he sat on his horse listening to the challenge. However, the trumpets for the charge sounded, and away went the knights straight towards each other like arrows, each one looking along his spear to see that it was aimed truly for his adversary—covering himself well with his shield. They went so fast that they could hardly be seen, and the crash when they met was louder than the loudest peal of thunder you ever heard.

The Princess shut her eyes at the sound. But she could not keep them shut, for the people were cheering very loudly. So she opened them reluctantly, and she seemed quite glad to see that the Knight of Sarragos had been thrown from his horse by the shock and was rolling in the dust. It was rather odd that she should be pleased at this, because as a rule she was sorry for the conquered knight; for myself I rather think she had wanted the Prince to win all along. Anyhow, she congratulated him warmly on his success when he came back to his seat, and for the rest of the day she did not seem much interested in the tilting, although some of it was very good, too.

So the first two days passed away and nothing particular happened. The Prince of India took his turn with the rest, till at last the third day came and there were only ten knights left. These, too, the Prince overcame, and it seemed as if all was over and he had gained the prize; but while the heralds were still calling for any one to come and defeat the Prince, and while every one was holding their breath in expectation, a loud blast from a trumpet sounded through the air, and at the other end of the lists a knight appeared. He was a very tall and splendid-looking knight—for his armour was of gold, and the crest on his helmet-top was a dragon carved out of a rose-red ruby of enormous size; and the point of his lance was made of one diamond, that sparkled in the sun a great deal more brightly than any dewdrop on a spring morning. And as to handsome, why he was a perfect blaze of handsomeness, so that there could be no objectionn to him. The only thing was, no one knew who he was, or where he came from.

So the Princess beckoned him to her, and he came and bowed low in his saddle.

"Who are you, Sir Knight?" she asked; "and where do you come from?"

"I am the Knight of London, your Majesty."

"London, London; where's that?—I've never heard of it."

"London is the capital city of England."

"But where *is* England?" she asked.

"I had thought that every one had heard of England," he said. "However, as no report of England has ever reached your ears, I will tell your Majesty. The British Islands, of which England is one, are a set of small islands off the west coast of Europe. They are composed of England, Scot—"

But here the Princess interrupted him:

"I thank you, Sir Knight, for your information, but just now the tournament is waiting for you, and I am not very fond of geography lessons."

The Knight bowed again, and retired to take up his place in the lists.

"How very handsome he is!" said the Princess to one of her maids-in-waiting.

And the lady answered:

"Oh, quite too handsome!"

However, by this time both the knights were in their places, and the Princess nodded to the heralds to give the signal.

"Laissez aller," they cried, which is the French for "Go."

And they did go with a vengeance—they went so fast that they looked all blurred together like streaks of lightning. And when they met, it was louder than thunder, louder than the shock of avalanches, louder than— well, louder than everything you ever heard, except perhaps when some one lets the tea-tray fall down the kitchen stairs.

And when the dust cleared up, the poor Knight of India was rolling on the ground in a heap, composed of himself and his horse. But the Princess did not seem very sorry for him—so wags the world.

The Knight of London, however, was seated in his saddle as firmly as if he were part of it; and as there seemed nothing else to do, he commanded his heralds to challenge any one who should wish to dispute his right to the victory. But no one came out, for either there was no one else left, or else the knights were afraid to enter the lists against one who had overthrown so easily so doughty a knight as the Prince of India. However that might be, no one turned up, so the Knight of London was declared the victor. The shout that was raised at this declaration was not very tremendous, for most of the people liked the Prince of India, whereas they did not care much for the new-comer. But he did not seem to mind it much, and he went smilingly to the Princess. As he came before the royal presence he made his horse kneel, and advance kneeling, till he was quite close.

Then he said:

"As no one appears to dispute my right I believe I am the victor, and in virtue of that right I claim your Majesty's hand."

But the Princess laughed.

"Oh, we'll see about that to-morrow; there'll be plenty of time then. Meanwhile, this evening we are going to give a ball at the palace, to which all who have taken part in the tournament are invited. Of course you'll come, won't you?"

"Of course I will, at your invitation, your Majesty, but——"

What he was going to say was drowned in an immoderate fit of laughter, which came from the Prince of India.

"Ha! ha! ha!" he laughed. "Can't you see who it is you're talking to?" he continued, talking to the Princess.

The Princess drew herself up.

"I believe I am talking to the Knight of London," she said severely.

"The Knight of London! why he's no more the Knight of London than I am. Why, your Majesty must be blind or mad, or both, not to see who he is. Blind's not enough to express it. You——"

But he got no farther, for the Princess called for the police to arrest him, but before they could get at him he had fainted; for the spear of the Knight of London had gone right through his side. So the Princess told the police to lift him up gently and to carry him to his house in the town.

But the Knight of London frowned:

"If I were you, your Majesty, I should order them to cut his head off on the first opportunity. To call you mad and blind—why, I've never heard of such a thing."

But the Princess said:

"That would never do. Why, he is an independent prince, and if I hurt him it would bring on a war with India, and goodness knows what else. However, I'll have him turned out of the kingdom as soon as he is well enough to go. However, I am going back now. Mind and be in time this evening."

So he went to doff his armour, and she drove home once more—this time without the poor Prince, who was being carried behind in an ambulance waggon. The rest of the day passed off somehow, and the night came at last, as nights are in the habit of doing, and with the night came knights— no longer dressed in steel armour, but gorgeous in velvet-and silk and evening dress. But, however gorgeous and fine they might be, the Knight of London outstripped them all, in dress, manners, looks, and everything else, and the Princess said he had the best step of any one she had ever known—and she ought to know, for she danced with him a great many times. In fact, by the end of the ball she had forgotten all about the poor Prince, for the Knight of London was a most enchanting person—although one thing did seem strange, and that was, that the Knight seemed positively afraid of the Owl; and at supper-time he actually refused to sit on the right hand of the Princess because the Owl was sitting on her right shoulder.

But the Owl took no notice of him at all, and never even looked at him, so she thought it was only a rather foolish prejudice on his part. However, the ball came to an end at last, and the Princess went to bed and dreamt pleasantly of some one, but it was not the Prince this time.

And the Prince lay tossing on his bed only half dreaming, and not pleasantly, of some one, and it *was* the Princess. As for the Knight of London, nobody knows what he dreamt about; and, to tell the truth, nobody cared. But the Owl sat at the head of the Prince's bed, and slept calmly—he did not dream; owls are not in the habit of dreaming—they are a good deal wiser.

When the next morning came, the Knight of London came with it, and he wanted to know when the Princess would marry him; but the Princess put him off—for somehow, although she liked him very much, she did not altogether relish the idea of marrying so soon. So she told him that he must wait until the Lords of the Council had given their consent, and they were not going to meet till the next day, so he would have to wait till then. But the Knight did not like this at all.

"At all events, my dear Princess," he said, "you might promise to marry me, for, after all, I did win the tournament, you see, and so—"

But the Princess put her hand to her chin and rubbed it softly as if she were thinking very deeply—and no doubt she was—and shook her head emphatically.

"No; I can't promise until the Council have given their consent, for you see that would be unconstitutional, and I can't be that even for you."

The Knight seemed quite angry.

"Bother the unconstitutionality," he said; "what does the stupid old Council want to blunder into such matters?"

But the Princess stopped him:

"Oh, you mustn't say that—please don't say that," she said; "it's not a stupid old Council, it's a very nice old Council, and it's much nicer than you are. When you get angry like that you're not at all nice—so just be quiet; now do."

And he had to be quiet, for he was afraid of making her really angry.

She too was afraid she had hurt his feelings by telling him to be quiet. So she asked him to join the hunt that was preparing outside, and he of course accepted her invitation, for you see he was only too glad to make it up. They rode out of the town, and soon a deer was started, and the chase swept through the tall trees after it over the thick carpet of fallen leaves and between the trunks of the beech-trees. As a rule the Princess's horse was swifter than any of the deer they started, but this one seemed an exception to the rule, for it went on at just the rate she did, keeping always at the same speed whether she pulled her horse in or let it go at the top of its speed. The Princess was quite annoyed at this. Gradually she passed all the knights and huntsmen who were labouring forward at full gallop, and then she came up with the hoarse-tongued hounds, who were running steadily along with their noses close to the ground. And then she passed them too, and their deep mouthing sounded behind, and gradually the shouts of the huntsmen and the cries of the dogs and all the sounds of the chase died away behind, and still the deer kept steadily forward. Just at this time she noticed the heavy gallop of a horse behind her, and looking round she saw the Knight of London cantering easily behind. So she slackened her speed a little to let him come up, and then she stopped to let the rest of the chase come up with her; and when she stopped the deer stopped too, and nibbled quietly at a flower that was growing at the foot of a tree.

By this time the Knight had come up with her, and she said:

"So here you are. What an annoying thing that deer is—I can't catch it up, do whatever I may, and my horse used to be thought the fastest in the world, except one," she added, after a moment.

"That is strange," said the Knight. "I used always to think mine the fastest in the world, and indeed, your Majesty, I think it is quite as fast as yours."

"I do believe it is," she said. "It's most annoying; every second person I see now has a horse as fast as mine. However, we'll try a race as soon as the rest have caught us up."

Just at that moment a hound's bay came from close behind them, and the deer started off again.

"There it goes," said the Princess; and again she started off, and the Knight kept close beside her. They went faster than ever, and she could hardly breathe because of the wind, but the Knight kept steadily by her side, and would not be out-distanced. Just at this moment she happened to look upwards, and there was the Owl sailing quietly along just over her head, flapping his wings lazily as if there were no need for exertion, although they were going at such a rate that the Princess could hardly keep her eyes open—just as when you put your head out of the window of a railway train that is going pretty fast—a thing, by the bye, that it is to be hoped you never do, or you might get your nose chopped off against a post. When she looked down from the Owl, to her surprise the deer had vanished altogether, and although she rubbed her eyes she could not see it anywhere; and although they galloped still farther on, no deer made its appearance, and the forest had become dark and thick and she had never been there before. So she drew her horse in so suddenly that its hoofs threw up the copper-coloured beech-leaves in showers, and the Knight shot some distance in advance. However, he turned and came back. So the Princess said:

"What are we to do now?"

"Go back, I suppose," he answered.

"But I don't know the way," she said, "and we are near the country of the Magi, and they're the most frightful creatures, who would tear us up and eat us if they knew where to find us."

The Knight smiled:

"I could save you from them," he said.

But the Princess said reflectively:

"I don't know so much about that, for you see they're very strong—and how dark it's getting; it must be past five, and it will soon be night."

I dare say if she had been alone she would have had a good cry, but that wouldn't do before strangers.

It was still getting darker and she began to feel very uncomfortable, for the howl of a wolf came down on the breeze, and a squirrel that had been searching for nuts darted home to its hole, scuttling along as fast as it could.

So she said:

"Come, let us be quick and get away."

"Promise to marry me first."

But she only said:

"Oh, I'll see about that when we're safe—so do come."

What the Knight would have answered was never known, for just then the Owl, who was seated on her shoulder, gave a mournful "Tu-whoo," at which the horse of the Knight jumped back nearly ten feet and almost threw him with the unexpected shock. But before she could do anything a hunter burst from the bushes near at hand and said:

"Hurry, Princess, hurry; the Magi have heard of your whereabouts, and they are coming at full speed here. Come, be quick."

But the Princess said:

"But what will you do, old man? for you have no horse."

But he smiled contemptuously.

"Horse! I don't want a horse—why, I can run as well as any deer. Come, come."

And he caught the bridle of her horse and away they went, and for the moment she forgot all about the Knight, for from behind came the sound of crashing branches, and she knew that the Magi were following them. But the old hunter ran in front of the horse, tugging at the bridle-rein, and shouting to her to go faster, so she leant forward and whispered in her horse's ear, and it stretched forward with such speed that it outsped the wind. Gradually the sounds behind began to get less and less, and the wood began to get lighter, and at last they jumped a little brook, and were at the end of the forest in a smooth meadow. Here the old man stopped.

"You are safe now," he said. And she drew a sigh of relief.

"At last!" she said; "but how can I reward you, my preserver? Would you like a lock of my hair, or a purse full of gold, or a—? well, that wouldn't do—you see I can't well offer to marry you, though that's what princesses generally do to their preservers. You'd better choose something for yourself. I will grant it, whatever it is."

But the old man shook his head.

"I want no reward, your Majesty; I only did my duty. I couldn't have done less. See, here come some of the hunters whom you left behind."

And just then several of them came up, and when they saw her they shouted and blew their horns to let the others know that the Princess was found. But the huntsman said:

"Good-day, your Majesty. I must go."

"But you haven't got your reward yet."

But he shook his head.

"I want no reward," he said; and before the Princess could say any more he stepped into the forest and was seen no more; so she turned her horse towards the town.

On her way she met the head huntsman, so she drew rein and said:

"Why did you not follow on the scent of the deer?"

"It lay so thinly, your Majesty, that the dogs could not follow, and they soon gave in."

"But you should have followed me, at any rate."

"Ah, your Majesty, we might as well have tried to prove the moon was made of green cheese. Besides, your Majesty had one cavalier; and sometimes two's company and three's none."

Just at this moment the Princess remembered the Knight.

"Good gracious!" she said, "what has become of the Knight—have none of you seen him?"

But none of them had, and although the question went far and wide no news came of him, nor could he be seen anywhere.

"He must have been caught by the Magi—if so, he will have been devoured to a certainty! Poor Knight!"

The chief huntsman seemed excited:

"Your Majesty has not been near the country of the Magi, surely?" he said.

"I was almost too near, and the poor Knight has probably been torn to pieces in trying to drive them back."

"Your Majesty should be thankful that knights are so faithful," said the chief huntsman; "but perhaps, after all, he has escaped by a different path."

But the Princess sighed:

"I am afraid not," she said.

However, she rode on to the town to consult Lord Licec as to what had better be done. But when she got there she found that he was out of town and would not be back till next morning. So the poor Princess had to go back home and wait—but she looked so pale that her ladies-in-waiting insisted on sending for the doctor. He came in a hurry, and asked her of course what was the matter, and when she told him he shook his head.

"I'm afraid he's got rather a poor chance, for these Magi haven't had a good meal of one of your Majesty's subjects for nearly three weeks, and they were uncommonly hungry. But if your Majesty will allow me to feel your pulse, I—"

So she gave him her hand, and he took out his watch and began to count. "One, two, three, four"; but just then he looked up and saw the Owl sitting on the Princess's shoulder, and his hand trembled so much that he dropped his watch, and it smashed to atoms on the floor.

"Oh, dear, there goes ten and sixpence," he groaned; "and I shan't be able to get another for ever so long. D'you know, your Majesty, I think you are somewhat feverish; and you had better go to bed. And meanwhile, the Owl is too exciting for you; if you could let it be put in a cellar and let it have nothing to eat for, say, three weeks, perhaps it might not be so fiery after that."

The Princess smiled:

"Perhaps you would like to take him there yourself," she said.

But the doctor said:

"Good gracious! no. I think he's perfectly capable of taking himself without any assistance. D'you know, your Majesty, I've got a very pressing case outside; and if you will excuse me I will retire."

And he retired so quickly that he left his umbrella behind him—for you see he was very frightened of the Owl.

Acting on his advice the Princess went to bed, and dismissed her ladies-in-waiting and told them not to come to the room again until she called for them.

And then she lay with her hand under her head thinking of nothing in particular, and the Owl sat on the top of the canopy over her bed.

Suddenly she heaved a deep sigh.

"I wish I knew what had become of him," she thought to herself.

"You wouldn't like it if you did know," said a strange cracked voice that seemed to come from nowhere in particular. She started up and looked all round the room, but there was no one to be seen; so she thought it was all imagination, and lay down again. And again she thought to herself, "How I should like to be with him."

"No, you wouldn't," said the voice.

This time she was sure it came from the Owl, so she asked quite softly, "Did you say that, cherished Owl?"

And the Owl answered:

"I did."

"But I thought you could not speak, dear Owl."

"Well, you see, I can sometimes—when it's necessary."

"But how did you know what I was thinking?—for I did not speak aloud."

"Ah! you see, Princess, I can't tell you that—it's quite enough for you that I can tell."

"But why do you say I should not like to see him?"

"Because you wouldn't."

"Why? Is he all torn to pieces by the Magi?"

"Torn to pieces!—not he," laughed the Owl.

"Oh! that is good news," said she quite joyfully. "Oh! do take me to him, dear Owl."

"Very well, Princess. But I warn you, you won't be pleased with what you see." But the Princess was quite confident.

"Oh yes, I shall, dear Owl—when shall we go?"

"At once, if you like—the sooner the better."

"Oh! you dear Owl. I'll go and get dressed at once."

So she ran into her dressing-room and dressed herself in no time, without bothering to call up any of her ladies-in-waiting about it. Then she went back to the room where the Owl was waiting for her.

He was sitting on the floor near the fire, blinking quietly at the coals, and he did not at first notice her entry, so she said:

"Well, good Owl, shall I send for the horse?"

"What for?" asked the Owl.

"To ride on, I suppose!" she answered.

"Oh, that's it, is it? That would never do. Just get on my back, and I'll see if I can't carry you somewhat faster than a horse could."

So she got on his back, although she was rather afraid she would crush him altogether. But somehow, when she sat down, she sank deep into his warm feathers—either she had grown small, or the Owl had grown very big all of a sudden. Without the least shock they passed through the wall, and out into the clear starlight.

"Good Owl," said the Princess, "you won't let me fall, will you?" for, to tell the truth, she felt rather afraid on the whole; but the Owl answered:

"No, of course not; you're quite safe, only you'd better keep close to me, for we shall go pretty fast, and the wind will be sharp enough to cut your hair off."

So she sat still, protected against the wind, and looking at the twinkling stars—for the Owl flew so high that he almost rubbed some of them out of their places.

The wind whistled loud in the wings of the Owl, but his flight was so regular that she almost fell asleep, and was quite happy—for you see she felt quite safe. Presently the straight flight of the Owl changed, and he began to circle round and round, and then they dropped quickly towards the earth, and the Owl stopped.

"You can get off now," he said, and she stepped off his back.

"Take care," he said next; and she rubbed her eyes in astonishment, for she found herself on the top of a roof.

"I told you you wouldn't like it if you came," he said. "But you'd better look down below if you want to see anything that's going on," and he gravely seated himself on her shoulder, for he seemed quite small again. So the Princess looked down, and she saw at some distance below a large fire that was blazing in a sort of courtyard, and then she saw that it was the battlements of a castle on which they were standing. Presently a horrible-looking old witch came within the glow of the fire—she was an awful old creature too, and she almost made the Princess cry out from fright. She seated herself near the fire, and began to beat the ground angrily with the handle of a broom that she carried, and every now and then muttered as she did so:

"How awfully late he is. Why don't he come?" and various other complaints of his lateness.

"But who is he?" asked the Princess of the Owl in a whisper.

"Wait, and you'll see," said the Owl.

Just then something peculiar happened down below—a couple of men appeared suddenly. They did not seem to come from anywhere in particular, but they were there all the same. The Princess almost screamed with astonishment, but she checked herself in time by stuffing a pocket-handkerchief into her mouth, for one of the men whom she saw was the Knight of London, and the other was Magog the King of the Magi; and the Knight of London did not seem to be on bad terms with the King of the Magi.

"You've come at last," growled the old woman, in a voice something between the squeaking of a slate-pencil on a slate and the growling of a bear with a sore head.

"I couldn't come any sooner, mother," said the Knight of London soothingly; "you see I had to wait for her to promise to marry me."

"Well, has she promised?" said the witch.

"Not yet."

"Then why on earth not?"

"She said she had to wait for the consent of the Council."

"Why didn't you eat her?" said Magog sleepily; and then, without waiting for an answer, he curled himself up close to the fire and went to sleep.

But the old witch went on:

"Well, and what are your plans now?"

"I'm going back to-morrow morning, and I'm going to take old Magog and pretend that he's my prisoner of war, and then the stupid old Council will say I've done a service to the State, and they will give me the hand of the Princess for my pains."

"But supposing they don't?"

"Then I shall cut them all to pieces, and kill the Princess, and make myself king by force—for you see nothing can cut through my armour, except one thing."

"And what's that?" asked the witch.

"Well, I don't mind telling you, mother, because you won't go and tell any one—it's *paper!*"

"That's a funny sort of thing to cut through armour."

"It may be funny," answered the Knight, "but it's true all the same, and if the Prince of India had found it out I should not be where I am now; only he didn't, you see."

"So much the worse for him," said the witch, "but is there nothing at all but paper that can cut through it?"

"Well, there is one thing that can—the beak of the Owl, to wit."

"Tu-whoo!" suddenly cried the Owl.

The effect of this sudden cry was tremendous. The Knight clung to his mother, and cried out in a piteous voice:

"Oh mother! mother! it's the Owl; save me!"

"How on earth can I save you if you hang on me like this?" said his mother. "Just throw some more wood on, so that we can see this Owl, and I'll fling my broom at it, and see if that won't bring it down."

But the Princess leant her head to the Owl, and said:

"Dear Owl, let's go. I've seen quite enough."

And the Owl seemed to think the same, for he said:

"All right. Just get on my back again, and we'll go."

So she did as she was told, and no sooner had she got on his back than she fell asleep, and remembered no more until she found herself lying on her bed with the early morning sun shining through the lattice.

She rubbed her eyes in astonishment, and it seemed as if it had been all a dream. But it all was so clear on her mind, and besides she had on her riding-clothes just as she had put them on to go with the Owl.

To make herself feel more sure she said to the Owl:

"Good Owl, was it a dream?"

And the Owl shook his head, but although she asked him several times to speak she could not get the least word out of him, although he always shook his head if she asked him if it was a dream.

Just then a tremendous noise in the street made her run to the window, and there she saw the Knight of London coming up to the door, dragging the King of the Magi behind him in chains, and the people of the town were following him in an excited crowd, which caused all the noise, for they were naturally very glad to see their old enemy in chains.

The Knight rode straight up to the palace door, and when he saw the Princess at the window he smiled and said:

"Good-morning, your Majesty—you see I am returned."

And the Princess said:

"Good-morning," as if she were very glad to see him, for she had not yet quite made up her mind about what she was going to do—for of course she could not marry him after what she had seen the night before. So she drew back from the window to think about it—for it would never do to try to get rid of him by force. At last she hit upon a plan—she had to think of it herself—for the Owl would tell her nothing.

She went to the door of her room, but there were no guards at the door—they had run down to see what the shouting was about. But just then the doctor came up the stairs:

"Good morning, your Majesty," he said; "have you had a good night?"

"A very good night, thank you, doctor. But that doesn't matter just now. I want the Prince of India."

"The *who*?" said the astonished doctor.

"The Prince of India."

"Then I am afraid he can't come. But if the Knight of London would do—"

"But he won't! I want the Prince of India at once."

"I fear your Majesty can't have him at once. You *wouldn't* have him once, you know."

"But why not?"

"Because at the present moment he isn't well enough to move."

"Oh, good gracious!—but why is that?"

"Well, your Majesty, if you'd been thrown from your horse with great violence, and had half a foot of spear stuck into you, besides being mortified at your overthrow, perhaps you would be rather unwell."

"Oh, poor fellow, I didn't know he was so bad as that. I'll go and see him at once."

"I think your Majesty had better not."

"Why not?"

"Because it might excite him too much, and besides, what would the Knight of London—"

But the Princess drew herself up and said:

"I beg your pardon, but I must ask you not to mention that gentleman's name, if you please."

"Whe—ew," ejaculated the doctor; "what's in the wind now?"

"I beg your pardon?" said the Princess.

"I—I only said—it's an east wind now, your Majesty."

Just then a page came running up, and said that the Knight of London wished to speak to the Princess.

"Tell him that I am not quite well enough to see him now, but I will send a message to him, if he will stop a moment. And on your way just ask Lord Licec to come to me, please."

"Yes, your Majesty," said the page, and he disappeared.

In a moment Lord Licec came.

"You sent for me, your Majesty, I believe?"

"I did, my lord. It was about this Knight of London. I have discovered that he is not what he pretends to be at all, for he is in league with the Magi; and this Magog whom he pretends is his prisoner is really nothing of the sort. He is one of his allies, and they are going to break out and kill me, and every one else, and make themselves masters of everything."

"Oh, my wig!" suddenly said the doctor, "I hope your Majesty won't let them; if you intend to I shall depart without delay, for I don't want to be eaten by this Magog."

"That's just what I wanted to prevent by begging the Prince of India to help us; only you said that I mayn't see him, doctor."

"Oh! on the contrary, your Majesty, it would be the best thing in the world—we'll go at once."

"Wait a moment," said the Princess, and turning to Lord Licec she went on:

"Now I want you to tell him that the Lords of the Council say that the last tournament was unfair, because he came in fresh at the end. And that if he wants to—to claim his rights, he must submit to go through another tournament. Of course he will—because he's quite sure of winning—but he won't this time."

"Are you quite sure, your Majesty?"

"Oh! quite. And as all the knights who tilted last time are still in the town, let it take place to-morrow."

"Yes, your Majesty."

"And if you could keep him out of the way for a few hours—so that he won't know what I'm going to do—so much the better."

"I'll challenge him to a game of 'Beggar-My-Neighbour'—that generally lasts for a pretty good time."

"That will do; the longer the better. Now I'm ready, doctor, if you'll conduct me to the Prince."

So they went out at a back door for fear the Knight of London should see them, and they soon reached the house of the Prince.

At the door was a servant, and they asked him where the Prince was.

"In the garden, your Majesty. I will go and announce your arrival to him."

But the Princess said:

"Oh no! never mind—you needn't trouble."

And they went through into the garden. On the way the Princess said to the doctor:

"I thought you said he was not well enough to get up?"

"I did, your Majesty, but he insisted that he must get up, and be off to India this afternoon, and he was excessively violent when I told him he had better not get up—in fact he—he kicked me downstairs; and if your Majesty has no present need of me I will retire, for to tell the truth he threatened to have me ducked in a horse-pond if I came near him again—and he meant it too."

So the Princess gave him leave to go—in fact she was rather glad he had gone; and she went on walking down the path. It was one of those old-fashioned manor-gardens, full of tall stiff hollyhocks, and damask roses, and beds of thyme and mint, over which the bees were humming so loudly that they could be heard over the whole garden. As the Princess could not see him down one path, she turned into another alley of stiff holly-bushes, but he was not to be seen down there either; however, she walked fast to the end of it—for you see she was rather impatient. Now it happened that just as she turned the corner, the Prince happened to be coming round too, and the result was that as they were going rather fast, and the Prince was the heavier of the two, the Princess was thrown back with violence against the hedge, and she couldn't help exclaiming:

"Oh!"—for you see he had trodden on her toe. As for the Prince, he could scarcely stand—for the shock and the sight of the Princess together produced a tremendous effect, as you may imagine—for she was the last person he had expected to see.

"My goodness!" he said, as soon as he was able to speak. "Your Majesty—I hope I haven't hurt you—I am really very sorry. I am very sorry—will you allow me to help you to a seat?—for I see I have trodden on your foot."

Her Majesty said:

"Oh no! not at all, thank you."

But all the same she let him give her his arm, and help her to a seat. It was a rustic seat—one of those queer seats made of branches of trees, and it stood in an arbour formed of rose-bushes, and there was plenty of room for two; so she said:

"Won't you sit down, Prince?"

But he answered:

"I really have not the time, your Majesty. I was just about to start for India, and if your Majesty has no further need of me I will go, and send an attendant."

But she did not seem to hear the last part of his sentence, for she answered:

"You were going away without saying good-bye to me. Perhaps, however, you intended to call as you passed the palace."

"I really had not intended to, your Majesty, for you seemed to have so many affairs that I might have interrupted, that I thought it as well to go without troubling you."

"You shouldn't have thought that. You see I have had so many affairs of State occupying me that I could not possibly get round to call, and you didn't choose to come and see me, which was rather, I think—however, that doesn't matter now. I have come to ask you to stop a little longer—till the day after to-morrow, if you won't stop after that."

But the Prince shook his head:

"I have to go immediately; affairs of State, you know, demand my presence in India, and I must go at once, your Majesty."

"Can't you really stop a little, Prince?"

"I really can't, your Majesty—that is—"

"Oh, please do; I'll tell you something, if you like. I've found out who the Knight of London is."

"And then, your Majesty?" inquired the Prince.

"I don't know what else. I—I thought that would be enough for you."

"I don't understand you, your Majesty."

"I mean that when I didn't know he was a wizard I thought he was very enchanting; but when I found out he was an enchanter, I thought you were enchanter—I mean more enchanting."

The Prince was just saying:

"Oh, your Majesty," when a peculiar noise from the back of the arbour made them both start, and the Princess jumped up so violently that the Owl, who had meanwhile gone to sleep, was nearly shaken off her shoulder.

"What was that?" she said.

"It sounded like somebody laughing, or trying to keep from laughing, rather. Just wait a moment, I'll see who it was."

And he went round behind the arbour. He soon returned bringing the doctor with him, and the doctor did not seem at all happy either.

"Why," said the Princess, "I thought you were going to leave me. How is it that you came like this behind the arbour?"

"I might just as well ask your Majesty why you came here."

"You might, but it would not be answering my question."

"I happened to come round there, your Majesty, to read a book in the shade, and I happened to drop off to sleep, and the noise you heard was my snoring."

"But how did you know we heard a noise if you were asleep at the time?"

"I—eh—I don't exactly know, your Majesty."

"It's quite clear you were listening. I'll excuse you this time, but if I catch you eavesdropping again I'll make the Owl take you up into the sky and drop you—that may be a drop too much for you. You can go now, but don't do so any more."

But the Prince had still hold of him.

"By the bye," he said, "there's a horse-pond near here; I think I'll just take you there and throw you in, as I said I would if I caught you again."

But the Princess said:

"Oh, let him go, Prince," and the doctor hurried off at a great rate.

"I don't think he'll come back again in a hurry," said the Prince; "meanwhile, what about the Knight of London?"

"I must get rid of him as soon as I can, and I want you to help me."

"I, your Majesty—but how?"

"The Council have decided that last tournament was not fair, because the Knight came in fresh and you were already tired out, so they have decided to have it over again, and you are requested to come and fight—for me."

"But what is the use of that? he'll knock me over just as he did before."

"Oh no! he won't, because I've found out his secret." And she told him about the paper.

At the end the Prince said:

"Oh! that's all right then. I'll be there, your Majesty."

"But are you strong enough, do you think?"

"Oh yes, your Majesty."

"And the affairs of State can be put off till the day after to-morrow. I promise to let you go as soon as you have got rid of the Knight for me."

"Oh, for the matter of that, there is no such great hurry. I really needn't go for some time."

"But you can go whenever you like, you know."

"Thank you, your Majesty."

"But—a—I don't want you to go, you know. In fact I should like you to stop, very much."

"Then I'll stop as long as you like, your Majesty—for ever, if you like, your Majesty."

"I should like it very much, Prince," she answered.

I don't exactly know what happened after that—perhaps you can guess— but they do say that the Owl, who chanced to wake at that moment, positively blushed; but then people are fond of exaggerating, and the Owl did not seem to object, so I suppose it was all right; and when the Princess went back to the palace, the Prince was quite good-tempered again, whereas before her visit he had been so angry that all his servants had left in a body— however, they came back when they found he was quiet again.

So the Princess was quite happy once more, as you may imagine, only there was one nasty thing she had to do, and that was to send a note to the Knight of London thanking him for having taken prisoner the King of the Magi, and hoping that he would be successful at the tournament on the next day—for you see she was not well enough to see him, and he was quite sure of winning, as he had done before, so he did not mind it very much.

The next day came, and the Princess was at the lists as before, and the crowd was just as great too, only there were very many less knights to fight, for the Knight of London was the challenger, and he—well, they had seen how he had treated the Prince of India, and they did not care to be tumbled over in such a very unceremonious way. However, two or three of the bravest in the world came and answered his challenge, but it was no use; they might just as well not have tried, for they were thrown from their horses so violently that they were most of them seriously hurt. So it seemed as if he was going to have it all his own way, for the Prince had as yet not put in an appearance, and the spectators began to call for him—for, as I said before, they liked the Prince better than the Knight; although he was so very handsome, still there was a something about him that they did not like at all. But the Knight had overcome all who had chosen to come against him, and his trumpets were sounding the challenge for the last time, and then their echoes died away and still no answering trumpet came, and the Princess was beginning to feel afraid that he had gone off to India and left her. But just as the Knight was advancing to claim his rights, a trumpet blast rang out brazen and shrill on the still air, and the Prince of India rode into the lists. He was still pale from his illness, but the people cheered him loudly, and the Princess gave a sigh of relief, and quite flushed with joy and excitement.

"He'll win this time," she said to Lord Licec, who was standing near her.

"I don't know so much about that," he answered, "for you see the Knight of London is in very good form to-day; and just look at the Prince's shield—it's made of cardboard, I should think—yes, it is. Ah—I am afraid his last defeat has rather turned his head."

The Princess smiled and nodded. Lord Licec thought she was nodding to him, but she wasn't; both the smile and the nod were meant for quite another person.

However, the combatants were already in their places, so she signed to the heralds to give the signal.

"*Laissez aller,*" they cried, and once again the Knight and Prince charged each other. This time they did not go so fast, and the spectators could see what took place. It was soon over. The spear of each of the combatants hit exactly the centre of the other's shield. But the spear of the Knight broke as if it had been made of a bulrush. It was not so with the Prince—for his spear pierced through and through the seven-fold shield of the Knight, and the Knight himself was thrown right off his horse on to the ground. He, however, was on his feet in an instant, and rushed at the Prince, who leapt off his horse and confronted the Knight.

The Knight made a pass at the Prince with his rapier, but the Prince caught the thrust on his shield, and the sword came to the same end as the spear. The Knight had still his heavy battle-axe, and he lifted it on high to swing it down on to the head of his opponent. The Prince made no movement to defend himself, and the axe came full on his crest—through the crest it hit its way, and through the steel helmet, but when it got past the steel it hit on a paper helm below, and the axe shivered at the touch as if it had been glass. Then the Prince caught the Knight by the wrist:

"Keep still," he said, "or I run you to the heart with my paper dagger."

"You can't," sneered the Knight.

"Why not?"

"Because I'm heartless; so you can't hurt my heart."

The Prince took no notice of what he said. He had turned to the Princess, who was clapping her hands for joy—which was rather an unprincess-like act; but she couldn't help it.

"What shall I do with him?" he said.

"Let him go, I suppose."

And the Knight was beginning to walk off as fast as he could. But a loud and commanding voice came from behind the Princess, and she looked behind her suddenly, and she almost fainted, for a marvellous change had come over the Owl, and it was still changing. She rubbed her eyes in astonishment, and all the people who could see him did so too, and then a great shout went up from all of "God save the King!" for it was no longer the Owl they saw—it was the old King.

"Stop!" he cried loudly to the Knight, who was slinking off—"you have not received your reward yet. Just wait a moment, and to prevent mistakes just take your ordinary form."

And again every one present rubbed their eyes in astonishment—for the handsome calm face of the Knight was shrivelling up, and his raven hair had become an ugly grey, and the people recognized him too as an old acquaintance, for he was—who do you think now? Why, he was Merry-mineral—it seemed as if that day gave two instances of old friends with new faces.

Although he didn't at all seem to want to stay, he was obliged to stop at the King's voice. So he stood in the middle of the lists looking very uncomfortable—for every one was looking at him. The King began:

"Now let us see how many crimes you have committed. You have broken your oath—isn't that right?"

"Oh! quite correct, your Majesty."

"And you have rebelled against my daughter?"

"Quite correct, your Majesty."

"And you have intended to murder her?"

"Just so, your Majesty."

"And you tried to marry her?"

"I should have been only too pleased, your Majesty."

"And you don't repent, do you?"

"Not at all, your Majesty."

"And the right punishment for each of your crimes is death?"

"Just so, your Majesty."

"But I don't care to sentence you to death—it's not hard enough. I sentence you to live underground for ten thousand years."

"Ten thousand years, your Majesty!"

"You can go at once, and if I catch you above ground—I shouldn't like to be you."

"No, your Majesty. Good-day."

And he kissed his hand to the Princess, and bowed gallantly to the Prince of India, and then the ground gave way under him—and he has never been heard of since. But the King turned to the Prince of India and said:

"You may go now, Prince."

The Prince looked astonished.

"I do not quite understand, your Majesty," he said.

The King looked at him and said:

"You seem to be uncommonly hard of understanding, cousin of India. I said, You can go."

"But I don't want to go, your Majesty," the Prince answered, getting a little red.

"Oh, don't you?" said the King; "from what I heard of a certain pleasant conversation in a certain summer-house you seemed to have important affairs of State that demanded instant attention."

Here the doctor suddenly remarked:

"If you will excuse me, your Majesty, I beg to differ from you when you refer to that conversation as pleasant. I myself heard it, or rather overheard it, and all I can say is I thought it most unpleasant—most. That is, if your Majesty will excuse my remark."

"But I won't," said the King suddenly. "I believe it was you that suggested I should be confined to a dark cellar for three weeks without food—eh!"

But the doctor suddenly remembered that he had an important case that demanded instant attention.

The King turned to the Princess and said:

"Well, I suppose you can settle it for yourselves, you two, because I'm going now. I shall come and see you every seven years. Good-bye."

And he suddenly turned into the Brown Owl, and flitted noiselessly off, before they could say "Good-bye," or anything else.

The Prince found that he could manage to postpone his affairs of State indefinitely, and in a few days the Prince and Princess were married and lived happily ever afterwards.

1891

Rocking-Horse Land

LAURENCE HOUSMAN

Prince Fredolin woke up, both eyes at once, and sprang out of bed into the sunshine. He was five years old that morning, by all the clocks and calendars in the kingdom; and the day was going to be beautiful. Every golden minute was precious. He was dressed and out of his room before the attendants knew that he was awake.

In the ante-chamber stood piles on piles of glittering presents; when he walked among them they came up to the measure of his waist. His fairy godmother had sent him a toy with the most humorous effect. It was labelled, "Break me and I shall turn into something else." So every time he broke it he got a new toy more beautiful than the last. It began by being a hoop, and from that it ran on, while the Prince broke it incessantly for the space of one hour, during which it became by turn—a top, a Noah's ark, a skipping-rope, a man-of-war, a box of bricks, a picture puzzle, a pair of stilts, a drum, a trumpet, a kaleidoscope, a steam-engine, and nine hundred and fifty other things exactly. Then he began to grow discontented because it would never turn into the same thing again, and after having broken the man-of-war he wanted to get it back again; also he wanted to see if the steam-engine would go inside the Noah's ark, but the toy would never be two things at the same time either. This was very unsatisfactory. He thought his fairy godmother ought to have sent him two toys, out of which he could make combinations.

At last he broke it once more, and it turned into a kite; and while he was flying the kite he broke the string, and the kite went sailing away up into the nasty clear sky, and was never heard of again.

Then Fredolin sat down and howled at his fairy godmother; what a dissembling lot fairy godmothers were, to be sure! They were always setting traps to make their godchildren unhappy. Nevertheless, when told to, he took up his pen and wrote her a nice little note, full of bad spelling and

319
.

tarrididdles, to say what a happy birthday he was spending in breaking up the beautiful toy she had sent him.

Then he went to look at the rest of the presents, and found it quite refreshing to break a few that did not send him giddy by turning into something else.

Suddenly his eyes became fixed with delight; alone, right at the end of the room, stood a great black rocking-horse. The saddle and bridle were hung with tiny gold bells and balls of coral; and the horse's tail and mane flowed till they almost touched the ground.

The Prince scampered across the room, and threw his arms around the beautiful creature's neck. All its bells jangled as the head swayed gracefully down; and the prince kissed it between the eyes. Great eyes they were, the colour of fire, so wonderfully bright, it seemed they must be really alive, only they did not move, but gazed continually with a set stare at the tapestry-hung wall, on which were figures of armed knights riding by to battle.

So Prince Fredolin mounted to the back of his rocking-horse, and all day long he rode and shouted to the figures of the armed knights, challenging them to fight, or leading them against the enemy.

At length, when it came to be bedtime, weary of so much glory, he was lifted down from the saddle and carried away to bed.

In his sleep Fredolin still felt his black rocking-horse swinging to and fro under him, and heard the melodious chime of its bells, and, in the land of dreams, saw a great country open before him, full of the sound of the battle-cry and the hunting-horn calling him to strange perils and triumphs.

In the middle of the night he grew softly awake, and his heart was full of love for his black rocking-horse. He crept gently out of bed: he would go and look at it where it was standing so grand and still in the next room, to make sure that it was all safe and not afraid of being by itself in the dark night. Parting the door-hangings he passed through into the wide hollow chamber beyond, all littered about with toys.

The moon was shining in through the window, making a square cistern of light upon the floor. And then, all at once, he saw that the rocking-horse had moved from the place where he had left it! It had crossed the room, and was standing close to the window, with its head toward the night, as though watching the movement of the clouds and the trees swaying in the wind.

The Prince could not understand how it had been moved so; he was a little bit afraid, and stealing timidly across, he took hold of the bridle to comfort himself with the jangle of its bells. As he came close, and looked up into the dark solemn face he saw that the eyes were full of tears, and reaching up felt one fall warm against his hand.

"Why do you weep, my Beautiful?" said the Prince.

The rocking-horse answered, "I weep because I am a prisoner, and not free; open the window, Master, and let me go!"

"But if I let you go I shall lose you," said the Prince. "Cannot you be happy here with me?"

And the horse said, "Let me go, for my great brothers call me out of Rocking-Horse Land, and I hear my sweet mare whinnying to her foals: and they all cry, seeking me through the ups and hollows of my native fastnesses! Sweet Master, let me go this night, and I will return to you when it is day!"

Then Prince Fredolin said, "How shall I know that you will return to me: and what name shall I call you by?"

And the rocking-horse answered, "My name is Rollonde. Search among my mane till you find in it a white hair, draw it out and wind it upon one of your fingers; and so long as you have it wound about your finger, you are my master; and wherever I am I must go or return at your bidding."

So the Prince drew down the rocking-horse's head, and searched in the mane, till he had found there the white hair; and he wound it upon his finger and tied it. After that he kissed Rollonde between the eyes, saying, "Go then, Rollonde, since I love you, and would see you happy; only return to me when it is day!" And so saying he threw open the window to the stir of the night.

Then the rocking-horse lifted his dark head and neighed aloud for joy, and swaying forward with a mighty circling motion rose full into the air, and sprang out into the free world before him.

Fredolin watched how with plunge and curve he went over the bowed trees; and again he neighed into the darkness of the night, then swifter than wind disappeared in the distance: and faintly from far away came a sound of the neighing of many horses answering him.

Then the Prince closed the window and crept back to bed; and all night long he dreamed strange dreams of Rocking-Horse Land. There he saw smooth hills and valleys that rose and sank without a stone or a tree to disturb the steel-like polish of their surface; slippery as glass, and driven over by a strong wind: and over them, with a sound like the humming of bees, flew the rocking-horses. Up and down, up and down, with bright manes streaming like coloured fires, and feet motionless behind and before, went the swift pendulum of their flight. Their long bodies bowed and rose; their heads worked to carry impetus to their going; they cried, neighing to each other over hill and valley, "Which of us shall be first? which of us shall be first?" After them the mares with their tall foals came spinning to watch, crying also among themselves, "Ah! which shall be first?"

"Rollonde, Rollonde is first!" shouted the Prince, clapping his hands together as they reached the goal; and at that, all at once, he woke and saw it was broad day. Then he ran and threw open the window, and holding out the finger that carried the white hair, cried, "Rollonde, Rollonde, come back, Rollonde!"

Far away he heard an answering sound; and in another moment there came the great rocking-horse himself, dipping and dancing over the hills. He crossed the woods and cleared the palace-wall at a single bound, and floating in through the window, dropped down on to the floor by Prince Fredolin's side, rocking himself gently to and fro as though panting from the strain of his long flight.

"Now are you happy?" asked the Prince as he caressed him.

"Ah! sweet Prince," said Rollonde, "ah, kind Master!" And then he said no more, but became the stock still staring rocking-horse of the day before, with fixed eyes and rigid limbs, which could do nothing but rock up and down with a jangling of sweet bells so long as the Prince rode him.

That night Fredolin came again when all had become still in the palace; and now as before Rollonde had moved from his place and was standing with his head against the window waiting to be let out. "Ah, dear Master," he said, so soon as he saw the Prince coming, "let me go this night also, and I will surely return before day."

So again the Prince opened the window, and watched him disappear, and heard from far away the neighing of the horses in Rocking-Horse Land calling to him. And in the morning with the white hair round his finger he called "Rollonde, Rollonde!" and Rollonde neighed and came back to him, dipping and dancing over the hills.

Now this same thing happened every night; and every morning the horse kissed Fredolin, saying, "Ah! dear Prince and kind Master," and became stock still once more.

So a year went by, till one morning Fredolin woke up to find it was his sixth birthday. And as six is to five, so were the presents he received on his sixth birthday for magnificence and multitude to the presents he had received the year before. His fairy godmother had sent him a bird, a real live bird; but when he pulled its tail it became a lizard, and when he pulled the lizard's tail it became a mouse, and when he pulled the mouse's tail it became a cat; then he did very much want to see if the cat would eat the mouse, and not being able to have them both together he got rather vexed with his fairy godmother. However, he pulled the cat's tail and the cat became a dog, and the dog became a goat; and so it went on till he got to a cow; and he pulled the cow's tail and it became a camel, and he pulled the camel's tail and it became an elephant, and still not being contented, he pulled the elephant's tail and it became a guinea-pig. Now a guinea-pig has got no tail to pull, so it remained a guinea-pig, while Prince Fredolin sat down and howled at this fairy godmother.

But the best of all his presents was the one given to him by the King his father. It was a most beautiful horse, for, said the King, "You are now old enough to learn to ride."

So Fredolin was put upon his horse's back, and from having ridden so long upon his rocking-horse he learned to ride perfectly in a single day, and was declared by all the courtiers to be the most perfect equestrian that was ever seen.

But these praises and the pleasure of riding about on a real horse so occupied his thoughts that that night he forgot altogether to go and set Rollonde free, but fell fast asleep and dreamed of nothing but real horses and horsemen going to battle; and so it was the next night too.

But the night after that, just as he was falling asleep, he heard something sobbing by his bed, and a voice saying "Ah! dear Prince and kind Master, let me go, for my heart breaks for a sight of my native land." And there stood his poor rocking-horse Rollonde, with tears falling out of his beautiful eyes on to the white coverlet.

Then the Prince, full of shame at having forgotten his old friend, sprang up and threw his arms round his neck saying, "Be of good cheer, Rollonde, for now surely I will let thee go!" and he ran to the window and opened it for the horse to go through. "Ah, dear Prince and kind Master!" said Rollonde. Then he lifted his head and neighed so that the whole palace shook, and swaying forward till his head almost touched the ground he sprang out and away into the night over the hills towards Rocking-Horse Land.

Then Prince Fredolin, standing by the window, thoughtfully unloosed the white hair from his finger, and let it float away into the darkness, out of sight of his eye or reach of his hand.

"Good-bye, Rollonde," he murmured softly, "brave Rollonde, my own good Rollonde! Go and be happy in your own land, since I, your Master, was forgetting to be kind to you." And far away he heard the neighing of horses in Rocking-Horse Land.

Many years after, when Fredolin had become King in his father's stead, the fifth birthday of the Prince his son came to be celebrated; and there on the morning of the day, among all the presents that covered the floor of the chamber, stood a beautiful foal rocking-horse, black, with deep burning eyes.

No one knew how it had come there, or whose present it was, till the King himself came to look at it. And when he saw it so like the old Rollonde he had loved as a boy, he smiled, and, stroking its dark mane, said softly in its ear, "Art thou, then, the son of Rollonde?" And the foal answered him, "Ah, dear Prince and kind Master!" but never a word more.

Then the King took the little Prince his son, and told him all the story of Rollonde as I have told it you here; and at the end he went and searched in the foal's mane till he found one white hair, and, drawing it out, he wound it about the little Prince's finger, bidding him guard it well and be ever a kind master to Rollonde's son.

So here is my story of Rollonde come to a good ending.

1894

The Reluctant Dragon

KENNETH GRAHAME

L ong ago—might have been hundreds of years ago—in a cottage half-way between this village and yonder shoulder of the Downs up there, a shepherd lived with his wife and their little son. Now the shepherd spent his days—and at certain times of the year his nights too—up on the wide ocean-bosom of the Downs, with only the sun and the stars and the sheep for company, and the friendly chattering world of men and women far out of sight and hearing. But his little son, when he wasn't helping his father, and often when he was as well, spent much of his time buried in big volumes that he borrowed from the affable gentry and interested parsons of the country round about. And his parents were very fond of him, and rather proud of him too, though they didn't let on in his hearing, so he was left to go his own way and read as much as he liked; and instead of frequently getting a cuff on the side of the head, as might very well have happened to him, he was treated more or less as an equal by his parents, who sensibly thought it a very fair division of labour that they should supply the practical knowledge, and he the book-learning. They knew that book-learning often came in useful at a pinch, in spite of what their neighbours said. What the Boy chiefly dabbled in was natural history and fairy tales, and he just took them as they came, in a sandwichy sort of way, without making any distinctions; and really his course of reading strikes one as rather sensible.

One evening the shepherd, who for some nights past had been disturbed and preoccupied, and off his usual mental balance, came home all of a tremble, and, sitting down at the table where his wife and son were peacefully employed, she with her seam, he in following out the adventures of the Giant with No Heart in His Body, exclaimed with much agitation:

"It's all up with me, Maria! Never no more can I go up on them there Downs, was it ever so!"

"Now don't you take on like that," said his wife, who was a *very* sensible woman: "but tell us all about it first, whatever it is as has given you this shake-up, and then me and you and the son here, between us, we ought to be able to get to the bottom of it!"

"It began some nights ago," said the shepherd. "You know that cave up there—I never liked it, somehow, and the sheep never liked it neither, and when sheep don't like a thing there's generally some reason for it. Well, for some time past there's been faint noises coming from that cave—noises like heavy sighings, with grunts mixed up in them; and sometimes a snoring, far away down—*real* snoring, yet somehow not *honest* snoring, like you and me o' nights, you know!"

"*I* know," remarked the Boy, quietly.

"Of course I was terrible frightened," the shepherd went on; "yet somehow I couldn't keep away. So this very evening, before I come down, I took a cast round by the cave, quietly. And there—O Lord! there I saw him at last, as plain as I see you!"

"Saw *who*?" said his wife, beginning to share in her husband's nervous terror.

"Why, *him*, I'm a telling you!" said the shepherd. "He was sticking half-way out of the cave, and seemed to be enjoying of the cool of the evening in a poetical sort of way. He was as big as four cart-horses, and all covered with shiny scales—deep-blue scales at the top of him, shading off to a tender sort o' green below. As he breathed, there was that sort of flicker over his nostrils that you see over our chalk roads on a baking windless day in summer. He had his chin on his paws, and I should say he was meditating about things. Oh, yes, a peaceable sort o' beast enough, and not ramping or carrying on or doing anything but what was quite right and proper. I admit all that. And yet, what am I to do? *Scales*, you know, and claws, and a tail for certain, though I didn't see that end of him—I ain't *used* to 'em, and I don't *hold* with 'em, and that's a fact!"

The Boy, who had apparently been absorbed in his book during his father's recital, now closed the volume, yawned, clasped his hands behind his head, and said sleepily:

"It's all right, father. Don't you worry. It's only a dragon."

"Only a dragon?" cried his father. "What do you mean, sitting there, you and your dragons? *Only* a dragon indeed! And what do *you* know about it?"

" 'Cos it *is*, and 'cos I *do* know," replied the Boy, quietly. "Look here, father, you know we've each of us got our line. *You* know about sheep, and weather, and things; I know about dragons. I always said, you know, that that cave up there was a dragon-cave. I always said it must have belonged to a dragon some time, and ought to belong to a dragon now, if rules count for anything. Well, now you tell me it *has* got a dragon, and so *that's* all right. I'm not half as much surprised as when you told me it *hadn't* got a dragon. Rules always come right if you wait quietly. Now, please, just leave this all to me. And I'll stroll up to-morrow morning—no, in the morning I can't, I've got a whole heap of things to do—well, perhaps in the evening, if I'm quite free, I'll go up and have a talk to him, and you'll find it'll be all right. Only, please, don't you go worrying round there without me. You don't understand 'em a bit, and they're very sensitive, you know!"

"He's quite right, father," said the sensible mother. "As he says, dragons is his line and not ours. He's wonderful knowing about book-beasts, as every one allows. And to tell the truth, I'm not half happy in my own mind, thinking of that poor animal lying alone up there, without a bit o' hot supper or anyone to change the news with; and maybe we'll be able to do something for him; and if he ain't quite respectable our Boy'll find it out quick enough. He's got a pleasant sort o' way with him that makes everybody tell him everything."

Next day, after he'd had his tea, the Boy strolled up the chalky track that led to the summit of the Downs; and there, sure enough, he found the dragon, stretched lazily on the sward in front of his cave. The view from that point was a magnificent one. To the right and left, the bare and willowy leagues of Downs; in front, the vale, with its clustered homesteads, its threads of white roads running through orchards and well-tilled acreage, and, far away, a hint of grey old cities on the horizon. A cool breeze played over the surface of the grass and the silver shoulder of a large moon was showing above distant junipers. No wonder the dragon seemed in a peaceful and contented mood; indeed, as the Boy approached he could hear the beast purring with a happy regularity. "Well, we live and learn!" he said to himself. "None of my books ever told me that dragons purred!"

"Hullo, dragon!" said the Boy, quietly, when he had got up to him.

The dragon, on hearing the approaching footsteps, made the beginning of a courteous effort to rise. But when he saw it was a Boy, he set his eyebrows severely.

"Now don't you hit me," he said; "or bung stones, or squirt water, or anything. I won't have it, I tell you!"

"Not goin' to hit you," said the Boy, wearily, dropping on the grass beside the beast: "and don't, for goodness' sake, keep on saying 'Don't'; I hear so much of it, and it's monotonous, and makes me tired. I've simply looked in to ask you how you were and all that sort of thing; but if I'm in the way I can easily clear out. I've lots of friends, and no one can say I'm in the habit of shoving myself in where I'm not wanted!"

"No, no, don't go off in a huff," said the dragon, hastily; "fact is, I'm as happy up here as the day's long; never without an occupation, dear fellow, never without an occupation! And yet, between ourselves, it *is* a trifle dull at times."

The Boy bit off a stalk of grass and chewed it. "Going to make a long stay here?" he asked, politely.

"Can't hardly say at present," replied the dragon. "It seems a nice place enough—but I've only been here a short time, and one must look about and reflect and consider before settling down. It's rather a serious thing, settling down. Besides—now I'm going to tell you something! You'd never guess it if you tried ever so!— fact is, I'm such a confoundedly lazy beggar!"

"You surprise me," said the Boy, civilly.

"It's the sad truth," the dragon went on, settling down between his paws and evidently delighted to have found a listener at last: "and I fancy that's really how I came to be here. You see, all the other fellows were so active and *earnest* and all that sort of thing—always rampaging, and skirmishing, and scouring the desert sands, and pacing the margin of the sea, and chasing knights all over the place, and devouring damsels, and going on generally— whereas I liked to get my meals regular and then to prop my back against a bit of rock and snooze a bit, and wake up and think of things going on and how they kept going on just the same, you know! So when it happened I got fairly caught."

"When *what* happened, please?" asked the Boy.

"That's just what I don't precisely know," said the dragon. "I suppose the earth sneezed, or shook itself, or the bottom dropped out of something. Anyhow there was a shake and a roar and a general stramash, and I found myself miles away underground and wedged in as tight as tight. Well, thank goodness, my wants are few, and at any rate I had peace and quietness and wasn't always being asked to come along and *do* something. And I've got such an active mind—always occupied, I assure you! But time went on, and there was a certain sameness about the life, and at last I began to think it would be fun to work my way upstairs and see what you other fellows were doing. So I scratched and burrowed, and worked this way and that way and at last I came out through this cave here. And I like the country, and the view, and the people—what I've seen of 'em—and on the whole I feel inclined to settle down here."

"What's your mind always occupied about?" asked the Boy. "That's what I want to know."

The dragon coloured slightly and looked away. Presently he said bashfully: "Did you ever—just for fun—try to make up poetry—verses, you know?"

" 'Course I have," said the Boy. "Heaps of it. And some of it's quite good, I feel sure, only there's no one here cares about it. Mother's very kind and all that, when I read it to her, and so's father for that matter. But somehow they don't seem to—"

"Exactly," cried the dragon; "my own case exactly. They don't seem to, and you can't argue with 'em about it. Now you've got culture, you have, I could tell it on you at once, and I should just like your candid opinion about some little things I threw off lightly, when I was down there. I'm awfully pleased to have met you, and I'm hoping the other neighbours will be equally agreeable. There was a very nice old gentleman up here only last night, but he didn't seem to want to intrude."

"That was my father," said the Boy, "and he *is* a nice old gentleman, and I'll introduce you some day if you like."

"Can't you two come up here and dine or something to-morrow?" asked the dragon, eagerly. "Only, of course, if you've got nothing better to do," he added politely.

"Thanks awfully," said the Boy, "but we don't go out anywhere without my mother, and, to tell you the truth, I'm afraid she mightn't quite approve of you. You see there's no getting over the hard fact that you're a dragon, is there? And when you talk of settling down, and the neighbours, and so on, I can't help feeling that you don't quite realize your position. You're an enemy of the human race, you see!"

"Haven't got an enemy in the world," said the dragon, cheerfully. "Too lazy to make 'em, to begin with. And if I *do* read other fellows my poetry, I'm always ready to listen to theirs!"

"Oh, dear!" cried the Boy, "I wish you'd try and grasp the situation properly. When the other people find you out, they'll come after you with spears and swords and all sorts of things. You'll have to be exterminated, according to their way of looking at it! You're a scourge, and a pest, and a baneful monster!"

"Not a word of truth in it," said the dragon, wagging his head solemnly. "Character'll bear the strictest investigation. And now, there's a little sonnet-thing I was working on when you appeared on the scene—"

"Oh, if you *won't* be sensible, cried the Boy, getting up, "I'm going off home. No, I can't stop for sonnets; my mother's sitting up. I'll look you up to-morrow, sometime or other, and do for goodness' sake try and realize that you're a pestilential scourge, or you'll find yourself in a most awful fix. Good-night!"

The Boy found it an easy matter to set the mind of his parents at ease about his new friend. They had always left that branch to him, and they took his word without a murmur. The shepherd was formally introduced

and many compliments and kind inquiries were exchanged. His wife, however, though expressing her willingness to do anything she could—to mend
things, or set the cave to rights, or cook a little something when the dragon
had been poring over sonnets and forgotten his meals, as male things *will*
do—could not be brought to recognize him formally. The fact that he was
a dragon and "they didn't know who he was" seemed to count for everything
with her. She made no objection, however, to her little son spending his
evenings with the dragon quietly, so long as he was home by nine o'clock:
and many a pleasant night they had, sitting on the sward, while the dragon
told stories of old, old times, when dragons were quite plentiful and the
world was a livelier place than it is now, and life was full of thrills and
jumps and surprises.

What the Boy had feared, however, soon came to pass. The most modest
and retiring dragon in the world, if he's as big as four cart-horses and covered
with blue scales, cannot keep altogether out of the public view. And so in
the village tavern of nights the fact that a real live dragon sat brooding in
the cave on the Downs was naturally a subject for talk. Though the villagers
were extremely frightened, they were rather proud as well. It was a distinction
to have a dragon of your own, and it was felt to be a feather in the cap of
the village. Still, all were agreed that this sort of thing couldn't be allowed
to go on. The dreadful beast must be exterminated, the country-side must
be freed from this pest, this terror, this destroying scourge. The fact that
not even a hen-roost was the worse for the dragon's arrival wasn't allowed
to have anything to do with it. He was a dragon, and he couldn't deny it,
and if he didn't choose to behave as such that was his own look-out. But in
spite of much valiant talk no hero was found willing to take sword and spear
and free the suffering village and win deathless fame; and each night's heated
discussion always ended in nothing. Meanwhile the dragon, a happy Bohemian, lolled on the turf, enjoyed the sunsets, told antediluvian anecdotes
to the Boy, and polished his old verses while meditating on fresh ones.

One day the Boy, on walking in to the village, found everything wearing
a festal appearance which was not to be accounted for in the calendar. Carpets
and gay-coloured stuffs were hung out of the windows, the church-bells
clamoured noisily, the little street was flower-strewn, and the whole pop-
ulation jostled each other along either side of it, chattering, shoving, and
ordering each other to stand back. The Boy saw a friend of his own age in
the crowd and hailed him.

"What's up?" he cried. "Is it the players, or bears, or a circus, or what?"

"It's all right," his friend hailed back. "He's a-coming."

"*Who's* a-coming?" demanded the Boy, thrusting into the throng.

"Why, St. George, of course," replied his friend. "He's heard tell of our dragon, and he's comin' on purpose to slay the deadly beast, and free us from his horrid yoke. O my! won't there be a jolly fight!"

Here was news indeed! The Boy felt that he ought to make quite sure for himself, and he wriggled himself in between the legs of his good-natured elders, abusing them all the time for their unmannerly habit of shoving. Once in the front rank, he breathlessly awaited the arrival.

Presently from the far-away end of the line came the sound of cheering. Next, the measured tramp of a great war-horse made his heart beat quicker, and then he found himself cheering with the rest, as, amidst welcoming shouts, shrill cries of women, uplifting of babies and waving of handkerchiefs, St. George paced slowly up the street. The Boy's heart stood still and he breathed with sobs, the beauty and the grace of the hero were so far beyond anything he had yet seen. His fluted armour was inlaid with gold, his plumed helmet hung at his saddle-bow, and his thick fair hair framed a face gracious and gentle beyond expression till you caught the sternness in his eyes. He drew rein in front of the little inn, and the villagers crowded round with greetings and thanks and voluble statements of their wrongs and grievances and oppressions. The Boy heard the grave gentle voice of the Saint, assuring them that all would be well now, and that he would stand by them and see them righted and free them from their foe; then he dismounted and passed through the doorway and the crowd poured in after him. But the Boy made off up the hill as fast as he could lay his legs to the ground.

"It's all up, dragon!" he shouted as soon as he was within sight of the beast. "He's coming! He's here now! You'll have to pull yourself together and *do* something at last!"

The dragon was licking his scales and rubbing them with a bit of house-flannel the Boy's mother had lent him, till he shone like a great turquoise.

"Don't be *violent*, Boy," he said without looking round. "Sit down and get your breath, and try and remember that the noun governs the verb, and then perhaps you'll be good enough to tell me *who's* coming?"

"That's right, take it coolly," said the Boy. "Hope you'll be half as cool when I've got through with my news. It's only St. George who's coming, that's all; he rode into the village half-an-hour ago. Of course you can lick him—a great big fellow like you! But I thought I'd warn you, 'cos he's sure to be round early, and he's got the longest, wickedest-looking spear you ever did see!" And the Boy got up and began to jump round in sheer delight at the prospect of the battle.

"O deary, deary me," moaned the dragon; "this is awful. I won't see him, and that's flat. I don't want to know the fellow at all. I'm sure he's not nice. You must tell him to go away at once, please. Say he can write if he likes, but I can't give him an interview. I'm not seeing anybody at present."

"Now dragon, dragon," said the Boy, imploringly, "don't be perverse and wrongheaded. You've *got* to fight him some time or other, you know, 'cos he's St. George and you're the dragon. Better get it over, and then we can go on with the sonnets. And you ought to consider other people a little, too. If it's been dull up here for you, think how dull it's been for me!"

"My dear little man," said the dragon, solemnly, "just understand, once for all, that I can't fight and I won't fight. I've never fought in my life, and I'm not going to begin now, just to give you a Roman holiday. In old days I always let the other fellows—the *earnest* fellows—do all the fighting, and no doubt that's why I have the pleasure of being here now."

"But if you don't fight he'll cut your head off!" gasped the Boy, miserable at the prospect of losing both his fight and his friend.

"Oh, I think not," said the dragon in his lazy way. "You'll be able to arrange something. I've every confidence in you, you're such a *manager*. Just run down, there's a dear chap, and make it all right. I leave it entirely to you."

The Boy made his way back to the village in a state of great despondency. First of all, there wasn't going to be any fight; next, his dear and honoured friend the dragon hadn't shown up in quite such a heroic light as he would have liked; and lastly, whether the dragon was a hero at heart or not, it made no difference, for St. George would most undoubtedly cut his head off. "Arrange things indeed!" he said bitterly to himself. "The dragon treats the whole affair as if it was an invitation to tea and croquet."

The villagers were straggling homewards as he passed up the street, all of them in the highest spirits, and gleefully discussing the splendid fight that was in store. The Boy pursued his way to the inn, and passed into the principal chamber, where St. George now sat alone, musing over the chances of the fight, and the sad stories of rapine and of wrong that had so lately been poured into his sympathetic ears.

"May I come in, St. George?" said the Boy, politely, as he paused at the door. "I want to talk to you about this little matter of the dragon, if you're not tired of it by this time."

"Yes, come in, Boy," said the Saint, kindly. "Another tale of misery and wrong, I fear me. Is it a kind parent, then, of whom the tyrant has bereft you? Or some tender sister or brother? Well, it shall soon be avenged."

"Nothing of the sort," said the Boy. "There's a misunderstanding somewhere, and I want to put it right. The fact is, this is a *good* dragon."

"Exactly," said St. George, smiling pleasantly, "I quite understand. A good *dragon*. Believe me, I do not in the least regret that he is an adversary worthy of my steel, and no feeble specimen of his noxious tribe."

"But he's *not* a noxious tribe," cried the Boy, distressedly. "Oh dear, oh dear, how *stupid* men are when they get an idea into their heads! I tell you he's a *good* dragon, and a friend of mine, and tells me the most beautiful stories you ever heard, all about old times and when he was little. And he's been so kind to mother, and mother'd do anything for him. And father likes him too, though father doesn't hold with art and poetry much, and always falls asleep when the dragon starts talking about *style*. But the fact is, nobody can help liking him when once they know him. He's so engaging and so trustful, and as simple as a child!"

"Sit down, and draw your chair up," said St. George. "I like a fellow who sticks up for his friends, and I'm sure the dragon has his good points, if he's got a friend like you. But that's not the question. All this evening I've been listening, with grief and anguish unspeakable, to tales of murder, theft, and wrong; rather too highly coloured, perhaps, not always quite convincing, but forming in the main a most serious roll of crime. History teaches us that the greatest rascals often possess all the domestic virtues; and I fear that your cultivated friend, in spite of the qualities which have won (and rightly) your regard, has got to be speedily exterminated."

"Oh, you've been taking in all the yarns those fellows have been telling you," said the Boy, impatiently. "Why, our villagers are the biggest story-tellers in all the country round. It's a known fact. You're a stranger in these parts, or else you'd have heard it already. All they want is a *fight*. They're the most awful beggars for getting up fights—it's meat and drink to them. Dogs, bulls, dragons—anything so long as it's a fight. Why, they've got a poor innocent badger in the stable behind here, at this moment. They were going to have some fun with him to-day, but they're saving him up now till *your* little affair's over. And I've no doubt they've been telling you what a hero you were, and how you were bound to win, in the cause of right and justice, and so on; but let me tell you, I came down the street just now, and they were betting six to four on the dragon freely!"

"Six to four on the dragon!" murmured St. George, sadly, resting his cheek on his hand. "This is an evil world, and sometimes I begin to think that all the wickedness in it is not entirely bottled up inside the dragons. And yet—may not this wily beast have misled you as to his real character, in order that your good report of him may serve as a cloak for his evil deeds? Nay, may there not be, at this very moment, some hapless Princess immured within yonder gloomy cavern?"

The moment he had spoken, St. George was sorry for what he had said, the Boy looked so genuinely distressed.

"I assure you, St. George," he said earnestly, "there's nothing of the sort in the cave at all. The dragon's a real gentleman, every inch of him, and I may say that no one would be more shocked and grieved than he would, at hearing you talk in that—that *loose* way about matters on which he has very strong views!"

"Well, perhaps I've been over-credulous," said St. George. "Perhaps I've misjudged the animal. But what are we to do? Here are the dragon and I, almost face to face, each supposed to be thirsting for each other's blood. I don't see any way out of it, exactly. What do you suggest? Can't you arrange things, somehow?"

"That's just what the dragon said," replied the Boy, rather nettled. "Really, the way you two seem to leave everything to me—I suppose you couldn't be persuaded to go away quietly, could you?"

"Impossible, I fear," said the Saint. "Quite against the rules. *You* know that as well as I do."

"Well, then, look here," said the Boy, "it's early yet—would you mind strolling up with me and seeing the dragon and talking it over? It's not far, and any friend of mine will be most welcome."

"Well, it's *irregular*," said St. George, rising, "but really it seems about the most sensible thing to do. You're taking a lot of trouble on your friend's account," he added, good-naturedly, as they passed out through the door together. "But cheer up! Perhaps there won't have to be any fight after all."

"Oh, but I hope there will, though!" replied the little fellow, wistfully.

"I've brought a friend to see you, dragon," said the Boy, rather loud.

The dragon woke up with a start. "I was just—er—thinking about things," he said in his simple way. "Very pleased to make your acquaintance, sir. Charming weather we're having!"

"This is St. George," said the Boy, shortly. "St. George, let me introduce you to the dragon. We've come up to talk things over quietly, dragon, and now for goodness' sake do let us have a little straight common-sense, and come to some practical business-like arrangement, for I'm sick of views and theories of life and personal tendencies, and all that sort of thing. I may perhaps add that my mother's sitting up."

"So glad to meet you, St. George," began the dragon, rather nervously, "because you've been a great traveller, I hear, and I've always been rather a stay-at-home. But I can show you many antiquities, many interesting features of our country-side, if you're stopping here any time—"

"I think," said St. George, in his frank, pleasant way, "that we'd really better take the advice of our young friend here, and try to come to some understanding, on a business footing, about this little affair of ours. Now don't you think that after all the simplest plan would be just to fight it out, according to the rules, and let the best man win? They're betting on you, I may tell you, down in the village, but I don't mind that!"

"Oh, yes, *do*, dragon," said the Boy, delightedly; "it'll save such a lot of bother!"

"My young friend, you shut up, said the dragon, severely. "Believe me, St. George," he went on, "there's nobody in the world I'd sooner oblige than you and this young gentleman here. But the whole thing's nonsense, and conventionality, and popular thick-headedness. There's absolutely nothing to fight about, from beginning to end. And anyhow I'm not going to, so that settles it!"

"But supposing I make you?" said St. George, rather nettled.

"You can't," said the dragon, triumphantly. "I should only go into my cave and retire for a time down the hole I came up. You'd soon get heartily sick of sitting outside and waiting for me to come out and fight you. And as soon as you'd really gone away, why, I'd come up again gaily, for I tell you frankly, I like this place, and I'm going to stay here!"

St. George gazed for a while on the fair landscape around them. "But this would be a beautiful place for a fight," he began again persuasively. "These great bare rolling Downs for the arena—and me in my golden armour showing up against your big blue scaly coils! Think what a picture it would make!"

"Now you're trying to get at me through my artistic sensibilities," said the dragon. "But it won't work. Not but what it would make a very pretty picture, as you say," he added, wavering a little.

"We seem to be getting rather nearer to *business*," put in the Boy. "You must see, dragon, that there's got to be a fight of some sort, 'cos you can't want to have to go down that dirty old hole again and stop there till goodness knows when."

"It might be arranged," said St. George, thoughtfully. "I *must* spear you somewhere, of course, but I'm not bound to hurt you very much. There's such a lot of you that there must be a few *spare* places somewhere. Here, for instance, just behind your foreleg. It couldn't hurt you much, just here!"

"Now you're tickling, George," said the dragon, coyly. "No, that place won't do at all. Even if it didn't hurt—and I'm sure it would, awfully—it would make me laugh, and that would spoil everything."

"Let's try somewhere else, then," said St. George, patiently. "Under your neck for instance—all those folds of thick skin—if I speared you here you'd never even know I'd done it!"

"Yes, but are you sure you can hit off the right place?" asked the dragon, anxiously.

"Of course I am," said St. George, with confidence. "You leave that to me!"

"It's just because I've *got* to leave it to you that I'm asking," replied the dragon, rather testily. "No doubt you would deeply regret any error you might make in the hurry of the moment; but you wouldn't regret it half as much as I should! However, I suppose we've got to trust somebody, as we go through life, and your plan seems, on the whole, as good a one as any."

"Look here, dragon," interrupted the Boy, a little jealous on behalf of his friend, who seemed to be getting all the worst of the bargain: "I don't quite see where *you* come in! There's to be a fight, apparently, and you're to be licked; and what I want to know is, what are *you* going to get out of it?"

"St. George," said the dragon, "just tell him, please—what will happen after I'm vanquished in the deadly combat?"

"Well, according to the rules I suppose I shall lead you in triumph down to the market-place or whatever answers to it," said St. George.

"Precisely," said the dragon. "And then—"

"And then there'll be shoutings and speeches and things," continued St. George. "And I shall explain that you're converted, and see the error of your ways, and so on."

"Quite so," said the dragon. "And then—?"

"Oh, and then—" said St. George, "why, and then there will be the usual banquet, I suppose."

"Exactly," said the dragon; "and that's where *I* come in. Look here," he continued, addressing the Boy, "I'm bored to death up here, and no one really appreciates me. I'm going into Society, I am, through the kindly aid of our friend here, who's taking such a lot of trouble on my account; and you'll find I've got all the qualities to endear me to people who entertain! So now that's all settled, and if you don't mind—I'm an old-fashioned fellow—don't want to turn you out, but—"

"Remember, you'll have to do your proper share of the fighting, dragon!" said St. George, as he took the hint and rose to go; "I mean ramping, and breathing fire, and so on!"

"I can *ramp* all right," replied the dragon, confidently; "as to breathing fire, it's surprising how easily one gets out of practice; but I'll do the best I can. Good-night!"

They had descended the hill and were almost back in the village again, when St. George stopped short, "*Knew* I had forgotten something," he said. "There ought to be a Princess. Terror-stricken and chained to a rock, and all that sort of thing. Boy, can't you arrange a Princess?"

The Boy was in the middle of a tremendous yawn. "I'm tired to death," he wailed, "and I *can't* arrange a Princess, or anything more, at this time of night. And my mother's sitting up, and *do* stop asking me to arrange more things till to-morrow!"

Next morning the people began streaming up to the Downs at quite an early hour, in their Sunday clothes and carrying baskets with bottle-necks sticking out of them, every one intent on securing good places for the combat. This was not exactly a simple matter, for of course it was quite possible that the dragon might win, and in that case even those who had put their money on him felt they could hardly expect him to deal with his backers on a different footing to the rest. Places were chosen, therefore, with circumspection and with a view to a speedy retreat in case of emergency; and the front rank was mostly composed of boys who had escaped from parental control and now sprawled and rolled about on the grass, regardless of the shrill threats and warnings discharged at them by their anxious mothers behind.

The Boy had secured a good front place, well up towards the cave, and was feeling as anxious as a stage-manager on a first night. Could the dragon be depended upon? He might change his mind and vote the whole performance rot; or else, seeing that the affair had been so hastily planned, without even a rehearsal, he might be too nervous to show up. The Boy looked narrowly at the cave, but it showed no sign of life or occupation. Could the dragon have made a moonlight flitting?

The higher portions of the ground were now black with sight-seers, and presently a sound of cheering and a waving of handkerchiefs told that something was visible to them which the Boy, far up towards the dragon-end of the line as he was, could not yet see. A minute more and St. George's red plumes topped the hill, as the Saint rode slowly forth on the great level space which stretched up to the grim mouth of the cave. Very gallant and beautiful he looked, on his tall war-horse, his golden armour glancing in the sun, his great spear held erect, the little white pennon, crimson-crossed, fluttering at its point. He drew rein and remained motionless. The lines of spectators began to give back a little, nervously; and even the boys in front stopped pulling hair and cuffing each other, and leaned forward expectant.

"Now then, dragon!" muttered the Boy, impatiently, fidgeting where he sat. He need not have distressed himself, had he only known. The dramatic possibilities of the thing had tickled the dragon immensely, and he had been up from an early hour, preparing for his first public appearance with as much heartiness as if the years had run backwards, and he had been again a little dragonlet, playing with his sisters on the floor of their mother's cave, at the game of saints-and-dragons, in which the dragon was bound to win.

A low muttering, mingled with snorts, now made itself heard; rising to a bellowing roar that seemed to fill the plain. Then a cloud of smoke obscured the mouth of the cave, and out of the midst of it the dragon himself, shining, sea-blue, magnificent, pranced splendidly forth; and everybody said, "Oo-oo-oo!" as if he had been a mighty rocket! His scales were glittering, his long spiky tail lashed his sides, his claws tore up the turf and sent it flying high over his back, and smoke and fire incessantly jetted from his angry nostrils. "Oh, well done, dragon!" cried the Boy, excitedly. "Didn't think he had it in him!" he added to himself.

St. George lowered his spear, bent his head, dug his heels into his horse's sides, and came thundering over the turf. The dragon charged with a roar and a squeal—a great blue whirling combination of coils and snorts and clashing jaws and spikes and fire.

"Missed!" yelled the crowd. There was a moment's entanglement of golden armour and blue-green coils, and spiky tail, and then the great horse, tearing at his bit, carried the Saint, his spear swung high in the air, almost up to the mouth of the cave.

The dragon sat down and barked viciously, while St. George with difficulty pulled his horse round into position.

"End of Round One!" thought the Boy. "How well they managed it! But I hope the Saint won't get excited. I can trust the dragon all right. What a regular play-actor the fellow is!"

St. George had at last prevailed on his horse to stand steady, and was looking round him as he wiped his brow. Catching sight of the Boy, he smiled and nodded, and held up three fingers for an instant.

"It seems to be all planned out," said the Boy to himself. "Round Three is to be the finishing one, evidently. Wish it could have lasted a bit longer. Whatever's that old fool of a dragon up to now?"

The dragon was employing the interval in giving a ramping-performance for the benefit of the crowd. Ramping, it should be explained, consists in running round and round in a wide circle, and sending waves and ripples of movement along the whole length of your spine, from your pointed ears right down to the spike at the end of your long tail. When you are covered with blue scales, the effect is particularly pleasing; and the Boy recollected the dragon's recently expressed wish to become a social success.

St. George now gathered up his reins and began to move forward, dropping the point of his spear and settling himself firmly in the saddle.

"Time!" yelled everybody excitedly; and the dragon, leaving off his ramping, sat up on end, and began to leap from one side to the other with huge ungainly bounds, whooping like a Red Indian. This naturally disconcerted the horse, who swerved violently, the Saint only just saving himself by the mane; and as they shot past the dragon delivered a vicious snap at the horse's tail which sent the poor beast careering madly far over the Downs, so that the language of the Saint, who had lost a stirrup, was fortunately inaudible to the general assemblage.

Round Two evoked audible evidence of friendly feeling towards the dragon. The spectators were not slow to appreciate a combatant who could hold his own so well and clearly wanted to show good sport; and many encouraging remarks reached the ears of our friend as he strutted to and fro, his chest thrust out and his tail in the air, hugely enjoying his new popularity.

St. George had dismounted and was tightening his girths, and telling his horse, with quite an Oriental flow of imagery, exactly what he thought of him, and his relations, and his conduct on the present occasion; so the Boy made his way down to the Saint's end of the line, and held his spear for him.

"It's been a jolly fight, St. George!" he said with a sigh. "Can't you let it last a bit longer?"

"Well, I think I'd better not," replied the Saint. "The fact is, your simpleminded old friend's getting conceited, now they've begun cheering him, and he'll forget all about the arrangement and take to playing the fool, and there's no telling where he would stop. I'll just finish him off this round."

He swung himself into the saddle and took his spear from the Boy. "Now don't you be afraid," he added kindly. "I've marked my spot exactly, and *he's* sure to give me all the assistance in his power, because he knows it's his only chance of being asked to the banquet!"

St. George now shortened his spear, bringing the butt well up under his arm; and, instead of galloping as before, trotted smartly towards the dragon, who crouched at his approach, flicking his tail till it cracked in the air like a great cart-whip. The Saint wheeled as he neared his opponent and circled warily round him, keeping his eye on the spare place; while the dragon, adopting similar tactics, paced with caution round the same circle, occasionally feinting with his head. So the two sparred for an opening, while the spectators maintained a breathless silence.

Though the round lasted for some minutes, the end was so swift that all the Boy saw was a lightning movement of the Saint's arm, and then a whirl and a confusion of spines, claws, tail, and flying bits of turf. The dust cleared away, the spectators whooped and ran in cheering, and the Boy made out that the dragon was down, pinned to the earth by the spear, while St. George had dismounted, and stood astride of him.

It all seemed so genuine that the Boy ran in breathlessly, hoping the dear old dragon wasn't really hurt. As he approached, the dragon lifted one large eyelid, winked solemnly, and collapsed again. He was held fast to earth by the neck, but the Saint had hit him in the spare place agreed upon, and it didn't even seem to tickle.

"Bain't you goin' to cut 'is 'ed orf, master?" asked one of the applauding crowd. He had backed the dragon, and naturally felt a trifle sore.

"Well, not *to-day*, I think," replied St. George, pleasantly. "You see, that can be done at *any* time. There's no hurry at all. I think we'll all go down to the village first, and have some refreshment, and then I'll give him a good talking-to, and you'll find he'll be a very different dragon!"

At that magic word *refreshment* the whole crowd formed up in procession and silently awaited the signal to start. The time for talking and cheering and betting was past, the hour for action had arrived. St. George, hauling on his spear with both hands, released the dragon, who rose and shook himself and ran his eye over his spikes and scales and things, to see that they were all in order. Then the Saint mounted and led off the procession, the dragon following meekly in the company of the Boy, while the thirsty spectators kept at a respectful interval behind.

There were great doings when they got down to the village again, and had formed up in front of the inn. After refreshment St. George made a speech, in which he informed his audience that he had removed their direful scourge, at a great deal of trouble and inconvenience to himself, and now they weren't to go about grumbling and fancying they'd got grievances, because they hadn't. And they shouldn't be so fond of fights, because next time they might have to do the fighting themselves, which would not be the same thing at all. And there was a certain badger in the inn stables which had got to be released at once, and he'd come and see it done himself. Then he told them that the dragon had been thinking over things, and saw that there were two sides to every question, and he wasn't going to do it any more, and if they were good perhaps he'd stay and settle down there. So they must make friends, and not be prejudiced, and go about fancying they knew everything there was to be known, because they didn't, not by a long way. And he warned them against the sin of romancing, and making up stories and fancying other people would believe them just because they were plausible and highly-coloured. Then he sat down, amidst much re-pentant cheering, and the dragon nudged the Boy in the ribs and whispered that he couldn't have done it better himself. Then every one went off to get ready for the banquet.

Banquets are always pleasant things, consisting mostly, as they do, of eating and drinking; but the specially nice thing about a banquet is, that it comes when something's over, and there's nothing more to worry about, and to-morrow seems a long way off. St. George was happy because there had been a fight and he hadn't had to kill anybody; for he didn't really like killing, though he generally had to do it. The dragon was happy because there had been a fight, and so far from being hurt in it he had won popularity and a sure footing in Society. The Boy was happy because there had been a fight, and in spite of it all his two friends were on the best of terms. And all the others were happy because there had been a fight, and—well, they didn't require any other reasons for their happiness. The dragon exerted himself to say the right thing to everybody, and proved the life and soul of the evening; while the Saint and the Boy, as they looked on, felt that they were only assisting at a feast of which the honour and the glory were entirely the dragon's. But they didn't mind that, being good fellows, and the dragon was not in the least proud or forgetful. On the contrary, every ten minutes or so he leant over towards the Boy and said impressively, "Look here! you *will* see me home afterwards, won't you?" And the Boy always nodded, though he had promised his mother not to be out late.

At last the banquet was over, the guests had dropped away with many good-nights and congratulations and invitations, and the dragon, who had seen the last of them off the premises, emerged into the street followed by the Boy, wiped his brow, sighed, sat down in the road and gazed at the stars. "Jolly night it's been!" he murmured. "Jolly stars! Jolly little place this! Think I shall just stop here. Don't feel like climbing up any beastly hill. Boy's promised to see me home. Boy had better do it, then! No responsibility on my part. Responsibility all Boy's!" And his chin sank on his broad chest and he slumbered peacefully.

"Oh, *get* up, dragon," cried the Boy, piteously. "You *know* my mother's sitting up, and I'm so tired, and you made me promise to see you home, and I never knew what it meant or I wouldn't have done it!" And the Boy sat down in the road by the side of the sleeping dragon, and cried.

The door behind them opened, a stream of light illumined the road, and St. George, who had come out for a stroll in the cool night-air, caught sight of the two figures sitting there—the great motionless dragon and the tearful little Boy.

"What's the matter, Boy?" he inquired kindly, stepping to his side.

"Oh, it's this great lumbering *pig* of a dragon!" sobbed the Boy. "First he makes me promise to see him home, and then he says I'd better do it, and goes to sleep! Might as well try to see a *haystack* home! And I'm so tired, and mother's—" here he broke down again.

"Now don't take on," said St. George. "I'll stand by you, and we'll *both* see him home. Wake up, dragon!" he said sharply, shaking the beast by the elbow.

The dragon looked up sleepily. "What a night, George!" he murmured; "what a—"

"Now look here, dragon," said the Saint, firmly. "Here's this little fellow waiting to see you home, and you *know* he ought to have been in bed these two hours, and what his mother'll say *I* don't know, and anybody but a selfish pig would have *made* him go to bed long ago—"

"And he *shall* go to bed!" cried the dragon, starting up. "Poor little chap, only fancy his being up at this hour! It's a shame, that's what it is, and I don't think, St. George, you've been very considerate—but come along at once, and don't let us have any more arguing or shilly-shallying. You give me hold of your hand, Boy—thank you, George, an arm up the hill is just what I wanted!"

So they set off up the hill arm-in-arm, the Saint, the Dragon, and the Boy. The lights in the little village began to go out; but there were stars, and a late moon, as they climbed to the Downs together. And, as they turned the last corner and disappeared from view, snatches of an old song were borne back on the night-breeze. I can't be certain which of them was singing, but I *think* it was the Dragon!

1898

The Deliverers
of Their Country

E. NESBIT

It all began with Effie's getting something in her eye. It hurt very much indeed, and it felt something like a red-hot spark—only it seemed to have legs as well, and wings like a fly. Effie rubbed and cried—not real crying, but the kind your eye does all by itself without your being miserable inside your mind—and then she went to her father to have the thing in her eye taken out. Effie's father was a doctor, so of course he knew how to take things out of eyes—he did it very cleverly with a soft paint-brush dipped in castor-oil. When he had got the thing out, he said:

"This is very curious." Effie had often got things in her eye before, and her father had always seemed to think it was natural—rather tiresome and naughty perhaps, but still natural. He had never before thought it curious. She stood holding her handkerchief to her eye, and said:

"I don't believe it's out." People always say this when they have had something in their eyes.

"Oh, yes—it's *out*," said the doctor—"here it is on the brush. This is very interesting."

Effie had never heard her father say that about anything that she had any share in. She said, *"What?"*

The doctor carried the brush very carefully across the room, and held the point of it under his microscope—then he twisted the brass screws of the microscope, and looked through the top with one eye.

"Dear me," he said. "Dear, *dear* me! Four well-developed limbs; a long caudal appendage; five toes, unequal in lengths, almost like one of the Lacertidæ, yet there are traces of wings." The creature under his eye wriggled a little in the castor-oil, and he went on: "Yes; a bat-like wing. A new specimen, undoubtedly. Effie, run round to the professor and ask him to be kind enough to step in for a few minutes."

"You might give me sixpence, daddy," said Effie, "because I did bring you the new specimen. I took great care of it inside my eye; and my eye *does* hurt."

The doctor was so pleased with the new specimen that he gave Effie a shilling, and presently the professor stepped round. He stayed to lunch, and he and the doctor quarrelled very happily all the afternoon about the name and the family of the thing that had come out of Effie's eye.

But at tea-time another thing happened. Effie's brother Harry fished something out of his tea, which he thought at first was an earwig. He was just getting ready to drop it on the floor, and end its life in the usual way, when it shook itself in the spoon—spread two wet wings, and flopped on to the tablecloth. There it sat stroking itself with its feet and stretching its wings, and Harry said, "Why, it's a tiny newt!"

The professor leaned forward before the doctor could say a word. "I'll give you half a crown for it, Harry, my lad," he said, speaking very fast; and then he picked it up carefully on his handkerchief.

"It is a new specimen," he said, "and finer than yours, doctor."

It was a tiny lizard, about half an inch long—with scales and wings.

So now the doctor and the professor each had a specimen, and they were both very pleased. But before long these specimens began to seem less valuable. For the next morning, when the knife-boy was cleaning the doctor's boots, he suddenly dropped the brushes and the boot and the blacking, and screamed out that he was burnt.

And from inside the boot came crawling a lizard as big as a kitten, with large, shiny wings.

"Why," said Effie, "I know what it is. It is a dragon like St. George killed."

And Effie was right. That afternoon Towser was bitten in the garden by a dragon about the size of a rabbit, which he had tried to chase, and next morning all the papers were full of the wonderful "winged lizards" that were appearing all over the country. The papers would not call them dragons, because, of course, no one believes in dragons nowadays—and at any rate the papers were not going to be so silly as to believe in fairy stories. At first there were only a few, but in a week or two the country was simply running alive with dragons of all sizes, and in the air you could sometimes see them as thick as a swarm of bees. They all looked alike except as to size. They were green with scales, and they had four legs, and a long tail and great wings like bats' wings, only the wings were a pale, half-transparent yellow, like the gear-cases on bicycles.

And they breathed fire and smoke, as all proper dragons must, but still the newspapers went on pretending they were lizards, until the editor of the *Standard* was picked up and carried away by a very large one, and then the other newspaper people had not any one left to tell them what they ought not to believe. So that when the largest elephant in the Zoo was carried off by a dragon, the papers gave up pretending—and put: "Alarming Plague of Dragons" at the top of the paper.

And you have no idea how alarming it was, and at the same time how aggravating. The large-sized dragons were terrible certainly, but when once you had found out that the dragons always went to bed early because they were afraid of the chill night-air, you had only to stay indoors all day, and you were pretty safe from the big ones. But the smaller sizes were a perfect nuisance. The ones as big as earwigs got in the soap, and they got in the butter. The ones as big as dogs got in the bath, and the fire and smoke inside them made them steam like anything when the cold-water tap was turned on, so that careless people were often scalded quite severely. The ones that were as large as pigeons would get into work-baskets or corner drawers, and bite you when you were in a hurry to get a needle or a handkerchief. The ones as big as sheep were easier to avoid, because you could see them coming; but when they flew in at the windows and curled up under your eider-down, and you did not find them till you went to bed, it was always a shock. The ones this size did not eat people, only lettuces, but they always scorched the sheets and pillow-cases dreadfully.

Of course, the County Council and the police did everything that could be done: it was no use offering the hand of the Princess to anyone who killed a dragon. This way was all very well in olden times—when there was only one dragon and one Princess; but now there were far more dragons than princesses—although the Royal Family was a large one. And besides, it would have been mere waste of princesses to offer rewards for killing dragons, because everybody killed as many dragons as they could quite out of their own heads and without rewards at all, just to get the nasty things out of the way. The County Council undertook to cremate all dragons delivered at their offices between the hours of ten and two, and whole waggon-loads and cart-loads and truck-loads of dead dragons could be seen any day of the week standing in a long line in the street where the County Council lived. Boys brought barrow-loads of dead dragons, and children on their way home from morning school would call in to leave the handful or two of little dragons they had brought in their satchels, or carried in their knotted pocket-hand-kerchiefs. And yet there seemed to be as many dragons as ever. Then the police stuck up great wood and canvas towers covered with patent glue. When the dragons flew against these towers, they stuck fast, as flies and wasps do on the sticky papers in the kitchen: and when the towers were covered all over with dragons, the police-inspector used to set light to the towers, and burnt them and dragons and all.

And yet there seemed to be more dragons than ever. The shops were full of patent dragon poison and anti-dragon soap, and dragon-proof curtains for the windows: and, indeed, everything that could be done was done.

And yet there seemed to be more dragons than ever.

It was not very easy to know what would poison a dragon, because you see they ate such different things. The largest kind ate elephants as long as there were any, and then went on with horses and cows. Another size ate nothing but lilies of the valley, and a third size ate only Prime Ministers if they were to be had, and, if not, would feed freely on boys in buttons. Another size lived on bricks, and three of them ate two-thirds of the South Lambeth Infirmary in one afternoon.

But the size Effie was most afraid of was about as big as your dining-room, and that size ate *little girls and boys*.

At first Effie and her brother were quite pleased with the change in their lives. It was so amusing to sit up all night instead of going to sleep, and to play in the garden lighted by electric lamps. And it sounded so funny to hear mother say, when they were going to bed:

"Good-night, my darlings, sleep sound all day, and don't get up too soon. You must not get up before it's *quite* dark. You wouldn't like the nasty dragons to catch you."

But after a time they got very tired of it all: they wanted to see the flowers and trees growing in the fields, and to see the pretty sunshine out of doors, and not just through glass windows and patent dragon-proof curtains. And they wanted to play on the grass, which they were not allowed to do in the electric-lamp-lighted garden because of the night-dew.

And they wanted so much to get out, just for once, in the beautiful, bright, dangerous daylight, that they began to try and think of some reason why they *ought* to go out. Only they did not like to disobey their mother.

But one morning their mother was busy preparing some new dragon poison to lay down in the cellars, and their father was bandaging the hand of the boot-boy which had been scratched by one of the dragons who liked to eat Prime Ministers when they were to be had, so nobody remembered to say to the children:

"Don't get up till it is quite dark!"

"Go now," said Harry; "it would not be disobedient to go. And I know exactly what we ought to do, but I don't know how we ought to do it."

"What ought we to do?" said Effie.

"We ought to wake St. George, of course," said Harry. "He was the only person in his town who knew how to manage dragons; the people in the fairy tales don't count. But St. George is a real person, and he is only asleep, and he is waiting to be waked up. Only nobody believes in St. George now. I heard father say so."

"*We* do," said Effie.

"Of course we do. And don't you see, Ef, that's the very reason why we could wake him? You can't wake people if you don't believe in them, can you?"

Effie said no, but where could they find St. George?

"We must go and look," said Harry, boldly. "You shall wear a dragon-proof frock, made of stuff like the curtains. And I will smear myself all over with the best dragon poison, and—"

Effie clasped her hands and skipped with joy, and cried:

"Oh, Harry! I know where we can find St. George! In St. George's Church, of course."

"Um," said Harry, wishing he had thought of it for himself, "you have a little sense sometimes, for a girl."

So next afternoon quite early, long before the beams of sunset announced the coming night, when everybody would be up and working, the two children got out of bed. Effie wrapped herself in a shawl of dragon-proof muslin—there was no time to make the frock—and Harry made a horrid mess of himself with the patent dragon poison. It was warranted harmless to infants and invalids, so he felt quite safe.

Then they took hands and set out to walk to St. George's Church. As you know, there are many St. George's churches, but, fortunately, they took the turning that leads to the right one, and went along in the bright sunlight, feeling very brave and adventurous.

There was no one about in the streets except dragons, and the place was simply swarming with them. Fortunately none of the dragons were just the right size for eating little boys and girls, or perhaps this story might have had to end here. There were dragons on the pavement, and dragons on the roadway, dragons basking on the front doorsteps of public buildings, and dragons preening their wings on the roofs in the hot afternoon sun. The town was quite green with them. Even when the children had got out of the town and were walking in the lanes, they noticed that the fields on each side were greener than usual with the scaly legs and tails; and some of the smaller sizes had made themselves asbestos nests in the flowering hawthorn hedges.

Effie held her brother's hand very tight, and once when a fat dragon flopped against her ear she screamed out, and a whole flight of green dragons rose from the field at the sound, and sprawled away across the sky. The children could hear the rattle of their wings as they flew.

"Oh, I want to go home," said Effie.

"Don't be silly," said Harry. "Surely you haven't forgotten about the Seven Champions and all the Princes. People who are going to be their country's deliverers never scream and say they want to go home."

"And are we," asked Effie—"deliverers, I mean?"

"You'll see," said her brother, and on they went.

When they came to St. George's Church they found the door open, and they walked right in—but St. George was not there, so they walked round the churchyard outside, and presently they found the great stone tomb of St. George, with the figure of him carved in marble outside, in his armour and helmet, and with his hands folded on his breast.

"How ever can we wake him?" they said.

Then Harry spoke to St. George—but he would not answer; and he called, but St. George did not seem to hear; and then he actually tried to waken the great dragon-slayer by shaking his marble shoulders. But St. George took no notice.

Then Effie began to cry, and she put her arms round St. George's neck as well as she could for the marble, which was very much in the way at the back, and she kissed the marble face and she said:

"Oh, dear, good, kind St. George, please wake up and help us."

And at that St. George opened his eyes sleepily and stretched himself and said, "What's the matter, little girl?"

So the children told him all about it; he turned over in his marble and leaned on one elbow to listen. But when he heard that there were so many dragons he shook his head.

"It's no good," he said, "they would be one too many for poor old George. You should have waked me before. I was always for a fair fight—one man, one dragon, was my motto."

Just then a flight of dragons passed overhead, and St. George half drew his sword.

But he shook his head again, and pushed the sword back as the flight of dragons grew small in the distance.

"I can't do anything," he said; "things have changed since my time. St. Andrew told me about it. They woke him up over the engineers' strike, and he came to talk to me. He says everything is done by machinery now; there must be some way of settling these dragons. By the way, what sort of weather have you been having lately?"

This seemed so careless and unkind that Harry would not answer, but

Effie said, patiently, "It has been very fine. Father says it is the hottest weather there has ever been in this country."

"Ah, I guessed as much," said the Champion, thoughtfully. "Well, the only thing would be . . . dragons can't stand wet and cold, that's the only thing. If you could find the taps."

St. George was beginning to settle down again on his stone slab.

"Good-night, very sorry I can't help you," he said, yawning behind his marble hand.

"Oh, but you can," cried Effie. "Tell us—what taps?"

"Oh, like in the bathroom," said St. George, still more sleepily; "and there's a looking-glass, too; shows you all the world and what's going on. St. Denis told me about it; said it was a very pretty thing. I'm sorry I can't—good-night."

And he fell back into his marble and was fast asleep in a moment.

"We shall never find the taps," said Harry. "I say, wouldn't it be awful if St. George woke up when there was a dragon near, the size that eats champions?"

Effie pulled off her dragon-proof veil. "We didn't meet any the size of the dining-room as we came along," she said; "I dare say we shall be quite safe."

So she covered St. George with the veil, and Harry rubbed off as much as he could of the dragon poison on to St. George's armour, so as to make everything quite safe for him.

"We might hide in the church till it is dark," he said, "and then—"

But at that moment a dark shadow fell on them, and they saw that it was a dragon exactly the size of the dining-room at home.

So then they knew that all was lost. The dragon swooped down and caught the two children in his claws; he caught Effie by her green silk sash, and Harry by the little point at the back of his Eton jacket—and then, spreading his great yellow wings, he rose into the air, rattling like a third-class carriage when the brake is hard on.

"Oh, Harry," said Effie, "I wonder when he will eat us!" The dragon was flying across woods and fields with great flaps of his wings that carried him a quarter of a mile at each flap.

Harry and Effie could see the country below, hedges and rivers and churches and farmhouses flowing away from under them, much faster than you see them running away from the sides of the fastest express train.

And still the dragon flew on. The children saw other dragons in the air as they went, but the dragon who was as big as the dining-room never stopped to speak to any of them, but just flew on quite steadily.

"He knows where he wants to go," said Harry. "Oh, if he would only drop us before he gets there!"

But the dragon held on tight, and he flew and flew and flew until at last, when the children were quite giddy, he settled down, with a rattling of all his scales, on the top of a mountain. And he lay there on his great green scaly side, panting, and very much out of breath, because he had come such a long way. But his claws were fast in Effie's sash and the little point at the back of Harry's Eton jacket.

Then Effie took out the knife Harry had given her on her birthday. It only cost sixpence to begin with, and she had had it a month, and it never could sharpen anything but slate-pencils, but somehow she managed to make that knife cut her sash in front, and crept out of it, leaving the dragon with only a green silk bow in one of his claws. That knife would never have cut Harry's jacket-tail off, though, and when Effie had tried for some time she saw that this was so, and gave it up. But with her help Harry managed to wriggle quietly out of his sleeves, so that the dragon had only an Eton jacket in his other claw. Then the children crept on tip-toe to a crack in the rocks and got in. It was much too narrow to get in also, so they stayed in there and waited to make faces at the dragon when he felt rested enough to sit up and begin to think about eating them. He was very angry, indeed, when they made faces at him, and blew out fire and smoke at them, but they ran farther into the cave so that he could not reach them, and when he was tired of blowing he went away.

But they were afraid to come out of the cave, so they went farther in, and presently the cave opened out and grew bigger, and the floor was soft sand, and when they had come to the very end of the cave there was a door, and on it was written: *"Universal Tap-room. Private. No one allowed inside."*

So they opened the door at once just to peep in, and then they remembered what St. George had said.

"We can't be worse off than we are," said Harry, "with a dragon waiting for us outside. Let's go in."

So they went boldly into the tap-room, and shut the door behind them.

And now they were in a sort of room cut out of the solid rock, and all along one side of the room were taps, and all the taps were labelled with china labels like you see to baths. And as they could both read words of two syllables or even three sometimes, they understood at once that they had got to the place where the weather is turned on from. There were six big taps labelled "Sunshine," "Wind," "Rain," "Snow," "Hail," "Ice," and a lot of little ones, labelled "Fair to moderate," "Showery," "South breeze," "Nice growing weather for the crops," "Skating," "Good open weather," "South wind," "East wind," and so on. And the big tap labelled "Sunshine" was turned full on. They could not see any sunshine—the cave was lighted by a skylight of blue glass—so they supposed the sunlight was pouring out by some other way, as it does with the tap that washes out the underneath parts of patent sinks in kitchens.

Then they saw that one side of the room was just a big looking-glass, and when you looked in it you could see everything that was going on in the world—and all at once, too, which is not like most looking-glasses. They saw the carts delivering the dead dragons at the County Council offices, and they saw St. George asleep under the dragon-proof veil. And they saw their mother at home crying because her children had gone out in the dreadful, dangerous daylight, and she was afraid a dragon had eaten them. And they saw the whole of England, like a great puzzle-map—green in the field parts and brown in the towns, and black in the places where they make coal, and crockery, and cutlery, and chemicals. And all over it, on the black parts, and on the brown, and on the green, there was a network of green dragons. And they could see that it was still broad daylight, and no dragons had gone to bed yet.

So Effie said, "Dragons do not like cold." And she tried to turn off the sunshine, but the tap was out of order, and that was why there had been so much hot weather, and why the dragons had been able to be hatched. So they left the sunshine-tap alone, and they turned on the snow and left the tap full on while they went to look in the glass. There they saw the dragons running all sorts of ways like ants if you are cruel enough to pour water into an ant-heap, which, of course, you never are. And the snow fell more and more.

Then Effie turned the rain-tap quite full on, and presently the dragons began to wriggle less, and by-and-by some of them lay quite still, so the children knew the water had put out the fires inside them, and they were dead. So then they turned on the hail—only half on, for fear of breaking people's windows—and after a while there were no more dragons to be seen moving.

Then the children knew that they were indeed the deliverers of their country.

"They will put up a monument to us," said Harry; "as high as Nelson's! All the dragons are dead."

"I hope the one that was waiting outside for us is dead!" said Effie; "and about the monument, Harry, I'm not so sure. What can they do with such a lot of dead dragons? It would take years and years to bury them, and they could never be burnt now they are so soaking wet. I wish the rain would wash them off into the sea."

But this did not happen, and the children began to feel that they had not been so frightfully clever after all.

"I wonder what this old thing's for," said Harry. He had found a rusty old tap which seemed as though it had not been used for ages. Its china label was quite coated over with dirt and cobwebs. When Effie had cleaned it with a bit of her skirt—for curiously enough both the children had come out without pocket-handkerchiefs—she found that the label said *"Waste."*

"Let's turn it on," she said; "it might carry off the dragons."

The tap was very stiff from not having been used for such a long time, but together they managed to turn it on, and then ran to the mirror to see what happened.

Already a great, round, black hole had opened in the very middle of the map of England, and the sides of the map were tilting themselves up, so that the rain ran down towards the hole.

"Oh, hurrah, hurrah, hurrah!" cried Effie, and she hurried back to the taps and turned on everything that seemed wet. "Showery," "Good open weather," "Nice growing weather for the crops," and even "South" and "South-West," because she had heard her father say that those winds brought rain.

And now the floods of rain were pouring down on the country, and great sheets of water flowed towards the centre of the map, and cataracts of water poured into the great round hole in the middle of the map, and the dragons were being washed away and disappearing down the waste-pipe in great green masses and scattered green shoals—single dragons and dragons by the dozen; of all sizes, from the ones that carry off elephants down to the ones that get in your tea.

And presently there was not a dragon left. So then they turned off the tap named "Waste," and they half-turned off the one labelled "Sunshine"— it was broken, so that they could not turn it off altogether—and they turned on "Fair to moderate" and "Showery" and both taps stuck, so that they could not be turned off, which accounts for our climate.

How did they get home again? By the Snowdon railway, of course.

And was the nation grateful? Well—the nation was very wet. And by the time the nation had got dry again it was interested in the new invention for toasting muffins by electricity, and all the dragons were almost forgotten. Dragons do not seem so important when they are dead and gone, and, you know, there never was a reward offered.

And what did father and mother say when Effie and Harry got home?

My dear, that is the sort of silly question you children always will ask. However, just for this once I don't mind telling you.

Mother said, "Oh, my darlings, my darlings, you're safe—you're safe!

You naughty children—how could you be so disobedient? Go to bed at once!"

And their father the doctor said:

"I wish I had known what you were going to do! I should have liked to preserve a specimen. I threw away the one I got out of Effie's eye. I intended to get a more perfect specimen. I did not anticipate this immediate extinction of the species."

The professor said nothing, but he rubbed his hands. He had kept his specimen—the one the size of an earwig that he gave Harry half a crown for—and he has it to this day.

You must get him to show it to you!

1899

From *Peter Pan in Kensington Gardens*

J . M . B A R R I E

Peter Pan

If you ask your mother whether she knew about Peter Pan when she was a little girl, she will say, "Why, of course I did, child"; and if you ask her whether he rode on a goat in those days, she will say, "What a foolish question to ask; certainly he did." Then if you ask your grandmother whether she knew about Peter Pan when she was a girl, she also says, "Why, of course I did, child," but if you ask her whether he rode on a goat in those days, she says she never heard of his having a goat. Perhaps she has forgotten, just as she sometimes forgets your name and calls you Mildred, which is your mother's name. Still, she could hardly forget such an important thing as the goat. Therefore there was no goat when your grandmother was a little girl. This shows that, in telling the story of Peter Pan, to begin with the goat (as most people do) is as silly as to put on your jacket before your vest.

Of course, it also shows that Peter is ever so old, but he is really always the same age, so that does not matter in the least. His age is one week, and though he was born so long ago he has never had a birthday, nor is there the slightest chance of his ever having one. The reason is that he escaped from being a human when he was seven days old; he escaped by the window and flew back to the Kensington Gardens.

If you think he was the only baby who ever wanted to escape, it shows how completely you have forgotten your own young days. When David heard this story first he was quite certain that he had never tried to escape, but I told him to think back hard, pressing his hands to his temples, and when he had done this hard, and even harder, he distinctly remembered a youthful desire to return to the tree-tops, and with that memory came others, as that he had lain in bed planning to escape as soon as his mother was asleep, and how she had once caught him half-way up the chimney. All children could have such recollections if they would press their hands hard to their temples, for, having been birds before they were human, they are naturally a little wild during the first few weeks, and very itchy at the shoulders, where their wings used to be. So David tells me.

I ought to mention here that the following is our way with a story: First I tell it to him, and then he tells it to me, the understanding being that it is quite a different story; and then I retell it with his additions, and so we go on until no one could say whether it is more his story or mine. In this story of Peter Pan, for instance, the bald narrative and most of the moral reflections are mine, though not all, for this boy can be a stern moralist; but the interesting bits about the ways and customs of babies in the bird-stage are mostly reminiscences of David's, recalled by pressing his hands to his temples and thinking hard.

Well, Peter Pan got out by the window which had no bars. Standing on the ledge he could see trees far away, which were doubtless the Kensington Gardens, and the moment he saw them he entirely forgot that he was now a little boy in a nightgown, and away he flew, right over the houses to the Gardens. It is wonderful that he could fly without wings, but the place itched tremendously, and—and—perhaps we could all fly if we were as dead-confident-sure of our capacity to do it as was bold Peter Pan that evening.

He alighted gaily on the open sward, between the Baby's Palace and the Serpentine, and the first thing he did was to lie on his back and kick. He was quite unaware already that he had ever been human, and thought he was a bird, even in appearance, just the same as in his early days, and when he tried to catch a fly he did not understand that the reason he missed it was because he had attempted to seize it with his hand, which, of course, a bird never does. He saw, however, that it must be past Lock-out Time, for there were a good many fairies about, all too busy to notice him; they were getting breakfast ready, milking their cows, drawing water, and so on, and the sight of the water-pails made him thirsty, so he flew over to the Round Pond to have a drink. He stooped and dipped his beak in the pond; he thought it was his beak, but, of course, it was only his nose, and therefore, very little water came up, and that not so refreshing as usual, so next he tried a puddle, and he fell flop into it. When a real bird falls in flop, he spreads out his feathers and pecks them dry, but Peter could not remember what was the thing to do, and he decided rather sulkily to go to sleep on the weeping-beech in the Baby Walk.

At first he found some difficulty in balancing himself on a branch, but presently he remembered the way, and fell asleep. He awoke long before morning, shivering, and saying to himself, "I never was out on such a cold night"; he had really been out on colder nights when he was a bird, but, of course, as everybody knows, what seems a warm night to a bird is a cold night to a boy in a nightgown. Peter also felt strangely uncomfortable, as if his head was stuffy; he heard loud noises that made him look round sharply, though they were really himself sneezing. There was something he wanted very much, but, though he knew he wanted it, he could not think what it was. What he wanted so much was his mother to blow his nose, but that never struck him, so he decided to appeal to the fairies for enlightenment. They are reputed to know a good deal.

There were two of them strolling along the Baby Walk, with their arms round each other's waists, and he hopped down to address them. The fairies have their tiffs with the birds, but they usually give a civil answer to a civil question, and he was quite angry when these two ran away the moment they saw him. Another was lolling on a garden chair, reading a postage-stamp which some human had left fall, and when he heard Peter's voice he popped in alarm behind a tulip.

To Peter's bewilderment he discovered that every fairy he met fled from him. A band of workmen, who were sawing down a toadstool, rushed away, leaving their tools behind them. A milkmaid turned her pail upside down and hid in it. Soon the Gardens were in an uproar. Crowds of fairies were running this way and that, asking each other stoutly who was afraid; lights were extinguished, doors barricaded, and from the grounds of Queen Mab's palace came the rub-a-dub of drums, showing that the royal guard had been called out. A regiment of Lancers came charging down the Broad Walk, armed with holly-leaves, with which they jag the enemy horribly in passing. Peter heard the little people crying everywhere that there was a human in the Gardens after Lock-out Time, but he never thought for a moment that he was the human. He was feeling stuffier and stuffier, and more and more wistful to learn what he wanted done to his nose, but he pursued them with the vital question in vain; the timid creatures ran from him, and even the Lancers, when he approached them up on the Hump, turned swiftly into a side-walk, on the pretence that they saw him there.

Despairing of the fairies, he resolved to consult the birds, but now he remembered, as an odd-thing, that all the birds on the weeping-breech had flown away when he alighted on it, and though this had not troubled him at the time, he saw its meaning now. Every living thing was shunning him. Poor little Peter Pan! he sat down and cried, and even then he did not know that, for a bird, he was sitting on his wrong part. It is a blessing that he did not know, for otherwise, he would have lost faith in his power to fly, and the moment you doubt whether you can fly, you cease for ever to be able to do it. The reason birds can fly and we can't is simply that they have perfect faith, for to have faith is to have wings.

Now, except by flying, no one can reach the island in the Serpentine, for the boats of humans are forbidden to land there, and there are stakes round it, standing up in the water, on each of which a bird-sentinel sits by day and night. It was to the island that Peter now flew to put his strange case before old Solomon Caw, and he alighted on it with relief, much heartened to find himself at last at home, as the birds call the island. All of them were asleep, including the sentinels, except Solomon, who was wide awake on one side, and he listened quietly to Peter's adventures, and then told him their true meaning.

"Look at your nightgown, if you don't believe me," Solomon said; and with staring eyes Peter looked at his nightgown, and then at the sleeping birds. Not one of them wore anything.

"How many of your toes are thumbs?" said Solomon a little cruelly, and Peter saw to his consternation, that all his toes were fingers. This shock was so great that it drove away his cold.

"Ruffle your feathers," said that grim old Solomon, and Peter tried most desperately hard to ruffle his feathers, but he had none. Then he rose up, quaking, and for the first time since he stood on the window-ledge, he remembered a lady who had been very fond of him.

"I think I shall go back to mother," he said timidly.

"Good-bye," replied Solomon Caw with a queer look.

But Peter hesitated. "Why don't you go?" the old one asked politely.

"I suppose," said Peter huskily, "I suppose I can still fly?"

You see he had lost faith.

"Poor little half-and-half!" said Solomon, who was not really hard-hearted, "you will never be able to fly again, not even on windy days. You must live here on the island always."

"And never even go to the Kensington Gardens?" Peter asked tragically.

"How could you get across?" said Solomon. He promised very kindly, however, to teach Peter as many of the bird ways as could be learned by one of such an awkward shape.

"Then I shan't be exactly a human?" Peter asked.

"No."

"Nor exactly a bird?"

"No."

"What shall I be?"

"You will be a Betwixt-and-Between," Solomon said, and certainly he was a wise old fellow, for that is exactly how it turned out.

The birds on the island never got used to him. His oddities tickled them every day, as if they were quite new, though it was really the birds that were new. They came out of the eggs daily, and laughed at him at once; then off they soon flew to be humans, and other birds came out of other eggs; and so it went on for ever. The crafty mother-birds, when they tired of sitting on their eggs, used to get the young ones to break their shells a day before the right time by whispering to them that now was their chance to see Peter washing or drinking or eating. Thousands gathered round him daily to watch him do these things, just as you watch the peacocks, and they screamed with delight when he lifted the crusts they flung him with his hands instead of in the usual way with the mouth. All his food was brought to him from the Gardens at Solomon's orders by the birds. He would not eat worms or insects (which they thought very silly of him), so they brought him bread in their beaks. Thus, when you cry out, "Greedy! Greedy!" to the bird that flies away with the big crust, you know now that you ought not to do this, for he is very likely taking it to Peter Pan.

Peter wore no nightgown now. You see, the birds were always begging him for bits of it to line their nests with, and, being very good-natured, he could not refuse, so by Solomon's advice he had hidden what was left of it. But, though he was now quite naked, you must not think that he was cold or unhappy. He was usually very happy and gay, and the reason was that Solomon had kept his promise and taught him many of the bird ways. To be easily pleased, for instance, and always to be really doing something, and to think that whatever he was doing was a thing of vast importance. Peter became very clever at helping the birds to build their nests; soon he could build better than a wood-pigeon, and nearly as well as a blackbird, though never did he satisfy the finches, and he made nice little water-troughs near the nests and dug up worms for the young ones with his fingers. He also became very learned in bird-lore, and knew an east wind from a west wind by its smell, and he could see the grass growing and hear the insects walking about inside the tree-trunks. But the best thing Solomon had done was teach him to have a glad heart. All birds have glad hearts unless you rob their nests, and so as they were the only kind of heart Solomon knew about, it was easy to him to teach Peter how to have one.

Peter's heart was so glad that he felt he must sing all day long, just as the birds sing for joy, but, being partly human, he needed an instrument, so he made a pipe of reeds, and he used to sit by the shore of the island of an evening, practising the sough of the wind and the ripple of the water, and catching handfuls of the shine of the moon, and he put them all in his pipe and played them so beautifully that even the birds were deceived, and they would say to each other, "Was that a fish leaping in the water or was it Peter playing leaping fish on his pipe?" And sometimes he played the birth of birds, and then the mothers would turn round in their nests to see whether they had laid an egg. If you are a child of the Gardens you must know the chestnut-tree near the bridge, which comes out in flower first of all the chestnuts, but perhaps you have not heard why this tree leads the way. It is because Peter wearies for summer and plays that it has come, and the chestnut, being so near, hears him and is cheated.

But as Peter sat by the shore tootling divinely on his pipe he sometimes fell into sad thoughts, and then the music became sad also, and the reason of all this sadness was that he could not reach the Gardens, though he could see them through the arch of the bridge. He knew he could never be a real human again, and scarcely wanted to be one, but oh! how he longed to play as other children play, and of course there is no such lovely place to play in as the Gardens. The birds brought him news of how boys and girls play, and wistful tears started in Peter's eyes.

Perhaps you wonder why he did not swim across. The reason was that he could not swim. He wanted to know how to swim, but no one on the island knew the way except the ducks, and they are so stupid. They were quite willing to teach him, but all they could say about it was, "You sit down on the top of the water in this way, and then you kick out like that." Peter tried it often, but always before he could kick out he sank. What he really needed to know was how you sit on the water without sinking, and they said it was quite impossible to explain such an easy thing as that. Occasionally swans touched on the island, and he would give them all his day's food and then ask them how they sat on the water, but as soon as he had no more to give them the hateful things hissed at him and sailed away.

Once he really thought he had discovered a way of reaching the Gardens. A wonderful white thing, like a runaway newspaper floated high over the island and then tumbled, rolling over and over after the manner of a bird that has broken its wing. Peter was so frightened that he hid, but the birds told him it was only a kite, and what a kite is, and that it must have tugged its string out of a boy's hand, and soared away. After that they laughed at Peter for being so fond of the kite; he loved it so much that he even slept with one hand on it, and I think this was pathetic and pretty, for the reason he loved it was because it had belonged to a real boy.

To the birds this was a very poor reason, but the older ones felt grateful to him at this time because he had nursed a number of fledglings through the German measles, and they offered to show him how birds fly a kite. So six of them took the end of the string in their beaks and flew away with it; and to his amazement it flew after them and went even higher than they.

Peter screamed out, "Do it again!" and with great good-nature they did it several times, and always instead of thanking them he cried, "Do it again!" which shows that even now he had not quite forgotten what it was to be a boy.

At last, with a grand design burning within his brave heart, he begged them to do it once more with him clinging to the tail, and now a hundred flew off with the string, and Peter clung to the tail, meaning to drop off when he was over the Gardens. But the kite broke to pieces in the air, and he would have been drowned in the Serpentine had he not caught hold of two indignant swans and made them carry him to the island. After this the birds said that they would help him no more in his mad enterprise.

Nevertheless, Peter did reach the Gardens at last by the help of Shelley's boat, as I am now to tell you.

The Thrush's Nest

Shelley was a young gentleman and as grown-up as he need ever expect to be. He was a poet; and they are never exactly grown-up. They are people who despise money except what you need for to-day, and he had all that and five pounds over. So, when he was walking in the Kensington Gardens, he made a paper boat of his bank-note, and sent it sailing on the Serpentine.

It reached the island at night; and the look-out brought it to Solomon Caw, who thought at first that it was the usual thing, a message from a lady, saying she would be obliged if he could let her have a good one. They always ask for the best one he has, and if he likes the letter he sends one from Class A, but if it ruffles him he sends very funny ones indeed. Sometimes he sends none at all, and at another time he sends a nestful; it all depends on the mood you catch him in. He likes you to leave it all to him, and if you mention particularly that you hope he will see his way to making it *a boy this time*, he is almost sure to send another girl. And whether you are a lady or only a little boy who wants a baby sister, always take pains to write your address clearly. You can't think what a lot of babies Solomon has sent to the wrong house.

Shelley's boat, when opened, completely puzzled Solomon, and he took counsel of his assistants, who having walked over it twice, first with their toes pointed out, and then with their toes pointed in, decided that it came from some greedy person who wanted five. They thought this because there was a large five printed on it. "Preposterous!" cried Solomon in a rage, and he presented it to Peter; anything useless which drifted upon the island was usually given to Peter as a plaything.

But he did not play with his precious bank-note, for he knew what it was at once, having been very observant during the week when he was an ordinary boy. With so much money, he reflected, he could surely at last contrive to reach the Gardens, and he considered all the possible ways, and decided (wisely, I think) to choose the best way. But, first, he had to tell the birds of the value of Shelley's boat; and though they were too honest to demand it back, he saw that they were galled, and they cast such black looks at Solomon, who was rather vain of his cleverness, that he flew away to the end of the island, and sat there very depressed with his head buried in his wings. Now Peter knew that unless Solomon was on your side, you never got anything done for you in the island, so he followed him and tried to hearten him.

Nor was this all that Peter did to gain the powerful old fellow's good-will. You must know that Solomon had no intention of remaining in office all his life. He looked forward to retiring by and by, and devoting his green old age to a life of pleasure on a certain yew-stump in the Figs which had taken his fancy, and for years he had been quietly filling his stocking. It was a stocking belonging to some bathing person which had been cast upon the island, and at the time I speak of it contained a hundred and eighty crumbs, thirty-four nuts, sixteen crusts, a pen-wiper, and a boot-lace. When his stocking was full, Solomon calculated that he would be able to retire on a competency. Peter now gave him a pound. He cut it off his bank-note with a sharp stick.

This made Solomon his friend for ever, and after the two had consulted together they called a meeting of the thrushes. You will see presently why the thrushes only were invited.

The scheme to be put before them was really Peter's, but Solomon did most of the talking, because he soon became irritable if other people talked. He began by saying that he had been much impressed by the superior ingenuity shown by the thrushes in nest-building, and this put them into good-humour at once, as it was meant to do; for all the quarrels between birds are about the best way of building nests. Other birds, said Solomon, omitted to line their nests with mud, and as a result they did not hold water. Here he cocked his head as if he had used an unanswerable argument; but, unfortunately, a Mrs. Finch had come to the meeting uninvited, and she squeaked out, "We don't build nests to hold water, but to hold eggs," and then the thrushes stopped cheering, and Solomon was so perplexed that he took several sips of water.

"Consider," he said at last, "how warm the mud makes the nest."

"Consider," cried Mrs. Finch, "that when water gets into the nest it remains there and your little ones are drowned."

The thrushes begged Solomon with a look to say something crushing in reply to this, but again he was perplexed.

"Try another drink," suggested Mrs. Finch pertly. Kate was her name, and all Kates are saucy.

Solomon did try another drink, and it inspired him. "If," said he, "a finch's nest is placed on the Serpentine it fills and breaks to pieces, but a thrush's nest is still as dry as the cup of a swan's back."

How the thrushes applauded! Now they knew why they lined their nests with mud, and when Mrs. Finch called out, "We don't place our nests on the Serpentine," they did what they should have done at first—chased her from the meeting. After this it was most orderly. What they had been brought together to hear, said Solomon, was this: their young friend, Peter Pan, as they well knew, wanted very much to be able to cross to the Gardens, and he now proposed, with their help, to build a boat.

At this the thrushes began to fidget, which made Peter tremble for his scheme.

Solomon explained hastily that what he meant was not one of the cumbrous boats that humans use; the proposed boat was to be simply a thrush's nest large enough to hold Peter.

But still, to Peter's agony, the thrushes were sulky. "We are very busy people," they grumbled, "and this would be a big job."

"Quite so," said Solomon, "and, of course, Peter would not allow you to work for nothing. You must remember that he is now in comfortable circumstances, and he will pay you such wages as you have never been paid before. Peter Pan authorizes me to say that you shall all be paid sixpence a day."

Then all the thrushes hopped for joy, and that very day was begun the celebrated Building of the Boat. All their ordinary business fell into arrears. It was the time of the year when they should have been pairing, but not a thrush's nest was built except this big one, and so Solomon soon ran short of thrushes with which to supply the demand from the mainland. The stout, rather greedy children, who look so well in perambulators but get puffed easily when they walk, were all young thrushes once, and ladies often ask specially for them. What do you think Solomon did? He sent over to the housetops for a lot of sparrows and ordered them to lay their eggs in old thrushes' nests, and sent their young to the ladies and swore they were all thrushes! It was known afterwards on the island as the Sparrow's Year; and so, when you meet grown-up people in the Gardens who puff and blow as if they thought themselves bigger than they are, very likely they belong to that year. You ask them.

Peter was a just master, and paid his workpeople every evening. They stood in rows on the branches, waiting politely while he cut the paper sixpences out of his bank-note, and presently he called the roll, and then each bird, as the names were mentioned, flew down and got sixpence. It must have been a fine sight.

And at last, after months of labour, the boat was finished. O the glory of Peter as he saw it growing more and more like a great thrush's nest! From the very beginning of the building of it he slept by its side, and often woke up to say sweet things to it, and after it was lined with mud and the mud had dried he always slept in it. He sleeps in his nest still, and has a fascinating way of curling round in it, for it is just large enough to hold him comfortably when he curls round like a kitten. It is brown inside, of course, but outside it is mostly green, being woven of grass and twigs, and when these wither or snap the walls are thatched afresh. There are also a few feathers here and there, which came off the thrushes while they were building.

The other birds were extremely jealous, and said that the boat would not balance on the water, but it lay most beautifully steady; they said the water would come into it, but no water came into it. Next they said that Peter had no oars, and this caused the thrushes to look at each other in dismay; but Peter replied that he had no need of oars, for he had a sail, and with such a proud, happy face he produced a sail which he had fashioned out of his nightgown, and though it was still rather like a nightgown it made a lovely sail. And that night, the moon being full, and all the birds asleep, he did enter his coracle (as Master Francis Pretty would have said) and depart out of the island. And first, he knew not why, he looked upward, with his hands clasped, and from that moment his eyes were pinned to the west.

He had promised the thrushes to begin by making short voyages, with them as his guides, but far away he saw the Kensington Gardens beckoning to him beneath the bridge, and he could not wait. His face was flushed, but he never looked back; there was an exultation in his little breast that drove out fear. Was Peter the least gallant of the English mariners who have sailed westward to meet the Unknown?

At first, his boat turned round and round, and he was driven back to the place of his starting, whereupon he shortened sail, by removing one of the sleeves, and was forthwith carried backwards by a contrary breeze, to his no small peril. He now let go the sail, with the result that he was drifted towards the far shore, where are black shadows he knew not the dangers of, but suspected them, and so once more hoisted his nightgown and went roomer of the shadows until he caught a favouring wind, which bore him westward, but at so great a speed that he was like to be broke against the bridge. Which, having avoided, he passed under the bridge and came, to his great rejoicing, within full sight of the delectable Gardens. But having tried to cast anchor, which was a stone at the end of a piece of the kite-string, he found no bottom, and was fain to hold off, seeking for moorage; and, feeling his way, he buffeted against a sunken reef that cast him overboard by the greatness of the shock, and he was near to being drowned, but clambered back into the vessel. There now arose a mighty storm, accompanied by roaring of waters, such as he had never heard the like, and he was tossed this way and that, and his hands so numbed with the cold that he could not close them. Having escaped the danger of which, he was mercifully carried into a small bay, where his boat rode at peace.

Nevertheless, he was not yet in safety; for, on pretending to disembark, he found a multitude of small people drawn up on the shore to contest his landing, and shouting shrilly to him to be off, for it was long past Lock-out Time. This, with much brandishing of their holly-leaves; and also a company of them carried an arrow which some boy had left in the Gardens, and this they prepared to use as a battering-ram.

Then Peter, who knew them for the fairies, called out that he was not an ordinary human and had no desire to do them displeasure, but to be their friend; nevertheless, having found a jolly harbour, he was in no temper to draw off therefrom, and he warned them if they sought to mischief him to stand to their harms.

So saying, he boldy leapt ashore, and they gathered around him with intent to slay him, but there then arose a great cry among the women, and it was because they had now observed that his sail was a baby's nightgown. Whereupon, they straightway loved him, and grieved that their laps were too small, the which I cannot explain, except by saying that such is the way of women. The men-fairies now sheathed their weapons on observing the behaviour of their women, on whose intelligence they set great store, and they led him civilly to their Queen, who conferred upon him the courtesy of the Gardens after Lock-out Time, and henceforth Peter could go whither he chose, and the fairies had orders to put him in comfort.

Such was his first voyage to the Gardens, and you may gather from the antiquity of the language that it took place a long time ago. But Peter never grows any older, and if we could be watching for him under the bridge to-night (but, of course, we can't), I dare say we should see him hoisting his nightgown and sailing or paddling towards us in the Thrush's Nest. When he sails, he sits down, but he stands up to paddle. I shall tell you presently how he got his paddle.

Long before the time for the opening of the gates comes he steals back to the island, for people must not see him (he is not so human as all that), but this gives him hours for play, and he plays exactly as real children play. At least he thinks so, and it is one of the pathetic things about him that he often plays quite wrongly.

You see, he had no one to tell him how children really play, for the fairies are all more or less in hiding until dusk, and so know nothing, and though the birds pretended that they could tell him a great deal, when the time for telling came, it was wonderful how little they really knew. They told him the truth about hide-and-seek, and he often plays it by himself, but even the ducks on the Round Pond could not explain to him what it is that makes the pond so fascinating to boys. Every night the ducks have forgotten all the events of the day, except the number of pieces of cake thrown to them. They are gloomy creatures, and say that cake is not what it was in their young days.

So Peter had to find out many things for himself. He often played ships at the Round Pond, but his ship was only a hoop which he had found on the grass. Of course, he had never seen a hoop, and he wondered what you play at with them, and decided that you play at pretending they are boats. This hoop always sank at once, but he waded in for it, and sometimes he dragged it gleefully round the rim of the pond, and he was quite proud to think that he had discovered what boys do with hoops.

Another time, when he found a child's pail, he thought it was for sitting in, and he sat so hard in it that he could scarcely get out of it. Also he found a balloon. It was bobbing about on the Hump, quite as if it was having a game by itself, and he caught it after an exciting chase. But he thought it was a ball, and Jenny Wren had told him that boys kick balls, so he kicked it; and after that he could not find it anywhere.

Perhaps the most surprising thing he found was a perambulator. It was under a lime-tree, near the entrance to the Fairy Queen's Winter Palace (which is within the circle of the seven Spanish chestnuts), and Peter approached it warily, for the birds had never mentioned such things to him. Lest it was alive, he addressed it politely; and then, as it gave no answer, he went nearer and felt it cautiously. He gave it a little push, and it ran from him, which made him think it must be alive after all; but, as it had run from him, he was not afraid. So he stretched out his hand to pull it to him, but this time it ran at him, and he was so alarmed that he leapt the railing and scudded away to his boat. You must not think, however, that he was a coward, for he came back next night with a crust in one hand and a stick in the other, but the perambulator had gone, and he never saw any other one. I have promised to tell you also about his paddle. It was a child's spade which he had found near St. Govor's Well, and he thought it was a paddle.

Do you pity Peter Pan for making these mistakes? If so, I think it rather silly of you. What I mean is that, of course, one must pity him now and then, but to pity him all the time would be impertinence. He thought he had the most splendid time in the Gardens, and to think you have it is almost quite as good as really to have it. He played without ceasing, while you often waste time by being mad-dog or Mary-Annish. He could be neither of these things, for he had never heard of them, but do you think he is to be pitied for that?

Oh, he was merry! He was as much merrier than you, for instance, as you are merrier than your father. Sometimes he fell, like a spinning-top, from sheer merriment. Have you seen a greyhound leaping the fences of the Gardens? That is how Peter leaps them.

And think of the music of his pipe. Gentlemen who walk home at night write to the papers to say they heard a nightingale in the Gardens, but it is really Peter's pipe they hear. Of course, he had no mother—at least, what use was she to him? You can be sorry for him for that, but don't be too sorry, for the next thing I mean to tell you is how he revisited her. It was the fairies who gave him the chance.

Lock-out Time

It is frightfully difficult to know much about the fairies, and almost the only thing known for certain is that there are fairies wherever there are children. Long ago children were forbidden the Gardens, and at that time there was not a fairy in the place; then the children were admitted, and the fairies came trooping in that very evening. They can't resist following the children, but you seldom see them, partly because they live in the daytime behind the railings, where you are not allowed to go, and also partly because they are so cunning. They are not a bit cunning after Lock-out, but until Lock-out, my word!

When you were a bird you knew the fairies pretty well, and you remember a good deal about them in your babyhood, which it is a great pity you can't write down, for gradually you forget, and I have heard of children who declared that they had never once seen a fairy. Very likely if they said this in the Kensington Gardens, they were standing looking at a fairy all the

time. The reason they were cheated was that she pretended to be something else. This is one of their best tricks. They usually pretend to be flowers, because the court sits in the Fairies' Basin, and there are so many flowers there, and all along the Baby Walk, that a flower is the thing least likely to attract attention. They dress exactly like flowers, and change with the seasons, putting on white when lilies are in and blue for bluebells, and so on. They like crocus and hyacinth time best of all, as they are partial to a bit of colour, but tulips (except white ones, which are the fairy cradles) they consider garish, and they sometimes put off dressing like tulips for days, so that the beginning of the tulip weeks is almost the best time to catch them.

When they think you are not looking they skip along pretty lively, but if you look, and they fear there is no time to hide, they stand quite still pretending to be flowers. Then, after you have passed without knowing that they are fairies, they rush home and tell their mothers they have had such an adventure. The Fairy Basin, you remember, is all covered with ground-ivy (from which they make their castor-oil), with flowers growing in it here and there. Most of them really are flowers, but some of them are fairies. You never can be sure of them, but a good plan is to walk by looking the other way, and then turn round sharply. Another good plan, which David and I sometimes follow, is to stare them down. After a long time they can't help winking, and then you know for certain they are fairies.

There are also numbers of them along the Baby Walk, which is a famous gentle place, as spots frequented by fairies are called. Once twenty-four of them had an extraordinary adventure. They were a girls' school out for a walk with the governess, and all wearing hyacinth gowns, when she suddenly put her finger to her mouth, and then they all stood still on an empty bed and pretended to be hyacinths. Unfortunately what the governess had heard was two gardeners coming to plant new flowers in that very bed. They were wheeling a hand-cart with flowers in it, and were quite surprised to find the bed occupied. "Pity to lift them hyacinths," said the one man. "Duke's orders," replied the other, and, having emptied the cart, they dug up the boarding-school and put the poor, terrified things in it in five rows. Of course, neither the governess nor the girls dare let on that they were fairies, so they were carted far away to a potting-shed, out of which they escaped in the night without their shoes, but there was a great row about it among the parents, and the school was ruined.

As for their houses, it is no use looking for them, because they are the exact opposite of our houses. You can see our houses by day but you can't see them by dark. Well, you can see their houses by dark, for they are the colour of night, and I never heard of any one yet who could see night in the daytime. This does not mean that they are black, for night has its colours just as day has, but ever so much brighter. Their blues and reds and greens are like ours with a light behind them. The palace is entirely built of many-coloured glasses, and it is quite the loveliest of all royal residences, but the Queen sometimes complains because the common people will peep in to see what she is doing. They are very inquisitive folk, and press quite hard against the glass, and this is why their noses are mostly snubby. The streets are miles along and very twisty, and have paths on each side made of bright worsted. The birds used to steal the worsted for their nests, but a policeman has been appointed to hold on at the other end.

One of the great differences between the fairies and us is that they never do anything useful. When the first baby laughed for the first time, his laugh broke into a million pieces, and they all went skipping about. That was the beginning of fairies. They look tremendously busy, you know, as if they had not a moment to spare, but if you were to ask them what they are doing, they could not tell you in the least. They are frightfully ignorant, and everything they do is make-believe. They have a postman, but he never calls except at Christmas with his little box, and though they have beautiful schools, nothing is taught in them; the youngest child being chief person is always elected mistress, and when she has called the roll, they all go out for a walk and never come back. It is a very noticeable thing that, in fairy families, the youngest is always chief person, and usually becomes a prince or princess; and children remember this, and think it must be so among humans also, and that is why they are often made uneasy when they come upon their mother furtively putting new frills on the bassinette.

You have probably observed that your baby sister wants to do all sorts of things that your mother and her nurse want her not to do—to stand up at sitting-down time, and to sit down at stand-up time, for instance, or to wake up when she should fall asleep, or to crawl on the floor when she is wearing her best frock, and so on, and perhaps you put this down to naughtiness. But it is not; it simply means that she is doing as she has seen the fairies do; she begins by following their ways, and it takes about two years to get her into the human ways. Her fits of passion, which are awful to behold, and are usually called teething, are no such thing; they are her natural exasperation, because we don't understand her, though she is talking an intelligible language. She is talking fairy. The reason mothers and nurses know what her remarks mean, before other people know, as that "Guch" means "Give it to me at once," while "Wa" is "Why do you wear such a funny hat?" is because, mixing so much with babies, they have picked up a little of the fairy language.

Of late David has been thinking back hard about the fairy tongue, with his hands clutching his temples, and he has remembered a number of their phrases which I shall tell you some day if I don't forget. He had heard them in the days when he was a thrush, and though I suggested to him that perhaps it is really bird language he is remembering, he says not, for these phrases are about fun and adventures, and the birds talked of nothing but nest-building. He distinctly remembers that the birds used to go from spot to spot like ladies at shop-windows, looking at the different nests and saying, "Not my colour, my dear," and "How would that do with a soft lining?" and "But will it wear?" and "What hideous trimming!" and so on.

The fairies are exquisite dancers, and that is why one of the first things the baby does is to sign to you to dance to him and then to cry when you do it. They hold their great balls in the open air, in what is called a fairy ring. For weeks afterwards you can see the ring on the grass. It is not there when they begin, but they make it by waltzing round and round. Sometimes you will find mushrooms inside the ring, and these are fairy chairs that the servants have forgotten to clear away. The chairs and the rings are the only tell-tale marks these little people leave behind them, and they would remove even these were they not so fond of dancing that they toe it till the very moment of the opening of the gates. David and I once found a fairy ring quite warm.

But there is also a way of finding out about the ball before it takes place. You know the boards which tell at what time the Gardens are to close to-day. Well, these tricky fairies sometimes slyly change the board on a ball-night, so that it says the Gardens are to close at six-thirty, for instance, instead of at seven. This enables them to get begun half-an-hour earlier.

If on such a night we could remain behind in the Gardens, as the famous Maimie Mannering did, we might see delicious sights; hundreds of lovely fairies hastening to the ball, the married ones wearing their wedding rings round their waists; the gentlemen, all in uniform, holding up the ladies' trains, and linkmen running in front carrying winter cherries, which are the fairy lanterns; the cloakroom where they put on their silver slippers and get a ticket for their wraps; the flowers streaming up from Baby Walk to look on, and always welcome because they can lend a pin; the supper-table, with Queen Mab at the head of it, and behind her chair the Lord Chamberlain, who carries a dandelion on which he blows when her Majesty wants to know the time.

The tablecloth varies according to the seasons, and in May it is made of chestnut blossom. The way the fairy servants do is this: The men, scores of them, climb up the trees and shake the branches, and the blossoms fall like snow. Then the lady-servants sweep it together by whisking their skirts until it is exactly like a tablecloth, and that is how they get their tablecloth.

They have real glasses and real wine of three kinds, namely, blackthorn wine, berberris wine, and cowslip wine, and the Queen pours out, but the bottles are so heavy that she just pretends to pour out. There is bread-and-butter to begin with, of the size of a threepenny bit; and cakes to end with, and they are so small that they have no crumbs. The fairies sit round on mushrooms, and at first they are well-behaved and always cough off the table, and so on, but after a bit they are not so well-behaved and stick their fingers into the butter, which is got from the roots of old trees, and the really horrid ones crawl over the tablecloth chasing sugar or other delicacies with their tongues. When the Queen sees them doing this she signs to the servants to wash up and put away, and then everybody adjourns to the dance, the Queen walking in front while the Lord Chamberlain walks behind her, carrying two little pots, one of which contains the juice of wallflower and the other the juice of Solomon's seals. Wallflower juice is good for reviving dancers who fall to the ground in a fit, and Solomon's seals juice is for bruises. They bruise very easily, and when Peter plays faster and faster they foot it till they fall down in fits. For, as you know without my telling you, Peter Pan is the fairies' orchestra. He sits in the middle of the ring, and they would never dream of having a smart dance nowadays without him. "P.P." is written on the corner of the invitation-cards sent out by all really good families. They are grateful little people, too, and at the Princess's coming-of-age ball (they come of age on their second birthday and have a birthday every month) they gave him the wish of his heart.

The way it was done was this: The Queen ordered him to kneel, and then said that for playing so beautifully she would give him the wish of his heart. Then they all gathered round Peter to hear what was the wish of his heart, but for a long time he hesitated, not being certain what it was himself.

"If I chose to go back to mother," he asked at last, "could you give me that wish?"

Now this question vexed them, for were he to return to his mother they should lose his music, so the Queen tilted her nose contemptuously and said, "Pooh! ask for a much bigger wish than that."

"Is that quite a little wish?" he inquired.

"As little as this," the Queen answered, putting her hands near each other.

"What size is a big wish?" he asked.

She measured it off on her skirt and it was a very handsome length.

Then Peter reflected and said, "Well, then, I think I shall have two little wishes instead of one big one."

Of course, the fairies had to agree, though his cleverness rather shocked them, and he said that his first wish was to go to his mother, but with the right to return to the Gardens if he found her disappointing. His second wish he would hold in reserve.

They tried to dissuade him, and even put obstacles in the way.

"I can give you the power to fly to her house," the Queen said, "but I can't open the door for you."

"The window I flew out at will be open," Peter said confidently. "Mother always keeps it open in the hope that I may fly back."

"How do you know?" they asked, quite surprised, and, really, Peter could not explain how he knew.

"I just do know," he said.

So as he persisted in his wish, they had to grant it. The way they gave him power to fly was this: They all tickled him on the shoulder, and soon he felt a funny itching in that part, and then up he rose higher and higher, and flew away out of the Gardens and over the house-tops.

It was so delicious that instead of flying straight to his own home he skimmed away over St. Paul's to the Crystal Palace and back by the river and Regent's Park, and by the time he reached his mother's window he had quite made up his mind that his second wish should be to become a bird.

The window was wide open, just as he knew it would be, and in he fluttered, and there was his mother lying asleep. Peter alighted softly on the wooden rail at the foot of the bed and had a good look at her. She lay with her head on her hand, and the hollow in the pillow was like a nest lined with her brown wavy hair. He remembered, though he had long forgotten it, that she always gave her hair a holiday at night. How sweet the frills of her nightgown were! He was very glad she was such a pretty mother.

But she looked sad, and he knew why she looked sad. One of her arms moved as if it wanted to go round something, and he knew what it wanted to go round.

"O mother!" said Peter to himself, "if you just knew who is sitting on the rail at the foot of the bed."

Very gently he patted the little mound that her feet made, and he could see by her face that she liked it. He knew he had but to say "Mother" ever so softly, and she would wake up. They always wake up at once if it is you that says their name. Then she would give such a joyous cry and squeeze him tight. How nice that would be to him, but oh! how exquisitely delicious it would be to her. That, I am afraid, is how Peter regarded it. In returning to his mother he never doubted that he was giving her the greatest treat a woman can have. Nothing can be more splendid, he thought, than to have a little boy of your own. How proud of him they are! and very right and proper, too.

But why does Peter sit so long on the rail; why does he not tell his mother that he has come back?

I quite shrink from the truth, which is that he sat there in two minds. Sometimes he looked longingly at his mother, and sometimes he looked longingly at the window. Certainly it would be pleasant to be her boy again, but on the other hand, what times those had been in the Gardens! Was he so sure that he should enjoy wearing clothes again? He popped off the bed and opened some drawers to have a look at his old garments. They were still there, but he could not remember how you put them on. The socks, for instance, were they worn on the hands or on the feet? He was about to try one of them on his hand, when he had a great adventure. Perhaps the drawer had creaked; at any rate, his mother woke up, for he heard her say, "Peter," as if it was the most lovely word in the language. He remained sitting on the floor and held his breath, wondering how she knew that he had come back. If she said "Peter" again, he meant to cry "Mother" and run to her. But she spoke no more, she made little moans only, and when he next peeped at her she was once more asleep, with tears on her face.

It made Peter very miserable, and what do you think was the first thing he did? Sitting on the rail at the foot of the bed, he played a beautiful lullaby to his mother on his pipe. He had made it up himself out of the way she said "Peter," and he never stopped playing until she looked happy.

He thought this so clever of him that he could scarcely resist wakening her to hear her say, "O Peter, how exquisitely you play!" However, as she now seemed comfortable, he again cast looks at the window. You must think that he meditated flying away and never coming back. He had quite decided to be his mother's boy, but hesitated about beginning to-night. It was the second wish which troubled him. He no longer meant to make it a wish to be a bird, but not to ask for a second wish seemed wasteful, and, of course, he could not ask for it without returning to the fairies. Also, if he put off asking for his wish too long it might go bad. He asked himself if he had not been hard-hearted to fly away without saying good-bye to Solomon. "I should like awfully to sail in my boat just once more," he said wistfully to his sleeping mother. He quite argued with her as if she could hear him. "It would be so splendid to tell the birds of this adventure," he said coaxingly. "I promise to come back," he said solemnly, and meant it, too.

And in the end, you know, he flew away. Twice he came back from the window wanting to kiss his mother, but he feared the delight of it might waken her, so at last he played her a lovely kiss on his pipe, and then he flew back to the Gardens.

Many nights, and even months, passed before he asked the fairies for his second wish; and I am not sure that I quite know why he delayed so long. One reason was that he had so many good-byes to say, not only to his particular friends, but to a hundred favourite spots. Then he had his last sail, and his very last sail, and his last sail of all, and so on. Again, a number of farewell feasts were given in his honour; and another comfortable reason was that, after all, there was no hurry, for his mother would never weary of waiting for him. This last reason displeased old Solomon, for it was an encouragement to the birds to procrastinate. Solomon had several excellent mottoes for keeping them at their work, such as "Never put off laying to-day because you can lay to-morrow," and "In this world there are no second chances," and yet here was Peter gaily putting off and none the worse for it. The birds pointed this out to each other, and fell into lazy habits.

But, mind you, though Peter was so slow in going back to his mother, he was quite decided to go back. The best proof of this was his caution with the fairies. They were most anxious that he should remain in the Gardens to play to them, and to bring this to pass they tried to trick him into making such a remark as "I wish the grass was not so wet," and some of them danced out of time in the hope that he might cry, "I do wish you would keep time!" Then they would have said that this was his second wish. But he smoked their design, and though on occasions he began, "I wish——" he always stopped in time. So when at last he said to them bravely, "I wish now to go back to mother for ever and always," they had to tickle his shoulders and let him go.

He went in a hurry in the end, because he had dreamt that his mother was crying, and he knew what was the great thing she cried for, and that a hug from her splendid Peter would quickly make her to smile. Oh! he felt sure of it, and so eager was he to be nestling in her arms that this time he flew straight to the window, which was always to be open for him.

But the window was closed, and there were iron bars on it, and peering inside he saw his mother sleeping peacefully with her arm round another little boy.

Peter called, "Mother! mother!" but she heard him not; in vain he beat his little limbs against the iron bars. He had to fly back, sobbing, to the Gardens, and he never saw his dear again. What a glorious boy he had meant to be to her! Ah, Peter! we who have made the great mistake, how differently we should all act at the second chance. But Solomon was right—there is no second chance, not for most of us. When we reach the window it is Lock-out Time. The iron bars are up for life.

1906

About the Authors and Illustrators

WILLIAM ALLINGHAM (1824–1889) was an Irish poet, whose circle included Thomas Carlyle, Dante Gabriel Rossetti, and Alfred Lord Tennyson.

SIR JAMES MATTHEW BARRIE (1860–1937) was the most successful British playwright of his generation, the author of such works as *The Admirable Chrichton* (1902) and *What Every Woman Knows* (1908). Among his novels are *The Little Minister* (1891), *Sentimental Tommy* (1896), and *The Little White Bird* (1902), from which *Peter Pan in Kensington Gardens* was excerpted (1906). His most enduring effort, however, is the play *Peter Pan* (1904), which he rewrote in 1911 as the novel *Peter and Wendy*.

CHARLES HENRY BENNETT (1829–1867) was a prolific author and illustrator of children's books, as well as an important *Punch* cartoonist. Among the books he illustrated are *The Fables of Aesop* (1857), *The Pilgrim's Progress* (1859), and Henry Morley's *Fables and Fairy Tales* (1860) and *Oberon's Horn* (1861).

FORD MADOX BROWN (1821–1893) was an early member of the Pre-Raphaelite Brotherhood. He was also the grandfather of Ford Madox Ford and illustrated his grandson's earliest books, *The Brown Owl* (1892) and *The Feather* (1893).

ROBERT BROWNING (1812–1889) was one of the greatest of Victorian poets. His works include *Dramatis Personae* (1864), *The Ring and the Book* (1868–1869), and, of course, "The Pied Piper of Hamelin," first published in *Dramatic Lyrics* (1842), the third part of *Bells and Pomegranates* (1841–1846).

DINAH MARIA MULOCK CRAIK (1826–1887) was a prolific author, best known in her day for the novel *John Halifax, Gentleman* (1856). She also wrote several children's books, the most important of which were *The Adventures of a Brownie* (1872) and *The Little Lame Prince and His Travelling-Cloak* (1875).

WALTER CRANE (1845–1915) was one of the most influential designers of the late nineteenth and early twentieth centuries. Associated with the Pre-Raphaelites, he was a leading exponent of the Aesthetic and Arts and Crafts movements. He made his most lasting contribution to book illustration, embellishing such fairy tale collections as Mary De Morgan's *The Necklace of Princess*

Fiorimonde and Other Stories (1880), *Household Stories from the Brothers Grimm* (1882), and Oscar Wilde's *The Happy Prince and Other Tales* (1888).

GEORGE CRUIKSHANK (1792–1878) was the greatest of England's nineteenth-century comic artists. He made his reputation with his pictures for Edgar Taylor's translation of the Grimms' *German Popular Stories* (1823 and 1826) and went on to illustrate Charles Dickens' *Sketches by Boz* (1836) and *Oliver Twist* (1838) among countless other books. His later work, such as his *Fairy Library* (1854 and 1864), was marred by temperance propaganda.

MARY DE MORGAN (1850–1907) knew the Pre-Raphaelites through her brother William De Morgan, the artist and author. She wrote several exceptional collections of fairy tales: *On a Pincushion and Other Fairy Tales* (1877), *The Necklace of Princess Fiorimonde and Other Stories* (1880), and *The Windfairies and Other Tales* (1900).

CHARLES DICKENS (1812–1870) was the pre-eminent novelist of the Victorian Age. *The Pickwick Papers* (1838), *Oliver Twist* (1838), *A Christmas Carol* (1843), *David Copperfield* (1850), and all his other books were as avidly read by children as by their parents. His only works written specifically for a juvenile audience were *A Child's History of England* (1852–1854) and *Holiday Romance*, first serialized in the American magazine *Our Young Folks* and Dickens' own journal *All the Year Round* in 1868.

RICHARD DOYLE (1824–1883) was one of the most popular comic artists of his day. He contributed to *Punch* and illustrated many books, including William Makepeace Thackeray's *Rebecca and Rowena* (1850) and *The Newcomes* (1855), *The Story of Jack and the Giants* (1851), and John Ruskin's *The King of the Golden River* (1851). His most ambitious effort was his suite of color wood engravings *In Fairyland* (1870), accompanied by verses by William Allingham.

FORD MADOX FORD (1873–1939), whose real name was Ford Hermann Hueffer, is best known as the author of the modern novel *The Good Soldier* (1915) and as the founder of the *Transatlantic Review*, but his earliest works were children's stories: *The Brown Owl* (1892), *The Feather* (1893), and *The Queen Who Flew* (1894).

SIR JOHN GILBERT (1817–1897) was a prolific illustrator, the first major artist to contribute to the *Illustrated London News*. His numerous books range from *The Illustrated Webster Spelling Book* (1856) to Mme. D'Aulnoy's *Fairy Tales* (1855).

KENNETH GRAHAME (1859–1932) was employed by the Bank of England (later as its secretary) and in his spare time wrote the charming books *The Golden Age* (1895), *Dream Days* (1898), and *The Wind in the Willows* (1908).

LAURENCE HOUSMAN (1865–1959), brother of the poet A. E. Housman, was an exceptional author and illustrator. Besides embellishing his own fairy tales with his exquisite pictures, he illustrated Christina Rossetti's *Goblin Market* (1893), E. Nesbit's *A Pomander of Verses* (1895), and George MacDonald's *At the Back of the North Wind* and *The Princess and the Goblin* (1900). His most famous work of literature was the play *Victoria Regina* (1934).

ARTHUR HUGHES (1832–1915) was the member of the Pre-Raphaelite Brotherhood who most diligently pursued book illustration as a profession. Besides
George MacDonald's fairy tales, the books he illustrated include William
Allingham's *The Music Master* (1855), Thomas Hughes' *Tom Brown's Schooldays*
(1869), and Christina Rossetti's *Speaking Likenesses* (1874) and *Sing-Song* (1872).

GEORGE MACDONALD (1824–1905) was ordained as a Congregationalist minister,
but quickly lost his pulpit due to his liberal religious beliefs. He devoted the
remainder of his life to writing, reflecting on spiritual matters in works of
fantasy, such as *Phantastes* (1858), *Dealings with the Fairies* (1867), *At the Back
of the North Wind* (1871), *The Princess and the Goblin* (1872), *The Princess and
Curdie* (1883), and *Lilith* (1895).

HAROLD ROBERT MILLAR (1869–1942) flourished between 1890 and 1935 as a
magazine illustrator, primarily for the *Strand*. Many of E. Nesbit's stories first
appeared in the *Strand* with his pictures.

HENRY MORLEY (1822–1894) became an editor of *Household Words* at Charles
Dickens' request. He was also a distinguished literary scholar and wrote two
collections of children's stories, *Fables and Fairy Tales* (1860) and *Oberon's Horn*
(1861).

"E. NESBIT" (1858–1924) was Edith Nesbit Bland, a prominent Fabian Socialist
whose friends included George Bernard Shaw, H. G. Wells, and G. K. Ches-
terton. She also wrote many fine children's books, including *The Book of Dragons*
(1900), *The Railway Children* (1906), the Bastable books, and the Five Children
trilogy.

MAXFIELD PARRISH (1870–1966) was one of the premier American illustrators
of the early twentieth century. After his first book, L. Frank Baum's *Mother
Goose in Prose* (1897), was published in England, he was commissioned to
illustrate Kenneth Grahame's *The Golden Age* (1899) and *Dream Days* (1902).

ARTHUR RACKHAM (1867–1939) was the outstanding British book illustrator of
his generation. He produced many lavish gift books, including J. M. Barrie's
Peter Pan in Kensington Gardens (1906), Lewis Carroll's *Alice's Adventures in
Wonderland* (1907), Charles Dickens' *A Christmas Carol* (1915), John Ruskin's
The King of the Golden River (1932), Christina Rossetti's *Goblin Market* (1933),
Robert Browning's *The Pied Piper of Hamelin* (1934), and Kenneth Grahame's
The Wind in the Willows (1940).

JOHN MCL. RALSTON was active as a watercolorist and a contributor to the
Illustrated London News between 1872 and 1881. Besides Dinah M. Mulock
Craik's *The Little Lame Prince and His Travelling-Cloak* (1875), the books he
illustrated include Charles Dickens' *A Child's History of England* (1873) and
John Bunyan's *The Pilgrim's Progress* (1880).

CHRISTINA ROSSETTI (1830–1894), the sister of the Pre-Raphaelite painter and
poet Dante Gabriel Rossetti and the art critic William Michael Rossetti, was
a distinguished poet in her own right. *Goblin Market and Other Poems* (1862)
is her most important book, but she also wrote a collection of children's verse,

Sing-Song (1872), and an imitation of *Alice in Wonderland, Speaking Likenesses* (1874), both illustrated by Arthur Hughes.

DANTE GABRIEL ROSSETTI (1828–1882) founded the Pre-Raphaelite Brotherhood with John Everett Millais and William Holman Hunt. He was as gifted a poet as he was a painter. He contributed illustrations to several books, including William Allingham's *The Music Master* (1855) and his sister Christina Rossetti's *Goblin Market* (1862) and *The Prince's Progress* (1866).

JOHN RUSKIN (1819–1900) became one of the most revered art and social critics of his day with the publication of his first book *Modern Painters* (1843). His only published work of fiction was the children's story *The King of the Golden River* (1851).

WILLIAM MAKEPEACE THACKERAY (1811–1863) was a cartoonist as well as one of the most important novelists of the Victorian Age. His works include *The Luck of Barry Lyndon* (1844), *Vanity Fair* (1847), *Rebecca and Rowena* (1850), and *The Newcomes* (1855), as well as a series of "Christmas Books" in imitation of Charles Dickens, the most famous being *The Rose and the Ring* (1855).

OSCAR WILDE (1854–1900) was one of the most flamboyant literary figures of the late nineteenth century. His reputation rests on a wide variety of writing, including his collections of fairy tales, *The Happy Prince and Other Tales* (1889) and *The House of Pomegranates* (1891), the novel *The Picture of Dorian Gray* (1891), his plays *Lady Windermere's Fan* (1892) and *The Importance of Being Earnest* (1895), and the poem *The Ballad of Reading Gaol* (1898).

WILLIAM BUTLER YEATS (1865–1939), perhaps the greatest modern poet in English, was a prominent member of the Irish revival called "the Celtic Twilight" after his book of 1893. Besides writing many exquisite poems based upon his native folklore, such as those in *The Wanderings of Oisin and Other Poems* (1889), he collected several volumes of Irish fairy tales and legends.

About the Editor

MICHAEL PATRICK HEARN is America's foremost man of letters specializing in children's literature and its illustration. The author of *The Annotated Huckleberry Finn*, *The Annnotated Wizard of Oz*, *The Annotated Christmas Carol*, and *The Art of the Broadway Poster*, and the editor of *The Andrew Lang Fairy Tale Book*, he has also provided introductions to such classics as *At the Back of the North Wind*, *Peter and Wendy*, *The Merry Adventures of Robin Hood*, and *Little Wizard Stories of Oz*. His articles have appeared in the *New York Times Book Review*, the *Washington Post Book World*, the *Nation, Graphis, American Artist*, the *Ladies' Home Journal*, and other publications. He is also the author of an original fairy tale, *The Porcelain Cat*, with illustrations by Leo and Diane Dillon.

Michael Patrick Hearn teaches the history of children's book illustration at Columbia University. He is currently writing *Classics Reconsidered*, a study of the masterworks of juvenile literature, as well as a biography of L. Frank Baum, author of *The Wizard of Oz*.